D0411137

THE
HUNGER
TRACE

THE
HUNGER
TRACE

EDWARD HOGAN

SIMON &
SCHUSTER

London · New York · Sydney · Toronto

A CBS COMPANY

First published in Great Britain by Simon & Schuster UK Ltd, 2011
A CBS COMPANY

1 3 5 7 9 10 8 6 4 2

Simon & Schuster UK Ltd
1st Floor
222 Gray's Inn Road
London WC1X 8HB

Simon & Schuster Australia
Sydney

A CIP catalogue record for this book
is available from the British Library

HB ISBN: 978-1-84737-124-9
TPB ISBN: 978-0-85720-510-0

Typeset by M Rules
Printed in the UK by CPI Mackays, Chatham ME5 8TD

To Emily

One of the most unusual auction sales Beamish & Fisher have ever held was conducted at Drum Hill Wildlife and Conservation Centre today. For the first time, exotic and dangerous animals came up for sale along with items associated with a wildlife park business.

The animals were viewed in their regular enclosures and the catalogue sale was conducted in the large entrance hall of the main residence. A female wallaby was sold for £510; a pair of Asian otters for £350; an ocelot for £110 and two lynx kittens for £190. The most expensive lots, however, were three life-size fibreglass dinosaurs. A triceratops fetched £800 . . .

Dispersal sale report in *The North Derbyshire Herald*, 25 March 2010.

EARLY SEASON

Grouse, ptarmigan, blackgame.

ONE

Such a thing had never before been witnessed in the village: a small herd of ibex skittering down Drum Hill towards the main road, their thick, ribbed horns blue in the small hours, their yellow eyes catching the streetlight. They turned left at the corner and quickened their pace. The icy pavements and unkempt verges of Derbyshire were not so far removed from their natural terrain. Their reflections shimmered in the Perspex of the bus shelter and the fake stained-glass windows of the White Hart pub.

Out on the road, the elder males bellowed. An HGV driver passing in the opposite direction brought his vehicle to a halt, and in his tired acceptance of all night wonders, reverted to hand-brake, neutral. From his high cockpit view, the driver saw them as a brown larval flow, sheathed by their own breath, the young in the middle borne by the power of the current.

The ibex passed the clock tower of the primary school and increased their speed, the raining clatter of their hooves echoing back from the bricks of the semis, bungalows and barn conversions on either side of the road. Scared and hungry, they sought higher ground. They headed for the rocky peaks, and for dawn.

Those villagers who rose early and saw the herd from their windows knew exactly where the animals were from. A mile away on Drum Hill, Maggie took the first of the calls, swaying like a water reed by her bed in the large, bowed room. She pulled on her jeans and boots, and zipped a padded coat straight over her bra. The Land Rover had been playing up lately and she hoped it would start. In the hall she left a note for her stepson: AN IBEX SITUATION HAS ARISEN.

Across the way, Louisa Smedley was washing meat for her hawks at the kitchen sink. Pink streaky water ran into the plughole. From the window, she could see Iroquois, the steppe eagle, on her perch on the grass. Iroquois roused herself in the blue dawn, and shook a light dusting of frost from her feathers. She turned her head sharply towards the field separating Louisa's cottage from Drum Hill Wildlife Park. Louisa followed Iroquois's gaze but could see nothing other than the silhouette of the big house, a shade darker than the sky. She waited, squinting. Moments later her neighbour came into view, running towards the cottage. Louisa sighed with irritation. She noted the upright gait of Maggie Bryant, the long-legged ease with which she swung over the wire fence, and the way she held back her dark curls with one hand. Louisa dropped the raw meat in the sink, and moved out of view.

On many occasions in the past, Louisa had crept onto the lawn of her neighbours' house, and stood outside the range of the intruder light, looking in through the large windows at David and his young new wife. Louisa had watched Maggie moving through the warm, yellow-lit rooms, before they had even been introduced. Despite her tendency to watch others – or perhaps because of it – Louisa did not like to be watched herself. She hoped that Maggie might assume the cottage was empty, although she knew this was unlikely.

Maggie knocked loudly on the door, but then entered without waiting for a reply and stepped quickly through the hall and into the kitchen. She smelled of the clean air outdoors, along with a faint cosmetic scent – the first in Louisa's house for some time.

'Louisa, thank God. I knew you'd be awake. I need your help,' Maggie said.

Louisa turned back to the sink. 'I'm busy. What is it?'

'We've had a breakout over at the park. Some of the ibex – the big goats—'

'I know what they are.'

'They got loose somehow, and they're on the road now.' Maggie took a long breath. 'If they get to the dual carriageway, we've got serious trouble.'

'*You've* got serious trouble. What am I supposed to do about it?'

'Well, the Land Rover won't start.'

Louisa took the keys to her van from her pocket, and threw them to Maggie. 'Take mine.'

Maggie wiped the watery smears of blood from the keys with her sleeve and looked up with an apologetic smile. 'I need *you*, as well,' she said. 'The trailer's at my house and we'll need to hook it up before we go.'

'Jesus,' Louisa said under her breath. But she could not refuse. She dried her hands on her jeans and followed.

Louisa had bought the maroon Transit van from a printing firm gone bust. A sticker on the back read *Am I courteous?* and gave an 0800 number. Maggie drove them over to the big house. Louisa, unaccustomed to human company in the van, noticed with some discomfort the state of her vehicle's interior. A fur of bird lint covered the dashboard, and tiny weeds grew in the footwell, spawned from the cuttings brought in on Louisa's boots.

When they'd attached the trailer, Maggie put a little wheelspin through the gravel path before they began the long drop down into Detton. 'Careful,' Louisa said. As they descended, the mist became water on the ground.

Louisa had watched plenty of women – usually older, and divorced – come and go from David's park, and had thought Maggie would follow them out. Anyone could see that the park was a money pit, and if the insufficient funds were not prohibitive enough, Christopher – David's outsized teenage son – was too much for most women. Even the hill road on which they now travelled was unwelcoming. It sloped almost vertically, bordered by knots of rusty grass and moss like body hair. Pines stood below the vehicle at alarming angles.

Louisa did not meet Maggie, in the conventional sense, until a week after she arrived. Of course, the men in the White Hart gossiped about David's new wife constantly. A lot younger, they said. One of them described her as exotic. Louisa thought them ridiculous. At close range, in daylight, a glance had told Louisa all she needed to know about the new Mrs Bryant: thin as a plant cane, early thirties, dusky skin, long curls, no muscle power or tits to speak of, tight jeans and pretentious cowboy boots with a fucking *heel*. She looked, to Louisa, like a Cherokee squaw. 'It's great to have another girl next door,' Maggie had said. Southern. Her words had the clarity of hail on an iron table.

Louisa had let her handshake do the talking, and felt the cartilage slide while Maggie talked about her intention to help out with the animals. She'd worked at 'Greenwich Park', apparently. She'd read some zoology textbooks and some Peter Scott. Louisa did not tell her that her wholesome ideas would soon be buried in lynx shit, or drowned in a bucket of 5 a.m. fish guts. Instead, she let Maggie continue. This one's talkative, Louisa thought. Perhaps loneliness would drive her off. Either way, Louisa had given her a month.

How many years had it been now? Three? She still wore those cowboy boots, but Louisa saw the scrapes and cuts on Maggie's long fingers when she changed gear, and the curls were shorter.

Maggie circled the roundabout four or five times. Louisa sighed. 'What are you doing?'

'If I was an ibex, where would I be?' Maggie said, looking east to where Morrison's supermarket glowed yellow, its huge synthetic awning like a frozen tidal wave. Two small limestone peaks rose up behind. 'The big rocks,' Maggie said.

She drove to Morrison's and pulled up in the car park. Louisa braced herself for a long morning, but Maggie's instincts proved right. The ibex had crossed the fields, taking the short route towards higher ground, and they emerged in the car park a few minutes after Louisa and Maggie. Louisa had to admit they were impressive animals, for ungulates, and she could see the predicament clearly. To get to the peaks, the herd would have to cross the car park and then the dual carriageway. Grass banks flanked the exit. The traffic on the carriageway was increasing as the sky began to lighten.

Maggie drove slowly, putting the van between the ibex and the car park exit. The van did not fully cover the escape route, and the ibex would have no problem, in any case, scaling the grass banks. 'What are you going to do?' Louisa said.

Maggie shrugged.

'Well, do you have any equipment?'

'Only what I could pick up as I was leaving the house. Tow-rope, a little feed, a couple of sedative darts.'

Louisa counted twelve animals. 'You should have brought dogs,' she said.

They both looked at the flash of cars in the rear-view mirror. 'If they get to that carriageway, it's a massacre,' Maggie said.

'We'll have to put ourselves in the way,' Louisa said.

'A toothpick in a canyon,' Maggie said, biting her lip.

Louisa looked down at her waist. It was a long time since anyone had called her a toothpick. Maggie stepped out of the van. 'Stay here,' she said. Louisa fought to control the anger that rose up to meet that command. She pulled the door closed and watched Maggie gather grit from the border of the car park and march towards the herd, who stepped about, waiting. There was an echoing crackle of horns as two males rose up onto hind legs and dropped briefly into engagement. Maggie stopped ten metres from them and threw the grit. She shouted and the whole herd backed off and re-grouped.

The workers on the early shift had just put out the trolleys. Louisa could faintly hear the delivery trucks at the back of the supermarket, but there was nobody around. Floodlights made pockets of yellow in the blue. The wind against the van brought blankness, a sort of silence.

Maggie turned to Louisa, held up her palm for her to stay and ran over to the supermarket entrance. She took hold of the back of a long line of trolleys and began to push. The clang of metal startled the herd and initiated a race, the ibex heading for the grass bank and the danger beyond, Maggie pushing the trolleys towards the van to cut them off in a big 'V'.

Louisa looked around, and saw that the gap between the van and the bank was too big. She slid into the warm driver's seat, turned on the engine and began to reverse. Maggie thought she was trying to save her vehicle and shouted, 'Wait', but Louisa put the van into first, slammed on right lock and jack-knifed the trailer to create a better funnel. The jolt stirred Louisa's blood. Everything began to converge on her: the noise of hooves and the skating wheels of the trolleys, the windows filling with the brown colour of the animals. Maggie arrowed the trolleys into the flank of the van to close the gap; the force of the blow knocked Louisa sideways. The ibex reared, bunched and bellowed, but could not turn out of the trap for the onrushing tail of their herd. Maggie got behind them, spread her arms at the base of the triangle. They were penned. Louisa watched for a moment, the ibex staring in at her, Maggie breathing hard behind them. Then she took the rope and got out.

Maggie whistled. 'Great job,' she said.

Louisa tried to control her racing heart. 'Would have been easier with dogs,' she said, looking at the trolleys against her crumpled bodywork.

The sky turned grey as they worked. The older ibex, compliant now, stepped up between them, all shine and steam. As they prepared to close the gate of the trailer, one of the kids broke for the bank. Louisa reacted first and gave chase. The kid was fast, and Louisa was not used to sprinting, but she began to gain on him. As she ran, she started to smile at the weirdness of it all: the ibex caught in the glow of the supermarket sign above them, the metallic ring of Maggie's boots following behind. Louisa's lungs felt raw, and Maggie overtook her as the kid reached the bank. Maggie scrambled up the incline on her hands and feet, snatched at the back legs of the ibex and knocked him off balance. He tumbled back down the bank. Louisa took him chest high and they both hit the ground, Louisa with her arm around the animal's neck.

'Bosh!' shouted Maggie.

Louisa could feel the kid's legs kicking against her own, and his underbelly rising and falling. She could hear the beat of his heart. His glassy eyes stayed wide open. Louisa coughed hard, as though she'd been resuscitated. Maggie got down on her knees beside her and secured the hooves until the kicking stopped.

'He's nice and warm, isn't he?' Maggie said.

Louisa could barely speak. 'It's a male?'

'Yeah.'

Louisa pushed her nose into the bristly neck of the beast, stayed clear of the budding horns. 'What will the neighbours say?' she said.

'What will *security* say?' Maggie said, pointing to the CCTV cameras trained on them from the roof of the supermarket. Maggie took hold of the ibex's fore-hoof and waved it, then turned back to Louisa. 'Listen, you were amazing. Thank you. I'll sort you out with some cash for the truck. For the damage.'

'Dead right,' Louisa said. The salty breath of the ibex kid

mingled with her own coffee tang. She was suddenly exhausted, and could not let go of the animal.

Maggie was sweating. She began to unzip her coat, revealing bare skin beneath. Louisa saw this and flinched. Maggie looked down. 'Oops,' she said, and zipped up. 'Shall we go?' she asked.

'Give me a minute,' Louisa said.

'You two take your time,' Maggie said.

Maggie drove back, making phone calls as she did so, and talking about possible ways that the ibex might have escaped. The history of the park was punctuated by break-ins. Students and animal rights activists had been the most frequent offenders, but thieves had sometimes targeted the more expensive animals.

'Did David ever tell you that story about the students who broke into the park in the early nineties?' asked Maggie.

'I was working there,' said Louisa.

'Course you were.'

David had chased them across the dark fields, caught one student scaling a fence, and sat on the kid until the police arrived with their torches to reveal the most beautiful nineteen-year-old girl David had ever seen. So he'd told Maggie that story. It irritated Louisa to think that David might have told Maggie stories about *her*. And she was not nineteen, and not beautiful. Although perhaps she had been, once.

Staff from the park were waiting for the trailer when the two women returned. They detached it immediately. Louisa looked at the cold, toad-skin stone of the house and saw the big blond head of David's son, Christopher, appear in the window. Maggie waved up at him, but he moved away.

'Can I get you some breakfast, Louisa?' Maggie said.

'No. I've got a busy morning. Slightly busier now.'

'I'd like to say thank you.'

'Taking me away from my work's not going to do it.'

'Okay,' Maggie said. 'I'll drive you home.'

Louisa frowned with confusion. 'Why don't you just get out here? It's my van.'

'I'd like to talk to you,' Maggie said, shrugging.

They drove the short distance back to the compact cottage on adjacent land. Louisa got out and inspected the dent in the panel. Maggie waited.

'Like I said, I've got a lot to do,' Louisa said after a few moments.

'I don't mind tagging along,' Maggie said.

Louisa fetched her bag and gauntlet from the cottage. Maggie followed her silently around the back, past the various moulting sheds to a horseshoe of weatherings, the wood furred with frost. They walked across the lawn, by the bank of open-fronted structures, the hawks and falcons watching them, some hunched like men in raincoats waiting for buses, some perched in the shadows. The display hawks screamed when they saw Louisa, but she ignored them. At the end of the row stood a separate chamber, built on breeze-blocks, where Louisa kept Diamond, her old tiercel peregrine. She had barely opened the mesh door before the bird was on her glove, tugging with his beak at the strip of beef between Louisa's fingers. Louisa curled the jesses through her fingers and rested her thumb against Diamond's breast. He turned away with his typical disdain. She hooded him.

The two women took the pea-shingle path back to the cottage,

Louisa carrying Diamond on the fist. Next to the kitchen was a weighing room with an outdoor entrance. Inside, the white-washed walls and bathroom tiles cast a cold blue glow over the gloves and lures hanging from nails. A reclining freezer stood along one wall, plastered with the faded stickers of yesteryear's lollies, but filled now with bags of quail, beef-shin, blast-frozen mice and day-old chicks.

Louisa put her finger under Diamond's tail and reversed him onto cast-iron scales modified with a perch at one end. She could feel Maggie behind her, taking everything in. A mobile phone vibrated, but Maggie made no move to answer it. This was the one sound in the room while both women looked at Diamond. His figure was stark against the white tiles behind. The covert feathers were the grey of wet stone, his breast was striped with black bars, and the top-knot of his hood spiralled up. His feet were the major weapons – his size fifteens, Louisa called them: huge talons grew from gnarled toes and arced back into the wood of the perch. He was an old boy now, and one talon was missing.

'He's a knockout,' Maggie whispered.

'Yeah,' said Louisa, writing his weight onto a large whiteboard covered with imperial figures in tiny squares. 'My number one guy.'

'You know, I met this falconer the other day, at the butchers. Guy called Mick?'

'I know him,' Louisa said. He was a leering psychobilly who had done time for hitting a neighbour with a sock full of batteries. But he loved his hawks.

'Do you? He's quite funny, isn't he?'

'If you like that sort of thing.'

'Bit of a ruffian, you know. He was saying his birds increased his appeal with the ladies.'

'He needs all the help he can get, I imagine,' Louisa said.

'Ha. Right. What was the phrase he used? *Bitch magnet.* That's it. He said the hawks were a bitch magnet.'

'Well. Here you are,' Louisa said. She watched the smile on Maggie's face fade as the insult registered. Maggie's breath curled up from her slightly open mouth.

'You didn't come here to talk about Mick, I presume,' Louisa said.

'No. I've been having trouble with Christopher. He isn't doing very well. He misses David, of course.' Maggie looked down at her boots, their pointed tips darkly discoloured from the wet grass of the bank. 'But he has his other issues, too.'

Louisa took Diamond back onto her fist by nudging his legs from behind, and they went back outside. She could not imagine why Maggie would want to talk to her about her family problems, but then she looked around to see no other houses within walking distance.

'I'm running out of ideas. I've been trying to get him back into college, but when I ask him what he wants to do he just says, "Formula One".' Maggie smiled, but Louisa did not. 'He used to love me, but nowadays I overhear him talking to the Samaritans and he calls me "The Traitor Maggie Green."'

Louisa nodded.

'The other day I saw him standing at the window watching you fly your hawks. You knew his father so well, and for a lot longer than I did,' Maggie said.

'Yep.'

'And you probably know Christopher better, too, having lived here all this time.'

Louisa did not respond. She remembered when Christopher was born. His mother, Cynthia, at one time the face and body of a TV advert for cereal, had hated the park from the moment she arrived. She had moaned about the smell of the place, and the coarse hairs of the various animals, which clung to her clothes. It had quickly become clear that Christopher was wired differently, and – with a little help from Louisa – Cynthia had left soon after the boy's third birthday.

'I just thought you might be able to show him the birds,' Maggie said. Her phone began to vibrate, and again she ignored it.

Louisa smiled and shook her head. 'I don't think so.'

'I don't mean teach him falconry or anything. If he really takes to it, I'll send him on a course.'

'It's not that.'

'Maybe he doesn't even need to handle them. He could just watch,' Maggie said.

'He could do that from the window.'

'He does.' Maggie frowned. 'I thought it might be nice for him to get closer. He seems interested in what you do.'

'Can't really let him near the birds.'

'But I thought you did falconry days for the public. The birds are manned, aren't they?'

Louisa noted the use of terminology. Maggie had clearly been reading up. 'Obviously my display hawks are fully manned. If he wants to come to one of the demonstrations in the summer, he can stand behind the rope. But I'm very busy, and besides, I can't have Christopher near the hawks. He's too unpredictable.'

Maggie fell silent. Finally, she said, 'Oh.'

Louisa saw Philip Cassidy, the head keeper at the Wildlife Park, approaching across the field. 'It would be irresponsible of me. To the birds and to him. People seem to think you can just—'

Maggie raised her hand. 'Okay,' she said. 'Okay.'

There was a moment of silence before Philip arrived. Maggie greeted him. When Philip spoke, Diamond turned his hooded head to the sound of the new voice. 'I've been trying to get you on the phone,' Philip said. 'But I suppose you've been busy.' He shot a look at Louisa. They had once been colleagues on the park.

'What's happening? Have you found anything?' Maggie said.

'It's bad news, duck. One down on the ibex headcount,' Philip said.

'Oh no,' Maggie said.

'And there's other animals missing. Four fences cut, and they broke into the medical centre.'

Maggie put one hand to her mouth and the other on Philip's shoulder. Louisa watched her long fingers extend. 'Jesus. I'll come straight back,' Maggie said. She turned to Louisa. 'Thank you, again, for today.'

Louisa nodded. She wanted to say that she was sorry about the missing animals, but she couldn't bring herself to do it.

On Christmas morning of the year that Maggie arrived, Louisa had stood at the boundary of her land and watched them. She was obscured from their view by a stand of birches, but could see Maggie and Christopher sprinting up the hill on David's 'Go', towards a trough of frozen water. Maggie let Christopher pass and win the race in his shorts and Wellingtons. He touched the trough and sank to his knees, spitting a greeny that he had to detach with his hand. 'I'm. Erm. Breathing out of my rump,' he shouted. Maggie dragged him up, lifting his hand in the air. 'The winner,' she cried. Even from that distance, Louisa could see the admiring look the boy gave Maggie.

Christopher and Maggie turned to the trough and on the count of three kicked through the crust of ice, Christopher squealing at the cold water splashing over his thighs. The miniature zebu came slowly out of the mist for their drink – perfectly proportioned tiny cows, screwing up perspective so you never knew how close they were until you touched them. David roared with laughter.

They were at the edge of Louisa's visual range, but starkly delineated against the milky fog. She turned back to her cottage.

Until then, Louisa had pinned her life to two desires: David Bryant and her hawks. At the age of forty-seven, she could look back and see that almost every decision had been taken with one or both of those concerns in mind. There was profundity in the care of a hawk: the relegation of needs, the pain taken over one ounce of weight, the thrill of watching them hunt. They were like gods to her, especially Diamond. As for David, she had come to realise that it was not so incredible to give a whole life to another person and receive so little in return. It was probably a lot like having a husband.

Seeing the three of them together on that Christmas day, Louisa had reached a decision. Having outlasted all of the glamorous women whom David had courted, Louisa had been defeated by five minutes of playtime.

After a few months of financial consolidation, Louisa had walked the hundred yards or so to the big house and quit her job as park falconer. David sat in his ground-floor office, the skin of dust on the threadbare red carpet given sheen by the weak light coming through the bow window behind his head. She squinted as she told him she was going solo; she'd maybe start breeding, or set up in avian clearance.

'You'll probably make out better than the park,' he said with a smile. 'You'll come back and do the odd show, won't you?'

'Not sure,' she said.

She slid her staff keys onto his desk. It was a purely symbolic gesture. The keys had made teethmarks in her palm, but she knew that David wouldn't notice. He studied the bunch. His blond-grey hair was lighter in colour than her own. 'Louisa, you know I brought you here, to the Drum Hill, because—'

'I brought myself here.'

'I know. But I *wanted* you here because of your skill. And your friendship. I never felt obligated because of what you did for me.'

She sighed.

'But I was always grateful.'

'Right,' she said.

She walked home, stemming the tears by force of will, mocked by the stupid moans of his misfit animals. In this way, she did her grieving early. When he dropped down dead on the hill that summer, she thought back to when they last spoke in his office, but could conjure nothing beyond his shape against the light behind his desk.

The first year after David's death, Louisa stayed out of the village as much as possible. She did not want to hear about the sorrows of others. She knew they called her a hermit, and when they did, she always thought of Anna Cliff, the reclusive woman from the village where Louisa and David had grown up, with her necklace of scar tissue. Perhaps it was penance that she should end up like Anna Cliff, the woman whose life they had destroyed. Louisa tried to push such thoughts from her mind.

In the end, there was nowhere else to go, and the only thing worse than the sly glances in her direction was the absence of such glances, so she returned to the White Hart for its sweet punishment. She suspected that everything she felt was sketched on her face, so she downed Guinness until the page was blank.

Louisa was in the Hart the day after they recaptured the ibex, suddenly greedy for news from the park. But the patrons soon began to irritate her. They talked about the break-in, which provoked polarised debate. Activists, some said. A couple of the regulars said the place was now a liability. Since David died, they said, things had gone slack. What if a young 'un happened upon one of those great big bloody cats?

Most of them felt sympathy for Maggie. Nobody mentioned Louisa's part in the rescue of the ibex, and Louisa did not say that she had seen a lone figure on the park the night before.

Richie Foxton, the butcher, his eyes nigh on the same colour as his pint of Pedigree, spoke up for Maggie. 'She's faced many a trial since David passed,' he said.

'Right enough. It's a tough ask,' said Bill Wicks, the landlord, 'running a place like that on your lonesome.'

Philip Cassidy smiled into his drink, refusing, as usual, to rise to the bait.

'Aye, she's a game lass though, in't she?'

Richie Foxton glazed over. 'Yeah, she's grand. Sommat about her, in't there? Sommat in her eyes.'

'A bloody dollar sign,' Louisa said. She'd had enough. Enough being six and a half pints. 'You don't know anything about her. What she's like. So before you start speaking ill of the dead—'

She slammed her glass down on the bar, knocking over Richie Foxton's as she did so. The accident broke her chain of thought. 'Oh shit. Sorry. Are you okay? Can I get you another?'

Foxton frowned. He looked childish and uncomfortable in his wet trousers. Philip Cassidy stood from his stool and stared at Louisa. She got out fast, feeling idiotic and hungry, but without the energy to contemplate a meal. From the bottom of the hill, the trees were like a mushroom cloud frozen in the second after detonation. She felt consoled by the thought of the nights drawing in.

Two

The walls of the gritstone gorge rose high above Detton village. In the soft light, the cliff-face looked tooth-marked and bruised, like half a discarded apple. Above the face lay a green scalp of land patched with enclosures, the big old house, a diving board, and the woods, through which Maggie carefully picked her way, looking for clues. Autumn's gravity created movement and noises everywhere. Clouds diffused the sun like lampshades, giving all objects an internal luminescence, their shadows falling at strange angles. Maggie found herself alert to the cascade of dead branches, and startled by the sudden appearance of the fibreglass triceratops, mottled as he was by fallen leaves.

A week had passed since the animals had been released, and she was alert to news from the village. The issue of the park's safety had been raised at the Parish Council meeting, and certain villagers were only too pleased to drum up panic. The stories resounded and grew, and by the time they got back to Maggie they were garish: dogs went into gardens to do their business and came back missing an ear; cats, if they came back at all, did so with acute nervous disorders and started pissing on the carpet. The Rileys said they saw something like a wolf in their garden, and Mrs Nettles reported a giant bird in her apple tree, although no birds had escaped.

It was the newspapers that infuriated Maggie. That week's *Derbyshire Herald* had taken the opportunity to resuscitate the perennial story of the big cat, known locally as the Beast of Belton. A farmer in Wirksworth had found one of his sheep 'torn to pieces', and his cattle had bolted across the road, smashing through an iron gate, to get away from the mystery predator. The article featured close-up photographs of paw-prints in mud, an archive head shot of a beautiful melanistic jaguar, and a good deal of hearsay and conjecture. The connection with Drum Hill Wildlife Park was explicitly made.

During her extensive searches in the village, however, Maggie found verifiable sightings rare. She had spoken to the children of Class 5A at the Detton Primary School, who had watched for ten glorious minutes as some kind of horned goat danced proudly across the coloured rings and game lines of the icy playground. Miss McArthur, their teacher, had allowed the pupils to crowd the window and watch. She told Maggie that the animal had slid through an impossible gap in the fence. It had left faeces and a few drops of blood in the playground. The children drew pictures for Maggie. It was the ibex – the yellow felt-tips made the eyes bright.

Reverend Sipson had killed the arctic fox in his Peugeot. He had the decency to bring the body to Maggie, wrapped in a tartan blanket. It had looked to him, he said, like a discarded bathmat, until it stood, late and alert against the left headlight. When she knelt to open the blanket on the doorstep, the red blood on the white fur – which was almost blue in the dropping light – reminded her of the fairy tales of her childhood. 'I'm so very sorry,' Reverend Sipson said. The man who had buried David. She looked up at him.

'It wasn't your fault, Reverend. She was blind.' Maggie rubbed her eyes. 'I don't know what to do.'

'Shall we pray?' he said.

'I don't think she was religious,' Maggie said, pulling the blanket over the dead fox.

As she emerged out of the trees now, Maggie wondered how she had ever got into this mess. By the woods stood the disused diving board. It was the high, platform type. The house had once belonged to a wealthy Lady with a young Olympian husband, although the pool itself had been filled with concrete many years before David's arrival. Along with the house on the hill, the diving board had become something of a Detton landmark, and many of the villagers had been grateful to David, who had arrived in 1987 to stop developers turning the place into a red-brick estate, with his odd menagerie of wallabies, ibex, zebu, European lynx, peccaries, otters and ocelots.

Commercially speaking, David had timed his venture disastrously – zoos were losing public favour, and you couldn't just buy a leopard anymore. The laws had tightened and visitor numbers had dropped. When Maggie first arrived at the park, David told her how people had boycotted the place for fear of foot-and-mouth, and then bird flu. He had built an assault course and commissioned the triceratops, stegosaurus, and tyrannosaurus in the woods for the infant visitors, stalling his own extinction with a brave smile. He was always better with the children than with the animals.

This is what Maggie had been left, and she had taken it with fervour, because – along with Christopher – the park was all she had of him. She looked up at the underside of the diving platform, where snails hung upside down near a hollow house martin's nest. She climbed the rusty metal steps. She stopped on the top step, and held the handrail. From there she could view the whole village. She could see the river and the brook pinching Detton between them, the traintracks slicing the landscape, and the fuck-you finger of the mill chimney.

She had met David in Greenwich Park, where she volunteered at weekends in the Secret Wildlife Garden. She took the unpaid work so she could be close to the deer. She had always been drawn to them; their silent ring in the centre of the enclosure was, for her, the steadily pulsing heart of the park. In March of that year, the vets and trained staff brought in two new stags which the Greenwich Park managers hoped would freshen the genetic mix. They had waited until spring, when the males had cast their antlers. It was a major operation. Maggie was not allowed to handle the animals, but she attended to deal with the minor administrative duties of the day, and to watch. She noticed a man viewing from the other side of the enclosure, talking to the managers. Somebody said he was there to observe the process, that he owned a park up north. She noticed the bulk and weight of him, and wondered why he did not help.

They had celebrated that night in a pub by the river which was furnished like someone's living room, low-lit with dark red lamps, sofas and a fireplace by which this man, David, stood to tell his stories. She had never seen anyone so closely shaved. In the red light, the sheen of David's aftershave was visible in a patch stopping halfway down his neck.

He told a story about a fight he once had with a huge rugby player, represented by two fists pressed thumb to thumb – 'hands that wide.' The rugby player had dumped him in an industrial bin. David had been woken early by a member of the local constabulary. 'Are you a police officer?' David had said.

'Yes.'

'Then perhaps you could tell me what I'm doing in this bin.'

Oh God, she thought, he's like a massive child, like one of my students. He was mischievous, all physical gestures. As the night wore on, he told his stories with fewer words and more sound effects, his hands like a rebus code. She repressed an urge to tell him to pipe down.

She looked him over. The lightly checked shirt stretched across the breadth of him. He wore grey trousers and a blue jacket. She could not imagine where he bought his clothes. So much of his life was beyond the scope of her imagination, and that made him attractive to her. He seemed as wide as the fireplace, the furrows of his white-blond hair motionless. His hands, which swelled with warmth, never stopped moving.

She knew exactly what she was feeling, but could not yet admit it. Maggie was suspicious of her desires, especially when they moved in such a new direction. She looked for a serious fault, and believed she had found it, for as David Bryant entertained his audience, his eyes kept shifting to one of the other volunteers, Grace. Grace was dangerously drunk. Her head swayed, and a fallen earring glinted in the gradually descending cowl neck of her top. Maggie watched this David character monitor Grace's loss of function from across the room. By midnight, Grace had passed out on one of the sofas. 'What shall we do with her?' someone said.

'Give her another drink,' David shouted. People laughed, but not Maggie. She kept him under surveillance for the rest of the night, and – sure enough – she found him with Grace later, sitting outside by the river, his hand on her back. He tried to tip some liquid into her mouth, with limited success.

'Excuse me. What's going on?' Maggie said.

'Well, I think it's bedtime for this one.'

'Right. And you know Grace, do you?'

'No, we've just met,' David said, 'Charming girl. Bit vomity.' He turned and saw Maggie's disapproval. 'Listen, you needn't think I'm going to have my way with her. I'm a sexual submissive. She's useless to me in this state. She couldn't hit a cow's arse with a banjo.'

Maggie squinted, unsure. A taxi pulled up, casting a little light onto the street, and his eyes. 'How do you know where she lives?' Maggie said.

'I don't,' he said. 'I'm going to tell the cabbie to take her around the block a few times and dump her in the river.'

Maggie laughed, in spite of herself.

'Are you going to give me a hand, or just stand there and accuse me of molestation?' David said.

Maggie took the ankles, and David held Grace under the armpits. They hoisted her towards the car. He looked at Maggie, and smiled. 'Their eyes met across a crowded body,' he said.

'You're relentless,' she said.

She put it down to the force of an unusual day – the romance of the new stags, the river outside – but each time she thought of him that month she reeled. People would later refer to the age gap, but Maggie's first impression of David was of someone with a child's view of the world. That freedom and fascination.

She couldn't stop thinking back to his big right hand beneath Grace's armpit as they carried her to the taxi, his thick fingers reaching all the way over her shoulder. Maggie had felt that same hand clasp the back of her head later that night, the latent force of it. The sensation had been dizzying.

The shock, when she found him in the viewing hide three weeks later, was coupled with the realisation that he must have been watching her for some time from behind the one-way glass. While the blood thumped in her head, he was garrulous and silly, asking loudly about mating rituals in front of a prim old couple in cagouls. The woman sighed and tutted. David took a bag of humbugs from his coat. 'Do you want a sweetie?' he said to the woman in the cagoul. Maggie laughed before she could stop herself.

She had spent her twenties in confusing relationships with evasive indie guys who were so closed they wouldn't even say what they wanted to drink, so it was a huge relief to be with this man who insisted on speaking his mind, telling her his plans. Once Maggie had accepted her attraction to him, there were no barriers. He knew what he wanted from the start. Maggie, it appeared, knew what she wanted ten minutes after she got it.

'Where are you even—? Where do you *live*?' she said, in the dark, sweet-smelling alley by the covered market in Greenwich.

His eyes became serious for once. 'I live in a castle,' he said.

The day after he died the family solicitor had visited, and she had ushered him upstairs, out of Christopher's way. 'He's left it to you,' the solicitor said. For a moment she did not know what he meant. She thought it was another of those vague commiserative phrases. 'Left what?' she said. The solicitor turned to the window, looked out at the park.

Maggie surveyed that same ground from the high berth of the diving platform now. She counted the beating human hearts around her. The park staff would go home in another hour, leaving Christopher, who was skulking around out of sight in his makeshift den by the brook, and Louisa. Maggie had spoken to the villagers about Louisa. They called her Crow Jane, after Tim Nettles heard those words blaring out of the tape deck of her van. It was a shame she was so hostile, they said, because she'd probably scrub up nice if she lost the attitude, stripped off that birdshit-covered coat, spent half a day at 'Hair Force One' and took a leaf from her own falconry book on weight-management. In whispered asides, they said they had never understood why David kept her hanging around. But Maggie knew.

She looked over to the cottage. A light came on. Louisa held parts of David within her: stories, reflections, physical gestures that she had picked up over the long years of friendship. That was precious.

Two people in a three-mile radius. It was a start.

Maggie climbed back down to the ground and began to make her way to the house. She came to the wire fence of the ibex enclosure. She noted the wisps of hair and the familiar sharp scent by the wooden posts. She already knew that the ibex had escaped from the opposite end of the park, because the wires there had been cut, but something caught her eye. She crouched down by one of the posts. The top of it was broken and spattered with blood, most of which had soaked into the grain. There were still some dark traces of it on the grass below. Maggie ran her fingers over the blood on the wire. The park felt impossibly big to her at that moment, and she did not know how to defend it.

*   *   *

Louisa had always felt her nightmares to be droll and transparent. Of course, there were dreams of Anna Cliff – the hermit – and her children. Those would haunt her forever. She dreamed of walking through the fields with David, the quality of the light on that day in February 1975. Otherwise, her dreams consisted of giving birth to avian spinal cords with teeth, or finding five-foot hawks, their feathers tacky with blood, behind hedgerows. She did not need a mystic to decode those crude images. After the break-in she began to dream of the ibex kid she had saved. Sometimes she lay on the bank with him, sometimes he was steel-clad and in her bed. In all of the dreams she felt the constant repetition of his heartbeat. In the encyclopaedia she read that the ibex was once coveted for its healing properties. People drank its urine, and kept the bezoar stones from its intestines as a charm against cancer. But the heart-beat did not soothe her – it was more like a one-inch punch.

One night, several weeks after the releases, the beat was strong enough to wake her. She went downstairs to find an envelope which had dropped between her boots by the door. It contained a cheque for a thousand pounds (twice as much as she would need to fix the van), and a postcard: *Mrs Muster as Hebe.* The painting featured a strong Renaissance woman, staring out. For a moment Louisa did not notice the eagle feeding from the plate in the woman's hand. She turned the card over:

Hey there Louisa,

Here's a cheque to cover the damage to your truck. Call me if it's not enough. Just wanted to thank you once more for your help the other day. I had fun in a weird way! I guess next time we could just go for a drink or something.

Bit worried about the missing guests. All it takes is for a curious schoolboy to get bitten, and I'm out of business. If you do see any of the animals, another of those fine tackles should do the trick.

Feel free to call round any time.

Love,
Mags.

Louisa sat down on the corduroy button-backed sofa and picked up her guitar, but she did not play, just looked at the flakes of finger-skin caught on the strings. She thought of the figure she had seen on the grounds that night. Even if she had wanted to tell Maggie, how could she explain her excellent vantage point?

She, too, had read the newspaper stories about the break-in. Maggie had responded to the scaremongering with an interview in the *Derbyshire Herald*, in which she spoke of the ignorance of the animal liberationists she assumed to be responsible. '*Many of the animals "set free" were in fact infants, or ill. They will not survive in the wild without their parents. One of the foxes released was blind. That's animal cruelty.'*

Clever girl, Louisa thought. She wondered what Maggie had done to get such coverage when the 'Lions on the Loose' angle pulled in the punters. The photograph was of an ocelot cradled in arms to show that it was not much bigger than a domestic cat. The arms wore a ribbed thermal undergarment, tight to the skin with a row of tiny buttons up through the cuff, and a coat over the top with a zip pocket in the sleeve. The arms were Maggie's and Louisa knew it; she was all straps and zips and buttons, that one.

These were the forms in which Louisa felt most comfortable dealing with people: cropped photos and handwriting, on newspaper and card.

THREE

Maggie stepped into the entrance hall of the house after her early morning rounds and waited for her eyes to adjust to the darkness. Powdery rays fell from the skylight onto the faded staircase runner, but for a few moments, all she could see was her breath.

They had once lived on the ground floor, but Christopher insisted that they move upstairs after David died. Maggie had told Christopher of his father's death in David's office, downstairs, and she recalled that she had been unable to cry. Christopher had curled into a huge ball on the floor, as still and silent as the stuffed foxes and hares that surrounded him.

She climbed the stairs. The second floor, where they now lived, was dusty and sparsely furnished. Planks of wood rested on garden rocks to serve as shelves, and smoky marks stained the walls above the defunct storage heaters. That morning, Maggie found the cold air heavy with the cedarwood and citrus of David's aftershave. She had to steady herself. In the bathroom she found Chris Isaak blaring from the radio, and the bath rimmed with the rusty splinters of Christopher's beard. A small pool of the aftershave dripped from the edge of the sink onto the bare floorboards.

As she walked through the hall, she could hear Christopher in the living room, and could tell from his tone that he was talking to the Samaritans. 'Anyway, I can hear my arch-nemesis approaching, so I have to go. What? No, no, I'm no longer suicidal. Erm. Okay, bye.' He laughed, and Maggie could discern, beneath his gravelly mirth, her late husband's laugh.

She gave him time to organise a video as an alibi, waiting until the rasp of motor racing came from the TV before entering the room.

'Morning, Christopher,' she said.

'Is it?' he said.

She looked at her watch. 'Well, yes.'

He was bulky, his large head lit by the dual burners of bright blue tinted contact lenses. His affected coolness was borrowed from 1950s Hollywood: he sat with one arm across the back of the sofa, and he often said, 'Howdy.' This morning the fingers of his right hand were speckled with the phosphorescent orange dust from a bag of Monster Munch. His limp lower lip was, as usual, split down the middle by a shining line of blood, which stained his front teeth and his dental brace. She crouched down by him, so their eyes were level.

'I don't suppose anybody has called about the missing animals?' she asked.

'How should I know? Anyway, you should hire security guards. I need to be in a secure environment in order to, erm, erm, flourish.'

Maggie smiled. It was a direct quote from his educational support document.

Christopher's face brightened spontaneously. 'Erm. I had the best breakfast in Christendom today. Guess what I had,' he said.

'Monster Munch?'

'That was for afters.'

'Then I can't guess. Weetos?'

'Nope. Whiskey and erm, cheesecake.'

'Do you think that's wise?' Maggie said.

'Erm. I like cheesecake.'

'You're wearing your dad's aftershave,' she said.

'Yes. And? *What if?*'

'It's nice. As long as you've not been drinking it.'

'That's disgusting.'

He had not washed his hair in the bath, and it rose in stiff golden clumps now. Maggie put her hand into one of the clumps, straightening out a few knots. Christopher looked at the television, but did not resist her touch.

'You know, I had a word with the history guy at the college,' Maggie said.

'Who you're in league with.'

'I'm not in league with him. I'm not in league with anyone. Anyway, he says you can do a personal project without doing the rest of the qualification. It means you can write about Robin Hood, get all Sherwood on their asses.'

He fell silent, and she knew she had achieved a small victory. 'Enrolment is Thursday,' she said.

He stood up quickly, and left her looking at the impression of his knees in his jeans. 'Where are you going?' she said.

'Pub,' he said.

'But they won't serve you.'

'They did last time. I look old enough. Why won't they?'

She rose to her feet slowly and looked up at him. He exhaled with a loud whistle through his nose.

'Because it's eight-thirty in the morning,' she said.

'Whose side are you on?'

She sighed on hearing this stock phrase of his. It was some-times possible to turn his extraordinary sense of cliché to her advantage, but with that smell in the room she did not feel like it. She felt, in fact, as sick as a parrot.

Christopher left, and sorrow gripped hard. The smell bloomed again, and she thought of the aftershave staining the wood of the bathroom floor. She found some newspaper to absorb it.

She had first met Christopher on a carefully arranged visit to Derbyshire, and it was David who had been more nervous in the moments before. 'Christopher has been briefed,' David said as they sat waiting in the neutrality of the White Hart. 'In many ways, he's excited to meet you.' She looked at her fiancé with abject alarm.

Christopher walked in. He froze when he first saw her, arms by his sides. She rose from her seat, identifying him immediately, and approached.

'Erm. Who's that?' Christopher said, looking at David, pointing at Maggie. The regulars did not need him to single her out – they were already looking.

'Christopher, come on,' David said. 'You know who it is.'

Maggie stopped between them.

'Erm. You're telling me that *this* is your new woman?'

37

'This is Maggie, yes.'

Maggie smiled, and allowed herself to be examined.

'Wowsers,' said Christopher. 'Erm. When was she born, yester-day? She's an absolute oil painting.'

'Nice to meet you,' Maggie said. 'You're not so bad yourself.'

He kissed her hand. 'What are you doing with this, erm, old coot?' he said.

Now, in the bathroom, the newspaper sagged under the weight of the liquid, which turned it brown – aged it in seconds. Maggie lifted the soggy paper and saw that the wood had already absorbed much of the aftershave. She imagined it soaking through the floor and dripping from the ceiling in the rooms below.

She sat for a moment, feeling the alcohol penetrate the cuts on her hands. And she was aroused. She felt the feeling rattle down her chest. She picked up the electric toothbrush and took it to bed. Her eyes remained open; there were no fantasies. Afterwards she lay still and stared at the ceiling. Such desires had gripped her occasionally and forcefully since David had died. She did not know what she was supposed to feel, but she was pretty sure it wasn't this.

*   *   *

Louisa kept her indoor lighting low, and rarely drew the cur-tains, so she saw Maggie coming from some way off. She wore a big red padded jacket. Louisa waited for her to knock and left it a moment before rising from her chair. When she opened the door, she saw that Maggie's hair was wet. Her eyes were wet, too, and a little wild. She looked, to Louisa, disproportionately pleased to be on her neighbour's doorstep. Perhaps she was drunk.

'Hiya, Lou. Did you get my note?'

'Yes. Thank you.' She pulled the cheque from her back pocket and returned it to Maggie. 'I don't need this.'

'Oh, come on. I wrecked your van. I insist.' Maggie pushed the cheque back but Louisa shook her head.

'I don't need it. I know a man who will do it cheap.'

'Right.' Maggie looked over Louisa's shoulder into the house. 'It's cold tonight.'

'You should wear a hat,' Louisa said.

'Yeah.' Maggie looked down at the cheque. 'Let's go and spend this,' she said.

'What?' Louisa said.

'It's quiz night at the White Hart.'

Louisa gave a derisive sniff. The irony of looking for answers in that place was crushing.

'Do you fancy coming down?' Maggie said. The wind flexed as she spoke, so that she had to shout, sounding more urgent than she probably intended. Louisa looked around. The moon was big and close, and the trees gave a crisp hiss.

'Can't really,' Louisa said.

'You busy, eh?'

'It's not so much that.'

'No. Me neither. I'm pretty busy in the day. Night-time? Not so very busy, I must say.'

Louisa did not speak.

'Come on. Christopher's out. Two hours. An hour. I'm buying. We need to get off this hill.'

'I just bathed.'

'And I just had a shower. Perfect. Sisters looking hot.'

Louisa found that remark distasteful, in many ways. 'No. Thank you. Anyway, I'd have thought you'd be staying at home in the evenings, after those break-ins.'

Maggie nodded, squeezed her eyes shut. 'Are you okay?' she said.

'Me? I'm fine,' Louisa said.

'Oh, that's good. I'm not fine, to be honest. And I don't much want to go down into the village and drink with those old buggers, but I quite fancied a drink with *you*.'

Louisa had no time for emotional blackmail. 'Listen. I don't expect you've ever been turned down. I'll put it down to inexperience, but you have this knack of only turning up here when you want something, so I can't help feeling like the bottom of the barrel. It's not a pleasant sensation, being scraped. I told your husband the same.'

Maggie shook her head and choked back some tears. She pointed to her house. 'I am in that ... *fucking* place on my jacks, waiting to be broken into. And I don't think my company is so poor that *I'd* be the only one to gain from us having a chat. And I know exactly what you told my husband. I just wonder what you tell your fucking self.'

She walked away. Louisa made sure she slammed the door quickly. The bloodrush made her giddy. She shut the lights off and watched Maggie through the window. Sixty paces from the house she was nothing more than that red coat lit by the moon.

Headless, legless. It was about then that Maggie screamed, 'For fuck's sake!' She didn't hold back on the volume.

Sleep proved difficult that night. Apart from the adrenal pump of the argument, Louisa panicked over what David had told Maggie. Had he told her about the second day of their hunting challenge, back when they were teenagers? Their silent, breathless walk through the glades and fields? It was the last day of February, and the last moment of pure beauty that Louisa could remember experiencing with another human. It was more likely he had told her of the moments following the walk, their lives split in two like rotten wood. She thought of David stumbling away from the hedgerow. She drifted off, and woke to find the moon so strong she thought it was afternoon.

At that moment, Louisa was truly aware of the exposed location of her cottage. And she could feel Maggie's presence, too. The walls of their houses seemed irrelevant, flimsy. She thought of Maggie trembling on the doorstep. It had been a long time since Louisa had provoked anger in another person, a long time since she had elicited emotion of any kind.

* * *

Training a falcon is unlike training a dog because a falcon does not – and will never – care for its owner. That was always the first thing Louisa said at falconry displays. The falcon comes from a world beyond society or hierarchy, and depends upon nobody. When she first received a falcon, Louisa would watch it bate from the glove, so sickened by her proximity that it would rather die than look at her. In practice, this mentality rendered punishment and censure utterly useless as training tools. The only way to proceed was to reduce the weight of the bird until it relented to the falconer as a source of food. Louisa had seen overweight hawks take off, even after several seasons, never to return.

People at the displays often asked Louisa what was in it for her. Falcons are so ungiving, they said. It's a one-way relationship. She replied that they worked together. When they went out on the moor, and her dog was on point, and Diamond rose to his pitch – even if Louisa could not see him through the cloud or the glare – they *knew* each other. She gave the signal, the grouse were flushed, and there he was, head over feet, plummeting. It was a privilege.

Diamond would come off the kill for her, and if that was because she was holding meat, then so what? If the respect was grudging, then it was earned. If you think human relationships aren't based on power, Louisa told the doubters, then maybe it's you who wants your head looking at. At least a falcon doesn't lie about it.

That week she received and trained a new lanner. On the Friday she looked down at the table in her kitchen, the needles and coping tools, the green stars of shit, the towels for swaddling, and the immature falcon. She realised she had not given the bird a name. There had been no need, for they were the only two beings in the house. If she was not talking to the lanner, she was talking to herself. Excepting those commands made to her dogs and birds, she had spoken perhaps forty words since the argument with Maggie on the doorstep almost a week ago. She read

Maggie's postcard again, and thought of the ibex's neck, hot against her face. She picked up the phone and dialled.

'I want to invite you and Christopher over for a short display. No, no trouble. It won't be anything special. He'll be fine. Can't be any crazier than me.'

FOUR

At that time of year, nature blended the boundaries. Leaves from the hilltop churchyard blew across the animal enclosures and onto Louisa's land. Wasps crawled drunk from grounded apples in the acidic fizz of afternoon light.

Louisa stood on the weathering lawn and watched Christopher and Maggie crossing the field towards her. Christopher wore a long waxed jacket which may have been his father's, and marched with his usual forward lean. Maggie looked small, steadying herself against him in the mud. Her voice carried in shards. Louisa had arranged Diamond and the new lanner, hooded, on Arab perches on the lawn, and put the Harris hawks, Fred and Harold, out of the way on bow perches. The hawks turned their heads, one after the other, to watch Maggie and Christopher approach.

'Well, hello there,' Maggie said to the birds, before smiling at Louisa without a hint of animosity. Louisa had braced herself for tension after the other night's rant, but there was none.

Christopher sipped from a can of Fanta and eyed the hawks suspiciously.

'I need your help with this one, Christopher,' Louisa said, pointing to the lanner.

'I'm not touching it,' said Christopher.

'You don't have to. He doesn't have a name, that's all. I wondered if you could help me name him.'

Christopher looked at the bird for a moment, and then at his feet. 'Steve,' he said.

'Okay,' said Louisa. 'Steve it is.'

Maggie laughed, and Christopher scowled at her until she stopped. 'So what do you think of them?' Maggie said.

'Erm. They seem daemonic,' he said.

'Christopher!' Maggie said. 'Sorry, Louisa. He says that about everything at the moment.'

'That's okay. I've called them worse.'

Christopher impersonated his stepmother: 'It's daemonic this, erm, daemonic that.'

Louisa took Diamond on her fist, removed his hood and began her standard lecture. She saw no reason to personalise the display. 'This is Diamond, a peregrine falcon,' she said. 'He's male. Males are known as tiercels, because they are a third of the size of females.'

Maggie nudged Christopher, who tutted.

Louisa continued. 'The world comes to Diamond differently. He sees polarised light. He sees ultraviolet. Most people know that a falcon's vision is long-range and acute, but what they don't know is that a peregrine sees the world *slowed down.*'

Maggie raised her eyebrows and nodded. Louisa put her face

close to Diamond, who looked away. 'The rate of signals from his eye to his brain is many times higher than that of a human. If Diamond watched TV, he'd just see a collection of static images constantly turning from dark to light.'

An insect buzzed around Christopher's drink.

'The wasp that just flew past your face in a blur,' Louisa said to Christopher, 'would not be a blur to Diamond. He would see it slowly passing by in perfect detail. He'd be able to see each beat of its little wings.'

Christopher batted at the persistent wasp, and then looked up at Louisa. 'So how fast is the wasp *really*, erm, going?' he said.

'What?' Louisa said.

'Well, if the wasp is going fast for me, and it's going slow for the bird, how fast is it *really* going?'

Louisa frowned. This is what happens when you ad-lib, she thought. She turned to Maggie, who was trying to suppress a smile. 'Maggie, do you know anything about the nature of time as an entity independent of human perception?'

Maggie laughed. 'Afraid not.'

'Life must be, erm, boring for them,' Christopher said. 'Even F1 would seem slow.'

Louisa had forgotten about his obsession with motor racing. Perhaps she could use it. 'Do you know anything about G-force, Christopher?'

His eyes widened and he began to stammer. 'Yes. Erm. Nigel Mansell sometimes underwent the force of up to two G during, erm, Grand Prix racing,' he said. He put down his drink and pulled his skin taut across his face.

'Pretty impressive,' Louisa said. 'How much G-force can a human stand, do you know?'

Christopher was delighted. 'Erm. That's easy. Six G.'

'God, well done you,' said Maggie, slapping Christopher's back.

'That's quite a lot, isn't it?' Louisa said.

'Six G is called, erm, G-LOC. The blood starts to drain from the eyes and consciousness is lost. It's not at all promising.'

Louisa nodded. 'You want to know how many Gs Diamond can take?'

Christopher stared at Diamond, who adjusted his feet on the glove. 'How many?' Christopher said.

'About twenty-eight G,' Louisa said.

'Horseshit!'

'Absolutely true.'

'That thing?'

'This very thing.'

Louisa looked at Diamond. 'He's pretty mean in character, but there's no way that Diamond could kill a grouse, which is almost three times his size, in a *straight fight*. So he pitches himself way up high – about a thousand feet – and then folds into this vertical dive, called a stoop. It's just about the finest, most ingenious thing you can witness. You can actually hear it. In the stoop, Diamond has a peak speed of two hundred miles an hour, increasing his killing weight from two pounds to sixty.'

'Jumping Jehosaphat,' said Christopher. He did some calculations and turned to Maggie. 'That's like thirty of me landing on you,' he said to her. 'Imagine that.'

'I'd rather not,' said Maggie.

'You'd be flattened,' said Christopher, clapping his hands together.

Louisa hooded Diamond, placed him back on his perch, and moved on to the Harris hawks. Fred was slightly larger, but they were both nearly chicken-sized, with big necks and chocolate feathers broken by rusty tones. Their feet and beaks were a strong yellow from the egg yolk she fed them. 'We're not going to fly Diamond today,' she said, 'We'll fly these two. Harris hawks don't mind people so much. You can bring them into your house, introduce them to the kids, sit them down at the dinner table, watch TV with them, or whatever it is you do of an evening . . . ' Louisa said, struggling a little for ideas.

'I like family values,' said Christopher.

'Diamond would go crazy if I tried that shit with him,' Louisa said. Maggie laughed again.

Louisa took Fred from the bow perch onto her glove, and then cast him into the trees surrounding the garden. He watched everything: the movement of Maggie's hand as she scratched her neck, the stone that Louisa kicked, the leaves. Louisa took out the rabbit lure – a strip of raw beef tied to a toy bunny, fixed to a length of string. She buried the lure in the undergrowth, and then whipped it out and ran with it. Fred descended from a nearby tree, gave a short chase, and crushed the toy. Maggie applauded, while Christopher tilted his head uneasily to watch Fred feed.

'Anybody fancy a go?' Louisa asked.

Christopher remained silent, and eventually Maggie stepped up. Fred flew to the high branches of a beech, and Louisa took off her glove, which steamed a little. She passed it over Maggie's long fingers and pulled it down. 'Almost fits,' Maggie said, squeezing a fist.

'It'll do,' Louisa said.

Louisa arranged Maggie's body so that the younger woman stood side-on to the bird, her head turned and her left arm extended. Louisa took a day-old chick from the bag and popped the yolk sac, placed it in Maggie's gloved hand, the blood and yolk darkening the worn leather. 'Call him,' Louisa said.

'Fred. Come on, sweetie,' Maggie said.

The bird leaned forward, stopped, and came. The silence was heavy as the wings beat and then held, the bird coming lower, inches from the ground before rising to the glove. Louisa looked at Maggie, because it was her first time. Maggie stayed still and kept her eyes on the hawk. She did not flinch. Louisa felt a slight disappointment, although she could not have articulated the source.

'Good boy,' whispered Maggie. Louisa could see the shock of it in her, a woman who worked with animals but was nevertheless excited by the level of control, and the simultaneous lack of it. Fred picked at the flesh, and Maggie released a little more of the chick's body.

'Okay, let him go,' Louisa said. Maggie cast Fred back into the air. He flew to the nearest tree and licked his feet.

'Will you give it a try, Christopher?' asked Maggie.

'No,' said Christopher. 'There's no point, now you've done it.'

'Come on,' Maggie said. 'It's another string to your bow.'

Christopher considered the phrase carefully. It was one of his favourites. 'Erm. Okay,' he said. 'One go.'

Louisa set him up. She had not been so close to the boy for

some time. She found the blue lenses strange, but more troubling was his silhouette, dark against the dropping light behind him. It was almost the same as David's, the paunch already thick, the legs strong, the shoulders sloping down. He was a little older than David had been when he and Louisa had gone hunting together that day.

Louisa placed another chick on the glove. 'Gross,' said Christopher. He bobbed the dead head against his fist. 'Call him in,' said Louisa.

'You do it,' said Christopher. Louisa tapped Christopher's glove and called out for Fred, who had the taste and required no second ask. He dropped from the tree.

Christopher's frown appeared to be inquisitive, nothing more, but when the hawk rose up through the last metre, Christopher screamed and hit the ground, flinging the chick away in a spinning spray of yolk and blood. Fred rose steeply and flew over to the roof of the old aviary, where he bristled. Louisa stood back and looked at Christopher.

'Bloody thing tried to kill me,' Christopher shouted, still on the ground, his arms over his head.

'Hey, what happened, sweetie?' said Maggie, walking over.

'Don't you come anywhere near me!' Christopher said, peering out from behind his hands. Maggie froze. 'And don't call me sweetie. I hate it. This is all your doing. You forced me to come here.' He was almost crying.

'Christopher, it's okay. It's a perfectly natural reaction,' said Maggie.

Louisa wasn't listening. She looked over at Fred, who seemed undisturbed, now, although he would make her pay later, for letting that boy snatch his food away. She took a guess at what a normal person would do. She crouched down to check on Christopher, who was still curled up in a ball. 'You're okay,' she said. She took him by the elbow, which he ripped around sharply into her face, knocking her over. She would later confess – though only to herself – to a feeling of exhilaration as she lay there on the grass.

'Jesus, Christopher, what are you doing?' said Maggie, running to Louisa.

'You can shut up,' Christopher said, standing. 'That bloody thing tried to, erm, kill me.'

'You can't just fucking hit people,' Maggie said.

'I'm fine,' Louisa said quietly, sitting up.

'It's your doing,' said Christopher again, pointing his big crooked finger at Maggie, dirt in the wrinkles. 'I never wanted to come here, and I never asked for you.'

He made a gesture of contrite protest to Louisa. 'I'm alright,' she said. 'Just taking five.' But he was quickly on his way, head down, shaking the glove onto the ground.

'I'm going to get completely inebriated,' he called back.

Maggie looked distraught. 'Well, he can make a good decision when he tries,' she said. She offered her arm to Louisa, who said she felt happy sitting down for a while. Maggie's eyes, swirling and opaque like a stick-stirred brook, gradually took their focus on Louisa, and then widened. 'He's cut you,' she said. Louisa dabbed at her lip, saw fresh blood on her fingers. 'Nah, I'm fine,' she said. 'It was just the shock that knocked me over.'

'That and the sixteen stone he weighs,' said Maggie.

After a few minutes, Louisa got to her feet, still shaky. She called Fred down from the roof, put the hawks in the weatherings, and knew she was done for the day.

Maggie took disinfectants and medical equipment from the weighing room, and ignored Louisa's insistence that she would treat herself. She made her go into the cottage and lie on the sofa. Louisa was secretly pleased, because she felt suddenly shattered.

She knew from her touch that Maggie was getting used to working with animals. The securing grip on the neck gave it away. Maggie washed the wound and stemmed the blood flow with cotton wool and petroleum jelly.

'I'm so sorry,' Maggie said.

'Forget it.'

'I'm sorry you had to witness that domestic scene, too.'

'Sounded pretty hurtful.'

'I'm used to it.'

Louisa thought back to how disagreeable she herself had been when Maggie first moved in.

'I appreciate what you did today,' Maggie said. 'I thought it was outstanding. When I called that hawk out of the tree, it felt like the first clear space I've had in my head for months. Does that make sense?'

'Big old beak and talons headed for you – tends to focus the mind.'

'I loved it.'

'I know you did.'

'I'd like to do it again,' Maggie said.

'I'm pretty busy.'

'So am I.'

'Which is also a problem. Too many people these days want to fly a hawk for a day, go back and tell their friends they touched the wilderness. I don't see shit burning any holes in their clothes. If you want to do this, it's got to be every minute.'

'I do know a little about the care of animals,' said Maggie.

Louisa managed half a nod of acknowledgment. The problem was the look on Maggie's face as Fred had risen to her fist. She looked him right in the eye, did not twitch. Louisa had spent most of her life fiercely guarding the secrets of her daily life with the hawks. She did not want people to know exactly what she did; she only wanted them to know that they could not do it themselves. And here was someone who perhaps could.

Christopher was still trembling when he arrived in the White Hart. The place smelled of blocked drains. He approached the bar. 'What do you want?' David Wickes asked.

'I want to settle down with a faithful woman and have some progeny, far away from this hell-hole,' Christopher said.

'I meant to drink.'

'Oh, right. Erm. A double Drambuie and a white wine, erm, spritzer.'

Wickes sighed. 'You're the boss,' he said, turning away to make the drinks. 'But your father didn't think Detton was such a hell-hole.'

'What do you know?' Christopher said, under his breath.

He was tired of the way people talked about his father in this pub. Before he died, they used to say, 'Your dad is a legend, youth.' Christopher would reply, 'Erm, incorrect. A legend must be, erm, deceased. It's part of the definition.'

Such definitions now contributed to his logic for the existence of a real historical Robin Hood. To be a legend, you have to die. To die, you must have lived. Therefore, it followed that Robin Hood had really lived. It also meant, he realised, that the men in the pub were now free to call his father a legend.

The problem, as with all legends, was that the stories the men told of his father changed and slipped. The details turned upside down, or were forgotten. The regulars never talked of how his father would take him garbage fishing in the brook; they never mentioned the pedal cart races around the enclosures. They spoke only of naked dancing at the big house on Drum Hill (strange), and of women and more women and better women (too much information). It was worrying to hear them get the facts wrong. When people got the facts wrong once, they rarely corrected them, in Christopher's experience. You ended up with an Australian Robin Hood and a father you didn't recognise.

Christopher took his Drambuie in a couple of gulps and started on the spritzer. Tim Nettles sat on a stool at the end of the bar, and nodded. 'Hello, lad. Any luck with that online dating malarkey?'

'That's classified,' Christopher said. He'd only just set up his profile, and couldn't remember talking to Nettles about it.

'Plenty of nice young ladies up on that hill, I'd have thought,' Nettles said.

'Erm, plenty of lunatics. With their idiot birds.'

'I can't think who you might be referring to,' Nettles said. Wickes smiled.

'I'll find my Marian,' Christopher said. He looked up at Wickes. 'Same, erm, again, please bartender.'

It was his father who had told him the stories of Robin Hood. It had been part of their nightly routine: they would watch Marx

Brothers films, and then his father would tell him tales in which Robin was a lithe, skinny child who used his cunning and slight stature to crawl through the legs of the sheriff. In David's stories, Robin could disguise himself as tumbleweed, or a green bouncy ball. Christopher had never resembled that ingenious boy, but he had loved the tales.

Since his father had died, Christopher had felt angry about those made-up, babyish yarns. Anyone could create such stories and what was the use of that? Christopher wanted something real. He had read widely about the historical figure of Robin Hood. In the old ballads, Robin massacred fourteen foresters because they forbade him to hunt on the king's land. Christopher was sure this was true because he had seen empirical evidence: there was a skull in a museum in Nottingham alongside a crossbow bolt they'd found rattling around inside. They had dug up thirteen bodies in a row. Pretty conclusive, Christopher thought. This Robin was no spry youngster; he was vengeful and he stalked through the woods like Christopher did, slighted and furious.

Christopher necked his drinks and took another round before he left. 'I need the alcohol to face, erm, going home again,' he told the regulars. Many of them could relate to that sentiment.

As he walked up the hill, he prepared himself for a clash with the Turncoat Maggie Green. So he'd elbowed someone in the face. That was nothing compared to Maggie's betrayals. He tried to list them: she rarely talked about his father, and when she did, it annoyed him; he suspected that she had not invited his real mother to his father's funeral, even though it would have been an ideal opportunity for a reunion; she made him go to the ridiculous bird display. The list went on.

When he got inside the big house, Maggie came down the stairs, which seemed to be spinning. 'Are you okay?' Maggie said.

'I don't want to hear it,' Christopher said. 'It was the bird's fault.'

'Why is David Wickes allowing you to drink so much?'

'David, erm, Wickes is my friend.'

As Maggie helped him up the stairs, Christopher tried to think of some of Groucho Marx's sayings about women, to insult her with. *A woman is an occasional pleasure but a cigar is ... something. Women should be ... something.*

It was difficult to remember the ones about women. When his father dropped him at school, he would say, 'Go, and never darken my towels again.' That was Christopher's favourite; the last laugh of the day and it wasn't even nine o'clock. Most afternoons, when his father collected him, Christopher would be upset or crying. His father would hold him in the car and whisper, 'If I held you any closer, I'd be on the other side of you.'

Christopher had a funny taste in his mouth and he thought he might be sick. Maggie tried to stabilise him. Christopher retched and stumbled towards the bathroom, with Maggie in tow. After he'd vomited, he dredged up another old Groucho quote, the same one he'd spontaneously remembered at the end of his father's funeral, the last time he was this drunk.

'I've had. Erm. A wonderful evening. Erm, erm. But this wasn't it.'

Louisa fell asleep for a long while, and when she opened her eyes Maggie was kneeling above her, dabbing a bag of frozen coffee below her lip. Louisa panicked and tried to get up, but Maggie pressed her down easily. 'It's okay,' she said.

'You don't need to do that,' said Louisa, noticing that Maggie had changed her clothes, and showered. Her skin smelled clean, and her hair glistened. She was dressed up.

'Couldn't find any frozen peas at home, so it's a middle-class substitute.'

'All that's in my freezer is dead mice.'

Maggie smiled. 'Christopher came home. He did get inebriated.'

'How long have I been asleep?'

'Not all that long, actually. He must have hit it hard and fast. He threw his guts up in the bathroom.'

'And there I was about to apologise for the mess in here,' Louisa said, looking back at the soiled newspaper and feathers on the kitchen table. Maggie took the cold away, and Louisa's face regained a little feeling. It was not welcome.

'I don't know what to do with him,' Maggie said, quietly. 'Christopher.'

Not many people sought Louisa's advice on human concerns. David had occasionally asked her opinion about one of his girlfriends. He had never asked her about Maggie, though.

'You could ask what's-her-name,' Louisa said.

'His counsellor?'

'No. His mother.'

Maggie looked away. 'What could I ask her?' she said.

'Well. Couldn't he go and live with her?'

'That's not the kind of solution I was looking for,' Maggie said. She looked at her watch, bracelets jangling as she turned her wrist. Nothing more was said. Louisa was dragged again into sleep, and the re-treading of old fields.

FIVE

Louisa had always been good on village folklore, and was familiar with Anna Cliff long before their lives collided so significantly.
Oakley, where Louisa and David grew up, was gentrified, fashionable, conservative. It was still quaintly agricultural in the 1970s
and had avoided the millhouse rows of nearby villages. But in
towns like Oakley, there is always a little squalor, and even people
with the best intentions fall down. Anna Cliff fell in a way which
became local legend.

She lived near the canal, on a patch of land which had been
cleared for development, but abandoned. It was rat-infested,
damp, plagued by floods, the light obstructed by huge sycamores.
The developers built one house and folded, so Anna got it cheap.
The Oakley locals speculated unkindly on the currency with
which Anna had paid. Such rumours followed her whatever she
did.

Anna's fiancé, Henry Morgan, had gone to war and never
returned, but his name was not carved into the memorial on the

local park. It was said that Henry, who had been a farm labourer in Oakley, had met a woman in France and fallen in love.

By the time Louisa was old enough to recognise her, walking the bridle path through the fields, Anna Cliff had a thick ring of scarred flesh at the base of her neck. The scar stood white against her dark – almost Mediterranean – skin. Louisa's older brothers, both living away from home, would spend Sundays telling gruesome stories about how Anna got her scar. Her colouring was unusual for the region in those times, and as a child Louisa had been struck by the dark richness of Anna's brown eyes. Without much care for historical accuracy, people called her Anne of Cleves when they saw the scar. They said she was a gypsy, or half-Indian. Louisa's brothers said she was a Nazi.

Over the years, villagers counted off Anna Cliff's four children, whose fathers were various. She tried to trap one man, a married farmer, into taking paternal responsibility, but the villagers rebuked her with such force, and from so many directions, that she never tried again. People like Louisa's parents often took guesses at the identity of the fathers. It became a dinner party joke. *'I saw the youngest Cliff child today. A real ringer for Tom Easter, it must be said.'*

In truth, the three boys and one girl all looked a lot like their mother. They ducked in and out of care, in and out of school, and if Anna was guilty only of distracted neglect, the children suffered plenty of mistreatment at the hands of their sometime classmates. Louisa was never party to such cruelty because she did not attend the state school, but she heard about it. And she heard when the children were finally taken away from their mother, to be distributed to foster parents across the Midland cities.

Richard Smedley, Louisa's father, was a social climber. He had worked hard in his job, and on his accent. He went shooting with the right people. Richard warned his young daughter that she would end up just like the Cliff woman if she kept on with her wild behaviour. Louisa figured that most Oakley girls had been told as much. It was one of her father's less inventive insults.

*   *   *

Louisa first encountered a bird of prey when she was five years old.

She lay on the back seat of the car, watching the slow swipe of the roadside lights through the dusk. Her parents sat quietly, as they always did after one of her tantrums, her father's retaliatory rage all spent, her mother exhausted by the confrontation.

Louisa's tantrums had the effect of temporarily suppressing her functions and needs, and she often recovered to find herself hungry or in pain. This time she needed urgently to urinate. She moaned.

'Louisa needs the toilet,' her mother said.

'There are none,' her father said.

'Richard, pull over, please.'

'Let her sit in it.'

Her father was always the last to relent, if he did so at all, but on this occasion another louder moan was all it took. He feared for his upholstery and soon pulled in to a layby. As Louisa prepared to leave the car he turned around and said, 'Who do you think you are?'

She often recalled that nasty remark in adulthood. What a thing to say to a child. She got him back in the end, she reasoned, simply by answering his question.

Louisa and her mother climbed the roadside bank, struggling against their skirts in a strong gale. Over the bank was a stubble field, and before that a tangle of bushes and weeds. Louisa squatted awkwardly with one hand on her dress and the other outstretched to her mother, for balance. She nearly passed out with relief.

The bird arrived as she was in mid-flow. She could not identify it. Now, when she thinks back, she sees an eagle but she knows that it was probably a buzzard, or a kite. The bird had perhaps been glanced by a car or attacked by crows, for it came down scared, and crashed into the bushes. The thrashing noise startled Mrs Smedley, who screamed and let go of her daughter's hand. Louisa stumbled slightly, pissing on her shoes, but she did not fall. She was quite calm. The bird righted itself, and they watched each other. It looked so big, so outraged. Three seconds passed until it recovered and took off, Louisa watching it all the way over the trees.

'Good God,' Mrs Smedley said, with a hand to her chest. She looked at the damp patch on her daughter's dress, but Louisa hadn't noticed. Louisa had never heard of falconry, but at that moment she had a fair idea of what she wanted to do. It was all over bar the shouting, of which there was plenty.

Her father had assumed falconry to be a regal sport, but soon found that – apart from a few famous exceptions – the majority of modern practitioners were working men. As such, he hoped

Louisa's fascination would pass, but she flung away the picture-books about dancing, and he found her burying her pony figurine in the flowerbed, digging with her hands. Two summers later, she was still talking about hawks, and Richard saw a notice promoting a small summer fair given for the council housing residents in the back-end of Staffordshire. He thought he could scare it out of her.

It was a bare, rough place; the smell of yeast from the nearby Marmite factory and brewery competing with the bad meat and burnt sugar of the food stalls. The wind whipped gravel off the hill-top car park. Richard Smedley saw the bony, half-dressed slum-clearance youths throwing hoops and wondered if he'd gone too far, whether this might turn nasty. He looked nervously back at his car.

Louisa could see nothing but the six birds, tethered and fenced off, raising their legs one at a time as if attempting to free them-selves from adhesive goop. She watched them, straight-faced, hands in the pockets of her unseasonal coat. She looked like a folded umbrella.

Roy Ogden stood on the pristine bowling green, the best patch of grass for ten miles in any direction. Forty yards away perched Banjo, an Indian eagle owl, his head turned to look at something in the firs behind. 'Anybody up for a goo?' Roy said.

Louisa pushed to the front, right hand still in her pocket, left hand out and bared. 'I would like to.' The small crowd noted the elocution, and looked at her father, who said, 'That's too big for you, dear.'

'No it is not,' Louisa said. 'I can hold a two-pound bag of sugar. He's not much more than that.'

Roy Ogden smiled. He'd been doing displays long enough to

know the voice of a falconer, whatever the size of the person it came from. He lifted her over the dividing wall.

Banjo would not come when Ogden called, and Louisa's top-lip whistle drew a laugh and an 'oo, a say' from the crowd. It also got the owl turning and dropping, the amber scorch of the eyes locked stone still within the nonsense of wings. Clambering into the upward arc, Banjo spread a shadow at the girl's feet, hitting the big glove hard. Louisa gasped.

While Banjo fed from her first, Louisa – heart going crazy – walked towards her father at the dividing wall. As she approached, Banjo raised his big wings for balance and Richard Smedley took a step back. Louisa witnessed the act with fascination.

It was the falcons she really wanted to fly when she saw them dipping over the scout hut at a brutal pace. 'Be a few years before you can handle one a them,' Roy Ogden said.

'That's not so long,' Louisa said.

Roy Ogden, black moustache on a thick face, and a way of biting the tip of his tongue when concentrating, fixed motorbikes in his own residential garage in Whatstandwell, working through the night to give himself daylight hours to fly falcons. He limped badly from the accident that had forced him to quit riding bikes, but his hawks moved with perfect grace and at his bidding.

Louisa's apprenticeship was a constant pushing at the boundaries of pleasure, until not long after her thirteenth birthday when she taught her first peregrine, Jacko, to stoop from out of pure grey nothing towards the grouse flushed from cover. The clatter of the contact was audible, and the stunned grouse gave up feathers like a trail of puffed cigar smoke, made a soft noise as it came down in the yellow tussocks. That day was the culmination of months of training for the falcon, and years of training for the girl. 'Nothing you can't do, now,' said Roy.

This was the seventies, before worldwide artificial breeding programmes, and the peregrine was teetering on the edge of oblivion. DDT pesticides had thinned the shells of peregrine eggs. Even obtaining such a bird was tricky and not always legal. There was a deathly zeal about hunting with a peregrine. The threat of imminent extinction was with them in the field.

The evening after Jacko's stoop, Louisa's brothers came for tea, but she felt unable to bear the presence of her family. It was a private feeling, this triumph – a lonely physical pleasure that she worried would show on her face. So she lay in the bath behind a locked door, turned up the radio and let the dirt drift off her arms. With her eyes closed she still felt tentacular, bound to her companions in the field, as though the dog was on point in the living room, Jacko was pitched hundreds of yards above the roof, and Roy Ogden was standing by the sink.

The hawking season coincided with the school term. There was no contest. The first couple of times she arrived at his house in the early morning, Roy drove Louisa the many miles back to school, but he eventually realised that he did not have the fuel money to win the war, and figured it was best to teach her well. She proved herself an asset in the field.

Mostly they took sandwiches, but they had occasional pub lunches where the landlords allowed children, and once stopped at a greasy spoon at the base of the Heights of Abraham, the cable cars swinging above them. These were Louisa's first few mouth-fuls of Derbyshire, and it was she who recommended Detton to David in later years.

On the days she attended school, Louisa went straight from feeding the birds, blood streaked across her hands. This did little for her popularity, about which only her mother cared. Mrs Smedley sometimes took the liberty of inviting other girls to tea, but Louisa always managed to sneak them into the shed, where they commented in whispers on the smell of the birds, and how it 'explained a few things.' Sometimes they cried over a hawk's messy consumption of a chick; one girl even vomited. Louisa assured her that the dog would clean it up.

The transition to secondary school had been a failure, and her teens promised a lack of all healthy conventions. It was in this lowly social state that she came across David Bryant.

Their schools were separated by gender, the icy hip of the A-road, and a field containing five magnificent Herefords, including a shaggy, horned bull. The lazy bulk of the cows made the trees and cars look small from where Louisa spent her lunchtimes – in the hilltop outwoods beyond the school fence.

One morning in December, whilst playing truant, she saw a group of six boys approach the field in their dark green blazers. She recognised the blond boy as he ducked down below the wall. The others crowded around him, their heads rocking back a second before Louisa heard the squawk of their laughter. In a moment, the blond boy was up and over the wall, naked but for his pointed shoes and grey woollen socks pulled up to mid-calf.

'Off you go, Bryant.'

'Tell them to be gentle.'

'With your arse.'

'Tell them you want commitment before you do it.'

David Bryant bounced from foot to foot, his hair shuddering. 'That one looks like Thompson's mother,' he said, pointing at a cow with a thick ginger fringe, as he set off towards the group of supine beasts. His sprint was compact and muscular, his cock – made shy by the frosty air – bobbing as he changed direction. The cows were uninterested but for one, who startled from a doze and sprang away, causing David to leap and call out, to the delight of his friends. After he passed the bull, he continued to run hard for the fence, his body steaming, his breath visible. He stopped twenty metres below Louisa, and laughed to himself quietly. Louisa could make out the damp brightness of his face, and the spots on his shoulders. She slid behind a tree, her smile set deep within her.

David did not see her. He turned to face his friends and raised his arms to acknowledge the applause and the shouts of *bravo*, while one of the boys tried to rouse the Herefords by throwing stones at them. Louisa looked at the hollows of his buttocks. The traffic slowed as it passed the scene.

Louisa was unprepared for the calamity of her feelings, and the hopelessness of the reality which met them. She knew him – he was the son of her father's friend – and now the mention even of stern, moustachioed Mr Lawrence Bryant made her reel. She despised such reactions in herself.

It was easy to re-order her short past around the few sightings of him. She remembered accompanying her father to the Bryant house, and seeing David, seven years old, sliding down the carpeted stairs on his backside. She remembered seeing him one Christmas near the canal with his two black labs. This now seemed hugely significant to her, for she had been out with her hawks that day, despite the fact that hunting was illegal on Christmas Day. He had seen her the way she saw herself, as a falconer.

When Mrs Smedley asked Louisa if she wanted to invite someone over for tea, Louisa, knowing her father was away on business, said Roy Ogden. Her mother relented, having long given up, generally, on what she had in mind. After tea, Louisa played her guitar loud enough so that her mother, washing dishes in the kitchen, could not hear her tell Oggie about David. He laughed gently and said, 'You want to fit everything in before you're fifteen, that's your trouble. You'll soon be ready to retire. Life is long, duck. Spread the butter thin.'

Love made Louisa despise a social world which she had thus far simply ignored. Some of the girls she knew already spoke of having had more than two lovers, and even her parents seemed to find such talk fashionable when they heard it on the television. People swung, cheated, or just moved on. Louisa could not compete in such a world and did not want to. She became puritanical as a result. There would be David Bryant, and nobody else.

She thought again about that Christmas morning: like Louisa, David had shunned the trivialities of celebration in favour of responsibility to his animals. He was the type of man who would understand.

The problem with Louisa's image of David Bryant was David Bryant himself. At fifteen he was a loud, drunk, happy, popular, rugby-playing nightmare. Unlike Louisa, whose politics had been broadened by Roy Ogden, David had no notion of life outside his class. He was pleased to be an integral part of the world she hated.

A week before the Pony Club Ball in Nottingham, Louisa realised she would have to infiltrate this world in order to drag him out of it. Her mother, on her knees at the hem of the dress, looked down at Louisa's wide, nicked feet spilling over the sharp edges of her small shoes, like rising white bread. 'You know we can curl your hair if you like. Or straighten it. You can have more than one look,' she said.

'I doubt it,' Louisa said.

Stepping backwards down the hall for a final appraisal, her mother fought the urge to wince. 'You do have an excellent bust,' she said.

Louisa looked down at her breasts and tutted.

She was so fired up by the time she reached the domed Council House that she feared a relapse into her childhood tantrums. She thought she might glass one of those groupie bitches who hung around the rugby team. The situation called for the same calm and responsive nature she had in the field. She had never really drunk, but thought it might help now. Sensibly, she by-passed the fruit punch, which was dangerously spiked, and walked over to where David stood with his friends, in his tuxedo. 'Have you got any beer?' she said.

'Louisa, isn't it? Our fathers know each other.' He looked at her breasts; she thought of her mother. 'Tommo has some vodka in his bag,' he said.

'I'm sure I can smell beer coming off you,' Louisa said.

David sniffed his shirt. 'It's Davidoff,' he said with a smile.

'I'll have a Davidoff then, please,' she said, with genuine innocence.

He said what he always said to girls – that he loved hunting. Banging on about *the ritual of the kill* had always done the trick, but he did not know what he was getting himself into. 'These people who eat meat but object to where it comes from,' he said. 'It's so hypocritical.'

'You eat fox, then, do you?' she said. She had no objections to killing vermin, only to the deceit, pomp, and phoniness of the aristocrats her father longed to be with.

'Oh, of course. You're the falconer. Actually, my family are into shooting, rather than fox-hunting, but I suppose you disapprove of that, too,' he said.

She was pleased to be 'the falconer'.

'I'm fine with shooting, actually. It preserves the grouse moors. Think of all that money the shooters pump into conservation, so they can have their pathetic little parties. It makes it possible for me to hunt with my falcons, which is a *real* art.'

'Yes, but falconry is no better than a cock-fight, is it?'

'A cock-fight? A cock-fight is fifteen toffs drinking rosé champagne in a field, talking about who has the biggest gun.'

David had never met with such provocation, and was intrigued. Louisa's orchestration was perfect. By ten o'clock they had organised a play-off between the two sports; she would take him hawking, and he would take her shooting. Then they would see which was best.

Later, the crowd spilled out into Nottingham Market Square in their dresses and suits – an easy target, Louisa thought, for the locals, but David did not seem to care. Somebody poured green dye and detergent into the water fountain, and Louisa watched from the outskirts as David danced in the eerie rising foam with his mates, the bib of his shirt stained with swampy streaks. She smiled at him. 'I hate you,' she whispered to herself.

Louisa would soon learn that she was not the only one with access to the woods. David and his friends had climbed up there weeks before the ball, and looked down on the other side of the hill, at the girls' sports field, where Louisa made heavy, asthmatic work of the sixty-yard dash. They called her 'Wheezer' Smedley behind her back. When one of the girls told her this, it disturbed her for only a moment, confirming as it did what she already knew: she was not pretty.

What she never found out was that, for several weeks after the Pony Club Ball, David Bryant was attracted to her. He liked her strong limbs and the cold soft redness of her face when she walked out on the first leg of their hunting challenge. He liked to see her bend to her haunches – the whipping sound of her inseams, the stretch of denim across her thighs. She looked like she could swim. He would certainly never tell his friends. After that first hunt with the falcons, they questioned him about Wheezer, and he tried to dismiss her fairly as a 'bloke with tits', but even this gave too much away. On the day they walked through the field together, on the second leg of their challenge, he stopped abruptly and she bumped into his back. He felt the give of her breasts against his shoulder blades, and tried to convince himself that he was aroused only by the thrill of carrying a firearm.

SIX

'Do you know any Jason Donovan, at all?' Christopher said.

'I'm afraid I do not,' Louisa said.

She had just finished playing 'Devil Got My Woman'. Christopher had come to her cottage to apologise for his 'savage and brutal behaviour resulting in facial injury' and then insisted that she play the guitar. She did not like to perform, but after a spell of silence, she thought it might make her forget he was in the room.

'Jason Donovan played Scott in *Neighbours*. He was world famous.'

'I've heard of him.'

'Jason's a good name. I'll probably call my progeny Jason,' he said.

'It's nice,' she said.

Another silence. Christopher became serious. 'Do you think Jason Donovan is, erm, gay, at all?' he said.

Louisa hesitated.

'Do you think he is strange in that way?' he said.

'I don't know him.'

After a little contemplation, they resumed negotiations about music, and settled on 'Sealed with a Kiss', Louisa playing the old Gary Lewis version while Christopher shouted 'quicker, quicker' and sang every third word. Louisa could feel the vibrations of his foot tapping from across the floor. When they finished he smiled greasily and slid down on the sofa. His brace shone, and Louisa noticed that one of his teeth originated from high on the gum.

'We're rocking around the music tree, now,' he said.

'Aren't we just,' Louisa said. She recalled the particular facial expression David wore when talking about Christopher. The sort of frozen, distant smile you affect when your horse comes a close third behind your mother-in-law's.

'This is a nice pad,' he said, stretching his arm across the top of the button-backed sofa.

'Thank you.'

'Could do with a clean,' he said. Louisa sighed, looked at her watch.

'Do you like Maggie Green?' he asked.

What a question. Louisa wondered if she had sent him.

'You mean Maggie who lives with you?' It was the first time she had heard her maiden name.

'Yes, my father's late wife.'

'Your late father's wife.' She corrected him automatically.

He looked at the floor. 'They are no longer married in the eyes of the law,' he said. 'Erm. Do you like her?'

'I really don't know her.'

'Do you think she's, erm, erm, ugly, at all?' He smiled.

'She certainly isn't that.'

Louisa felt a degree of discomfort. She reasoned that it may have resulted from the pleasure she took in the conversation.

'She's not my mother, you know,' Christopher said.

'I know. I know your mother.'

'Do you?' he said, leaning forward.

'I *knew* her. Before.'

'Before she, erm, flew the roost.'

'Yes.'

'Erm. Do you think Maggie Green is a gold-digger, at all?'

'I don't know her,' Louisa said.

'I think she is. It's a bit of a, erm, coincidence, isn't it? She moves in, the younger woman, and then ... all hell breaks loose.'

Christopher remained thoughtful. It was Sunday morning, and the light came through the window in great bars that reached over his legs. His face was in darkness beyond the dust motes.

'Have you ever been to Eden, at all?' he asked.

'Eden?'

'It's a lap-dancing club in Derby.'

'Well in that case, no. I have not been to Eden.'

'It's pretty distracting, I must say, when a woman is, erm, erm, gyrating her pelvis in your face.'

'I don't doubt it. Although perhaps I'm not the person to talk to about such things.'

'Oh, right,' he said, lapsing into a silent reverie – probably flashing back to some private dance – of which Louisa was powerless to disapprove.

Then he sat back slowly, raised both arms in the air and pointed both index fingers down at his crotch. He stared at Louisa through his blue lenses. She shook her head slowly and grasped the neck of the guitar, ready to swing it if he made a move. She knew the dog was outside. '*What are you doing?*' she said.

He leaned forward, still pointing downwards. 'Toilet,' he whispered.

It took Louisa a moment to understand. 'Jesus,' she said, closing her eyes with relief. 'Yes, yes, go. It's upstairs.'

Louisa put her hands over her face as he left the room. She had thought briefly of the irony of being sexually attacked by David's son. She laughed to herself.

He flushed twice before coming downstairs, still buckling up. 'Erm, erm, I've had a whale of a time,' he said as Louisa showed him to the door. 'This could be the start of quite a friendship.' Louisa smiled, and he carried on. 'A friendship based on Mutual Assured Destruction.'

'Oh?'

'Well, I've told you sensitive information. About Eden and the gold-digger,' he said, touching his nose. 'I hope you won't betray me to Maggie Green.'

'I will not.'

Louisa let him go, thinking he had misunderstood the concept of Mutual Assured Destruction, until he turned and said, 'And I won't tell Maggie that you hang around the garden at night.'

They'd been vying for control of the woods for years. Louisa remembered a time on Bryant's land, back in the nineties, when, leaning against the fibreglass stegosaurus, she'd been shocked by a crashing sound behind her. She turned to see that David's little boy had fallen from an ash tree. His leg was bleeding, and he was in shock from the fall. He was whimpering, and still held the branch that had broken in his hands. 'You might want to, erm, help me instead of just standing there,' he said.

'Are you okay?'

'No. Get my, erm, daddy.'

As something of an uninvited guest on his land, Louisa saw that as a last resort. 'Who else is working on the park today?' she asked. 'Perhaps someone—'

'Not someone. Daddy!' he screamed. Some of the animals called back.

'Okay, okay,' Louisa said.

As it happened, she came upon David first anyway, in his Stetson and long coat. They ran back to Christopher and carried him to Louisa's cottage because it was nearer and she had a better medical kit. Louisa's attempts to treat the boy met with kicking and screaming and the word 'fiend', so David took over, kneeling before the sofa on which Christopher lay.

'Now Christopher,' said David. 'Look at me and tell me honestly: what were you doing up that tree?' He applied the rag gently to the edge of the wound as he spoke. Christopher hissed, but answered the question.

'Because Robin Hood has a tree house. You said, in your story. I was looking to see if there might be any, erm, ruins.'

'Robin Hood?' said David. 'He didn't live in a treehouse, you ninny, he lived in a cave. I mean ... Not a cave. Cave's too dangerous.'

'A den,' Louisa said.

'Perfect! Yes, a den. He lived in a den,' David said.

Christopher narrowed his eyes and looked at them both in turn. 'What are dens made of?' he asked.

'We'll make you one, down by the brook, won't we Louisa?'

'I suppose. I just pulled down the old mews, so there's a lot of wood and iron hanging around. We could use that. It'll be like a treehouse, only on the ground,' she said. David beamed. 'A treehouse on the ground,' he said, and then stopped smiling and addressed Christopher. 'As long as you promise, no more trees,' he said.

'Erm, erm, as long as you promise a den,' Christopher said, excited by the prospect of an infinite conversation.

When his knees were wrapped in the gauze Louisa used to treat her hawks, they left Christopher to rest and went through to the kitchen. Louisa made tea. They stood by the sink. 'You look well,' Louisa said, with a hint of sadness.

'I feel good,' David said. 'Better than I have for a long time. Since I was a kid, I suppose.'

Louisa nodded slowly and sighed. 'Good,' she said. 'I'm glad.'

'It's taken a long time. It was a terrible thing that happened to us. You saved me, you know. I wouldn't have coped.'

Louisa sniffed and looked away.

'Anyway, what about you, Smedley?' David said, lightening the tone. 'I see precious little of you these days.'

'Well, it's not like I *go* anywhere. You know where I am.'

'You're in my garden,' he said. Louisa reddened, but David became serious. 'If there's ever anything I can do for you,' he said.

They looked at each other for a moment. The kitchen lights were off, but the twilight made the place orange, threw patches of furtive heat across them both. Steam slinked up from the coiled clay mugs. Louisa's knuckles stung.

Christopher hobbled into the room. 'Daddy, I want to go home, now. This house smells funny.'

'Christopher, for God's sake.'

The moment was gone. Louisa turned away, towards the sink, the pan handles thrusting forth from water gone tepid. No plates.

'Louisa, he doesn't mean that. He's just tired.'

'So am I,' Louisa said.

The next day, Louisa dropped the materials for the den at their house, but left them to it. So David, with help from Christopher, built the den into the bottom of the slope, not far from the brook. They could often be seen fishing for beer cans and old shoes. Later, when Christopher was older and hoarding God knows what secrets, Louisa would see him crawling into the tin shack alone, hiding from the world.

Christopher's policy of speaking the brutal truth had not abated. Had he not said something similar, about the state of the house, on his most recent visit? Louisa thought of his bright gums, of her own swollen mouth, and of the unquantifiable disfigurements of the animals her birds had killed. Faces peeled off, eyes speared, every kind of cave-in. Diamond had once slashed a partridge after a fulsome stoop, and when it hit the ground it split in two, from head to tail. She thought of David in that field, all those years ago. The horror of it. Louisa could not sleep, and when she heard Maggie calling her dog on the first round of the morning, she stood from a bed on which she had only sat.

*　*　*

The day after visiting Louisa, Christopher sat at the computer, wrapped in a blanket, and checked his profile on the dating website. His photograph was just a picture of his bright blue eye.

I'm a big handsome Robin looking for a Marian to Sher the Wood with. Excellent family values absolutely crucial. Interest in motorsport optional. I won't let you down, unlike certain others.

Shivering, he laughed at his pun about Sherwood Forest. They could see that he had a GSOH, he thought, even if he didn't have GCH. There was a message in his inbox from a girl named Carol-Ann.

So it could have been a good day, but his nemesis on campus that afternoon was Mr Stephen Cullis, tutor and supervisor, who was intent on convincing Christopher that there were no decent grounds for the existence of a real, historical Robin Hood. Christopher believed that William Fitzooth, a twelfth century landowner, had been dispossessed by King John while accompanying Richard the Lionheart during the crusades. Such a catastrophe, it seemed to Christopher, would be enough to create the violent outlaw who inhabited the early Robin Hood ballads.

Christopher had trapped Cullis in the corridor after class. He didn't like the way Cullis nodded to the other students who passed slowly by, watching the scene. 'This is an important, erm, historical issue,' Christopher said.

'Listen, Christopher. Can't we talk about this some other time?'

'It's not very nice to be usurped,' Christopher said. 'I've had a similar experience myself. I know how Robin Hood must have felt.'

'That's what I'm talking about,' said Cullis. It was not their first argument on the subject. 'Robin Hood is always a product of his times. He tends to be most popular in eras of tyrannical leaders, unjust wars and revolution. People turn to a moral hero who pulls down the pants of the men in charge.'

'Pulls down their pants?'

'Figuratively,' said Cullis, looking over his shoulder towards the staff-room.

'Oh, right.'

'Each Robin Hood is created in line with the society he comes from. You yourself have created a Hood with your own sense of … well, a man with your issues at heart. Injustice, and such like. An angry man.'

'But what about the corpses?' said Christopher. 'What about the evidence?'

Christopher reminded Cullis of the crossbow bolt, the skull, the rank of bodies. Cullis pushed his fingers under his spectacles and rubbed his eyes. He wore an overlarge denim shirt tucked into what Christopher would have called 'school trousers'. The skin at his neck hung loose and smooth. 'Nottingham's got the worst per capita gun crime in the country, and every time a body turns up they blame it on Robin Hood,' Cullis said.

Christopher considered this. 'Whose side are you on, exactly?'

'Look. Your essay is shaping up well. You can analyse the *texts*. How does the psychotic vigilante of the ballads compare to the all-American code of Kevin Costner? It's good stuff.'

'He wasn't psychotic. It's understandable that he'd be, erm, erm, aggrieved. How would you like it if someone usurped you?'

'Christopher, you've got to let go of him being real. He was a tree-sprite.'

Christopher walked away at that point. He considered the 'tree-sprite' comment to be sacrilege. Figurative pants. But he knew, on some level, that it might be true.

In the canteen he had lentil soup, nostalgic for his years of vegetarianism. His refusal to eat meat had come from his fear of the animals on the park, the fear of retribution. His father had talked him out of it. 'Protein is the building bollocks of life,' David had said. His father had a way of swearing which was different to other people. He made it sound kind and funny, like a hiccup. There was nobody to tell Christopher what was right and wrong now. Nobody to tell him what was true or mythical about Robin Hood, or anything else.

When he listened to the stories of Maggie Green and the villagers, it was hard to hold on to the real memories of his father. Maggie Green sometimes tried to tell him that old story of how they met, in the deer enclosure in London. Christopher used to like that story, but now it just sounded like the tale of how she wangled her way onto the park. Anyway, why should he believe such a story? Where was her evidence? Everything was uncertain.

His building bollocks of life, it seemed, had tumbled to the floor.

As she drove to collect Christopher from college, Maggie remembered his fifteenth birthday, when they had set up a treasure hunt in the woods. Maggie and David had spent the day writing clues for Christopher, riddles about Madge and Harold from *Neighbours*, and Ayrton Senna. David found a tree with two protrusions at chest height and he tied a bikini on them, pasted a picture of Dannii Minogue's face above. That night, in the beam of the lanterns, she had watched Christopher dry hump the tree while David told him to stop through his laughter. She could not remember ever having had so much fun.

It was dark when she arrived at the campus, the only illumination coming from her headlights and a bulbous lamp placed in the path-side bushes. Christopher stood on the edge of the glow, shifting his weight awkwardly in the doorway and chewing the lip of his cardboard coffee cup. Three students taunted him. He tried to retaliate, but it only made them laugh.

Maggie got out of the truck, felt the rain coming down the inside of her jacket, felt her endorphins firing up.

'Erm. Why do you have to use such vulgar language?' Christopher said. 'Anyway, I haven't got anything stuck in my, erm, brace.'

'Your *embrace*? What are you talking about?'

Maggie noted the pun, the voice with all regional traces squeezed out of it. She knew this sort of student from her days working in colleges. They were the worst kind – the children of the governors, who would bully a kid half to death, then breeze into the disciplinary meeting with a haircut and a suit.

'Hi, Christopher,' she said.

He crumpled out of the light when he saw her. 'Erm. What are you doing here?'

'Come to pick you up,' she said, with an apologetic smile.

'This your woman?' one of the students asked.

'No!' shouted Christopher.

'Go home, before I call your daddies to come and get you,' Maggie said to the students.

'Hey, steady on,' one of them said. 'You don't know what happened here.' The boy pointed to Christopher. 'He said Mark had herpes.'

'Christopher, that's ridiculous,' said Maggie. 'Who'd shag *him*?'

She looked at the students, one of whom smiled. Christopher marched past her and got into the Land Rover. Maggie stepped closer to the group. 'I don't want to see you near him again,' she said.

'Are you sure? I would have thought you'd be delighted he had a few mates.'

The comeback tripped her. She was out of practice.

Another of them spoke up, his skinny jeans concertinaed about the knee, as though his legs were drinking straws. 'To be honest, we'd be pretty grateful if you could keep him away from *us*.'

The rain fell like splinters through the light. She looked at Christopher in the Land Rover. He stared ahead, chewing his coffee cup. She turned back to the students. 'Just be nice,' she said. 'Have a think about what it's like for him, eh?'

'It's not somewhere I want to go,' one of the students said. Maggie realised it was a girl, her fringe pushing through the hood, her face plush and full in the cold.

'That's what I mean,' Maggie said. 'That's exactly what I'm trying to say.'

The group moved away slowly, a wet sheen coming off their

pleather jackets. Maggie walked back to the truck and sat next to Christopher. 'Alright, kiddo?' she said.

'Erm. Yes. Can we get chips and fishcake with curry sauce on the way back?'

She saw a red wedge of coffee cup stuck between his brace and his teeth, but decided not to mention it. They drove on, collected chips, wound up the hill.

'Did you go and see Louisa?' she asked.

'Who told you that?'

'Nobody. I saw you walking over there. It's absolutely fine. I'm pleased. Did you talk over what happened the other day?'

'It's, erm, classified information. What we talked about.'

'I think she's a good person to talk to. She knew your dad really well. Did you talk about your dad with her?'

'Classified.'

'Okay. Consider my memory wiped.'

'It obviously is.'

Maggie looked at him. It seemed like a cruel snipe, but he may not have intended it. Sometimes Christopher, in trying to be disagreeable, stumbled upon something raw.

SEVEN

Louisa found a folded note in her letterbox:

KNOCK-DOWN MEAT IN YOUR FREEZER, LOVE MAGS.

The door of the weighing room was ajar, and Louisa entered to find striped bags of beef and quail neatly packed in her reclining freezer. Louisa sighed and read the post-script of the note, which explained that Foxton's butcher's had suffered a powercut.

THE MEAT WAS GOING FAST OR GOING OFF. DIDN'T THINK YOU'D MIND ME BREAKING IN. XX

Louisa thought of Maggie kneeling above her with the frozen coffee. Money was tight, and the extra food for her hawks was welcome. She regretted what she had said about shipping Christopher out to his mother.

And so, in late October, Louisa took Maggie lamping. She

called at the big house around midnight, knowing that Maggie would be awake. This time she answered the door in a skirt and a silky white top, the straps radiating from a wooden circle above her breasts. Her nipples pressed at the surface as the night cold hit her. Louisa did not consider the details at that time. 'Get your kit on,' she said. 'I've got a job for you.'

Squinting into the headlights of the van, Maggie took a moment to make her decision. 'Give me five minutes,' she said.

Maggie brought the warm fragrances of garlic and a musky perfume into the van. She turned around and looked at the Harris hawk, boxed and secured in the back. 'What are we up to, sweetie?' she said with relish, the streetlight slipping over her jeans.

'*No good*, hopefully,' Louisa said.

They took the narrow off-road track, cut onto John Salt's fields, stopped and got out. Maggie looked confused as Louisa took Fred from his box. The eyes of the bird popped with red flashes in the brake light. 'Jesus, can he see in the dark now, too?' Maggie said.

'Only when you turn the light on,' Louisa said, nodding at the lamp.

'I get it,' Maggie said, strapping the lamp battery round her waist and turning on the light. Fred tuned his vision to the end of the beam. Louisa taped his bell, for silence.

They walked out into the open together, the sky fringed with pallor from the villages, but moonless. Maggie revealed the world in silver arcs of lamplight. Louisa usually hunted alone, and had not prepared herself for the rush of feeling and the memories of that time she had gone hunting with David. Her legs began to shake. She tried to concentrate on the technical details of hawking.

'You need to move over to the side,' she whispered to Maggie. 'So his wings don't block the light. You see a rabbit, you keep the light on it, everywhere it goes. If he misses, cut the lamp. Fred'll go to ground. Then turn the light on me, and he'll come back to my fist.'

'Okay. Jesus, this is some crazy shit.'

The first rabbit was too close to cover, but Fred gave good chase on the second – an old bunny who kept the hawk in a shaky line until the last second, when it switched direction, spinning out from under his elevated right wing.

Later, in the van, Maggie would say that the time just after the lamp went off was the strangest time, because it was so dark she could barely believe that the drama she had just witnessed had happened at all. And that was a strange time for Louisa, too. As she waited in the darkness she could hear the private shifting of the hawk in the field, and her own heartbeat, which seemed much louder now that she had human company. At first all she could see was the cooling bulb of the lamp across the way, but soon Maggie's belt buckle and coat buttons started to gleam, followed by the rest of her appearing in violet as Louisa's eyes adjusted, as though light was a falling formative powder.

Maggie shone the lamp on Louisa, blinding her. Louisa stuck out her meated glove and Maggie's beam found it, as did Fred, who looked like a bleached, giant moth gliding out of the dark. 'Your turn,' Louisa said. They took a break before swapping, ate biscuits.

'What do you think?' Louisa said.

'Strangest, most incredible thing I've ever done,' Maggie said.

'If you'd have told me, ten years ago, that I'd be out in a field in Derbyshire at two a.m., killing rabbits with a hawk ... '

'We haven't bagged any yet. Some nice flights, though.'

'He's getting closer. How did you train him for this?'

'I took two sequins off an old dress, and pinned them on the face of a rabbit lure. Sparkly eyes.'

'Oh, now that's wasteful,' Maggie said. 'I could have had that dress. I like sequins.'

'I didn't take them off the nipples; it's still wearable. You might even grow into it one day.'

It took them a while to find another rabbit, and the first one they saw just froze. Maggie slipped Fred from her fist as the rabbit flung herself out towards the trees. Fred was up quickly into the funnel of light, the band above his tail glowing white, his wings banking at every turn the rabbit took. They almost reached the end of the beam and Louisa began to follow, running. Fred's feet came out, and he checked, rose, kicked at the rump, which is usually a mistake but this time threw the rabbit off balance. The rabbit bashed into a thick clump of grass, flipped over, and came down skidding and rolling like tumbleweed. She kicked out in the air, but Fred was above her, his feet clenched around her face, the hind toe digging deep into the tender flesh at the base of the neck. The rabbit's skull collapsed. Fred rode her until she stopped, and then mantled, his wings up and out. The rabbit had surrendered six inches from the thicket.

They jogged over, Maggie coming into the light and pulling meat from the bag, ready to take Fred off the kill. 'Wait. Let him have a taste first,' Louisa said.

'Thought he'd lost her when he went for the rear,' Maggie said.

Louisa took out the knife but there was no need for dispatch. The rabbit's head, deeply depressed on one side, had been wrenched backwards, and was hanging on by gristle. Suddenly, in the wavering grey beam, Louisa saw a child's face with punctured brown eyes. She caught her breath.

'Okay. Take her off, take her off.'

Maggie crouched down with some meat, and Fred stepped up quickly to the glove. Louisa went to gather the rabbit, and both women saw the slick pink protrusion from the belly, the even black dots. 'What's that?' Maggie said.

'Pups,' Louisa said. 'Were going to be.'

'Oh.'

Louisa cut the mass free, left it for the foxes, hauled the mother, and stood.

They loaded Fred and the equipment into the van by the light of the lamp. 'Did Christopher come and talk to you?' Maggie said.

'He did. He came to apologise.' Louisa dropped her lower lip to reveal the healing cut.

'I'm glad. It's a good thing for him, having you around.'

They fell silent for a while. Fred was still alert, peering beyond them into the field. 'I'm sorry about what I said before,' Louisa said eventually. 'About his mother.'

Maggie nodded.

'How has he been?' Louisa said.

'No better, really. I tried so hard to get him into the college, but the kids are being such *bastards*,' Maggie said.

'Is he being any kinder to you?'

'No,' she said. 'Did he mention me, when you spoke?'

Louisa recalled their pact of mutual assured destruction. 'No, not really.'

Maggie nodded. 'He was so nice to me when I got here.'

Louisa knew. She had seen them, racing to the trough of frozen water on Christmas Day. Through the big window, she had seen Maggie on his shoulders, changing a light bulb in the dining room.

Maggie looked at Fred. 'Did David like the birds?' she asked.

Louisa frowned. 'He liked to look at them. After a certain stage, hunting didn't interest him anymore. He lost the blood lust.'

'Oh yeah. He was a softie.'

'So he never talked about my hawks to you, then?' Louisa said.

'No,' said Maggie, then shook her head. 'But he talked about *you* all the time.'

Louisa laughed immoderately. 'I doubt that.'

'He did,' Maggie said. 'He absolutely loved you.'

'I doubt that,' Louisa said, quieter.

Maggie began to laugh and then cry. Louisa thought it might only last a few seconds, but it didn't. She rummaged in the van's dark interior for something with which Maggie could wipe her eyes, but could find only towels smeared with blood and bird shit. Maggie did not wait; she wiped her nose on her sleeve, and then folded the cuff over, tutting. 'I haven't had a good cry in ages,' she said. 'You must think I'm a terrible baby,' Maggie said.

'You *are* young,' Louisa said.

'It's just . . . This isn't how I saw things working out.'

Louisa looked around and smiled in a tired way. 'No. I'll bet.'

'I would give anything to make Christopher happy again,' Maggie said.

'Well. What does he want?' Louisa said.

'What does he *want*? I don't know. A family? He talks about having a family a lot. Getting married and stuff. He's just a kid.'

Louisa nodded, seeing the many barriers to that goal beyond Christopher's youth.

'I don't think there's much I can do to help him with that,' Maggie said. 'Short of getting him a mail-order bride, which, I believe, he has already looked into.'

Louisa smiled. Maggie put her arms out to the side. 'I just don't know what to do,' she said.

'You could do what I do,' Louisa said.

'What's that?'

'You take all the feelings, and you screw them into a big ball and bury them in the pit of your stomach.'

Maggie laughed and put her hands on Louisa's face, one on each cheek. The left hand was still warm and damp from the glove, the other very cold. Louisa flinched.

Louisa's hallucinations continued that night, but they weren't all malevolent. Waking, she saw a fragment of Maggie picked out by the lamp: her arm, the buttons on her sleeve leading deep into the glove. Then, later, more white flashes of her.

That screwed up ball of feelings, buried in her stomach, had begun to unravel.

*   *   *

Over the next month their days took on a tentative rhythm. On the mornings when Louisa did not have a clearance job, Maggie helped her to weigh, feed and fly the hawks. Louisa had bought a female peregrine with the future intention of breeding Diamond, and she allowed Maggie to help train her. In homage to the 1980s naming style of Christopher, they called the bird Caroline.

In the afternoons, Louisa helped Maggie on the park, repairing fences, and feeding the animals. Louisa could see the relentlessness of Maggie's desire, the need for work and the craving for exhaustion. It was invigorating to watch. Philip Cassidy occupied himself with other jobs in the enclosures, and kept his own company on the afternoons when Louisa helped out, but that was no surprise.

Out there on the park, the weather drowned the voices of the two women. They had to lean close to talk. They tramped through the long grass, watching the hedgerows tugged back firmly and slowly like pulled hair. Wallabies bounded uphill.

Sometimes they were afforded an hour of calm in the late afternoon, the brassy light clearing the shade off the hill at the pace of a falling man, the pines casting shadows with a beneficent lean. These were the hours that Maggie would remember later that season, when everything had been lashed to tatters by the floods.

On 5 November, they went up to the roof of the big house, which was green with moss and bad drainage. There, with old duvets and beers, they sat on ancient garden furniture and watched the fireworks.

As they clinked bottles, Maggie silently recalled her early exchanges with Louisa. After David died, a consortium of local businessmen and developers had tried to buy the park from Maggie, and she remembered Louisa standing at the back of the

Church Hall during the meeting. Maggie had held firm, despite the prising fingers. 'David did a great job with the park,' one of the businessmen had said. 'But I think he'd agree, it's time for a change.'

'You're looking at it,' Maggie had said. Philip Cassidy had escorted Maggie through the throng of disgruntled suits, but Louisa had been the first to leave, banging out through the fire exit.

Maggie looked at Louisa now, hunched up in her coat and blanket, like one of her preening birds. 'Lou,' she said.

'Yeah.'

'Don't take this the wrong way, but when David died, were you one of the consortium that tried to buy me out?'

Louisa held her gaze. 'Yes,' she said.

'Did you really want them to build flats on Drum Hill? Next to your cottage?'

'I didn't care. I was going to sell my land and my home – everything that David left me – to the consortium, and just move away.'

'Where?'

'I don't know. Anywhere but this hill. I couldn't stand it.'

'But when the bid fell through, you stayed here.'

'Nobody would've bought my place on its own, as it was. Without David's house and land, mine was worth nothing.'

'If you'd have explained, I would have bought the land from you,' Maggie said.

'And you were the only person in the world I wouldn't have sold it to.'

Maggie sipped from her drink. 'I'm glad you didn't sell it,' she said, not expecting a reply.

'So am I,' Louisa said.

That night, finally, Louisa talked. She talked about her father, whose big ears glowed red when he got angry, and her brothers, who sometimes fought each other in the middle of the road. She talked about her dream of starting a breeding business, the dual chambers she would build, and her part in the original peregrine breeding programme – the hand-reared bird who, believing himself to be human, took Louisa for a mate. She had collected his seed in a rubber hat she wore. 'You're saying you fucked your falcon?' Maggie said.

'No. He fucked me. He was the man. That was very clear.'

Maggie put a hand to her mouth, scandalised and disbelieving; Louisa offered to fetch the hat as proof, and so Maggie conceded. Rockets whistled in the distance.

Maggie herself spoke of her time back in London, her tight group of friends who had long given up calling. 'I couldn't expect them to understand this life,' she said. 'Or how I felt about David. How I still feel.'

She felt the tone of Louisa's silence change at the further mention of David's name, and so she desisted, happy enough to quietly recognise David's part in this new and unexpected friendship.

When the sparklers had died, when the burger vans had taken their headlights away and the sprays of colour had faded to faint purple scrapes of smoke, they contented themselves with watching the many bonfires down in the valley, the crumpling guys at their centres.

Walking home, Louisa felt the happiness rising inside her and managed to curb the instinct to strangle that good feeling. It lasted far into the night, and even alone in her bed she recalled snatches of conversation. Lord knows how long it had been since someone had thrown back their head and laughed at anything Louisa had said. There was a moment of panic, when she thought of all the things she had revealed to Maggie, but for once, the panic passed. After all, there were other stories, more deeply buried.

EIGHT

On the first leg of the Hunting Challenge, Louisa and David took Jacko out. It rained heavily, and he would hardly fly. The session lasted an hour and Louisa felt crushed. It was one of the only times a falcon had failed her, and even then it seemed more like her own physical deficiency. David apparently perceived this, and promised to tell his friends that Louisa Smedley couldn't get it up.

Much happened in the intervening weeks: the weather cleared, and spring arrived. The smell of cut grass and cold stone spiked the air, and birthing sheep lay prostrate and helpless. The hawking season drew towards its close, and for once, Louisa did not feel like locking herself in the moulting shed for six months.

The Bryant household was tense in February 1975. The previous year, Leicestershire, along with much of the region, had swung back to Labour. There was talk of change at local level, and Lawrence Bryant, fearing for his job, came down with what he called 'flu'. Until his early twenties, David believed that the symptoms of influenza were blocked sinuses, moodswings and acute paranoia. David's father spent the day before the second leg of the challenge in bed.

Even had Lawrence been well, David saw no sense in asking for permission to use his gun. David had always been told that when he was seventeen he would be old enough to purchase his own shotgun, and therefore old enough to make his own decisions.

As a child, David had watched his father's last driven shoot, somewhere near Foston. He remembered the cold, and little else. Lawrence suffered a back injury soon after, which forced him into a bitter retirement from his hobby. So while many of his country friends were being introduced at a very young age to all aspects of field sports, David was permitted only a small air rifle – a .410 – with which he had killed about six rabbits in the extensive family garden. Once, when he was drunk on his mother's port, he had shot a squirrel from his bedroom window, but the pellet went straight through the torso, and the vermin escaped up the tree trunk with no apparent injury. That was the total of his life's bag.

With his father bedridden, and his mother occupied with worry, it proved no great feat for David to enter his father's shed, which stank of linseed oil and damp, take the old twelve-bore along with a box of cartridges, and put them in his cricket bag. When his family woke to find his bed empty, they assumed he was walking the dogs, as usual.

Louisa waited for him at the boundary gate of the field on the outskirts of the village. The cold grip of night loosened drip by drip from the fence planks and the roadside lamps. She could hear the canal. David was late. It appeared that he was unaccustomed to

rising at dawn, but Louisa had already developed an uncharac-
teristic patience with David rivalled only by her forbearance when
training eyasses.

She was also aware that letting David triumph in their hunting
wager (which he would now surely do) might work in her favour.
In her mind, the relationship had progressed quickly, and she had
begun to see herself as a stabiliser, a scaffold for him. In this way,
he had given her a purpose which she had otherwise failed to find
outside of falconry. She admired his extrovert nature and his
talent with people; to someone so lacking in these areas, he was
like a magician.

When she saw him slogging up the hill with his cricket bag and
a black spaniel, she did not know what she had been expecting; a
Labrador and a couple of Land Rovers, perhaps. Or a large group
of aristocratic men. The dog got to her first and licked the palm of
her hand. 'Where are we going?' Louisa said.

He nodded to the woodland enclosure beyond the first field.
Louisa knew it. She also knew the sour old owner of the surrounding arable land, the stubble fields and corn. 'It's a bit close to
home,' she said. 'Is your dad the tenant? I couldn't get permission
to fly my hawks here. Maybe you could have a word—'

'My dad's not the tenant. I happen to know that the tenant is
absent.'

They climbed the stile and began to walk the bridleway, which
was cattle-trod, peaked and frosty in the shade. 'So we're poach-
ing,' she said.

'Nobody's going to miss a few rabbits.'

Louisa shook her head. In the early days, she had been just as
rash, trespassing on farmland to steal eggs, hunting magpies in

the orchards of her neighbours. These days, though, she asked permission.

'I was expecting good quality plonk and high-class people. Isn't that what happens? *The ritual of the kill?*'

'Yes, well. I've become solitary,' he said, frowning, and then laughed at his own nonsense.

In fact, the thought of watching a driven shoot from the sidelines, with all that snooty affectation and the grating subservience of the beaters, had filled Louisa with nervous dread. She liked the idea of David as a rough shooter, even if the signals said he did not want her to meet the family just yet.

At the outskirts of the woodland, as he sent the dog into the pillow softness of the ferns, she studied the back of his neck. It was strong, the collar flush against the skin, tiny blond hairs dampened by a milky sweat, like sap. When he stopped in front of her, she leaned into him, not without intention.

Around mid-morning, a rabbit bolted from the grass, and David fired his right barrel, missed. The noise startled a murder of crows and he swung the gun upwards and fired again, into the black. He hit fresh air. 'You didn't follow through,' Louisa said.

David looked around, listened to the atmosphere settle. Louisa was worried about the possibility of a gamekeeper, but there was no human reaction. 'Looks like the only person around here who's going to miss a couple of rabbits is you,' Louisa said.

They shared Louisa's sandwiches, standing up. David was ravenous, his body clearly baffled by the early start.

'What are you thinking about?' Louisa asked.

'My father. He's afraid of losing his job. And he's not well, really.'

'He's a powerful man, though, right? What's wrong with him?'

'He thinks the world is going to end.'

Louisa looked around. 'Nice day for it.'

They finished their food quietly and walked on in the silence that the shoot demanded. Louisa hoped that David felt the same satisfaction she did. Perhaps she was the person with whom he could shed his clown act. She relaxed into that cradled space she inhabited when out with her hawks. Across the stubble fields, through the corn and the bracken, their shadows stretched, David's crumpled like a garment over the fences. The light was soft, and their breathing slipped in and out of synchronicity. They did not find any release pens; feed hoppers leaked corn for the pheasants but the birds were not to be tempted out of hiding. The only other signs of men were in the angular stands of commercial woodland. The sky ruled, spilling blueness onto the patches of straw-like grass that bordered the fields. Later, they saw a barn owl, the head so human, so still. David's gun hung empty and open over his arm for much of the walk, but that seemed irrelevant somehow.

'You ready to head back?' David said.

Louisa looked at the sun, which was large and low now. 'Yes, let's go.'

As they crossed the final field and approached the canal bridge, Louisa saw a flash of iridescent green in the tangle of overgrown hawthorn acting as a hedgerow. She turned to David; he had seen it too. He loaded cartridges as the dog stalked through the long grass. 'David,' Louisa whispered. 'The dog needs to get behind the hedge, flush towards us.'

'It's a pheasant,' said David. 'It'll go vertical. We'll walk it up.'

Louisa shook her head. They moved to within thirty yards of the hedgerow. The light was poor, but if the bird came up above the height of the first houses of the village, it would be nicely silhouetted against the sun.

David had little control over his dog, which charged into the cover of its own will, flushing the cock pheasant, which came up briefly and then dipped lower, curling away from the back of the hedge. David fired twice, once as the cock rose, and again when it dropped lower. There was the echo, and the silence. 'I think I got it,' David said, marching to the scene.

'Too close to the dog for my liking,' Louisa said, following ten paces behind.

She would always remember him, opening his weapon, walking towards the sun. She did not even have to squint, because the light was so soft. The noise he made on recoiling from the hedge was strangled and inarticulate. It was a cattle noise, the kind you make when you surface from a bad dream. She was surprised that he should be so upset by a dead bird. But then she saw the pheasant gliding, tar-black, into the distance, and she knew something was wrong. She moved towards the hedge. David walked past her in the opposite direction, coughing and heaving.

A child lay behind the hawthorn. Louisa had already worked with animals long enough to know death when she saw it. She did not beg the child to wake, or reach through the thorns to shake him. She walked briskly to the gate, went through to the other side, and examined the body.

The gun had a tight choke. Shot had ruptured the right eye, and smashed the skull like damp wood. There had been no time to scream. Louisa looked with some wonder at the boy's left ear, which was perfect and intricate, untouched by the damage.

The disturbance which finally pierced Louisa's shock was a rapidly growing sense that she recognised the boy. How could this be? He wore scruffy clothes: a ragged little coat, grey shorts, socks pulled up to the knees. She guessed him to be five years old. He was weak and dirty. She lifted his left eyelid and saw the stunning brown eye of Anna Cliff. The breath went out of her. But they had taken the children away from her years ago, hadn't they? Louisa could not understand. 'Shouldn't be here,' she said. Blood ran from the child's nose, down the side of his face.

Louisa went back to the gate to find David walking away, the gun and his cricket bag lying in the grass.

When she caught up with him, he seemed calm, but he began to cry freely and horribly the moment he looked at her. 'I'm sorry, I'm sorry,' he said. He spoke violently through his tears, like he was issuing a command, as though, she thought later, he could drive the feeling away. She took him by the shoulders to stop him walking and he dropped to his knees, taking her down with him. He convulsed against her. 'Maybe he was already dead. Maybe it wasn't me,' he said. They both knew better. The blood was fresh. There was no doubt. 'No, David,' Louisa said.

'We'll lose everything,' David said. 'I'm sorry. I'm so sorry.'

Louisa rubbed the bones in his lower back, then pulled out his shirt from his trousers, and rubbed the bones again, her hands on his skin. She kissed him on the neck, on the line of his jaw, feeling for the first time the shoots of stubble against her lips.

Once she had made her decision, the flush of power within her was thrilling. 'Pick up your bag, David. Leave the gun in the grass. Pick up your bag, and go home. Get out of here. Don't say a word to anyone.'

He tensed for a moment and then gradually broke away from her embrace. He held his breath. She watched him stand up, collect his bag, and walk away across the fields, giving himself time to regain composure. When he had gone, Louisa began to run with her eyes closed. She crossed the canal bridge, ran along the bridleway, and emerged onto the road to find that the world, with its cars and pavements, continued to exist.

She calmed herself in the phonebox by reading the spiky letters carved into the black metal of the coin tray. The initials of lovers. She dialled the emergency services, another flash of power running up through her legs. When the call was answered she licked her cold lips. It was hard to form the shape of the words, but she did. 'I've killed a boy,' she said.

NINE

In late November, Maggie and Louisa rescued Diamond from a pond, where he had bound onto a duck. They arrived back at Drum Hill bedraggled but in high spirits. In the cold hallway, Maggie took off her boots and jeans. Her wet socks slapped against the stone floor. 'You're completely dry!' Maggie said, pointing at Louisa.

'That's because I wear proper boots, waterproof trousers and a technical coat,' Louisa said, smiling.

'*A technical coat,*' Maggie said, with a wry nod. She took off her top, revealing a crosshatch of scratches from the branches over-hanging the pond. She wore matching underwear – sheer pink pants with an ornate leaf design at the waistband. Louisa turned away.

Maggie gathered her wet clothes, and said, 'Come on. I've got something to show you.'

She bounded up the stairs on the balls of her feet. Louisa watched her go. She thought of David walking away from her in the field. Hawking with Maggie brought the memories back. It made her want to leave, but she forced herself to climb the stairs.

By the time Louisa reached the second floor, Maggie was wearing a dressing gown. She handed Louisa a towel to dry her hair and turned on the TV and VCR.

It took Louisa a moment to discern the grainy grey image of her van pulling into Morrison's car park. Moments later, the herd of ibex trotted into shot.

'How did you get this?' Louisa said.

'I wrangled it off the security guard. Look.'

The picture quality was poor, but Louisa could make out the single ibex kid bolting for the bank, and her own laboured pursuit. Maggie followed, bending at the waist.

'What were you doing? Were you sick?' Louisa said, pointing at the screen.

'No. I was laughing.'

'At me?'

'Well. It was really funny,' Maggie said.

If she squinted at the screen, Louisa could see the end of it all, her body wrapped around the bucking kid, and Maggie waving a hoof at the camera. A fine grey morning. The date and time were incorrectly recorded in the corner of the screen as 1 January.

When Louisa looked up from the TV, Maggie had left the room. Louisa wandered out into the hallway, and heard running water. She found Maggie in the bathroom. The door was open, and Maggie was dabbing awkwardly at the scratches with cotton wool, her dressing gown pulled down to the elbow. The place smelled of TCP.

'Ouch,' Louisa said, startling Maggie. 'You need a hand with that?'

'No, ta. I think someone else would be too delicate.'

'Not something I'm known for,' Louisa said. She stood on the threshold for a moment, unsure of whether to enter the bathroom until Maggie half-turned.

Louisa came to the mirror, took a tube of Zovirax from her pocket and smeared it on the cold-sore which had formed over the gash on her lip. They smiled knowingly at each other in the glass; the brown of Maggie's eyes and the pale green of Louisa's were the only colours picked out by the dim natural light. Maggie took some foundation from a little make-up bag. 'We're like a pair of girls getting ready to go out on the town,' Maggie said.

'It's been a while since I've done that,' Louisa said. A hundred years, she thought.

'Yeah, me too. Don't remember it being quite like this.'

'Cuts and cold-sores? No,' Louisa said.

'Good company though.'

Louisa nodded.

'You know, next month they're having a Christmas do in the Church Hall,' Maggie said. 'Rosie Wicks from the pub asked if we'd come.'

'I sincerely doubt that I am invited.'

'You are. Rosie asked specifically.'

Louisa felt herself becoming angry. There was another feeling, too, a sort of jealousy. 'It's not my kind of thing. Those people.'

'They're okay,' Maggie said.

'Nobody is stopping *you*. Go. If you like,' Louisa said.

'No,' Maggie said, still smiling. 'I don't think I'll bother.'

Louisa sighed. She was pleased that Maggie would decline, though she felt a little guilty about it. Maggie flattened her long fingers on the sink and Louisa recalled the threadbare borrowed glove her friend used when out in the field. She rushed out and came back with a piece of paper, took a make-up pencil from Maggie's bag. She placed the paper on the toilet lid. 'Put your hand down on this,' Louisa said.

'Louisa, you make the strangest requests,' Maggie said.

But she eventually complied, kneeling. Louisa got down beside her and traced the hand onto the paper, the pencil's tip spreading to create a thick line. Maggie flicked up her index finger involuntarily when the pencil touched the soft skin at the base. She laughed and shook her head. 'Great,' Louisa said, when she had finished. She took the impression and stood. Maggie rose and went back to the mirror. Louisa walked to the door but turned back. She noticed a small mark on Maggie's neck, higher than the cuts she had treated, and different in nature. It was a fading contusion, with a speckle of burst capillaries. Little red dots on a smoky blue patch.

'Sorry Louisa, did you need the toilet?' Maggie asked.

Louisa did not know how long she had been standing there.

*   *   *

Colour drained from the sky like blood from a clenched fist, leaving them with a high dome, smooth and cold as polished granite. On the ground, winter revealed the secret structures – trees like whalebone corsets, the bare wiring of the undergrowth, nowhere to hide but the soil, and yet everything gone.

One afternoon, they fed salmon to the otters, whose electric squeals rose from the converted well as they spooled and dived.

'I've got plans for this place, Lou,' Maggie said. 'It's over-crowded, now. I want to cut the number of species, widen the enclosures.'

She had read of the psycho-pathologies observed in captive animals: sexual disorders, auto-aggression, the consumption of faeces and the paintwork from cages. She had the drawings for the improvements in her bag.

'Sounds like a decent idea,' Louisa said.

'You're the first person to say that. Most people reckon I should leave the park as it is. They say this was how David wanted it.'

Louisa shrugged. 'David was ... ' She struggled to complete the sentence. 'He was a good man. But he didn't know anything about animals.'

Maggie looked down into the water. The rings of light on the brown surface made it look like melting celluloid. 'I'll need some help,' she said. 'Someone I can trust.'

Louisa opened her mouth as if to object but then stopped. 'Okay,' she said.

'I've got to convince the staff first,' Maggie said.

'Maybe it's best if you handle the people side of things,' Louisa said.

They found Philip Cassidy helping to fit a heavy anti-intruder gate on the entrance to the main enclosures. The flattened tips of his thick fingers curled through the wire, and when he put down the door, the imprints remained.

'Phil, I need you to organise a meeting for all the staff at the end of the month. I'll be outlining some changes we're going to make to the park,' Maggie said.

'*We?*' Philip said, with a quick glance at Louisa.

'We, the staff,' Maggie said.

'Right-o,' said Philip. 'I'll sort it. Nothing too drastic, I hope.'

Maggie put a hand on his shoulder. 'I'm promoting you to MD,' she said, with mock seriousness.

Philip smiled at the joke and straightened an imaginary tie at his neck. He rubbed the white stubble on his cheeks, and leaned towards Maggie, away from Louisa. 'Some more news this morning. A couple of missing animals found. Jack rabbits.'

'And?' said Maggie.

'Dead,' he said.

Maggie closed her eyes. Philip continued. 'Also, yesterday there was a sighting of what could have been the ibex on a building site near the city. Climbing on rubble. I sent a couple of lads up there, but they didn't see oat.'

'Okay. Thanks Philip. Appreciate it,' Maggie stroked his arm and the two women departed for Louisa's cottage. After a few strides, Maggie turned to Louisa, laughing and said, 'I think he likes you.'

'I think he'd like to feed me to the pigs,' Louisa said.

'Do you ever think about it? Meeting someone, I mean?' Maggie said.

Louisa shook her head. 'You?'

'Too busy with this place. And Christopher. He's the man in my life at the moment.'

'That's a lot of man,' Louisa said.

Maggie laughed. She looked at Louisa, the root-like tangles of her light hair. Once, Maggie had wanted to befriend Louisa for her connections to David, for the prized vault of her memories. These days she saw Louisa as a friend in her own right.

The cottage came into view above the contours of the land, and the hawks began to scream, as if they sensed the women approaching.

*   *   *

Louisa poured another whisky and watched Maggie spread the plans on the kitchen table. The wintery light bent through the coloured glass of the lightshade, and made green and orange patterns on the paper. Louisa studied Maggie's neck, but her curls had fallen over the mark there.

The idea, Maggie said, was to restrict the park to animals currently or formerly resident in the British Isles. Like Noah's Ark, Louisa thought.

'I'm changing the name to Drum Hill *Conservation Centre*,' Maggie said, 'And I've started to apply for state funding. The admission receipts are a pittance, anyway. There's hardly any visitors.'

'You can't rely on people forever,' Louisa said.

'Well, I figure they'll come back after the changes,' Maggie said.

Louisa nodded. Maggie's plans seemed solid, progressive, and Louisa felt a flare of excitement along with her usual caution. She knew the consequences of friendship and its bitter twists. She was on her third drink, though, and that helped.

'I've been thinking about your breeding programme, too,' Maggie said. They had been to an autumn sale with falcons lined up on Astroturfed bars under tents, and Arab men wrapped in fur coats drinking tea while their agents bought the palest ashgar saker for twenty grand. 'I think you should do it,' Maggie said.

'I don't have the capital. It's beyond my means.'

'It's not beyond *ours.*' Maggie said. 'David put aside some money, and after the work on the park, there'll still be—'

'I couldn't. I couldn't involve you financially. It would be an obligation, and ... ' Louisa trailed off. A month ago she would have dismissed such an offer immediately, but things had changed.

'Think of it as David paying you back,' Maggie said. 'For all the hard work you did here.'

Louisa looked up sharply, and Maggie met her eyes. It may only have been the quality of the light that triggered the memory, but Louisa thought back to standing in the phone box, waiting for the police to come. She took a sip of whisky.

'I like it when you're a bit drunk, Lou,' Maggie said, blinking slowly. 'You lick your finger before you pick up your drink. Like you're turning the page of a newspaper.'

'I do not,' Louisa said.

'You do. It's nice.'

Maggie laughed and sat back in her chair. Louisa eventually began to smile, too. She watched her friend look out of the window, back towards her own house. Something seemed to occur to Maggie. She straightened up, a little tense.

'Lou, do you think you'd be able to take Christopher out tomorrow night? Just to the pub. He's miserable at the moment, and I've got so much paperwork to sort out.'

'Sure.'

Maggie relaxed again. 'He called you his *partner in crime* yesterday. He says he's got something he needs to talk to you about, actually.'

'Sounds ominous,' Louisa said.

'It's *classified*,' Maggie said.

TEN

When the police car arrived at the phone box, Louisa took them to the field where the boy lay dead. She stood back with the older policeman, and watched the young constable pick a path through the grass to the hedge. He crouched down for a moment, and then quickly jerked his head away. After a few seconds, he turned to look at Louisa, and exhaled. He nodded to his partner.

The police station was like school, only more open about its brutality. As she waited on a wooden bench, she could see a bloodied hockey stick in a clear plastic bag behind the front desk. Thick drips of white paint had dried, tacky and shiny, in the grooves between the bricks.

Louisa remained unmoved as she gave her statement to the same young constable who had found the body; she had as much respect for him as she did for her teachers. She said she had borrowed the gun from her friend David Bryant, who had parted with it only on the condition that it be used on a supervised shoot.

She said she had taken it to the field alone, and fired into the hedge at the pheasant.

For a moment she imagined David at home, packing his bags, leaving a note and running to the train station. But he wouldn't do that. He was a good man, she thought. The right man.

She regained her composure, and enjoyed taking David's place in the rest of the story. She felt the warmth of inhabiting his body. It was her composure, in fact, which caused the constable's one fleeting suspicion. 'You seem very calm, I must say,' he said. 'You *do* know what's happened, don't you? You *do* know what you've done?'

Soon after that, however, Richard Smedley arrived, and Louisa's behaviour began to show signs of disturbance. They argued in the corridor. 'I have worked so hard to get you where you are,' Richard said. Louisa looked around and nodded.

'And you just want to tear this family down.' He got close to his daughter, so the constable could not hear. 'Why did you call the police? Why didn't you call *home*, girl?'

'I didn't want to end up like that little boy.'

He slapped her for that.

As they left the station, Louisa saw that a middle-aged drunk had taken her place on the bench. He was crying, and his face was ridden with ashen tracks, dirt clogging around his eyes like make-up. Louisa thought that she might like to cry, if only to feel the dry tightness in her face afterwards.

For a few days, Oakley felt like the moon to its residents. They found themselves awake at odd times, watching the alien lights of police cars spinning through the grey fog towards the canal, and

Anna Cliff's house. As the story crept out, news came of Anna's initial response: it was said she had spent all night searching the woods and fields for her boy, unaware of what had happened, but too afraid of the police to report her son missing.

Garish tales of the Social Services visit to the Cliff house filtered into the village. The more outlandish stories told that the beds of the other, long-gone children had yet to be made, and that a drove of pigeons unfolded from the dead boy's bedroom when they opened the door.

Somebody started a rumour that Anna's house was in reasonable condition, that she had made a careful new start with this boy, whose name was apparently Charles. That particular story was dismissed because people found it much easier to be appalled by Anna Cliff than to imagine her sane, in a room, being told that her child was dead. She never returned to the village.

David's father, apparently over his flu, played a significant part in the proceedings following Charles Cliff's death. He had always been taught, he said, that one's weapon is one's own responsibility. Around those parts, such codes were commonplace. Louisa never spoke to him, or asked him how much he knew, or suspected. Like everyone else, he seemed to accept Louisa's admission of guilt.

She watched her own father reduced to bowing and snivelling before Lawrence Bryant, who called in favours from his contacts in law enforcement. Louisa had a licence for a small air rifle she used to kill sparrows to feed her hawks, and this was taken into account.

In her school uniform, although she would not go to school that day, Louisa listened to the coroner return a verdict of accidental death. She looked around the court one last time for David, but he was not there. She felt a hollow sense of panic. It seemed that her act of sacrifice had backfired, for she had not seen him since that day in the field. Surely he had not abandoned her. She wondered if he had been forbidden from speaking to her by his parents. It was as if, she thought with a sad smile, they'd been caught sleeping together.

At first the changes seemed subtle, and perfectly bearable. In the dinner hall, Louisa heard the girls whisper *'murderer'* as she walked past. Somebody put a small wig covered with fake blood in her bag, but in the dark of her rucksack she thought the wig to be the meat-darkened pigeon feathers of her lure, and ignored it. The cool reaction scandalised her classmates more than any screaming or crying would have.

Still she hadn't seen David, but heard that he barely spoke at school. Louisa did not care about the stain on her name, but she wanted it to mean something to him.

*   *   *

At night, the glow which crept out of Roy Ogden's underground garage was eerie. It looked like the house might detach from its foundations at any moment. Louisa had been too busy to visit since the accident, but the great thing about Oggie was that he was outside of her life, separate from the awkwardness of school and the anger of home. She walked down the steps into the workshop. Nelly Carter, one of Ogden's local apprentices, was down there too, working on an engine part that looked like a human skull.

'Fucking hell, here she is,' Nelly said.

'Nelson,' said Ogden as he emerged from the back of the garage.

'What?' said Nelly.

'I've had enough a you. Bugger off, lad. Go on, get out of it.'

Nelson shrugged, and tossed the engine part onto the workbench. 'Right-o. I'm off for a bath and a wank,' he said.

'Wash your hair *first*, eh?' Louisa said, as Nelly left.

Ogden wiped his hands ineffectively with a rag, for a long time. 'Y'rate lass?' he said, eventually.

'Not so bad. All things considered.'

'Aye.'

'Are you out with the hawks this weekend, Oggie?' she said. 'Down the reservoir? I could do with getting out in the field.'

He limped towards her and stood under the bare bulb. 'Not really,' he said.

'I can probably do Monday next week, then. Teacher training day, so there's no school.'

Ogden pinched his moustache. 'Can't really do it, kid, to be honest.'

'What do you mean?'

'I don't think it's a good idea no more, you coming out with me.'

The shock silenced Louisa. For a moment she wondered if he was referring to the accident, but then she realised. Her father had got to Ogden first.

'What's he paying you?' she said.

'Who?'

'My dad. Do you think I'm thick, Oggie?'

'It in't like that.'

But it was. Louisa knew Ogden's garage was underground for a reason, and his customers paid cash. That money, along with his disability benefit, kept his hawks in meat. Louisa imagined her father standing where she stood now, jumper over his shirt and his driving gloves on, pointing out that those two sources of income were incompatible, legally.

'Okay, look, he came 'round. But he made some decent points and I agree with him. Upshot is, schooling's got to come first. You need to take care with that. And you live bloody miles away. Anyway, you don't want to be hanging around with a . . . '

Louisa, who had been shaking her head throughout the speech, swiped a socket wrench from a toolbox and hurled it into the dark recesses of the garage, where it smashed into the shelves of parts and tins. Ogden stopped speaking but did not flinch.

'If you want to carry on with the falcons, I've got some names of people closer to home, but you must promise not to tell your old man I gave them you.'

'You know what, forget it, Oggie. You can piss off. You're a sad old coward.'

She turned and took the steps quickly because she knew she would cry.

In the end, their parents did forbid David and Louisa from meeting, and Louisa took the decision with a shrug. What did it matter, anyway, when he was avoiding her? But a week after her father made his decree, she found a note speared on the bushes by her house, telling her to go to the roadside trailer that sold tea and bacon cobs just outside the village. The note was written in David's sharp, slanted hand.

He was waiting behind the trailer, and as she approached him in the shadows she thought he looked cleaned-up, leaner, his shirt crisp. Just as she'd feared – he had moved on. 'Where have you been hiding?' she said.

'Louisa, I'm sorry for what happened,' he said. 'It was all my fault and I couldn't deal with it.' For all the apparent maturity of his admission, Louisa, now feet from him, could see that he had not recovered. The glossy fullness of his lips actually came from a haze of surrounding dry skin and the balm used to treat it. Louisa could almost see the roots of his fair hair, like those of the dolls her father had once bought her. His weight loss was unhealthy, and forks of broken blood vessels emerged from his nostrils.

'You didn't tell anyone what really happened, did you?' she said.

'No. Your secret's safe,' he said.

'*My* secret?'

'I mean mine.'

'*Our* secret,' Louisa said.

'I'm sorry,' David said.

'Don't be sorry,' Louisa said, grasping his wrist, noting the desperation in her own voice. She collected herself, relaxed her grip into a slow rub with her fingers. She tried to smile. 'Don't be sorry for me. Be grateful.'

She could already feel him slipping away. *Don't be sorry for me.* How she had meant that when she first said it. But she learned to take what she could get.

ELEVEN

Louisa looked at Christopher's face in the lamplight of her cottage, and saw again the resemblance to his father. His phone beeped twice as 'Crow Jane' played on the stereo.

Christopher looked at the phone message and laughed. His expression grew more serious as the song progressed. 'Erm. I don't like that song. I think it's against women.'

'Strange to hear that coming from someone who goes to Derby's only lap-dancing club,' Louisa said.

'Certain women are different.'

Louisa nodded. 'And all men are the same.'

He frowned. Louisa stopped the CD, picked up her guitar and played a few bars of 'Too Many Broken Hearts' from a tab she had downloaded. He laughed and then became thoughtful. 'Louisa. *You're* a woman ... '

Louisa raised her eyebrows.

'Do you think a woman likes a man to have a mortgage, at all?'

'I would say she'd prefer him not to.'

Christopher looked puzzled. 'But I'd like to have a wife and a mortgage, one day.'

'Oh, I see. You mean you'd like to *buy a house*, some day.'

He nodded. 'Do you, erm, think a woman would prefer you to other men if you had, for example, a GCE Advanced Level Certificate, and, erm, a Batchelor's Degree?'

'I think that would be a little shallow of her.'

'Oh right.' He paused. 'I've gone back to college, but I'm finding it hard to concentrate on my essay about the Hooded Man because I've got love on the brain. But then I know I'm going to need a qualification to stand a chance with the, erm, lucky lady.'

'So you're stuck between a rock and a hard place.' Louisa said. Christopher's eyes widened. Louisa was learning fast.

'Erm, erm, yes!'

'Who's the girl?'

'Her name is Carol-Ann. Erm, erm, erm. It was just love at first. Erm. We send each other in the region of ninety texts a day.'

'Jesus wept. Was that her who texted just now?'

'Yes,' he said, and grinned. 'Do you mind if I check my emails?'

'Sure. What did she say?' Louisa asked.

'Erm. Classified.'

'Course. None of my business.' But Louisa could not help it. 'She go to your college?'

'Nope.'

'Where'd you meet her?'

'Erm. Cyberspace.'

'Oh.'

'The problem is, she makes ten K a year. How am I supposed to compete with that?' He walked over to the computer.

'I don't know. Maybe it doesn't have to be a competition,' Louisa said.

'I believe a man should look after his woman,' said Christopher. 'Family values.'

Louisa did not reply.

'I've told her she means the world to me. I feel like I have a purpose, at last. Erm. I'm going to be the breadwinner and look after Carol-Ann and her child.'

'Whoa. Hold on there,' Louisa said.

'What?'

'This girl has a child?' Louisa said.

'A baby, yes. Simon, it's called.'

'It? I mean, you have to be careful here. You haven't even met this woman. You don't really know her.'

Christopher waved his mobile phone. 'Erm, erm. Hello? In the region of ninety texts per day.'

'Yes, but you can't make promises like that without *really* knowing a person. You're a young man. She could be trapping you into something you're not equipped to deal with.'

Christopher stood up. 'You're just like *her*,' he said, pointing his finger in the direction of the big house. He walked towards the door.

'Chris,' she said, following him.

'It's *Christopher*,' he bellowed. Then, in a quieter voice, he said, 'If you're writing it down, and you're in a hurry, I'll accept Xtopher.'

'Looking after a child is a big thing.'

'How would you know? Whose side are you on?'

'I'm not on anybody's side,' Louisa hissed. 'Sit down, now.'

She pointed at the sofa. Christopher flinched, and the force seemed to drain from him. He sat down.

'I'm not on anybody's side. But *she* is,' Louisa said, nodding towards the park. 'She's on yours.'

'Maggie Green is in it for the money,' Christopher said.

'Nonsense.'

'She's probably going to sell the park.'

'She'd make a loss if she did, you fool,' Louisa said. Christopher looked up, surprised.

'She doesn't care about Dad.'

'At the moment, all she talks about is you.'

'About how she's going to, erm, conspire against me.'

'No!' Louisa shouted. 'About how she wants to help you. She wants you to have friends, a girlfriend. To be happy. She, on the other hand, is up there, completely alone. And what are you doing to help? Whose side are *you* on, apart from your own?'

Christopher punched his thigh, and stared hard at the ground. He had lost a contact lens; Louisa could see that one of his eyes was bright blue, while the other remained grey. He got down on the floor to search, and eventually Louisa bent down to help him. It was under the sofa, furred with dust. It appeared that he hadn't noticed the shotgun.

'You know what we should do?' Louisa said.

'Erm. What?'

'We should go down to the White Hart, and get ... shit-faced. What do you think?'

'Erm. I think there's no need for that language, but I suppose we could go to the pub. Although at college they say I'm not comfortable working in group situations,' he said.

'But which came first, the chicken or the egg?' said Louisa. Christopher smiled.

They descended the hill together, and although Christopher stomped off into the dark to begin with, he soon slowed down and walked behind Louisa, occasionally placing his hand on her back as he resisted the slope.

The best part of the evening was seeing the collective discomfort of the regulars when they entered. Bill Wicks looked jaundiced in the light reflected from the optics. Christopher slouched on the bar. 'This must be the quietest pub in Christendom,' he said. He put Dr Hook on the jukebox to liven things up.

They drank heavily, offering flaming sambucas to the regulars, although Richie Foxton was the only man game enough to drink one, blowing first on the blue flame as though it were a birthday candle. Louisa and Christopher laughed when he asked if Maggie would be coming down. The other patrons shook their heads, and whispered amongst themselves. Christopher proposed a toast. 'To the two biggest loons this side of the Pecos!'

Louisa half-raised her glass and smirked.

The night wore on, and Christopher spoke of Robin Hood. 'People have this idea of him as a, erm, jolly character, but he mutilated Guy of Gisbourne's face with an Irish knife.'

'Does that make you like him more, or less?'

'Erm. Times were hard and men were men. Sometimes you have to get nasty. Dad used to say it's every man for himself. Sometimes you have to rock someone back to their ancestors, that's what Dad used to say.' Christopher tried to suppress a belch. He was wildly unsuccessful.

'Doesn't sound like David,' Louisa said. 'Never saw much violence out of him ... and I don't see how your violent Robin Hood
is compatible with your family values.' The word 'compatible'
was something of a struggle.

'Well, it's like me and Carol-Ann. Marian knew who the breadwinner was.'

'Not to mention the fact that, likely as not, he would have stunk
to high heaven,' Louisa said.

Christopher considered this. 'No,' he said. 'He was a stalker.
Like you. I think he would have been unusually clean.'

Back at Drum Hill, Christopher took the side entrance, to escape
a rain shower. Louisa heard him begin to climb the stairs and
then come back down to vomit on the doorstep. There was a note
of tired acceptance in his retching.

Louisa was drunk and relapsing. She would later tell herself
that it was the unusual light from the house which drew her into
the front garden, but on some level she admitted the futility of the
excuse. It was true, however, that she had never seen a light in
the third ground-floor window before. She had never seen David
in there, and had always assumed it to be some kind of storage
room. Now she saw that, although small, the room contained a
large armchair, and a disused fireplace in which stood a portable
heater and a desk lamp trained on the ceiling, so that shadows
extended from the bodies within.

Louisa had never seen the man before. His nakedness was
made more shocking by Maggie's state of dress. She wore a tight
black shirt and boots; her jeans were crumpled around her knees.
The man knelt before her as she sat in the armchair, her long legs

over his shoulders. She put a hand through her hair as he lowered his head between her legs. It did not take long, Louisa noticed, before Maggie slid down in the chair. She reached out for the back of his head, and hesitated, perhaps fearing the intimacy of the gesture. But then she took hold of him anyway, and pressed him to her. His erection grew taut, and soon he pulled off her jeans and boots. Maggie left the chair and straddled him where he knelt on the floor, her legs behind his back and her head turned away from the window. In the dim light Louisa could barely discern the man's features. He had rocky outsized shoulders and buzz-cut hair.

Standing there in the darkness, Louisa began to feel cold. Tears came to her eyes. This was nothing new. She thought of herself in her school uniform, in the coroner's court all those years ago.

Maggie held on to his arms and arched her back. In the garden, the soundlessness was the strangest thing – or rather the discordance of the outside sounds: the sporadic wet hiss of distant cars, the leaves shaking themselves of water, the hum of some giant generator coming from God knows where, the animals, all accompanying this apparently silent act.

MID-SEASON

Coot, snipe, wildfowl.

TWELVE

The morning after seeing Maggie with the man, Louisa woke early but stayed in bed. She watched the light glide across the carpet and illuminate the doorway. The jamb had splintered from her repeatedly slamming the door the previous night. Ugly channels of light wood showed where the white paint had come off, and debris covered the floor. The hinges had been damaged, too, and the door hung at a slight angle. She could not explain it, but she would not have to because nobody would know.

She was due to meet Maggie at the big house at 7.30 a.m. She lay in bed and waited for that time to pass. Shortly afterwards, her mobile phone rang. She threw it across the room. When it rang again, she rose to retrieve it and removed the battery. From her window she could see the tiny figure of Maggie in the distance, peering over at the cottage.

Fragments of their past conversations came back to Louisa throughout the morning. *'You're the only person I can talk to,'* Maggie had said. *'I feel like I can tell you anything.'* They had talked about men. She remembered Maggie saying that she was too busy for a relationship. Too busy with Christopher. *'He's the man in my life at the moment.'*

Louisa tried to focus on that remark, that lie. She tried to feel angry on Christopher's behalf, but she knew that the hurt she felt was for herself. It wasn't just the plans they had made, to work together on the park. There was something else, something deeper.

The next day, she could see Maggie across the fields, planning out the boundaries for the new, more spacious lynx enclosure they had talked about. Louisa felt a twinge of sadness, a momentary wish to be out there with Maggie, but she dismissed it sharply.

She had spent so much of her life avoiding people; it was really not so difficult. She slipped out of the back door of her cottage, put Diamond in the van and drove away, gunning the engine and heading for the reservoir.

Even out in the field, the images came to her frequently. Watching the clouds for Diamond, Louisa suddenly recalled the light fanning from the upturned lamp, the shadows around the big armchair, Maggie's hand on the man's neck, the slow control of his movements. She felt the blood begin to move in her body, felt her pulse quicken and her temperature rise. She had to call Diamond to the fist and sit in her van to calm down.

Travelling home she thought of David, and all the women he had brought to the house. After his first marriage failed, there were several, all of them practically the same: divorcees with a passion for cocktails and double-barrelling their surnames. Louisa

had watched them all drive away, but she could not help but feel
that she had spent her life being *replaced*.

Maggie visited in the afternoon. Louisa was in the living room listening to the bating of her hawks; the short bursts of frantic
wingbeats were like someone trying to start a car. The light was
already changing, the contours of her furniture dissolving before
her eyes. Preliminary sketches of the dual-skylight breeding
chamber lay on the table before her, fading into dark.

She could hear Maggie outside, talking to Iroquois. She could
hear boots on the path as Maggie walked to the door. Louisa did
not rise when Maggie knocked, and she had bolted the door this
time.

'Lou? You in?'

A few moments later Maggie was at the window, hand to her
brow, squinting into the living room. Louisa knew that Maggie
would not be able to see her, because of the dusky light outside
and the darkness within the house. She sat there in the shadows
with immunity, her pupils blacking out the colour, until Maggie
took two steps back, and then turned away.

She saw the man arrive at the big house again, shortly after
Christopher had left for his Sunday afternoon session in the Hart.
The last hope that she had witnessed a strange one-night stand
was gone. He parked his red Volkswagen Golf at the back of the
house. It was almost dark, and impossible to discern his features
from that distance anyway, as he walked through the beam of the
outside light. He moved with the stoop of a tall man, and had a
youthful bounce in his step. He gave a tap on the side door,

which presumably led to the seedy little room. The door soon opened.

Louisa turned away from the window. Women like Maggie, they could marry, bury their husband, and find another man within – what? – two years. All that talk of grief: what did it mean?

She paced around her living room for half an hour, tempted to walk across the fields and face Maggie with her accusations. But she admitted to herself that those accusations – when put into words – amounted to little of rational substance. She could not, however, stay in the house, and so she got in her van, rolled it down the hill, and parked across the road. She waited.

In the van she picked over the last few months, trying to think of signals she had missed. She could recall nothing. All of this had clearly been happening on her doorstep and, despite the watchful eye she kept on the house, she had missed it. I confided in that woman, she told herself, and she took me for a fool. She wondered about the nature of the relationship between Maggie and the man. She wondered if she had the power to destroy it.

When the Golf reached the junction at the bottom of the hill, she could see the man through the windscreen. His lips were pursed as he surveyed the road. He was young, maybe mid-thirties. Maggie's age. He rubbed at his short hair, which stood up in spikes like the comb on a set of hair clippers.

He turned left and she followed him through Detton to Fulbrook, a cheaper little village a few miles away. He parked on a quiet terraced street. Park Avenue, it was called. Louisa snorted. She pulled over a hundred yards behind, by the take-away on the corner. She watched him get out of his car and walk into his narrow mid-terrace. After a few moments she drove slowly past his door, which was painted with black gloss. The windows were clean, but she could not see into the living room for the wooden blinds – a sensible precaution, she thought, in a house with a street-level window. She stopped a little way down the street.

It was 6 p.m., and the lights on the dashboard were glowing. Louisa felt a warm satisfaction, a sensation which had disappeared from her life in the past few days. She thought of Maggie back at Drum Hill, and of her own proximity to the man. A light came on inside the house, and Louisa drove away.

* * *

It was not long before she was back on Park Avenue, waiting for him after dawn. Sleep had deserted her again. She parked by the take-away. Her mouth was dry, and her hands shook slightly, but she felt better than she did at home.

Fortunately, he left the house early, in a green uniform, and she followed him to a golf course out in the countryside. When he turned into the entrance, Louisa drove by, made a u-turn at the next roundabout and positioned the van at the back of the car park, far away from his car.

She could see him out in the rough which bordered the fairway. He had a strimmer buckled to his hip, and wore orange ear defenders and a visor of plastic mesh. He looked like a giant insect. She watched him work in a cloud of grass cuttings and smoke. He spent the morning alone, breaking once to raise his visor, drink from a flask and smoke a cigarette. He massaged his shoulder and wiped his face, then coughed.

For the next few days Louisa could find no real comfort unless she was tracing the man's movements. When she followed him, time seemed to pass with merciful speed, and she found that she was no longer alone with her wretchedness. There was comfort in abandoning oneself to the life of another.

She watched him for three days, and the plain rhythms of his life emerged quickly. When the first golfers arrived, he would go into the clubhouse for a few hours, and leave for Fulbrook soon after lunch. After spending some time at home, he would come out drinking pink liquid from a container that looked like a child's beaker.

Louisa followed him to a gymnasium. She parked outside but caught sight of him occasionally, through the large windows. On the second day she could see him buckled into some complex contraption, straining against himself, his image reflected in the mirror beyond.

Through the afternoons and evenings, he visited various houses in the villages around Detton. Never the same ones. Were it not for his casual clothing, Louisa would have guessed that he was a salesman.

On the Tuesday night, he stayed late at a block of flats in Fulbrook. The night was cold, the streetlights a sickly red. Louisa went home before he came out.

Driving back to the hill, she saw Christopher making his way back from the White Hart. She passed him quickly and did not look back. The sight of him made her feel ashamed about what she was doing, although she could not work out why. She told herself she would not follow the man again.

That night, in the moments before sleep, she saw him on the golf course – the green insect – rubbing his face beneath the black grid of his face guard. She imagined the fibres of grass that he spat into the sink when he arrived home, and the sad face which met him in the bathroom mirror. The noise of her boiler became the motor of his brushcutter. Her eyes remained open.

She stayed away until Wednesday tea-time. Children were playing football by streetlight on Park Avenue, and his car was still outside his house. He came out at 7 p.m., and she followed him to the Black Swan, a pub on the outskirts of Derby. She resolved to go in; her pulse was so strong she could feel it behind her eyes. The feeling was different from when she had spied on David, watching a life she already knew everything about, featuring a man who probably wouldn't have been surprised to find her in his garden. There was danger in this pursuit. If he spotted her, or Maggie found out, it would be the end of Louisa, a humiliation from which she would never recover. She would probably have to leave the hill. Somebody would. At the thought of Maggie, she got out of her van and entered the pub.

Thankfully, the place was crowded and dark. Early twentieth-century streetscapes and pictures of old boxing champions hung on the walls. Louisa sat down by the anomalous red pool table on the other side of the bar and watched him drinking lime and soda alone at a table with a red candle melting into a port bottle. He removed his jacket and she could imagine the heat coming from him as the sweat of his earlier exercise resumed. He blinked slowly, and looked – for one second – as though he might cry. He opened his eyes and shook the expression of sadness away. It was a private moment, but Louisa could not stop herself from looking. She felt a wish to console him, a sudden sense that she *could* console him, better than Maggie, better than anyone. Someone pressed the button to release the balls in the pool table behind her, and in the silence following that deep rumble, Louisa was reminded of the sad fact of what she was doing. She thought about leaving, but at that moment the door opened, and a woman came in. The draft made the gig notices flutter. She wore a black coat and a shapeless silky dress. Her hair was reddish, and Louisa could detect the smell of a recent dye-job – like washing-up liquid – as the woman walked hesitantly past and scanned the room.

The man stood, his face restored to the serious pursed-lip look. He moved purposefully now, in much the same way as he walked the fairways at the golf club. His tall man's stoop had confused Louisa, because now, in a room filled with other men, she could see that he was quite short. It was the closest she had been to him, with no windows in between.

Louisa watched the woman register his presence, saw the feeling hit home. He greeted her with a firm hand placed above her hip. He kissed her. The woman went to his table, while he ordered at the bar. Louisa could not hear his voice, but she saw a bottle of wine in a metal ice-bucket placed before him.

The woman looked at him, and then caught Louisa's eye and smiled. Her lipstick shone. Louisa turned away and left the pub, aware of some laughter over by the pool table.

So he was a cheat, Louisa thought as she drove home. She

thought of his hand on the woman's hip, and she thought of Maggie. What she felt was a surge of power. She could not help it.

Arriving at the top of the hill, she watched the shadowy shape of the big house emerging. It seemed to tilt in the sky as she drove past. Floodlights trained on the façade picked out patches of stone in the darkness. Louisa knew she could not tell Maggie what she had seen without revealing secrets of her own. She liked the feeling the knowledge gave her.

* * *

Oh, the numb comfort of afternoons in a village nobody has ever heard of. Louisa sat in her van at the bottom of Drum Hill and watched the light fade as though the trees were growing at five inches an hour, the branches closing like latticed fingers over the road. She watched the windows of the nearby houses turn yellow like crocus buds bursting out of season. Louisa knew the man was with Maggie, on one of his visits, and she expected his car to descend at about 3.30 p.m. She had the heater on full blast.

The Golf arrived at the junction, as usual, but this time things were a little different. He wore a light grey suit, a white shirt and a red tie like a tugged-out tongue. Louisa could tell that he had showered. As usual, the car was pointing to the left, but this time he swung it to the right at the last moment and then disappeared over Jack O' Darley Bridge. Louisa made a three-point turn, to the displeasure of two sides of oncoming traffic.

She caught up with him on Eaton Bank, where the sun shone – a last blast before it went down. Louisa kept her distance, unsure about the change of territory. Eventually, he turned left up Woodlands Close. She didn't know the road, and by the time she took the same left, he was out of sight.

It was a narrow hill, a steep incline with cars parked on both sides. Louisa took it in second gear, looking along the rows of cars. She reasoned that he couldn't have had time to parallel park. As she reached the mid-point of the climb, she saw that the road widened at the brow into a turning space; it was a cul-de-sac. The houses looked incredibly tall. He must have parked somewhere up there, she thought.

But he had not parked. He had turned his car around, and was now descending, quite deliberately, towards her. Stop then, she thought. Let me by. But he made no move to accommodate her van, and Louisa realised that she had been rumbled. There was only room for one vehicle between the stationary cars. She was trapped. He came down slowly, releasing the brake until they were just feet apart. Louisa could see the droplets of water from his shower soaking through his shirt. She could see the two-tone of his tie. His face was obscured by the glare of the sun on the windscreen. She let the van roll backwards. Her descent was halting. The light glinted off her wing mirrors, causing her to squint. She twitched the steering wheel, guiding the van through the narrow gap. When she reached the bottom of Woodlands Close she saw that the main road was now teeming with cars. The school run. She put on the handbrake. 'Back off,' she shouted. 'Just back off.' Then she stopped, knowing that he could not hear her, and that he'd probably be pleased if he could.

He stepped out of his car, leaving the motor running. He looked at the ground, his lips pursed, hands in pockets, the flaps of his jacket up and out. His suit had a cheap purple lining. He rubbed the flat of his hand across the top of his head, as she had seen him do before. Water came off and his short hair was immediately dry. He signalled that she could roll down her window, but mercifully approached the passenger side.

He bent down. She glanced at him long enough to notice the little gap between his teeth, and then stared forward. He seemed poised to knock on the window so she hit the button twice, letting in the noise and cold air and his breath.

'Alright?' he said.

Surprisingly wry. A strong North Derbyshire accent.

'Yes,' she said.

'Bit blocked in, are we?'

She shook her head stiffly as he smiled.

'You a dick?' he asked.

'I beg your pardon?' she said, turning to him.

'A PI. Private dick.'

'No I am not.'

'Working for one?'

'No.'

'Doing a bit a snoopin' about for a friend?'

'You could say that.'

'For a fella?'

'No.'

'Oh.' His tone became lighter. 'Well, in that case.' He patted his pockets, brought out his wallet and offered a card to Louisa. 'Adam,' he said. *Adum.* He dropped the card accidentally into the footwell of the passenger seat, and so pulled out another one. She took it, reluctantly, and put it in the pocket of her fleece. She felt him notice the bird smell, intensified as it was by the heat pulsing from the dashboard.

'Is it you?' he said.

'Is what me?'

'The *friend* you're snoopin' about for. Is it you? No shame in it.'

'I don't know what you're talking about,' she said. She was relieved that he had not connected her to Maggie.

'Alright, alright. Fair-do's.'

'Are you going to let me out?'

He looked back at his car and laughed. 'Oh aye. Give us a minute.' He tapped the van twice.

In spite of herself she called out to him as he walked to his car. 'Never seen you in a suit before.'

'Well how long have you been following me?'

She shrugged. He laughed and shook his head. 'Going to court, aren't I?' he said.

'Really?' she said.

'No,' he said, a flash of anger in his voice. 'And you shouldn't be doing this, you know. It's not on.'

She flushed, but he was quickly in the car, reversing up the hill with that satisfying whiz. She followed him and turned the van around. He watched her do it and let her go without pursuing. She managed not to cry until she got over the bank, but she was helpless then, her chest jumping so hard she could barely hold the wheel.

By the time she arrived back at the house the tears had ceased. She remained in the van, took the card out of her pocket. *Adam Gregory. Home visits and public accompaniment.* The conversation she had with him shifted into place, along with his late-night movements. She experienced a new feeling of disgust. But her thinking, as she looked over at the big house, became cloudy. Disgust had always been a simple emotion for Louisa, but that – she realised – was because she had always known, quite firmly, with whom she was disgusted. These days, she wasn't so sure.

THIRTEEN

The night before the staff meeting, Maggie set off to Louisa's cottage again. She needed an ally, and hoped that Louisa would fill
that position. In the dark, the bordering fields had become wild
again; the wind animated the black shapes around her. It had
been a while since she had thought of a border between them, but
now – even as she imagined the reasonable explanations for
Louisa's recent absence – she could feel those old walls coming
up. The van was parked outside the cottage. Iroquois strained
against her leash, screaming.

'Are you the bouncer?' Maggie said to the eagle.

She did not bother with the door this time, but stepped across
the lawn and knocked on the window. She looked inside; the
living room seemed untouched, but she could only see along the
tunnel of moonlight which burrowed into the smooth sofa, half of
the coffee table, and a section of the white wall. The corners of the
room were invisible to her. It had been almost a week since she
had last spoken to her friend. A couple of times she had seen

Louisa in the mornings, coming out of the cottage to deal with the birds, but she was too far away to call out to. More often, the van was already gone when Maggie rose. She tried to tell herself that the unanswered phone calls were a result of the bad signal on the hill, and hoped that Louisa was not relapsing into those old hermitic habits. 'Lou?' she shouted, one last time. 'Are you okay?' She turned and walked back to the house.

Maggie spent the night – as she spent many of the lengthening nights – in the office, filing papers and working on funding applications. When she was too tired to continue, she visited a deer webcam set up on a farm in Norfolk. It was empty now, as it was most of the time – just a grainy clearing in the bramble – but it was worth the wait for the occasions when the stags came into view, and wallowed in the steaming mud, their tines like writhing fingers in the mist. Maggie watched the seconds pulse on the digital clock in the corner of the screen.

It was the weird collisions she had loved, back in Greenwich. The Greenwich deer had a bloodline dating back to the time of Henry VIII and yet, out in the enclosure, the low grey ghosts of aeroplanes yawned overhead; you could hear the laser chirp of green parakeets and see the top deck of a bus sliding above the brick wall that shut them off from the wind-scoured roads of Blackheath. She had loved the physical signs of their seasonal desires, too, the antlers growing as the hormones raced, the blood-rich velvet nourishing the hard bone beneath and then peeling raggedly. She loved the ugly, aching bellow. It was an unmajestic, hurt sound. During the rut, the neck of a red deer stag increases exponentially in muscle mass; such spontaneous gains are unrivalled in the animal world. And at the end of the season, the antlers fell off, one by one.

Her own desires had waned now. The empty physical longing she had felt throughout the autumn had begun to subside. She had cancelled her last two appointments with the man from Fulbrook. It wasn't what she needed any more.

The deercam was best in the early hours, when a hind would sometimes turn and face the camera, pulling her hooves through the grass, eyes like molten metal in the floodlights. But tonight, the camera showed nothing but a tangle of briars. She knew how crazy it was to sit there watching for an elusive glimpse of a wild animal when there were hundreds in her garden, but there were no deer at Drum Hill, and deer made her nostalgic for her early moments with David. These days, and these nights, nostalgia was the feeling she longed for.

*　*　*

The keepers and volunteers sat in David's old office while Maggie, alone, explained the proposed changes to the park. Scattered rectangles of livid red stood out from the faded carpet, where she had removed the cases of stuffed animals.

She told them of the plan to reduce the stock to those species which were native – or had been native – to Britain. Talks were underway with the local university and the Nature Conservation Committee to captive-breed several species, including red squirrel, with a view to re-introducing them into wild habitats. She was particularly keen to obtain a herd of red deer, and she planned to buy another ten acres of woodland. She had hired a consultant zoologist, and spoken to conservation groups who had urged her to purchase vulnerable wolf cubs from fur farms in Romania. Fewer species meant more space for those that remained. Deer in, miniature zebu and wallabies out. She would also require staff to undertake training. Some of the volunteers looked at each other when she said that, some just groaned.

'Why are we getting rid a the zebu, anyway? I love those little buggers,' said Yvonne, a quiet sixty-year-old volunteer for whom Maggie felt great affection.

'I love them, too, Yvonne. But they're used to a tropical climate, and the cold is making them sick. It's cruel.'

She couldn't hear what the staff were muttering, but she could guess. Visitor numbers had further slackened as the cold weather began. People were beginning to think that her obsessions would destroy the park. She had heard the keepers talking about 'the spirit of the place.' More ghosts.

When Philip got up to leave with the others, she called him back.

'I can't really stay,' Philip said. 'The wife is picking me up, and I don't like to keep her waiting.'

'You didn't say much in the meeting.'

Philip looked down at his hands. He did not wear his cap indoors, and Maggie noticed the lustre of his oiled hair, the surprising thickness of the strands.

'I needed a little support, there,' she said, trying to smile.

Philip coughed.

'What's up, Phil?' Maggie said.

'I shan't be doing the training. I will understand if that means you have to terminate my contract.'

'Oh, Phil. Surely you've not taken it personally. I know how skilled you are.'

'It's not a personal thing, but I'm not going back to school.'

'Look, Philip. Firstly, nobody is terminating any contracts. You should see this training as an opportunity.'

Philip shook his head. 'I'm sixty-seven years old. I'm weary.'

'*I'm* doing it. It won't cost you anything. I'm paying for it.'

He looked up sharply. They held each other's gaze.

'Philip, if there's something you need to say to me, then feel free. We've always been very open. If you think I *don't understand*, or that I'm *not from around here* ...'

'I've never said anything of that sort. When someone comes to this part of the world, they can either shut themselves off from people, or they can get involved in the community. When you first got here, I saw you as someone who'd fit right in. Someone who'd get involved in the village.'

'I do get involved.'

'*She* doesn't count,' Philip said, with a sudden burst of anger. The fury immediately dissipated, and he sighed.

'I see. It's Louisa you have a problem with. I know Louisa is difficult sometimes, but she is a good person. I spend time with her because she knew my husband better than anyone. Better than I did.' Maggie thought of Louisa's current retreat from their friendship.

'Oh, that's true,' said Philip.

'I *know* she was in love with him, if that's what you mean.'

Philip frowned in confusion, his skin stretching over the thick ridges of his forehead. *'In love with him?* She sabotaged him at every bloody step. She's got nothing but bitterness, that woman. She tried to snatch this place, which is ours – *yours* – from under your feet. Don't you remember? You should have heard the things she said about you, and all.'

'I can imagine what she said about me in the early days, thank you.'

Philip tried to reclaim his composure. Maggie had never seen him like this. He dropped his hands by his sides. 'There are a lot of good people in this village,' he said.

'I know that.'

'People who respect you. People who really like you.' Philip paused, seemed to deliberate. 'Richie Foxton—'

Maggie laughed suddenly, and then stopped when she saw the dismay on Philip's face.

'Oh I see,' Philip said. He turned to leave. 'Fair enough.'

'Philip, I didn't mean – Richie is a great guy.'

'When David died,' Philip said, turning back to her, 'you said that you had wanted to start a family with him. There's no reason why you can't move on, eventually. '

'I've put all of my energies into this park,' Maggie said.

'Believe it or not, I want what's best for you. And there's a lot I could say now, but I'll settle for this: you continue to keep the company you're keeping, and you'll end up with nothing. No park, no family, nothing.'

He cut the air in front of him with a chopping motion. Maggie thought again of the ironic timing of Philip's attack on Louisa. He wasn't to know. She reached out to him, and took his hand. She looked down and saw the difference in colour between their skin – his raw pink flesh beneath the net of callouses, her own fingers light brown. 'Okay,' she said, to calm him. 'Okay.'

*   *   *

A few hours later, Christopher stepped halfway into the office, covering his body with the door like a shower curtain. 'I'm going out for a mammoth, erm, session,' Christopher said.

'Well, it's probably healthier than being on the internet all day,' Maggie said.

'You don't know anything,' Christopher said.

'It's a majority view,' Maggie said with a smile. 'Who are you going out with?'

'Erm. I'm going to call on Louisa Smedley,' Christopher said.

'Oh,' Maggie said. She frowned. 'Have you seen her recently?'

'No. I mean, erm, erm, what's it to you?'

'Doesn't matter. Will you tell her I said hello?'

'I'm not making any promises,' Christopher said, sliding out.

Maggie stood at the window, and waited for Christopher to come into sight. The light from the house gave his clothes a purple hue as he leaned forward into the wind. She could hear him swearing, and knew his curses were probably for her.

They had once been part of a family. He had always loved to hear the story of how Maggie and David met. He would ask questions about the drunken woman they had carried to the taxi ('Was she completely inebriated? Did she lose bladder control, at all?). Mostly he would just listen, enraptured, his laughter fading into an open-mouthed smile. 'It's like in days of, erm, yore,' he once said. 'With all those deer prancing around in the background. The squire and the, erm, buxom wench.' After a pause he said, 'I like true love.'

Maggie went back to the computer. The graph line of the park's income dipped across the years. Looking at the dates, she recognised that a landmark had slyly passed: she had now known Christopher longer than she had known David. She turned back to the window, but his shape had already melded with the dark. Maggie sighed. She saw the light of Louisa's cottage twitching behind the waving branches. Maybe her neighbour could restore the boy to his former self.

Louisa was back into the habit of turning off the lights when she saw a figure approaching from the big house. She did so now, then poured herself a drink and sat in the dark. He banged loudly on the door, rhythmically and unceasingly for nearly a minute. 'Come on, erm, Louisa. We're the two biggest loons this side of Christendom,' he shouted. 'Let's return to the theatre of war, and repeat our former glories. Erm, in the pub, I mean.' He was more persistent than his stepmother, but she could feel the darkness and the silence begin to threaten him. After a while longer, he said, 'Erm. Erm. Bye.'

When she was sure he had gone she licked her thumb, picked up her glass of whisky and then froze, noticing the gesture for the first time. She threw the glass across the room. The contents spattered on the wall and the floor but the glass itself lodged between a cushion and the seat of the armchair, still intact.

The card lay on the table in front of her. She thought of the man appearing at the window of her van, gesturing for her to roll down

the window with the rotation of his closed fist. The same movement as turning a spit. She thought of his tie and the lining of his
suit, the muscles of his jaw like stones beneath the skin. She
thought of Maggie's hands in his hair.

'Pull yourself together,' Louisa muttered. She retrieved the
glass, poured another drink and dialled the number, unsure of
what she was about to say.

'Yep,' the voice said.

'Do you see Maggie Bryant?' Louisa said.

'Eh?'

'Maggie Green.'

A silence. 'I don't give out such information.'

'Do you know what I'm talking about?'

'Look. Best thing to do in a situation such as this, is talk to the
person in question. I provide a service, but I don't ever knowingly
provide that service to someone in a relationship unless it's with
the consent of partner.'

'It's not like that. I just want to know if she pays you, like it says
on your card, or if you're seeing her because you like her.'

'You're the woman from the van, aren't you?'

She wanted him to remember. She wanted her face to appear in
his imagination.

'Yes, it's me,' she said.

He was quiet for a moment. 'I shouldn't really be having this
conversation, to be honest.'

'Why not?'

'There have been ... There's been a few incidents in the past.'

'What kind of incidents? Are you accusing me of stalking
you?'

'Well, you are. Anyway, that's not the point. I've had a few conflicts of opinion with folk who don't approve of what I do, that's all.'

'What, you mean religious people?'

He laughed. 'Husbands, mainly. Unsurprisingly. I've been given some very specific legal advice concerning such matters.'

Louisa heard an undertone of curiosity in his voice. 'You're not how I expected, on the phone,' she said.

'How did you expect me to be? How am I meant to speak to someone who follows me around?'

'What's that supposed to mean?'

'Well. You need to think on what you've been doing the past few ... however long. Think on whether you're behaving properly.'

'Oh, says *you*.'

'I know what *I'm* doing. I'm square with it. I go into it with my eyes wide open.'

'That's too much information,' she said.

'Aye. It probably is. According to the advice of my solicitor, I should have hung up by now.'

'But you haven't.' Louisa said.

She heard the dial tone.

'Bastard,' she said. She counted to one hundred, aware of a growing sense of excitement. Then she dialled 141 and called again.

'Yep.'

'I was talking to you,' she said.

'You were talking *at* me. Drinking at me, too, I reckon. Look—'

'Are you scared of me, or something?' she said.

'No. I'm not. But I can't do this all night.'

'Got appointments, have you?'

'Aye, I have actually. Do you want one?'

'Yes,' she said, immediately.

Momentarily, he seemed taken aback. But not for long. 'Do you want to go out? I can do Notts, Leeds or Sheffield if you don't want to stay local.'

Louisa tried not to think too hard about what she was saying. 'I don't want to go out.'

'You want me to call round? Where do you live?'

'Drum Hill, in Detton.'

Silence. 'Oh. You're the neighbour,' he said.

'Yes.'

'I can't believe I didn't figure it out.'

'I'm very clever,' she said.

'What about—'

'Leave your car at the bottom of the hill,' Louisa said. 'I'll collect you. Can you do tomorrow?'

'No. I'm busy all weekend. Are you free Monday?'

She didn't need to check. 'Yes. Seven-thirty onwards.'

'Fine. It's one-fifty an hour, four hundred for a stop-over. What's your name?'

'Louisa. You won't be stopping over.'

'You never know.'

She put the phone down as soon as it occurred to her to do so.

Maggie woke at 3 a.m., on hearing something smash downstairs. Still tense after the break-ins, and disturbed by the rebel spirit of the park staff, she put on a jumper and crept halfway down the stairs. From there she saw Christopher pissing up against the radiator in the hall. He whistled, stumbled slightly, and began walking upstairs.

'Oh hi,' he said, raising his hand briefly. 'I've had an absolute, erm, skinful.'

Maggie caught the sugary chemical smell from a good distance away.

'Are you okay?' she said. 'Did you see Louisa?'

'No. She was, erm, hiding in her lair. I had to go on my own, but that's okay. I'm a lone, erm, erm, wolf,' he said. Then he howled, and laughed like David. He walked past her, stepped into the bathroom, flushed the toilet and went to his bedroom, supporting himself by leaning against the wall. Maggie could see the dust collecting on the sleeve of his jacket.

She went to her own bedroom and laughed for a moment with her head in her hands. But she found she could not sleep for worrying. What would happen to Christopher if he carried on like this? With Louisa retreating, Maggie resolved that she would have to deal with him alone. She turned on her bedside lamp, and opened her laptop. She had recalled the bedroom of a schoolfriend who had a poster of the actor Michael Praed, dressed in Robin Hood gear, kneeling before a giant antlered spirit. The TV series had first aired in the 1980s, and it was not so difficult to find online. Maggie promptly ordered the box set.

She fell asleep with the deercam open, the grey light beaming into her face until the battery ran down, leaving the room in darkness.

FOURTEEN

Adam spent Monday morning in the rain, sawing overhanging branches from the beeches that lined the tenth fairway. When he switched off the brushcutter, the sounds of the golf course remained muted outside his ear defenders. All he could hear was the fierce roar of his own blood.

As he bagged the branches, the thought of his evening appointment reared again. This woman, Louisa, was different. He recalled the feeling he had in his car, as it dawned on him that he was being followed: the double-take as he looked in his rear-view mirror and realised that the kidney-coloured van had been there yesterday, and the day before. The shock had been visceral, almost exhilarating.

He could smell the petrol fumes from the brushcutter now, and the soaked mulch of crushed nettles. These past few days, his senses had sharpened. He saw his surroundings as though for the first time. He marvelled at the crimson colour of the two-stroke fuel as he filled his machine for tomorrow, and at the bristling of the long grass which seemed blue beneath the cloudy sky. The rain came down on his ear defenders in tiny clicks. He removed them, and the world flooded in. He was done for the day.

Adam tried to tell himself that his Golf GTi did not look so out of place in the car park of the country club, though he was the only man covered in grass cuttings. He sat with the door open and brushed down his trousers, swapped his toe-capped boots for trainers. He smoked a cigarette.

Much of Adam's business came by word-of-mouth but this Louisa, he suspected, had not arrived at his name by the usual route. It seemed strange that she wanted to meet at her house, but did not want the neighbour to know. He recalled the smell of her vehicle as he closed the door of his own. He thought of her staring ahead on the hill as he spoke to her through the window of her van. Her quick glance in his direction. The vulnerability of that glance. He felt a strange pressure in his skull.

The roads home were narrow, bordered by dry-stone walls. The tarmac was uneven, and rainwater had begun to settle in the dips. The day after he realised she was following him he had secretly observed her movements, pretending that he hadn't noticed. She had waited outside the gym and followed him home. At one set of traffic lights, she had come to a stop only a few yards behind him, in the next lane. He had seen her face quite clearly – the strong jaw, and the light eyes like a husky.

He checked his mirrors now, and saw the fields and the golf course unravelling behind him. For a moment he thought he saw a flash of red, and squinted, but it was just a golf bag. When he looked back at the road he saw that the bend had come upon him too quickly and, just beyond it, a herd of sheep was crossing from one field to another. He locked the brakes, then tried to pump them, but aquaplaned off to the right through a big puddle, the road disappearing from view, replaced by the spinning green of the land, as the car took a wooden gate off its hinges and smacked against a stone wall. On impact, the passenger airbag inflated, but – inexplicably – not his own and he was thrown sideways, banging his head slightly against the window.

In the stillness, Adam took a huge breath, released the pressure on the pedals and looked at the powdery white balloon filling the other side of his car. He cast a glance in his mirrors, but there was nobody on the road behind. 'Get it together, lad,' he said to himself, rubbing his neck. He opened the door, stepped down into the mud and looked at the crumpled nose of his Golf. The wall had bent his left front wheel on its side.

The farmer approached him. 'What the fuck are you doing?'

'Not much now, pal,' Adam said.

Several miles away, Louisa was out with Diamond, hunting to work off her nervous energy. A pheasant went into cover, and when they flushed it, the bird was so waterlogged it could hardly get into the air. Diamond put in two short stoops and stunned the thing with the second, as though disconnecting a wire. The pheasant made a splash when it hit the ground, its head amputated on contact, spraying water as it spun away from the body.

The sky was like grey shag-pile rubbed in places against the grain. Louisa finished early because she could not concentrate. She wished that the memory of the phone call she had made would stop bolting through her torso. The rain quickened as she drove home. Other falconers had been saying that it would be a bad year for rain, that you had better get out there now, because the end of the season would be a wash-out.

Adam's confidence began to fade that evening on the train to Detton. Something about the dissolving day dragged at him. He tried to blame it on the dark weather and the sight of his car being towed away. Without meaning to, he recalled the feeling of power as he trapped the woman on the hill, and made her roll back down towards the main road.

The floor of the train was covered in a silty filth, imprinted with soles. The carriage was empty but for a couple of old boys going out to the factories for the night shift, and a man with his infant daughter.

Adam wondered if what he was feeling was nerves. He tried to remind himself of the guidelines he had created for his behaviour with clients. He never spoke of his family: his estranged mother back in Belton, the former industrial village where he had grown up. He did not smoke on a visit. Of course, he never mentioned his child. He did not speak about his work, or his other clients. That rule would be particularly relevant in this case, the woman living in such close proximity to another client. He never swore, but spoke in a firm, forthright manner; the women had called him, and should not have to ask twice.

That, perhaps, was the difference with Louisa. Most of the women he saw relied on him to seduce them; as soon as he had left their houses (sometimes even their bedrooms), he was dead to them. A source of shame. But this was a woman who had pursued him through the streets. He had seen her buy a drink from the take-away near his house. She had bought two more for the little boys playing football in his street. He recalled her bouncing on her haunches, passing the cans to the children. *I'm very clever*, she had told him on the phone. That seemed true enough.

The little girl in the train carriage began to scream for her mother. She was blonde, her face dark pink, so that she looked like a half-chewed saveloy. The screaming settled into a rhythm, with the stress on the second syllable. 'Mu-*mee*, Mu-*mee*.'

The father turned to Adam. 'I'm sorry about this,' he said.

'It's no bother, youth,' Adam said. 'She's saying what we're all thinking.'

Usually he could swallow his emotions. It was just as important to his job as any sexual technique. When he felt particularly bad, he consoled himself with this: nobody could see into his mind. As the train slowed down, the windblown rainfall was like an animal clambering across the roof of the carriage. He tried to pull himself together. Maybe it's just the time of day, he thought. The early evening was a dark, penitent time for him, heralding the changeover from one life to another. He patted the pockets of his jeans as the train stopped. He'd forgotten his phone.

Louisa bathed, looking down at the outcrops of her belly and breasts, the dismorphic limbs beneath the glass-green water. Bubbles quaked in her leg hairs. After all those private years, her body now felt like a diary left in a café. She flushed with the outrage of her vanity. She would shave for no man, she thought. And yet she felt the pull of shame.

Her mind went back to the entrance hall in the big house, the echo of Maggie's coughing as she took off her clothes on the day they had rescued Diamond from the pond. Maggie had stepped from her jeans like a hawk trying to free herself from the leash. Louisa remembered the shimmer of the netted fabric of her underwear, the neat thin strip of pubic hair. All sorts of wonders. Louisa hoped Adam would not be expecting such things from *her*.

She stood, and put her right foot on the edge of the bath. She soaped the lower part of her leg and then took hold of the disposable razor with which she usually shaved her armpits. She dragged the blade upwards from her ankle and immediately felt the blunt pluck of it. Dots of blood mixed with the green soap on her skin. 'Sod it,' she said. 'I'm paying.'

She dropped the razor into the water where it twisted slowly. But when she had unplugged the bath, she took a new blade from the packet and started again.

She tidied, tucked the stock of her shotgun under the sofa and boiled coffee bags to cover the bird smell although she could no longer detect it herself. For the first time in many years, she applied make-up, and tried to keep thoughts of her own hypocrisy at bay. She was, after all, doing exactly what Maggie had done.

She waited, drinking Guinness and then Scotch. The drink bloated her, made her feel ridiculous, so that by 7 p.m. she no longer wanted him to come. It was a grotesque idea. Why had she entered into this so rashly? What if someone found out? What if she didn't fancy him when she saw him up close? He could have grown a moustache. What if the whole thing was awful?

The phone rang at half past and she heard his young voice. 'It's Adam Gregory.'

Oh God. Here he was calling her, with his *surname*. 'Oh. Hello,' she said.

He was surely calling to cancel and, after all her reservations, she was desperately disappointed by the prospect of spending the evening alone.

'I'm at the station,' he said.

'The police station?'

'No.' He sounded offended. 'The train station.'

'Why?'

'Car's fucked. Sorry. 'Scuse the language. My car is done-in, basically.'

'Golf GTi, right? You boys thrash those things to within an inch of their lives.'

'It was a crash, actually,' he said. 'But I'm alright. I'll have a courtesy car soon. I wouldn't normally have to take the train, like.'

'I'm sure,' she said, enjoying the shift of power, but trying to put him at ease.

She felt him relax slightly. 'Wouldn't say much for my work if I couldn't afford to run a car, would it, eh?'

'I'm sure you're good enough to run a whole fleet,' she said, catching her eye in the mirror and shaking her head, almost unable to believe in the conversation, and her part in it.

'Well. We'll soon see,' he said. 'So ... '

'Oh sorry. Of course. I'll come and pick you up.'

The rain was still hammering down as she arrived at the station. The sky was thick and purple. He stood, exposed as could be, lit up in the old red phone box, surrounded by the gelatine corpses of spiders. He left the phone box and started jogging towards Louisa before she flashed the lights because, of course, he recognised her van.

As soon as he got in beside her, Louisa began to fully appreciate the extent of her intoxication. She could hardly remember how she'd got there. She drove back at twelve miles an hour, noticing him glance at the speedometer. He seemed unnerved. She worked hard not to laugh at the thought of being pulled over by the police, drunk, with a prostitute in her Transit van.

They spoke, briefly, about the damage to his car, but Louisa found she had to further slow the van in order to concentrate, so in the end they sat in silence. Driving sobered her enough to bring back the nerves. She turned off the lights as they reached the top of Drum Hill, and cast an anxious glance at the big house. She parked as close as she could to the cottage.

Adam became more animated when he got out of the van and saw Iroquois under shelter on the lawn. 'Sake!' he said. Louisa thought of the well-tended lawns of the houses she had seen him visit. She felt her life about to go on show, and could barely guess what would be considered eccentric, although a steppe eagle in the front yard was an obvious one.

'What a belter,' Adam said. 'Can I touch him?'

'Her. You can if you want to be eviscerated.'

'I'd like to know how it feels.'

'To have your guts ripped out?'

'No. The feathers and that.'

Iroquois had already lost interest. She had a look of judgment about her. Adam continued to stare as he walked by.

'Bitch magnet,' Louisa whispered to the bird as she opened the door.

In the light of the hall, she looked at Adam.

'What's up?' Adam said.

'Nothing,' she said. 'I'd forgotten that you were ... I'd forgotten what you looked like.'

He sighed. 'It's a height thing, isn't it? You're thinking I'm too short.'

He was right, but was this the same super-confident bloke who had trapped her on Woodlands Close? 'No,' she said. 'Your height is the least of my concerns. Besides,' she said, slipping into a Derbyshire accent, 'you're all same lying down, aren't you?'

He gave a weak smile.

'Are you usually this touchy?' Louisa said.

'No. Sorry. Been a weird day. It's just that people sometimes mention it. "Thought you'd be taller." One of the reasons I don't work for one of them seedy agencies. Women just come out and say it: *no short men. Must be six foot plus.* Not much I can do about it, is there, apart from going on rack? It's like racism.'

Louisa laughed. 'That's a bit strong.'

'Well, imagine the uproar there'd be if men started saying, "No fatties".'

Adam said this as Louisa removed her coat, revealing her belly and big hips. He blushed and looked away. Louisa saw the blush. 'Well, well,' she said. 'Now that we know what we think of each other's *physiques*, shall we have a drink?'

Adam closed his eyes. 'Sorry. I'm not normally this ... '

'Doesn't matter. But if you think men don't request slim women, you need your bloody ears testing. And your eyes. Now. What do you want?'

'You got beer?'

She patted her stomach. 'You know it.'

She noticed that his hands were shaking. 'Are you alright?' she said.

'Yeah. I just ... I just need a fag.'

She opened the door again, and let him out into the cold air. In the kitchen she poured the beers and watched the throbbing red dot of his cigarette in the dark.

For the first few moments, she tried to guess his thoughts. She looked for signs of some tired routine, but he appeared to be honest, quiet – the sort of person who would not make her uncomfortable by asking too many questions. After half an hour, Louisa's bitter, paranoid voices quietened. She did not even feel drunk any more.

He asked her about 'the birds', and she told him the basics of what she did: the clearance, the displays, the hunting.

'I remember this time,' he said, 'I were about eleven years old and we were playing in the junior football tournament at a carnival. I goes over to take a corner, and this massive golden eagle from the falconry display swoops down on me. Really went for me.'

'What did you do?' Louisa said.

'I hit the deck. All my mates are laughing at me. Referee didn't know what to do.' He became thoughtful. 'Me mam was there, and all. I remember looking over and she was hysterical with laughter.'

'Where was it? The carnival?'

'Belton Rec.'

'I think that might have been Oggie's eagle,' Louisa said. 'I was probably there myself, assisting. A lot older than you.'

'Really?' he said.

'We did all of those carnivals.'

'Imagine that,' he said quietly. 'We were both there on Belton Rec that day, and now we're here. Funny how things work out, in't it?'

'I'd say it's hilarious,' she said.

They sat in the warm and they talked and drank and laughed. In the brief silences, they listened to the rain. Louisa had taken the unusual step of turning on the central heating, and – as Adam sat by the radiator – his jeans gave off a pleasant heated fug that mixed with the almond smell of his wet hair wax.

Louisa had planned to talk about Maggie, but she dismissed the impulse when it came to her. She did not want to ruin the night, and she realised now that there was something to ruin. She looked at his strong neck. 'Do you need anything? Another drink?' she said.

'No ta, duck. I feel much better.'

To Louisa, that felt like an unguarded compliment. She went into the kitchen to fetch another drink for herself and he followed her, talking. The contents of Diamond's crop lay by the toaster: a neat line of washed bones and fur. She thought about trying to hide it, but Adam didn't appear to mind.

'What's all this?' he said, picking up the skull of a mouse.

'That's the last bloke who came here,' Louisa said.

Adam laughed. 'There was me worrying about my size.'

'Yeah, but he was hung like a horse,' said Louisa.

Adam held the mouse head up to the light, and the colours

from the glass lampshade swirled on his hand. 'I like it,' he said.

'I feel a bit strange being the one to say this,' said Louisa. 'But you don't have to do anything you don't want to. Just having the company is fine.'

Afterwards she decided that he must have made the move, because she would have over-thought it, even in that relaxed state. What shocked her, after all those years, was desire. He leaned against her so hard that she lost her balance and flailed behind with one arm, reaching blind for the kitchen wall like a bad swimmer. He brought her back with a forearm around her waist.

Jesus wept, the warmth and the breath and the moisture. He kissed her neck and she felt the long pulse of his desire – the duration of a muscle cramp. She knew he was not faking it. People have it within them, she thought, those same people who seem so distant and closed in everyday life. And now she felt it coming from this man who was so near to her that he was just a colour, a shape, an eye, an ear. Belt buckle and fervency.

She heard a moan – that remembered sound, charged with the frustration of not being able to crash right through the other person, the impatient wish to sit inside their ribcage, or eat them. She realised that the moan came from her.

Louisa woke at four to find him incapacitated by a young man's sleep. They were still on the living room sofa, where they had made love. He lay with one leg hanging down, his big toe touching the carpet, while she sat at the end. Her shirt was nearby; she put it on. His sweat felt cool on her thigh.

She brought a blanket from the bedroom and laid it over him.

When he finally rose, Louisa was already making breakfast. She felt glad that she could not see his face. While he slept, her doubts had crept back in. He must have done this a thousand times. He must have done it with Maggie, a few hundred yards away – though Louisa had never seen him stay the night there. She had become suspicious of the desire which she had found so flattering last night. For some reason, she found herself thinking of David again, their one kiss. She had seen the reluctance in his face afterwards, and she feared that she might be met by a similar expression when Adam walked into the room.

She could hear him dressing in the lounge now, the glide of the various fabrics. His movements were slow. She turned back to the eggs before he arrived in the kitchen, dressed in his boxer shorts and red T-shirt.

'Good morning,' she said. 'I've made breakfast. There's easily enough here for two, but if you don't want it, I'll feed it to the dogs. Or I can eat it myself. That's more likely, to be honest. I'm fairly hungry, as it goes.'

He rubbed vigorously at his soft, bristly hair. 'I really don't know what to say about last night,' he said.

'You could just have coffee. If you want.'

'I would love some coffee.' He sat down at the kitchen table.

'Help yourself. And help me. My mug is there. It says "mug" on it.' She laughed unsteadily.

Louisa put two plates of eggs, bacon, black pudding and toast on the table, and sat down. Adam smiled and looked away. 'Ta,' he said.

'Well,' she said. 'You said you might stop over, but I didn't think your tactic would be to just pass out like that.'

'I'm so sorry.'

'I'm not,' she said.

'No. I mean. Neither am I. But it doesn't count as a stop-over.'

'Whoa there. It does to me, young man. The notch is on the bed-post and I've told all my friends.'

He laughed. 'I didn't mean that.'

'Listen, don't worry. It doesn't matter. It's natural for a man to fall asleep after sex. At least you didn't nod off while we were ... These things happen.'

'No they don't. This is not how I do things. I drooled on your sofa.'

She laughed with a mouthful of toast. 'My God. You're not too clever at the old morning-after chat, are you, given your business?'

'Louisa, most of my visits are in villages. Half of them are in the daytime. This is not something I'm used to. And last night ...'

'It must be a bit disturbing, waking up to me. The whole clotted mascara, morning breath thing.'

He sat back and looked at her. She felt abruptly aware of her appearance: she knew that the small amount of eye make-up she had applied was probably a spidery mess, and could feel her ponytail slipping to the left. She was bra-less in a large US Air Force T-shirt. She searched his face for that expression of regret.

'You look nice,' he said, and smiled.

FIFTEEN

For the first year after the accident, David continued to meet Louisa at the cob van once a fortnight, and she admired him for that. His family had closed around him protectively, and he could have excised those few months from his life, gone back to his friends and lived normally. She hoped he continued the meetings through need, rather than duty.

They spoke quietly while the generator powering the trailer rattled on. If a trucker, or sometimes two, emerged from the bushes, they fell silent, and drifted into the dark. He was dealing with a crime for which he felt sorry, but for which he had received no censure. Louisa told him now was not the time to confess. 'It'll dig everything up again, and we don't need that. *I* don't need it,' she said.

'But I can't get the pictures out from here,' David said, tapping his head. 'I can't concentrate on anything else. It's like I'm in love with it.' He would say these things quickly, and then become sheepish. 'What about you? It's worse for you. What am I complaining about?'

'I'm fine. We've got each other, haven't we? We're lucky.'

Though his face did not project feelings of good fortune, though he did not kiss her, she hoped there was time for that.

'Do you ever get that thing where you wake up, and you're convinced that it hasn't happened?' he said, with the first glimpse of a smile.

'No,' she said.

On one of those nights, a year after the accident, Louisa saw her father's car as she was walking to the trailer. He must have worked late. She turned away and obscured her face with her hair, but she could hear him slow down and pull over. He pipped the horn. She carried on for a moment and then relented, marching over to his window. It was his birthday, and she had told him she had to miss supper to stay late at school. He was a man who felt vulnerable and mawkish on his birthday, and he looked hurt as he leaned over and opened the door. 'Hi,' she said. 'The school thing finished early.'

'Get in,' he said.

'No. I'm meeting some friends.'

'I know who you're meeting,' he said. He must have seen David waiting by the trailer. 'I'm not going to take you home. Just get in for a second. It's cold.'

She sat in the passenger seat, keeping the door open and one foot on the kerb.

'*Happy birthday, Daddy,*' he said.

Louisa sighed, and felt her father bristle. 'Shall I postpone dinner until you get back?' he said.

'No. I'll get a cob from the van.' She pointed up the road.

He shook his head. 'Eating from a *van*,' he said.

'Jesus,' she whispered, and began to get out of the car.

'Wait.'

'What now?'

'Just watch you don't get left behind.'

'What are you talking about?'

'I can't understand it,' he said, quieter, so that she involuntarily leaned towards him. 'I just can't understand it. That boy isn't fit to lace your boots.'

And with that old sporting phrase, he shocked Louisa for the first time in many years.

Her world did not collapse, it eroded. School became something of a waste of time; the teachers, she noticed, stopped reprimanding her. Punishments were meted out at arms' length, with minimal eye-contact, and she was left to drift towards her hawks. She kept company with the older boys who worked with Roy Ogden. Good, gentle types like Baz Tiler, who could have a bird flying free in four days, and harsher boys like squinting Nelly Carter who clicked his tongue whenever he saw her, made remarks about her 'posh accent' and one day, when she bent over to peg a bow-perch, said, 'Eh up, look at that bit a tail. 'Bout creamed me sen.'

'Yeah, I heard you had a hair-trigger,' Louisa replied, standing and pressing down on his toes as though she was running a red light. Nelly smiled through the pain, and Baz Tiler looked away.

Sessions concerning further education undoubtedly took place at her school, but either Louisa was not invited, or she failed to attend. In any case, the concerns of the girls in her class seemed alien to her now, and trivial. She scored high on biology tests, and could identify the fungus *Aspergillus fumigatus* in a closed jar before the teacher, but that was the limit of her academic success. She was so far from comprehending the rites and motivations of her peers, she did not imagine that the same conversations about the future might be taking place in the boys' school across the road.

At sixteen, she took a job on an estate in Derbyshire, lived in the old mews, and slept in a woolly hat. Her falcons, and those of the master, resided in purpose-built quarters next door. The master did not bother her, and she felt happy to be left alone with her work. Her father did not object to the residential position, and her mother had become distant since the accident, as if she had fired the gun herself. A few times a year Louisa saw Baz and Nelly, who had taken night-shift work so they could fly their birds by day. They were not bitter about her live-in falconry job, being mammy's boys, both. The early starts and long days meant their meetings in the Patternmaker's Arms were swift and moderate, full of bushwhacked whistles and stone-me-youths.

On her rare free days, Louisa strove to make it back to the van on the outskirts of Oakley. They never discussed the possibility of David making the trip to Derbyshire. His parents didn't like her to call his home, so she called a phone box near his house at 7 p.m. every Wednesday. There was no phone line in the mews, and Louisa enjoyed the romantic idea of them speaking from identical phone boxes, miles apart. He usually answered, in the beginning. But David's social life soon resumed. She grew to recognise the strain in his voice, and his tendency to suppress his inquisitive nature, swallowing questions lest they prolong the conversation.

Sometimes she thought she heard people talking outside the phone box. She began to feel sick of phone calls which *started* with the words 'I'm on my way out, actually.'

'Where to?' she asked him, one day in May.

'Leavers' Ball,' he said, clearly distracted. Another ball, she thought, without her this time. No pointy shoes.

'Leavers' Ball? Where are you going?'

'Bristol,' he said quickly, and then swore under his breath. 'To university.'

Re-heating cock-a-leekie on the portable stove, she thought of him down there at university, thought of what he might be up to. She had little experience of the social life, but she had a bitter imagination. She had let him slip from her grasp. Warming her hands above the soup, she knew she had made a terrible mistake.

Louisa went back to Oakley when she heard about the reunion at the OAP hall. She waited outside, in her big shapeless coat, which was as green as the moss on the war memorial against which she rested. She could not help but think back to that night she had first approached him. To say she would do it all the same again was to make a murderer of him, but she could not help what she wanted.

The revellers came out before midnight, into late spring rain, talking about the bus to town. For a moment Louisa felt superior to their frivolity. A pink, spatulate girl saw her first, took thirty seconds to make the identification and still failed to muster any restraint. 'Oh God, it's *her*. Where's David? David? Darling?'

'Yes? We're heading for the Coconut,' he said, trying to light a cigarette. The girl pointed, and whispered in his ear. 'What are you talking about?' he said, half-walking, half-dancing towards Louisa in his suit. Louisa's eyes had adjusted to the dark hours before, but David's had not. He stopped suddenly when they did.

'Christ,' he said.

'Close. The Holy Ghost,' she said. 'Boo.'

He looked over at his friends, who had gathered on the steps of the OAP hall, to watch. 'Will you give me a minute, chaps?' he shouted.

'A bloody minute?' Louisa said. 'Not much time for an old friend.'

He smiled hesitantly at her. 'Or perhaps you could come into town with us ... ' He pointed over his shoulder, but lost conviction.

'I don't think so, do you?' she said, smiling.

'No. Probably not,' he replied. 'What brings you to these parts?'

'You, David. I can't seem to get hold of you on the phone.'

'Been busy.'

'Aye, so I see,' said Louisa, thankful for the darkness, because the 'aye' which slipped out had made her cheeks burn. She saw it all quite clearly: the students had come to this party intent on showing each other how they had matured during their years away. But it was she who had changed most, without wishing to. Perhaps her difference could be used to her advantage. She doubted it.

In any case, she told him he owed her more than a minute, so he reluctantly waved goodbye to his friends for the night. Louisa watched them go, surprised at how few she recognised. She surmised, from their unwillingness to approach, that they all recognised her.

Louisa and David walked uphill, passing her old haunts, and the places where she had flown Jacko. David looked nervous, scared perhaps that they would somehow arrive at the canal. He'd never had much directional sense. He talked about the reunion, about Bristol, and about the nightclub the others were going to. 'It's nowhere special,' he said, with an unconvincing shrug. 'Pretty small town stuff, really. Plays some hot music, though. Do you manage to get out much, where you are?'

'What do you mean?' Louisa said.

'Do you go to clubs?'

Louisa thought of Nelly and Baz, of the colours of the well-lit dartboard in the Patternmaker's. 'No. I'm beyond all that, to be honest. I've too much work to do.'

They reached the fenced limits of her old school, from where she had looked down at David running naked across the field. Now, the field was packed tight with tents, erected as part of an open-air sale. The rain, falling forcefully, made a rolling putter as it hit the canvas. The tents were like dull bulbs, their colours diffused.

'Do you still think about what happened?' she said.

'I try not to,' he said.

'I see,' she said.

'I mean, I do. Of course I bloody think about it. Every single day. Every time I see a kid. Every time I see—'

'Who do you talk to?'

'I don't talk to anyone. If it gets really bad, I just try to go to sleep.'

'You used to talk to me,' she said. 'About everything.'

He had grown an inch since she had last seen him, and his hair was now flecked with seeds dislodged from bushes and trees by the rain as they had walked to the top. She kissed him, and pushed him against the coated wire fence which gave slightly with their weight. He unzipped her coat, and put his hand on her waist, ran it up the side of her jumper and took hold of her left breast. Then he pulled away and inhaled audibly as though he'd been underwater. He stared at her with alarm, breathing fast.

'Don't stop,' she said, unbuckling his belt.

'I can't do this.'

'Why not?' she said, but she saw, as she stood back and examined his face, that there were reasons, and she did not want to know them.

She had read books and seen films, and she knew that most girls would have insulted him, or ran away, shamed, at that point. But she wanted him to think she was something different, that her commitment had transcended such self-regard. So she put her arms around him, and twined her fingers through the fence behind his back. 'Don't worry,' she whispered. He was shaking – cold, perhaps.

She walked him home, but felt him get twitchy as they neared his road. 'I'm sorry, Louisa.'

'Don't be sorry,' she said, again. 'And don't forget me.'

'How could I?'

SIXTEEN

Sensual overload had suppressed Louisa's morbid outlook for a couple of hours after Adam left the house, but she knew her irascible soul and there was no escape from it. By 2 p.m. that day, she was imagining Adam and Maggie in bed together, laughing at her.

He had refused any payment. Taken by a crazy mood, she had said, 'Well then, I'll have to buy you dinner instead, won't I?'

'I think you probably will have to, aye.' He had sounded sad to Louisa, almost resigned.

He must loathe me, she thought now.

She did not call him that afternoon, and thanked herself for it later in the evening, when she dressed in last night's clothes and looked in the bedroom mirror at the place on her neck he had kissed. Tufts of blonde hair curled there, along with a couple of wiry white ones. She pulled her shirt up over her face and left it there for a long time, inhaling and exhaling until she had made a wet patch which felt the same against her belly as his sweat and spit had felt.

She removed her clothes and sat on the bed with her eyes closed. She thought of his arm going between her legs to take hold of the back of her thigh, and then sliding on up. But in her imagination, her legs became Maggie's legs. Louisa pondered this vision and let it play for a moment. Then she opened her eyes, picked up the knickers from the pile of clothes and took them through to the kitchen.

She had been making a bumper leash – an elasticated tether to soften the impact on Diamond's fragile legs. She punched holes in a strip of leather, sheared off the elastic from the top of the knickers with a knife, and threaded it through the holes. She stitched the ends together, twanged the leash and placed it carefully back on the table, ready.

By Wednesday she could no longer stand it. She stood at her living room window and watched Maggie's house. The thought of Adam pulling into her neighbour's drive made Louisa want to drink fence paint. But he did not. Was *she* supposed to call *him*? Wasn't that the way his job worked, after all? (And it was just a job, she reminded herself.)

The old voices were back, loud and strong. Maybe he had visited Maggie, but he had driven the courtesy car that replaced his Golf. Maybe she had missed him. Yes, the voices were back, but it was the whisper of a good feeling that sickened her. She resolved to eliminate that in her usual manner. She would follow him, see him on one of his 'appointments', and confirm to herself how crushingly pointless the whole thing was. Even as she picked up her coat, she felt the rush of adrenaline.

Outside, she examined her van. The dent, where Maggie had driven the trolleys into the door still remained, like a sucked-in cheek. *If you didn't want me to see that you were stalking me,* he had said, *you wouldn't have done it in that maroon monstrosity.* Well, if he could have a courtesy car, then so could she. She got into the van and set off for the garage.

As it happened, she saw him catching the bus from the top of his road. Even under the cover of a black Corsa, she stayed way behind. When Adam alighted in Duffield, she pulled into the Co-op car park. She had to take a deep breath when she saw him. At that cautious distance, she could not see the face of the woman who greeted him at the door of the small end terrace, but she could see that the woman was young. She had dark hair and wore boot-cut jeans and a T-shirt with writing on the front. Louisa turned on the heater and waited.

She woke an hour later to find him sitting next to her. 'Oh shit,' she said.

'New motor?' he said.

'It's a courtesy car,' she said, unable to look at him.

'Well you're not being very fucking courteous with it, are you?'

She had a bitter taste in her mouth. She looked at him, feeling the same toppling attraction as she had that night at her house. He was quiet, his breathing quick and shallow. 'This isn't what it looks like,' she said, but even as she spoke she felt herself leaning towards him.

'I don't even want to say what it looks like,' he said, but his voice was quiet.

They kissed and then stopped, Louisa glancing around, seeing kids come out of a nearby school. She looked back over at the house he had just come from, and shook her head.

'You were quick,' she said, their faces still close. Louisa was frightened of picking up the scent of another woman.

'You must've been asleep for ages,' he said. He kissed her again.

The disgust she felt had become so mixed with arousal that she could no longer tell them apart. 'What was she like?' Louisa asked.

'She's nice.'

Louisa wanted to hit him. 'I see,' she said.

'I'm biased, mind. She's my sister.'

'Right,' Louisa said, relieved, and then appalled with herself.

'She gets mate's rates.'

Louisa sighed. He put his hand on the back of her neck, and she heard the unfamiliar vehicle adjusting to their movements.

'I couldn't get a spare car, on my insurance,' Adam said. 'Can you give me a lift home?'

She nodded.

'Okay,' he said. 'You know the way.'

Louisa had often wondered about the inside of his house, imagining the earthy smell of football boots and an overflowing bin, a big plasma TV and an unpleasant glass table. She was right about the TV, but the place was tastefully done, if a little sparse. He had clearly bought wrecked wooden furniture and worked it up himself. His coffee table was a school desk with the legs cut off, the drawers still intact. There was a nautical feel to the lounge: a barometer, pebbles and shells, and a caged light on the table, which looked like something from an old boat. 'You do know that Derbyshire contains the most landlocked inch of Britain, right?' she said.

'Aye. Exactly. That stuff reminds me of me holidays.'

A few small family pictures stood discreetely on the bookshelf. In one, a young Adam sat with his mother and sister on a Spanish beach, drinking from a glass bottle of 7UP that was as big as his arm. His skin was darker, but the facial expression was unmistakable – the lips pursed as though he had narrowly avoided some catastrophe. Louisa turned to see him wearing that same expression now. 'Will you stay for a cuppa?' he said.

The afternoon faded fast into that sad hinterland, but he did not bother to turn on the lights. They made love against the door jamb, one foot in the living room, one in the hall. Without alcohol the pleasure was more shocking, their bodies colder but no less willing. They ended up lying on the carpet, his stomach glistening like glass in the almost dark. After a few moments, he turned on the boat lamp and she suddenly remembered what the window looked like from the street.

She asked him about his sister. He said it was the usual thing: he visited Sophie to hear news of those family members who no longer spoke to him. 'Bit a joy, bit a torture.' He hadn't been back to the family home in Belton for ten years.

'Because of your job?' Louisa asked.

'No. They don't know about that. Other stuff.'

Sophie knew about his evening work, and she didn't really want him around her children. She never said it, but he could tell. 'As if I'd pimp them out or sommat.'

Louisa pulled a blanket down from the sofa and covered them both. 'How did you get into this job?' she asked him.

'Careers Advisor.'

She cuffed his head. 'Seriously.'

'Just fell into it, really.'

'Oh, come on.'

'I'm serious. I had a thing with this lass. Just a thing, like. Sex, you know?'

Good God, Louisa thought. Just his saying the word was enough to cause that feeling in her stomach.

'Anyway, that finished, but she rings me a few months later and says it's her mate's birthday the next week and they'd had a whip round. Asked me if I could do oat. She laid it on thick, like. Said I was dead good in sack.'

'Well,' Louisa said.

'Said they'd raised two hundred pounds. Couldn't believe it. I was skint. Birthday girl'd had a bad run, apparently.'

'That was the first one?'

'Aye. Grew from there.'

'Did you – *do* you – advertise?'

'No. None of that. It's all word of mouth.'

'Which is the title of your new movie, I suppose,' she said.

'You what? Oh aye. Them kind of jokes are an occupational hazard. Fortunately I'm not too swift on the uptake.'

'*Mmm. Uptake.*'

He laughed.

'Can I ask another question?' she said.

'Aye, go on. As you're in your stride.'

'Do you take drugs?'

He frowned. She had offended him again. 'No. I don't touch any a that shit.'

'I'm sorry. I'm just trying to work out why you—'

'I've got a kid, an't I? From when I were young. Send most of the money to her mam.'

'Jesus Christ.'

'It's nothing I meant to hide. I don't usually tell folk.'

She tried to pick through the layers of that remark for a moment. 'Where are they now?'

'Out west.'

'*Out west?*'

'Aye. Shropshire somewhere.'

Louisa laughed for a second and then stopped. 'Sorry. Do you see her at all? The child?'

'Nope.'

'That must be—'

'Way it goes, in't it. I might not be there, but me money's there.'

'How old is she?'

'Fifteen.'

'My God. You can't be much older than that yourself.'

'Oh, I'm at least twice that age,' he said.

His life began to open up to Louisa. She could imagine his parents' house in Belton – the damp mossy stone, the tidiness of the rooms, the smell of apples in the kitchen, the thin walls.

He took a cushion from the sofa, lifted her head from the carpet, slid the cushion underneath. He turned to face her. 'What's going on with you and your neighbour, then?' he asked. Louisa felt her eyes widen. She sat up.

'Why, what did she say?'

'She never said oat.'

'I thought you didn't talk about other clients. You didn't tell her about this, did you?' She was aware of shouting the last few words, but Adam remained calm.

'No. And she's not my client any more.'

'Really?'

'She stopped it. It was four or five weeks. That's all. I knew it would be.'

Louisa let her head fall gradually back on the cushion. 'What did you think of her?' she said.

He shrugged. 'Looked like she was feeling bad about herself. Oftentimes I see people in that state.'

'She's grieving.'

'What happened?'

'Lots of stuff.'

'You seemed quite eager to get one over on her.'

'I was looking out for her.'

'No you weren't.'

Louisa was quiet. 'She was my friend.' It hurt to say it, and she felt, with panic, that she might cry.

'What did you fall out over?'

She did not have the heart to tell him. She hadn't spoken to Maggie for weeks now, and she couldn't imagine doing so after this, but there had been no confrontation. 'I can't even remember. Do you think it's only going to be four or five weeks with me?'

He shook his head. 'Different. Completely different thing.'

She thought of Maggie and Adam together, as she had seen them that night. The vigour and eagerness of them. She felt the blood move inside her. She felt sick. It was tough to hold on to the tears. 'I want you to tell me what it was like with her,' she said.

'No you don't.'

'That good, eh?'

'Didn't say that.'

'She had this mark on her neck. It was a love-bite, wasn't it? It was you.' Louisa remembered watching Maggie from the doorway of her bathroom. The cold light and the discolouration on her skin.

'You don't want to talk about this. It's not your thing, and I'm not fucking telling you, anyway.'

She nodded and turned away. 'I've managed to piss you off as well, haven't I?'

'No,' he said. 'You don't get away that easy.'

Seventeen

Adam stood just inside the automatic doors at Morrison's and listened to them opening and closing behind him. His trousers were covered with a pelt of wet grass. He was tired, but he didn't care, because Louisa was coming for an early supper. They had spent almost every night together for the past two weeks.

He marched the aisles, picked up the ingredients for steak sauce. At the meat counter he chose a couple of rib-eyes. He turned away to sneeze. 'You allergic to grass?' the assistant from the meat counter said, looking at his work clothes.

'Aye. A bit.'

'Looks like you're in the wrong game,' the assistant said.

'You're probably right,' Adam said.

His mother had worked in a supermarket. He remembered once, when he was eight years old, that she had slipped on some spilt oil at work and broken her arm. Adam had been mute for three days. His mother had raised him with passion and care, but she had always had the power to destroy him with a single sentence. Emotionally annihilate him. Once, in his teens, she caught him talking dirty to a girl on the phone, and lost her rag. 'If you start getting into all *that* at your age, you'll never find out what else you're good at.' They both had a fair handle on the future, powerless as they were to influence it.

Belton, where he grew up, was a town of fine lines. Arkwright's Mill – a World Heritage Site – was just down the road. It was the home of the Industrial Revolution, the catalyst for the modern world, but half of the current population didn't have a job. When Adam was young, most of the unemployed lived on St Mark's Estate, down by the colourworks, where the brook sometimes ran pink. Most of them took smack. But it didn't have to be that way. Adam's father had a job, and Adam himself could have followed his old man into construction.

Now, in the supermarket, he felt the cold of the giant refrigerators. The beeps and pips from the checkout sounded like a life-support machine. The hollow sound of these places always made him remember.

At fifteen, he had failed to heed his parents' warnings about the older girl who worked on the checkout with his mother. When he had thought about the trouble he could find on St Mark's Estate, putting his hand up some lass's NafCo 54 sweatshirt seemed like the soft option, and he'd be damned if he'd spend his life wringing it out over the blonde one from *Roseanne*.

'I'm late,' she had said, meeting him outside the shops.

'No you're not. We said half past.'

It had been an honest mistake, and he'd felt sorry for the girl. He had promised to pay for the child, and he was a man of his word. He recalled sitting in the waiting room during one of the early appointments, staring at the green Nike Air Max he had received for his fifteenth birthday (he knew how hard his parents had saved to get them). The girl's grandparents had come over from Shropshire, and everyone was shaking their heads and casting glances in his direction. He had expected there to be tests in life, but he had not expected the final exam to come so early, or that his failure would be so irredeemable in the eyes of others.

These days, his wages from the Golf Club went towards child maintenance, and he used the money he made from his night job to pay the rest, and cover his own bills. He hadn't accepted an appointment, however, for two weeks. He reached for some broccoli, but decided to go up-market, and chose asparagus instead.

The last time Adam had seen his daughter, she was four months old. Her name was Elizabeth, although he had once heard her mother call her Lizzie on the telephone. He had thought of her a lot more since meeting Louisa. Of course, he had always thought of her, but now he allowed those thoughts to linger.

When he spoke to Louisa, told her stories, he could make her laugh under her breath. He knew that took a special sort of skill. Sometimes, when he was on a roll and she was laughing easily, he opened his mouth with this great wish to say something else, to tell her something he could be proud of. He wanted to talk about his daughter. But he knew nothing about her, and so had nothing else to say. He didn't even know what a Shropshire accent was like.

The picture in his mind was of a tall, sensible girl with her mother's features. Perhaps she would look him up one day. The thought made him more anxious than excited – it only seemed to strike when he was leaving the house of a client. She would be disappointed if they met, but he knew that in all likelihood they would continue to live eighty miles apart, without contact, and clever Lizzie would probably despise the idea of him without any details to confirm her instincts. That, perhaps, was the best he could hope for.

He swung his basket down the frozen foods aisle, trying to guess which ice cream Louisa would like. Plain, she would claim, but he already knew her better than that. A woman in a trouser suit sailed towards him with a deep trolley, holding the hand of a little boy. It was too late for Adam to turn around, and he knew what was coming. The woman raised her eyebrows in recognition, her lips parting with good humour as she prepared to greet him. Adam waited for the circumstances of their meeting to dawn on her. The woman's face froze, her eyes a little wider. She coloured, averted her eyes, and pushed the trolley on. 'Thomas, get here. Now,' she said to the little boy, who had disengaged to look at the desserts.

Adam stood still and waited for the woman and her son to pass. Last Christmas, that same woman, who had claimed to be called Collette (though Adam had seen household bills addressed to Linda) had pleaded to be allowed to suck his cock. He loitered by the bags of ice for the short time he knew it would take her to curtail her shopping trip, before making his own way to the check-out.

The machine at the till rejected his debit card. It had been a bad month, with the car repair and his moonlight sabbatical. He emptied his pockets onto the conveyor belt: a wallet with no money in it, £9.20 in change, his keys, half a blister pack of painkillers and a condom which he quickly shifted to his other hand.

The checkout girl sighed loudly and began to sort through his coins and goods, trying to work out what he could afford. Adam had already done the maths. 'Can I leave these vegetables here, duck?' he said.

'No law against it,' she said.

'I was probably getting ahead of myself, anyway, buying asparagus,' he said. The girl didn't even look up.

As he drove home he thought of Louisa. The previous night he had been to her house. She was always nervous when arranging a meeting, and she'd told him to park in the village and walk up through the pines. Her anxiety soon wore off, and she had reluctantly agreed to play the guitar. He loved the way her face stayed almost still while she played, just the odd raise of the eyebrows, a tightening of the mouth, her scarred fingers sliding smoothly down the neck.

When he left the cottage, she had walked with him. 'I'll just go to the end of the path,' she had said. And then she had continued all the way down to the village with him, looking away with a little smile, daring him to mention it.

When he drove away from their early meetings, the purity of his feelings were contaminated by the pull of wherever he was heading next. So he had begun to cancel his appointments.

In the mornings, the reality of the situation was clear: his choices had been made many years ago; there was no room for the feelings he had now; the whole thing with Louisa was impossible. But throughout the day she would just fill him up. The thought of her enlivened him, gave him an oblivious sense of hope. He'd never asked himself if he could live without his night-job. His feelings of anxiety – the need to please a stranger every day – Louisa was smashing all that to pieces.

The clouds above his road were blue and yellow. He caught himself checking his mirrors as he passed the take-away, to see if she was following. He smiled.

Louisa knocked and waited, holding the gift in her fist. She had treated the mouse skull he had picked up that first night at her house and attached an old falcon bell and a chain to make a key-ring. She thrust it at him as he opened the door.

'A say, look at that! Is that the mouse from—'

'The very same.'

He smiled broadly, revealing the gap in his teeth, and attached the charm to his bunch of keys. 'That's mint, that. Eh up, isn't this what you use to find your hawks?'

'Well, we use transmitters now, but yes. Same principle.'

'So it's another way of you stalking me.'

'That's the idea,' she said.

'Good,' he said.

Louisa laughed and scratched her neck. Reciprocation was a novelty, and sometimes a frightening one. She could smell meat in the kitchen, and the wild boozy stench of mushrooms cooking in sherry. It smelled like a home.

'I'm a bit worried about my hawks, actually,' she said above the noise of the extractor fan as he poured her a Guinness. 'It's difficult to get them out, what with the weather.'

'And the sex,' he said.

Louisa ignored him, trying not to grin. 'It's important that they get exercise. There's a few of them that I'm trying to cut down.'

'Cut down?' Adam said.

'Reduce their weight.'

'Why?'

Louisa rolled her eyes. He was evidently interested by what she did, but he was not as intuitive as Maggie. 'To get them keen and sharp. You feed up a captive hawk and it won't do the business. It's not so easy to get a fat bird to do what you want in *my* game.'

'I'm shocked and appalled.'

'No you're not,' Louisa said.

The food was sticky and good, and she told him that a simple salad was just as tasty as any fancy-dan asparagus when he apologised for the lack of it. They were in bed before seven.

Adam's bedroom was quite bare, with white linen and soft lamps with papery shades in the corners. Louisa would have sneered at such décor a month ago. Now, she held his hands beneath the sheets.

'I'm not the first, am I?' she said.

Adam frowned. 'What do you mean? I'm not a virgin.'

'This must be something that happens. A fling. You have this kind of thing with clients all the time, right?'

'I don't have this kind of thing with anybody,' he said. It was difficult to distrust him.

'Are you going out tomorrow night?' she asked.

'No.'

'Is business usually so slow?'

'I'm taking a little break from that side of things,' he said.

Louisa paused. 'Do you think that's wise?'

She disliked herself the moment she said it, and saw the

glimmer of hurt in Adam's face. He looked at her sincerely. 'Look. As for Detton, I won't go—'

She shushed him with a finger over her lips.

For the moment, this was how she dealt with the feelings his job aroused in her: the odd joke, avoidance, and a little snipe now and again. She was always aware of his mobile phone in the room, set to silent vibrate. To her surprise, she found herself wondering about the women in the village – women she had thought boring before. Tim Nettles' sister, a divorcee, often wore leggings, and her thighs were toned and firm for a woman of her age. When Rosie Wicks served her a pint in the Hart, Louisa tried to imagine the older woman's desires. Her husband was fat, and often drank ale well into the night with the regulars. Did Rosie ever become lonely or frustrated? And of course there was always Maggie, lean and supple, across the way. Don't think of it, Louisa told herself. Just don't. It was easy, at that time, to avoid the issue, because they were together all the time.

At a corporate hawking display, Louisa addressed a group of account executives on the lawn of a country club. 'Take a look at the size of Fred's eyes,' she said, holding the Harris hawk on her fist. 'Proportionally, they are much bigger than those of a human.' She went into her usual rant. As she spoke, she flashed back to her nights with Adam, the roughness of his fingers on her shoulder, the surge of feelings through her skin. 'The hawk has a sensual world which is far superior to ours,' she said. She smiled, because, at last, she realised she was wrong.

EIGHTEEN

Maggie walked the hardcore paths of the park, early one morning in December, wondering about the lone ibex and where he might be. Could an animal like that survive in the semi-urban wilderness of Derbyshire? There had been no news since the false alarm at the building site.

From a distance, she saw Button, one of the otters, rise to the surface of the dark pond, sniffing the air for the scent of the little boy who stood by the barrier. Maggie watched their stand-off through the mist, the boy sucking on the end of a Mars bar while Button ducked in and out of the reeds for a better view. The boy bent down, picked up a stone and hurled it at Button, who was quick enough to dodge, but the boy threw another, which hit the surface just as Button disappeared beneath it.

Maggie raced over to the boy. 'What the hell do you think you're doing?' she said, taking him by the arm, which had the effect of raising him on to one foot. She had not realised how small he was. He did not seem perturbed.

His mother caught up with Maggie. She was dressed in tight jeans and an expensive-looking raincoat. 'Get your hands off him,' she said.

'He threw a stone at one of the animals,' Maggie said.

The woman shook her head, almost wearily. 'If you don't let go of his arm, I'll call the police,' she said.

'What?' Maggie said, relinquishing her grip on the boy. She had pulled his coat out of shape. 'It's me who should be calling the police,' Maggie said.

'Go ahead. Call the police on a six-year-old boy for throwing a stone at a . . . ' The boy's mother gestured to the pond, which contained only the noises of Button's underwater lightning switches.

The woman shook her head and took hold of the boy's hand. She looked back at Maggie as they walked away. 'Stupid,' she said, quietly.

After a moment staring at the water, Maggie made her way back towards the house. From the corner of her eye she saw the high vertical jump of the lynx. By the time she turned her head, the lynx was hidden in the foliage on top of his wooden shelter. Maggie recalled the time just after David died, when she had come into the living room to find the lynx lying on the sofa, his paws bandaged, his face swollen with sleep. Philip had told her the lynx was tame, and drowsy from his medication, but Maggie had hardly been sure, listening to his almost human cries through the house that week.

Maggie had been anxious in those days, intimidated by the size of the grounds, but now the park made her feel enclosed. She had a sudden urge to smash the network of rails and barriers, as the intruders had done; to sweep the whole lot off the top of the hill. The place would be better as open grazing and woodland, the animals managing it themselves. Just red deer, horses.

She had to admit that deer were not endangered in the least. She only wanted deer on the park because she loved them. In her mind she heard the warnings of her neighbour and former friend. *'It's ignorant and disgusting to invest animals with human characteristics.'*

'Oh leave me alone,' Maggie mumbled. Then, much quieter, with a brief look to the west, she said, 'Don't.'

She walked back to the house, and in the hallway, Philip abruptly curtailed a conversation with the vet and nodded at Maggie.

'I know what species we need to get rid of, now, Phil,' she said.

'Oh aye?' said Philip.

'Fucking people,' she said.

Philip smiled. 'Got a call from Post Office, Maggie. They've got a parcel for you,' he said.

'Can't they bring it up?'

'Not enough postage.'

Maggie pressed the heels of her hands into her eyes and watched the bursts of light.

*   *   *

'Do you want to eat out tonight? I know somewhere quiet,' Louisa said, as they made their way through Detton in the Golf.

'Can't,' he said.

They fell silent. Adam was back to his moonlight job, and how could Louisa complain, when she had practically suggested it. They stopped at the lights and Louisa saw Maggie come out of the

Post Office with a small box, her shoulders hunched against the cold as she took the pedestrian crossing. Louisa ducked down in the passenger seat, untied and re-tied her boot laces, trying to whistle casually, not realising that she was whistling the theme from *Jaws*.

'She's gone,' Adam said.

'Who?' Louisa said, rising slowly.

Adam laughed.

'It's not because of you,' Louisa said. 'The sneaking around.'

'Oh aye. Turn you on, does it?' he said.

'No, actually,' Louisa said.

'Me neither. Maybe we need some privacy. Maybe I should take you away.'

'No. There's no need.' She looked at him. 'Would you? Would you do that?'

'Aye.'

'When?'

'How about today? Just somewhere we could relax a bit.'

'Where?'

'Matlock.'

At that time of year, the town had a snow-globe beauty. The steep stretch of the cliffs dwarfed the buildings; motorbike lights and Christmas lights blinked through the grey. Louisa recalled the places she had sometimes eaten with Oggie – her real past, as opposed to the one she had fantasised with David.

They rode a cable car above the town. Louisa remained silent and vertiginous in the swinging booth. As they neared the middle of the line, where the cars stopped for a moment, she saw that

Adam's eyes were closed and his hands gripped a bunch of his jacket. 'You don't like heights?' she said.

'I'm shitting it,' he said.

'Why did you suggest the cable cars, then?'

'Didn't want you to think I was a pussy.'

They remained arm-in-arm for the rest of the journey and were so pleased to arrive on firm ground that the rest of the afternoon took on the quality of a second life. Louisa found a good chip-shop and took great pleasure in the meal: the hotness of the tea going down, the radioactive greenness of the mushy peas, the white linen folds of the haddock. She looked across to see if Adam felt the same. He was shovelling it in. 'This fish is like crack,' he said.

Back in Detton, he stopped the car at the bottom of the hill, out of sight. She could see that he had retreated into himself, for both their sakes. He looked down the road when she kissed his cheek. 'Thank you,' she said, 'for today.'

She climbed the hill, feeling shaken, smashed, and better than she ever had. When she reached the cottage she put her head against the door and sighed.

'Hello.'

Louisa spun rapidly with her key forced between her knuckles. It was Maggie. 'Jesus Christ,' Louisa said and put a hand to her chest.

'Sorry,' Maggie said, wincing. 'I didn't mean to frighten you.'

Louisa could still smell Adam on her skin. A man that Maggie, amongst others, had been fucked by. She waited for Maggie to speak.

'I haven't seen you for such a long time, so when I saw you coming up the hill, I made a run for it.'

'Hi,' Louisa said.

'I bought these Robin Hood DVDs for Christopher, kind of an early Christmas present, and I was just wondering if you might like to come over and watch them with us tomorrow night,' Maggie said. 'He breaks up from college tomorrow.'

'Can't,' Louisa said. She was seeing Adam.

'Okay. Well, how about tonight? I could sure eat some food.'

'I've eaten.'

'Oh yeah? What did you have?'

It may well have been an innocent question springing from a good appetite, but to Louisa it felt like a criminal interrogation. 'Look. I'm just not ... I've got an early start in the morning.'

'Okay. I hear you,' Maggie said. Louisa detected a little terseness in her neighbour's voice, and had to control her instinct, which was to respond in kind.

'I'd love to bend your ear on a few park matters, too. When you've got a minute,' Maggie said, in such a way that it seemed to be a reminder of the plans they had made together. Louisa gave the faintest of nods.

Maggie held up her hand and began to walk away. Louisa turned towards the cottage door with some relief.

'Oh, one more thing,' Maggie said. 'Christopher sends a message. I don't know if you'll be able to decode it. He says, "Mutual Assured Destruction."' It was a passable impression of his voice.

'Right,' Louisa said.

Maggie nodded, waved.

Safely locked in the cottage, Louisa allowed herself to think of Adam again, but only for a moment. She went to the window and watched Maggie trudging back to the big house.

Adam was not, at that moment, on his way to an appointment. He was travelling, instead, to his sister's house, this time with a very clear objective.

He had resumed his evening job four nights ago, but already the differences were clear. Severing the link between his body and his mind was never a problem, and he was physically still able to perform. The after-effects, however, were more difficult to take. He woke with sliding limbs in his mind, and no matter how much he washed he could not rid himself of the smell of the clients.

He had begun to find the personal items in other people's houses unbearably depressing. The feeling made him want to steal things and dump them in the river: postcards from cork-boards, children's toys, digital alarm clocks. Such objects would all be sailing out to sea if he had his way. He could not explain it.

Money was a problem. Lizzie's mother had split from her man, and the pressure fell back on Adam. Why shouldn't Lizzie go to college? Why should she pay for her parents' mistakes? Adam agreed.

Sophie was smoking on the doorstep in a long padded coat that made her look like a chrysalis. When she saw his car, she shooed the children out of the hallway and up the stairs. She poked her head further into the street and looked both ways before letting him in.

Her youngest boy stood at the top of the staircase, naked, and peered through the banister spindles. Adam nodded to him in greeting. The boy disappeared.

'Leon's back from work in a bit,' Sophie said. 'Do you need tea?'

'No ta, Sis.'

Adam sat on the edge of the sofa, which was low and soft. The multi-coloured plastic play pen stood between them. 'How's the lad? With his leg?'

'He's fine. He goes to physio once a week. Fine.'

A year ago, Adam had loaned Sophie two thousand pounds so her eldest could have a private operation on his foot.

'That why you're here?' she said.

'I was just wondering how you were doing in terms of freeing up some cash for the repayments,' he said.

She shook her head and bit her lip, as though his mentioning the loan was an unjustified imposition. 'There isn't any *free cash*, Adam. Things are tight at the moment.'

Adam, without meaning to, looked at the holiday photograph on the mantelpiece. It was a recent picture of the family in Lanzarote, the black rocks and sea in the background.

Sophie laughed. 'Jesus. What? You begrudge us a holiday? Your nephews?'

Adam held up his hands. 'Course not, kid. I wouldn't ask, obviously, but I'm struggling myself.'

She smiled and gave a couple of quick blinks – a trait she had carried from childhood. 'Business slow, is it?'

He nodded. 'Well, it's too wet for golf, isn't it? We're working day on, day off.'

'Golf,' she said, and snorted.

'Listen, my cash is *okay*, isn't it?' he said. He did not speak aggressively, he just wanted to get past the brittleness that money always brought to their conversations. 'I mean, you don't have a problem with letting me help you out once in a while, do you?'

Sophie tilted her head and blinked again.

'I don't want the full amount, Soph. Just anything you can spare. I've got Lizzie's payment coming up at the end of the month.'

'I don't know why you have to keep paying for her,' Sophie said.

'You'd know quick enough if you were on your own with these kids.'

'Oh that's nice. Thanks for that.'

'Come on, Sis, give me a break.'

Sophie looked as if her resistance was about to collapse, but then she smiled, as if possessed of some brilliant new idea. '*Mum's* coming round tomorrow,' she said slowly, with mock brightness.

Adam looked at his feet.

'I think she's got a bit of money stashed. I can have a word if you like. Explain your situation. About how slow *work* is at the moment. *Golf*. Maybe she'll be sympathetic.' Sophie smirked.

'I see,' Adam said.

They sat in silence for a moment, Adam staring at her, trying to be resilient, trying to get her to see that the nature of her victory was nothing to be proud of.

'Is everything okay, otherwise?' she said.

'Surprisingly well,' he said. 'Unusually well.'

Sophie did not probe further. Despite her threats of disclosure, she could not stomach the details of his life. But Adam realised that he wanted to tell her about Louisa. It made him feel better just thinking about telling her.

'We'll be back up to speed with the repayments next month,' she said, all the tension and animosity gone from her voice.

'Right-o.'

He could feel the eyes of the children on him, and turned to see them peering through the banisters. He stuck out his tongue, and they bundled out of sight, giggling. He turned back to Sophie, and stuck out his tongue at her, too.

NINETEEN

The hairy, spongy chairs in Cullis's office smelled to Christopher like cigarettes and bananas. It was the last day before the Christmas break, and Cullis was skimming over the Robin Hood essay. Christopher had finished the first section ('Hooded Man/Psycho Killer'), which left him with two remaining chapters: 'Love on the Brain', on which he was currently working, and 'Death'.

Cullis looked up from the paper. 'Christopher, there are gaps in your logic. You've got to get over these people being real. It's only natural that as time passes, Robin should gain a fictional love interest in the guise of Maid Marian.'

Love interest, thought Christopher; the kind of phrase used only by turncoats and seasoned backstabbers.

'Can you imagine a play, or even a Hollywood film, without a leading lady?' Cullis continued. 'People might question what Robin Hood was *doing* in the woods with his merry men, all dressed in tights.'

'There's, erm, no historical evidence to suggest that he wore –
hold on. Are you, erm, saying that Robin Hood was *strange*, at
all?'

'Look, all I'm saying is that a homeless, dispossessed vagrant,
even a fictional one—'

'Not fictional.'

'—would find a willing wench hard to come by. No dating
websites in those days, Christopher.'

Dating websites? Christopher wondered whether Maggie
Green had been on his computer, and then fed the information to
Cullis. He decided to ignore the comment and concentrate on
frying bigger fish.

'So you're standing there, erm, telling me that Marian de Lacy
didn't really, erm, exist?'

'Actually, *you're* telling *me* that,' Cullis said.

Oh that is absolutely typical, thought Christopher.

'Christopher, you believe in the psycho – the aggressive killer
of the early ballads, don't you?'

'Yes. Erm. What if?'

'Well there's no mention of Marian in Robin Hood literature
until the eighteenth century. You can't have it both ways.'

Christopher tore at his coffee cup. He knew it was true. It was
true, and no Marian meant no progeny, no family values.

'Love in the forest is a pleasant romantic notion, Chris,
but—'

'My name is not, erm . . .'

'—life is just not that simple.'

With his leading ladies and unwilling wenches, Christopher
thought Cullis was a treacherous bastard. He could almost have

provoked Christopher to use such language out loud. *Life's not that simple?*

'Erm, erm, erm. Tell me something I don't know.'

Christopher took the bus home. While the other students wore tinsel and Santa hats, and sniffed poppers, Christopher brooded on the unsatisfactory nature of his own love-life. He had arranged to meet Carol-Ann, from the dating website, tomorrow. At first they had agreed that she would bring along Simon, her baby son, who – for Christopher – was very much part of the package. In a recent text message, however, Carol-Ann had informed Christopher that Simon would stay at home with his grand-mother. This was to give Carol-Ann and Christopher some proper time to get to know each other, Carol-Ann said. *Get to know each other?* Christopher had thought. After the promises they had already made, he viewed this as a significant retreat. Despite his determination that his thoughts on love should remain pure, Christopher could not help but detect the stink of betrayal.

His suspicions had been further aroused by a text two days later, changing the venue from a pub in town to the Little Chef Travelodge off the A52, and moving the time forward to mid-afternoon. Christopher had received the text in one of Cullis's classes. 'Ding-ding. Alarm bells,' he had said aloud, to the confu-sion of several other students. Cullis had ignored the mumblings Christopher made as he typed his reply:

> WHY ALL THE SHIFTING ABOUT? I HOPE YOU
> HAVEN'T GONE COLD FEET ON ME. I WANT OUR
> LIVES TOGETHER TO START POST-HASTE. XX

In the next reply, Carol-Ann blamed her father, saying that he had insisted on neutral territory and daylight hours. Christopher did not see why a modern woman in her late twenties with a baby and a job needed her father's advice. So much for the power of love. He was not, however, about to ruin his one shot at domestic happiness.

On the bus home, he leaned his head against the cool condensation of the window, and tried to think of what his father would have advised. But his father's sayings about women blurred with those about bullies. *Do it to them before they do it to you.* That probably wasn't relevant, Christopher decided.

He had always thought his father had done well to land himself a humdinger like Maggie Green, but then again, he had been blind to her traitorous ways. Christopher searched his memory harder. He saw his father slapping his own face with both hands. He saw him raising his leg and lowering his elbow to fart. He heard him whistle through his teeth with exasperation. He saw him crying. These were things most people had never seen. Most people, thought Christopher, just remembered what a legend David Bryant was, in his Stetson with his animals and his pint of bitter.

In any case, Christopher reasoned, this current problem could not be solved by those who would never again darken anyone's towels. How was he, Christopher, going to get to a hotel on the A52? He certainly wasn't going to ask Maggie Green. Fighting the vibrations of the window, Christopher wrote 'C-A' in the condensation with his finger. Within seconds the letters were sagging with strings of moisture.

When Christopher arrived at the den, he saw two boys playing in the pools of standing water in the field across the brook. They pointed their torches at him, whispered for a moment, then continued splashing. Christopher stooped under the corrugated roof.

Inside the den, he crouched down and retrieved the plastic folder of correspondence with Carol-Ann, which he had printed at home but liked to read in the secrecy of his favourite place. By the white light of his mobile phone, he could just about read through the plastic. *I want to be a provider,* he had written, in one of the later emails. *You and me and Simon could be joined by a whole band of our own progeny.* Christopher smiled, and sang, to the tune of the Queen song: 'Don't stop me now, I'm having lots of children!' His voice echoed, and he heard laughter out in the field. He had forgotten about the two boys, who were now flashing their torches again. Christopher poked his head out of the den. 'Erm, erm. You shouldn't be in this field,' Christopher shouted. 'You need to get the eff out of, erm ... '

'It's not *your* fucking land, is it?' one of the boys said.

'No, but that's because I've been dispossessed,' Christopher said.

'You what?' the other boy said. 'Sing us another song, you big freak.'

Christopher retreated. It was their problem if they drowned, he decided, but he knew they wouldn't, because his father had shown him the storm drain.

Once or twice a year, the field which bordered Bottleneck Brook would briefly flood. It was only natural, of course. Detton was in the elbow of two rivers, sliced through by their various tributaries, and the field was at the bottom of a steep hill. It was like a basin. When Christopher was a boy, he had hated the times when the field flooded. The standing water brought not only what Christopher described as 'mortal danger', it also brought boys such as those outside now, to his most sacred of hideouts.

One day, on hearing his complaints, Christopher's father had walked him into the middle of the field to see the concrete culvert pipe. The pipe emerged like a worm from the mud and lush green life, and was fitted with a metal grate, so that it looked like a mouth. 'This bit is like a plug-hole,' his father said. 'When the field gets flooded, the pipe collects all the water that overflows from the brook, along with all the extra rain, and it takes it down under the railway line, under all the houses, and it flushes it out into the big river.'

'Jeepers,' Christopher said. He liked the idea of the underground tunnels, and he liked the word 'culvert', which sounded foxish and clever. But something played on his mind. 'Dad? What about when, erm, erm, erm? You know when the plug gets blocked in the bath?'

'Yes.'

'What about that?'

'Well, the pipe is prepared for a one hundred year event.'

'What does that mean?'

'It means there will only be enough water to block the drain every one hundred years.'

'*One hundred years?*'

'Yes.'

'That's absolutely, erm, ages,' Christopher said. 'That's millenniums.'

His father had smiled, and rubbed his head. A hundred years did seem like a long time when you were young, Christopher thought now. But he didn't know how long it had been since the last one hundred year event.

It wouldn't happen tonight, anyway. The two boys left the

field, shouting insults as they went, and Christopher could hear the water draining into the pipe to be carried beneath the village.

He went to visit Louisa before going home. It had been a while since his last attempt, and he wondered if the message about the pact of Mutual Assured Destruction had hit home. He could hear the birds as he walked up the path – their sudden and contagious shifts.

When his knock went unanswered, Christopher looked through the window of the cottage and saw something quite unexpected. Louisa, wearing a black slip which rode the contours of her belly and buttocks, stood before the mirror in her living room, painting her eyelashes with crude flicks of the wrist. Christopher felt momentarily captivated, if only by the solid strength of her calves and the brightness of the lamplight caught in the silk at her lower back. She turned around and Christopher ducked down below the sill.

He stayed crouching with his hands on his head for less than a minute, until the door opened. Louisa was now wearing jeans and a jacket, although Christopher could see the sheen of the slip tucked into the waistband. 'What do you want?' she said.

'I just need some help with a particular matter,' Christopher said, standing slowly. He took his hands off his head.

'I don't have time. Why don't you go and ask Maggie?'

'Why, erm, don't *you* go and ask Maggie?'

'What?'

'Well I don't see you over there very much any more.'

'Look, Christopher, I really have got things to do.'

'Oh, right. So Maggie didn't deliver my message then.'

Louisa opened her mouth, then paused. She closed her eyes and took a deep breath. Christopher smiled, pleased with his foothold in the conversation.

'It shouldn't, erm, take a moment,' he said. 'I just wondered if you thought women like a man to have a vehicle, at all.'

'No,' Louisa said. 'It gives him too much independence. Listen, come back tomorrow. There's no need for any assured destruction. Just knock on the door. It's creepy, spying on people.'

'Says you,' Christopher said. 'Anyway, it might be too late by tomorrow. All hope could be lost by then.'

He began to walk away. Then it came to him – it must have been the sight of the diaphanous undergarment. 'Erm. Anyone who says they can see through a woman is missing a lot.'

'What?' Louisa said.

'Oh nothing. Just something my dad used to say.'

Louisa closed the door.

When Christopher arrived at the house, Maggie was running a pet-hair remover over his green jumper in the living room. He could smell the rich saltiness of bean stew from the kitchen. Again.

'Hey sweetie,' she said. 'I've got a surprise for you.'

'Erm, chance would be a fine thing,' he said.

The surprise, it transpired, was indeed a fine thing. Maggie passed him the box set of *Robin of Sherwood*. Christopher had heard of it, read of it, but never seen it. 'I can't believe I didn't think of it before,' Maggie said. 'Robin Hood *and* the eighties! My friend back home used to fancy the absolute nuts off Michael Praed.'

Christopher took some beers from the kitchen, while Maggie set up the DVD. Hail and rain lashed the windows as they sat down. 'It just adds to the pagan atmosphere,' Christopher said.

The DVDs were not in order, but Christopher did not mind. He could not look away from the screen. Sherwood was eerie, and reminded him of how he felt in his own woods, especially Herne, the dark, antlered figure who appeared like a vision to Robin and guided him.

'*Nothing is forgotten*,' Herne said, rather a lot.

'I like, erm, deer,' Christopher said. 'I can tolerate them because they remind me of days of yore.'

'Me too,' Maggie said, encouraged. 'We should get some for the park.'

The fourth episode they watched was called 'Cromm Cruac', taking its name from a childless but otherwise idyllic village where the outlaws briefly sheltered. Will Scarlet found his wife, Elena, in Cromm Cruac, which was something of a shock, for Elena had been dead for several years. When John and Robin realised that the village was full of ghosts and devil worshippers, they decided to leave, but Will Scarlet did not want to. He wanted to stay with his wife. So he changed his name back to Scathlock and put a bit more gel in his hair.

Christopher enjoyed the episode immensely, although it took a while to get used to Jason Connery, who seemed to have replaced Michael Praed in the title role. Maggie laughed at Connery's LEGO haircut, and at the demon which controlled the village – a rubberised sock puppet. But Christopher noticed that she did not laugh when Will Scarlet found his dead wife. She didn't laugh when he danced with Elena, swinging her around at the village disco while Clannad played his theme, 'Scarlet inside'.

'She doesn't say much,' Christopher said of Elena, drawing a weak smile from Maggie.

In the end, Little John told Scarlet that his wife was dead, that he was living with a demon, a creature. This riled Scarlet, who came out of the hut to fight. The hut, along with the rest of the village, burned to the ground (Marian, pulling her weight like all good living wives, had destroyed the sock puppet), and John held Scarlet while they watched the Elena incarnation screaming in the flames, her hair scorched off.

'That last part was really, erm, quite unpleasant,' Christopher said with a smile.

Maggie sighed.

'Shall we, erm, watch another episode?'

'You can watch another if you like, but I don't really feel like it tonight.'

'Oh, right,' Christopher said as Maggie walked over to the window and looked out on the blackness. After a moment, she left the room.

While Christopher watched another episode, Maggie went down to the office and turned on the computer. She stared at the shadowy forms on the deer webcam for a while. Then she picked up the phone and called the farm in Norfolk.

'Sorry to ring so late,' she said. 'I'm calling from Drum Hill Conservation Centre, in Derbyshire. I'd like to make an enquiry about red deer.'

'Drum Hill? Never heard of you,' the man said. 'We do trophies and that. Antlers. We can get you a nice pair of twelve-pointers for the hallway. Nice present for the husband.'

'I'm enquiring about breeding stock,' she said.

He went quiet. When he started talking again, he asked her

some general questions about hybridisation, body weight, and the price of venison. He was testing her, and she passed. Eventually, he quoted her a figure. Each nought erased another species from the park, but she was much more determined to get them now that Christopher had shown an interest. She wanted to visit the farm, make some preliminary observations, see her potential stock in action. They arranged a date in February.

Maggie recalled seeing a man walking through the shot of the webcam one day, and wondered if she might be speaking to him. 'What do you look like?' she asked.

'Oh, hang on,' he said slowly. 'Is this a wind-up? One of those sexy calls? Did the boys put you up to this?'

'No,' she said, with convincing finality, and hung up.

She could hear Christopher laughing at the TV upstairs. She thought about the village in the programme, the outlaw and his dead wife. It was silly, really, she told herself. You can never tell what's going to get you.

But it had been good to see Christopher so engaged. Maggie went online and searched the local cinema listings.

TWENTY

Louisa woke to a familiar banging on the door. Easing herself out of the bed so as not to disturb Adam, she went to the window and looked down at the swirls of Christopher's uncombed hair. She thought about waiting for him to leave, but she knew of his pathological patience. She had told him to come back today, after all.

She put on a large T-shirt and went downstairs, her mouth dry with silence. Christopher's colours were blurred behind the frosted glass panels in the door. She opened it.

'Oh hi, Louisa,' he said, stiffly raising his hand.

'Shh,' Louisa said. 'You'll wake the birds.'

'Oh right. Erm. My sworn enemy Maggie Green told me I should come around here any time I want.'

'Do you always do what your sworn enemies tell you?'

'Erm. What?'

'Nothing. Come in and sit down.'

He followed her into the living room without commenting on her partially dressed state. He sat on the arm of the sofa, and then stood again. 'My nerves are sky-high. Erm. Through the roof.' He gestured upwards.

'I'm going to make some coffee,' she said.

'Oh right.'

'Do you want one?'

'No. I've already had a drink this morning. Erm, guess what it was.'

'Whisky.'

'Nope. It was champagne. I had a champagne and cheesecake breakfast. I like cheesecake. I was pampering myself because today I'm going to meet the woman of my dreams.'

'Positive thinking. I like it,' Louisa said. She went into the kitchen, leaving the door open.

'I'm going to meet Carol-Ann,' Christopher said.

'The woman from the internet?'

'She's from Nottingham. Erm, I think she's from the part ... '

Louisa was spooning out coffee, and so she didn't understand why he had stopped speaking. It did not take her long to guess.

'Louisa, what's that noise?' he said. 'I think someone's, erm, coming.'

Adam's footsteps fell heavy on the stairs. Louisa came back into the living room to see his ill-fitting socks, slightly swollen with the ghosts of his toes, descending into view. She and Christopher watched. 'Oh,' Louisa said. '*That* noise.'

'Eh up,' said Adam.

Christopher's eyes became so wide that Louisa feared his lenses might pop out. He looked at her, and pointed to Adam. 'Who's that?' he said.

Louisa relaxed slightly. She had worried that Christopher

would recognise Adam from his visits to Maggie. Clearly, he did not. Maggie must have been more discreet than Louisa had given her credit for. 'This is my friend Adam,' she said. 'Adam, this is my friend Christopher.'

'Y'rate, youth,' said Adam.

'Friend who stops over?' Christopher said, smirking.

'Looks that way,' Louisa said. 'Coffee, Adam?'

'Aye. Ta, duck.'

Louisa went back to the kitchen, knowing she should have stayed, but not quite capable of enduring it. She heard Adam sit down and take a few deep breaths, which whistled through his pursed lips. This meant he had a hangover. She knew such details, now. She turned occasionally to see Christopher staring at Adam, biting the skin of his fingertips.

'You don't know score from last night, do you, pal?' Adam said.

'Erm. What?' Christopher said.

'Derby. Football.'

'No I do not. Erm. Football is a mug's game. I was once bullied by someone called Peter Greggs. He thought he was going to be a megastar footballer. He used to say, "One day you'll be watching me on TV, you, erm, spaz." Erm. I don't like being called a spaz.'

'I'll bet. What happened to him, then?' Adam asked.

'He suffered a career-threatening injury, and now he plays for the Bridge Inn.' Christopher looked away, as though recalling some old mystery. 'I'm glad his career's gone down the, erm, pan,' he said, as Louisa came back in with the coffee.

'He sounds a right knob-end,' Adam said.

'He was that, yes.'

Louisa scowled at Adam. He smiled back.

'You've got an accent,' said Christopher.

'Aye. 'Appen,' said Adam.

'It sounds a bit rough.'

'That'd be right.'

'Are you and Louisa, erm, getting down to it?'

'Christopher, Jesus Christ!' Louisa said.

'It's alright,' Adam said.

'Who says it's alright?' Louisa said. 'You?'

'Aye. Me and Christopher are having a good, straight-talking chat.'

Christopher laughed. 'Yeah, Louisa. Erm, we're just having a man-to-man.'

Christopher's amusement caused him to lose his trail of thought, and he did not follow up on his original question. Louisa changed the subject before he had chance to remember. 'So what was it you wanted to talk about, Christopher?' she said.

'Well. It's a erm, erm, massive day for me, as you know. Absolutely crucial day. I'm meeting Carol-Ann at the Travelodge on the A52.'

'You're meeting her at the *Travelodge*?' said Louisa.

'That's the one by the flyover, in't it?' said Adam.

Louisa glared at him. Christopher continued. 'I think it's a good idea, because that way we can book straight into a room if all goes well. Erm. Sparks could, erm, fly. Although her father is going to wait for her in the car park.'

'Shit,' said Louisa, quietly.

'That's no way for a lady to speak,' Christopher said.

Louisa rubbed her eyes.

'Anyway,' said Christopher. 'The tragedy of this whole situation is that the Travelodge is thirteen miles away, and I have no way of getting there.'

'I see,' Louisa said.

'Erm, erm. Hint, hint,' Christopher said.

'Well. To be honest, I'm pretty busy,' Louisa said.

'Oh right,' Christopher said. He looked thoughtful for a moment. 'Maybe I'll just, erm, tell the Turncoat Maggie Green that you two lovebirds have got too much, erm, erm, loving to do. She is the last resort.'

Louisa pushed back her hair. 'What time do you want to go?'

'Three p.m. Daylight hours. Erm, erm, all the better to see you with.'

'Okay. I'll take you. If that's what you want.'

'Thanks Louisa. I knew you'd pull through, because we're such a great team.'

'Yeah, yeah. No problem.'

Christopher stood, mission accomplished, and wiped the seat of his chinos. 'See you at one-thirty sharp, then,' he said. He turned to Adam and waved. Adam winked.

Christopher put a hand to his mouth, as if to whisper, but said loudly to Adam, 'I'm going to get my rocks off.'

'Good lad,' Adam said.

As Christopher opened the door, Louisa took his arm. 'Christopher?'

'Yep?'

'If you have to go ... take a cold shower first, and lay off the whole Red Riding Hood thing.'

'Oh right.'

'It's not what the ladies are after.'

'Oh right. Robin Hood, not erm, Riding Hood.'

'That's it.'

'Erm. What's *your* advice?' he said, pointing to Adam.

'Don't swear,' Adam said.

'I hate swearing.'

'You'll be rate then, won't you?'

When Christopher left, they sat in silence for a while, Adam grinning. 'That's my neighbour,' Louisa said.

'Right,' said Adam.

'He's going to get his rocks off,' Louisa said.

'Aye. I know. He said.'

'Do you want to come along?' Louisa said.

'You bet.'

*   *   *

'Have you ever had a beard at all, Adam?' Christopher said. They all sat up front in the van, Adam in the middle seat. Louisa drove, in the hope that it might take her mind off the tension she was feeling.

'No. I can't really have a beard because of my job.'

Louisa looked at him for longer than was safe on a dual car-riageway.

'You mean you have to be smart for the office?' Christopher said.

'Aye, sommat like that,' Adam said.

'I started to grow a moustache once but I was afraid I looked

219

like the one out of Freddie Mercury,' Christopher said. 'Erm. Do you think Freddie Mercury was strange, at all?'

'I think he was barmy, youth,' Adam said. 'But I reckon it went beyond facial hair.'

'Oh right,' Christopher said.

A film of rain sheathed the windscreen between each beat of the wipers. The ruddy bricks and grey roofs of Spondon stood below the flyover, the colours of a pebble beach. When the windows began to steam up, Louisa turned on the heaters. She soon felt Adam start to sweat beside her. He smiled, apparently in no discomfort.

'I just want the simple life, Louisa,' Christopher said.

'Yeah, I know,' Louisa said.

'Do you think she'll be my Marian?'

'Let's wait and see.'

'I wonder what she'll be wearing. Erm. I bet she's hot just like an oven.'

'Careful, kid. I'm feeling fragile,' Louisa said.

Adam laughed. He put his hand on the back of Louisa's head-rest and stretched. Louisa felt the presence of his arm, could smell his wrist.

'Have you not seen a picture of her?' he said to Christopher.

'Not full length. I haven't seen a, erm, full frontal,' Christopher said.

'Could be in for a surprise, then,' Adam said.

'Yes,' Christopher said. He looked out of the window. 'Erm. Of course, it was all jerkins and bodkins in those days,' he said.

Louisa weaved quickly through the Saturday afternoon traffic. She tried not to think of Christopher explaining this road trip to Maggie.

'People always say, "be yourself", but I don't think that's, erm, the right thing to do in all situations,' said Christopher.

'Well, I don't think you should put on airs and graces,' said Louisa.

Christopher nodded his approval at the phrase. 'No way. Erm. But I don't want her to think I'm the biggest loon this side of Christendom.'

'Just ... you know,' said Louisa. She curtailed her advice to overtake a horsebox, got a flash of the chestnut rear of the beast within. Adam assumed her role in the conversation. 'There's nothing wrong with *acting* a certain way. We all do that a bit. As long as you don't tell lies,' he said.

'Oh right. It's just that sometimes I think it might be a good idea, rather than being myself, to be someone else a bit better,' said Christopher.

'Yeah, but who?' Louisa said, distracted.

Christopher seemed to ponder this for a while. Then he smiled. 'Louisa, do you think Carol-Ann will run across the marble floor, and jump into my arms, at all?'

'Don't reckon it'll be marble,' Louisa said, 'in the Travelodge.'

She felt Adam look at her. She could not tell if it was curiosity, desire, or disapproval.

'Oh, right,' Christopher said.

Spiky roadkill blemished Brian Clough Way. They drove out from under the weather, the clouds like blue ink from a black ink pen, petroleum rainbows climbing up the spray. 'Erm. Next exit to Brooklyn,' said Christopher.

They came off the carriageway and pulled into the car park, which was almost empty. Adam took out a cigarette.

'Not in the van,' Louisa said.

'No?'

'Bad for the hawks.'

They all got out, leaned against the doors.

'Can I crash one of those?' Christopher asked. Adam took a Marlboro Red from the pack, lit it with his own cigarette, and gave it to Christopher, who held it like a flute. He sucked a little bit, and exhaled immediately. 'Mmm. These are good,' he said.

Adam laughed.

'Do you think women like men to smoke, at all?'

'I don't do it when I'm with a lass,' said Adam, winking at Louisa.

'Oh right,' said Christopher.

'What do you think, Lou?' said Adam.

Louisa loved the taste of cigarettes on a man's mouth. Adam had smoked on that first night, despite his pronouncement. 'I think it's not good,' Louisa said.

'I might take it up, anyway,' Christopher said.

'You mean you don't smoke?' Louisa said.

'I do now,' Christopher said. Louisa witnessed his first nicotine rush and shook her head. He steadied himself against the van. 'Do you think it's cool, at all?'

'Nothing cool about emphysema,' Adam said.

'Oh right,' Christopher said.

Louisa could see the head of a man in an old Volvo estate parked near the hotel entrance. She took him to be Carol-Ann's father, as did Christopher. 'He doesn't need to be here, erm, protecting her,' Christopher said. 'I care about Carol-Ann just as much as he does. I feel like saying something to him.'

'I don't think that's a good idea,' Louisa said.

'I feel like asking him if he thinks I'm some kind of psycho. Some kind of Peter Sutcliffe wannabe.'

'Listen,' Louisa said. 'It might not even be him. And for God's sake don't mention Peter fucking Sutcliffe.'

Adam spluttered with laughter, which set Christopher off, and soon Louisa surrendered to it, too. The laughter lasted for nearly a minute. Adam's face turned red, and he looked a little helpless, as though he wanted to stop.

'It's just not first date material,' Louisa said through her tears.

'I was only going to say it to her dad,' Christopher said.

Adam whooped. 'Oh, that's alright, then,' he said, wiping his eyes.

Louisa looked away and tried to stop smirking. A growl rolled in the back of Christopher's throat for a few seconds after he had stopped.

'Hey, it's time to get in there,' Louisa said.

'Aye. You don't want to keep a lady waiting,' Adam said.

'That's right. I approve of chivalry,' Christopher said.

'Go on then.'

He did not move. 'Erm. Thanks, guys,' he said.

'That's okay,' Louisa said.

'Erm. Guys?' he said.

'Yes, Christopher,' Louisa said.

'I hope that you two get a mortgage together.'

Louisa's shoulders dropped. She did not reply.

'Thanks, mate,' Adam said. 'Although, to be honest, I think I might have some trouble filling in the forms.'

'Oh right. I hate bureaucracy.'

They fell silent for a moment, and then Christopher revved an imaginary engine. 'Erm. Erm. Mansell versus Piquet, Silverstone, 1987,' he said, and left the van.

'Goo on lad,' Adam said.

Louisa watched him cross the car park. He headed for the Volvo, but veered away at the last moment and disappeared through the glass doors. Adam and Louisa got back in the van.

'Fucking Ada,' said Adam. And then, 'Are you alright, duck?'

'Yes,' she said.

'What's on your mind?'

'Nothing. I was just thinking of this time in a car park.'

She thought of the herd of ibex, stomping, and scanning the horizon, their hooves like high heels on the concrete. The beat of the kid's heart against her chest. Adam put his hand on her leg.

It had taken all of her effort to deal with how she felt about Adam, to acknowledge her desires, and to satisfy them. She had avoided considerations of the future. And now, with Christopher's blessing, the full weight of reality came down on her. The *future*. There would be no mortgages, no family, no real relationship. How could there be? The futility of it was crushing.

'Are you – *working*, tonight?' she said.

He nodded, and there was only the sound of the heater. What she found hardest was Adam's reluctance to rise to the bait, and his consistent kindness to her. If he was going to descend into the surrounding villages every evening to fuck other women, then he could at least act like the sort of person who did such things.

The knock on the window made her shout. It was Christopher. He had been gone for less than five minutes. She buzzed down the window. 'You scared the shit out of me, Christopher,' she said. The man in the Volvo had turned around.

'What's wrong, youth?' Adam said. 'You forget sommat?'

'Erm, erm, let me in,' he said.

'It's open,' Louisa said.

Christopher got back in the van. 'Erm. Let's get the eff out of Dodge,' he said.

'Hey,' Louisa said. 'Just relax. It'll be fine. You're just nervous, that's all. Relax. Get back in there and have a chat with her.'

'I did,' Christopher said.

'What happened?' Louisa said.

'Erm. Not my type.'

'*Not your type?*' Louisa said.

'She's a few too many rungs down the evolutionary ladder for my liking,' Christopher said.

Louisa glanced at Adam, who pretended to clear his throat with his hand over his mouth. Christopher began to chew the skin on his fingers. Louisa looked towards the Travelodge. The man in the Volvo drove closer to the entrance. A woman came out and got in the passenger seat. Louisa could not see her face.

'Right,' Louisa said, starting the engine. 'No point hanging about, then.'

'Nope,' Christopher said. 'Let's leave Dodge behind.'

'Are you okay?'

'I'm fine, thank you. Erm. It's a crying shame things didn't work out between me and Carol-Ann, but it's for the best.'

Louisa hung back and waited for the Volvo to get onto the carriageway. Then she put the van in gear.

'You're probably right,' Adam said. 'Good lad.'

They waited to join the traffic. 'I could see her, erm, bending over a hot stove,' Christopher said, and Louisa knew what was coming because she had heard it from David, had watched the film with him. 'But I couldn't see the, erm, stove.'

* * *

That night, Adam's vibrating phone crawled across the table, the face lit green. Nothing could change a mood like it. They looked at each other like gunslingers, Louisa's smile still fading from an earlier joke. He picked up the phone and read the text.

'That your mother, was it?' Louisa said.

'No. My mother an't spoke to me for years. You know that.'

'Sister?'

He shook his head.

'You could at least do me the service of lying,' she said.

In the early days she had been pragmatic. She told him she knew the deal; it didn't matter. She could not imagine ever having felt like that now. She went upstairs and got dressed, listening to the mumbled voice. The laughter. He came in a few moments later. 'Look, I won't go if you don't want me to,' he said.

'Don't be stupid.'

'It's just one visit – I can afford to miss it.'

'I can't believe you can stand there and tell me it's about the money. It's nothing to do with money – it's in your nature. You enjoy it.'

'That might have been true, in the past. But it's not now.'

He paused. 'Look. What if I stopped? Altogether. We could both get proper jobs, pool our earnings.'

'*Proper jobs?* What do you think I do all day?'

'How much do you make a year? From the birds?'

Louisa fidgeted. She added a thousand pounds to the true total. 'Six,' she said.

'You live on *six grand a year*?' he said.

'My hawks do. I live on my savings. Anyway, that's not the point. I'm not going to work in a stupid office where some idiot schoolkid tells me—'

'I'll quit,' Adam said. 'We'll get by. I'll find the money for the lass. We'll get by. You could teach. They must want teachers for this kind of shit at the agricultural college. I'll go back on the building sites. We could get a place. A normal life. A good one. I've been thinking about it almost since I met you. You've made me think it's possible. I'll quit, for you.'

There followed a silence in which Louisa slowly shook her head. 'Don't you go making it about *me*, Adam. Don't put me in that position.'

He laughed once and then stopped, waited for her to continue. When she did not, he left.

She watched from the window as he got in his car and slammed the door. It wasn't that she didn't want a life with him, she just didn't think it was possible.

As it happened, Adam did not get as far as the roundabout that afternoon; he was back in four minutes. Louisa thought it was Christopher calling again, and was about ready to burst when she came to the door.

'There's a lot of traffic,' Adam said, without meeting her eye. 'So I cancelled.'

They went into the living room. The rush of relief enabled Louisa to postpone any more big talk for the time being. She reached for the gin with one hand, his belt with the other, and ignored the look of defeat on his face.

TWENTY-ONE

The lights rippled up and down the triangular peak of the Odeon's plastic awning. From the roof, the CCTV cameras filmed the retail park: the expanse of orange brick, and the childish blocks of DFS and B&Q. Maggie parked the Land Rover and walked towards the cinema. Through the glass front of the building she could see the toad-green mass of Christopher huddled over the bright wall of pick-and-mix. She went to buy the tickets.

They had loved coming to the cinema together, before. David would drop them off and then go to the pub. They used to play air-hockey before going in, Christopher's size and forthright politeness scaring off the youths who haunted the arcade area.

Maggie had noted, amongst the teen flicks and blockbusters advertised in the newspaper, that the film club were having an eighties season and showing *ET*. She figured it was worth a try. She walked over in time to see Christopher swipe a fistful of sweets. The moustaches of dirt beneath his fingernails were stark against the pink shrews.

'I hope you're not eating as you go,' Maggie said. 'Because that's a felony. Here's your ticket.'

Christopher looked at it. 'Of all the features in Christendom,' he said.

'What's wrong?'

'*E.T.: The Extra-Terrestrial*, that's what's wrong.'

'I thought you liked it.'

'One: I don't like animals.'

'He's not an *animal*. '

'And B: this is a student ticket.'

'You're a student,' Maggie said.

'I don't want to be associated with, erm, institutions and repressive, erm, regimes.'

'Principles cost money, kiddo. *You* didn't have to pay for the tickets.'

'Neither did you.'

Maggie was sick of that argument. She closed her eyes slowly, and when she opened them she was just quick enough to spot the expression of care disappearing from Christopher's face. 'Why are we doing this, anyway?' he said.

'Well, I thought it would be nice. I thought it would remind us of the Good Old Days,' she said, trying a catchphrase.

'Why, erm, would we want to do that?'

Maggie took a big breath and tried to keep smiling. 'Well, you know. We used to have a good time. Me and you, off to the movies.'

'*Movies* is okay, but I hate it when people say, erm, *cinemas*. Erm. "I'm going to the cinemas." Stupid. I'm only going to *one* cinema.'

'Yeah,' Maggie said.

'So we're travelling through time then, are we? A blast from the past?' His arm shot out to simulate a rocket.

'I guess so.'

'Like, erm, Marty McFly.'

'Yeah.'

'I like *Back to the Future*,' Christopher said.

'It'll probably be on in a few weeks. They're doing a whole season.'

Christopher puffed out his cheeks and exhaled in a long, sweet whistle.

'Oi. Give us a shrew,' Maggie said.

Maggie hadn't been to the cinema since David had died. They took seats by the aisle. She realised that their clothes smelled of the outdoors: metallic in her case, fungal and damp in Christopher's. The couple in front of them seemed to notice this, too, and ceased their embrace in order to sniff the air and half turn against the light of the screen. Maggie figured the smell of the hotdog and nachos which she had purchased for her stepson would crowd out their alien odours.

She watched Christopher bite into a nacho loaded with various mush. He closed his eyes while he chewed, and sighed with pleasure, as if he'd just taken some life-saving antidote. Crisp shards fell into his hand, which he had readied below his chin for that purpose. He pushed the crumbs in, too. Against all odds, it was fun to watch. When had Maggie last enjoyed food to such an extent? She laughed, and Christopher laughed, too, unable to contain his pleasure.

When the film started they watched quietly until the scene in which the young Drew Barrymore sees E.T. in her brother's room. 'Holy shit,' shouted Christopher, when Barrymore screamed. The couple in front looked at each other, united in their sense of injustice. Maggie opened her mouth to whisper a warning to Christopher, but she thought of David, how he would laugh guiltlessly at Christopher's public histrionics. She shifted her feet, unsticking her boot heels from the floor.

'She turned into an absolute, erm, humdinger, that Drew Barrymore,' said Christopher, not whispering. 'I'd like to make an honest woman of her.'

'Good luck with that,' Maggie said.

'She just needs to, erm, settle down a bit.'

The man in front of them received a shove from his girlfriend and turned around. 'Look. Could you keep it down please?' he said into the space between Maggie and Christopher.

'We're sorry,' Maggie said.

'I can speak for myself, you know,' Christopher said to her.

'I know, kiddo,' Maggie said. She turned back to the man. 'I didn't realise I was talking so loud. Sorry.'

The woman turned around now. 'It's not so much the talking as the eating. Can't you get him to eat with his mouth closed?'

'Oh come on,' Maggie protested. 'Have you seen the size of those hot-dogs?'

The woman tutted and turned back to the film. Maggie had tried to joke it off, but she was hurt by the couple's reaction. She looked at Christopher and saw that he was almost crying. 'Hey,' she whispered. She put her hand on his arm but he stood and addressed the couple. 'Oh, I'm *really sorry* for eating. At least I'm not, erm, virtually having coitus in a public place. I mean, there's a time and a place for that sort of, erm, copulation, and it's the bedroom. Or maybe the stairs if you can't, erm, wait. Erm, eff off.'

He tramped up the sloping aisle, his body tilted into the gradient.

'Cheerio,' the man said, shifting back into his seat.

Maggie paused for a moment, and then leaned towards the woman in front. 'What you said was very cruel,' she said. The woman did not turn round.

She followed Christopher out into the car park, where he was already trying the door of the Land Rover. Maggie unlocked it and went round to sit in the driver's seat. She rubbed her face with her hands.

'It's not you that should be, erm, upset,' said Christopher.

'You mustn't listen to people like that, Christopher. They're ignorant.'

'It's all very well saying that now, isn't it?'

'What do you mean?'

'You're a substandard wingman. Louisa Smedley would have been all over them like a bad, erm, rash. Smack.'

'Yeah, well, Louisa Smedley didn't take you to the cinema. She's not *here*, in case you hadn't noticed.'

Maggie felt like saying more on the subject, but she did not want to poison the friendship between Louisa and Christopher.

'I need a drink,' he said.

'So do I,' she said.

'Alone,' he said.

Maggie started on cocktails as soon as she got home. She drank Pisco sours, like her mother used to make. She mixed the drinks in an empty biscuit tin, which was the only suitable receptacle she could find. After four of these, she felt acidic and needy. She called Louisa and got a dead tone. These days, she felt disinclined to knock on the door. It seemed like a wasted walk. A mood of resentment struck her, and then gave way again to the simple wish to be with her friend.

What she remembered was autumn, when they had seemed to find a possible way of living, pulled by the magnetism of the animal rhythms, and the arc of light over the hill. She recalled that day out by the reservoir, Diamond coming down from on high, and taking the duck into the pond, riding him, drowning him. Louisa had waded in after them, to take Diamond off the kill. She threw the limp mallard to Maggie, who stood on the bank, watching in awe as Louisa, breathing sharply against the cold of the pond, held her left hand up high above her head with Diamond perched on top, feeding. As Louisa waded back to the bank, Maggie held out a thick branch. Louisa took the branch and dragged her into the water, Maggie bouncing like a colt. She might have laughed, had she been able to breathe.

In the van, on the way home, the radiator had bitten through the coldness of their clothes and created a heat haze. Maggie nipped at the whisky flask Louisa kept in the glove compartment. She had been tired in a way she had never been before. She felt healthy, and knew that she could get out there tomorrow and do the same again. She knew that she would have company, help, a purpose.

Perhaps her mistake had been to imagine that could go on indefinitely. People seemed only to exist in her memory these days. That needn't be true of everyone, she thought. With an aching need, she reached for the phone.

* * *

He got there just before it started to rain, his head pounding. 'I can't remember from last time,' he said, when she met him at the side door. 'Do I take my shoes off?'

'Well. Eventually,' she said, and walked on into the little room. She had a swaying, high-shouldered walk. She was drunk. He followed her.

'Actually,' she said, turning to look at his shoes. 'They *are* very muddy. Did you have an outdoor appointment?'

'I took a cab to the main road, and strolled up through the pines. For the sake of discretion, you know?'

'That's thoughtful of you, but there's no need. I can honestly tell you that nobody around here takes a blind bit of notice of what I do.'

Adam opened his mouth to sympathise, but stopped himself. Maggie shut the door behind him. The room felt cold, as though there was damp in the walls.

'I thought it would be a problem,' Maggie said. 'You know what they say about small villages and nosey neighbours. But I've been having difficulties of a quite opposite ... ' She trailed off.

She poured a lemony liquid into a glass. 'Cocktail?' she said.

Adam smiled. 'Yeah. If that's all you've got.'

She brought him the glass, sipping from it as she walked. She turned on the little heater and the desk lamp by the empty fire-place. The shadows flared.

'I wouldn't mind, to be honest, if the neighbours were a bit nosier. Came and visited, even.' She looked out of the window. Adam felt the veins in his head constricting with the first bitter sip. Maggie whispered theatrically. 'The people around here are very hard. Unpredictable. I get myself into trouble, no matter what I say. But now I have company. So thank you for that.'

She turned so that her back was against his chest, and she took his wrists and wrapped his arms around her. Adam noticed that they were about the same height. She shuffled back into him, put her hands behind his thighs and pressed him against her. They were both breathing heavily: he from the walk and she from the drinking.

'I was surprised when you called,' he said. 'I thought maybe . . . '

'Maybe what?' she said.

'I don't know,' he said. He heard a noise from outside and flinched.

'It's an old house,' she said. 'The guttering can't cope.'

Adam drew his arm away and Maggie stumbled slightly, adjusting her footing.

'Had a few jars, have we?' he said.

'What's it to you, Constable?' she said, smirking.

'Nothing,' he said. 'I just . . . I don't want to make you do some-thing you'll regret in the morning.'

She turned to look at him, regaining some sobriety. 'I know what I'm doing,' she said. 'And, in case you've forgotten how this works, it's *me* that's forcing *you*.'

'Yeah, I suppose. Listen, is there a toilet down here?' Adam said.

'End of the corridor. I'll put some music on,' she said.

In the bathroom he fumbled in his pocket for the painkillers, and his keys came with them. He detached the mouse-head charm from the key-ring and stared at it in his hand. It rolled in his palm and the bell clinked. Louisa had once told him that birds swallow stones, which they use to grind up the food in their stomachs, because they have no teeth. He himself had often dreamed, as a child, that he was choking on stones, and would wake suddenly, coughing and spitting. Now he could hardly swallow the paracetamol. The taps were tight, the water shockingly cold.

He recalled his last argument with Louisa. *Don't make it about me,* she had said. As if it could be about anyone else. It was a kick in the guts, after he had laid himself bare like that. Maybe she was right. Maybe his proposal of a life together was hopeless and unrealistic.

He looked at himself in the mirror. Loud music came from the other room. Maggie sang a line, and then stopped. She was his age and she liked the music he liked: The Pixies, Pulp, Pavement.

The bathroom window was frosted, the swirls like scars. Behind it was a blue-blackness, and – somewhere – Louisa's cottage. He tried to make a mental list of the saleable items in his house, totted up the value. Maths was never his strong suit, but he knew the answer was a pittance.

Maggie was opening her buttons when he came back in. She was sitting in the armchair now, holding his gaze. He knew his expression was as serious as hers, and that she had mistaken it for desire.

'I have to go,' he said.

She did not respond immediately, but pulled her shirt closed. He could still see the rich creamy colour of her bra strap.

'What did I do?' she said.

'It's not you, love. I swear. My mind's not right.'

'Well no,' she said, as if that was a given. 'Mine neither.'

Maggie looked around for a moment and then seemed to accept the rejection.

'Okay,' she said. 'You want to stay for a drink?'

'I can't.'

'Right,' she said.

He turned to go and then stopped. 'I think you're wrong, you know, about nobody around here caring about you,' he said.

'What do you mean?' she said.

'I don't know,' he said, trying to withdraw. 'Just strikes me that people around here are alright.'

Maggie shook her head with bewilderment. 'I don't know what's going on any more.'

'I'll just ... I'll go,' he said.

She stood, but he raised his hands. 'I'll let myself out.' He turned back to her at the door, but there was nothing more to be said.

TWENTY-TWO

Louisa had watched Cynthia Driscoll, David's first wife, flinch back from a barking dog on the day she arrived at Drum Hill, and she had known that she had the power to make her leave. But Cynthia was not frightened of people. She described herself as an emotionally sensitive woman. She was in touch with her feelings, she said. What that really meant, as far as Louisa could see, was that her emotions were more important than anyone else's, and you had better keep yours to yourself if they were likely to upset, contradict, or irritate her. Many of her acquaintances compromised their feelings to avoid judgment, or the hassle and embarrassment of a scene. As a consequence, she considered most people she met to be repressed, which further fuelled her opinion of her own exceptional emotional range.

Louisa afforded Cynthia grudging respect for the way she controlled David. It had taken Louisa years to eradicate her angry streak in order to please him, to put him first. She had kept everything inside to maintain the balance, but he remained unimpressed. And here was this woman who cried and stomped and threw her handbag out of the car window, and David was on his knees.

The first time Cynthia visited Louisa's house, she did so alone. Louisa saw her walking towards the window, tilting her head to check her hair in the reflection, unaware that Louisa stood behind it. Inside, Cynthia said little as she toured the rooms. 'Is this a supporting wall?' she asked. She knocked on the wall with one sharp knuckle and listened. Louisa found herself being unusually placid and careful. It really was impressive. Cynthia looked at her watch. 'Do you have anything to drink?' she said.

Jealousy, Cynthia had explained to David, was disgusting. It destroyed relationships. She was a model – it was her job to look good, and she would not apologise for that. There would be attention, obviously, and he would have to accept it. 'David knows the deal, in that regard,' Cynthia told Louisa.

So Louisa was surprised, and – she had to admit – delighted when Cynthia berated David in the White Hart for spending too much time at the cottage across the field. She was less surprised to hear David describe the accusation as preposterous.

He repeated the word to her, later.

'It's not preposterous,' Louisa snapped. 'It's not *true*. There's nothing in it. But the idea itself is not preposterous.'

He curbed his visits.

David tried to provide entertainment and society for Cynthia. He bought her a basic model white BMW to enable her to get around. Her sales rep car, she called it. The one area in which David would not compromise was the park, and that was the most devastating defeat for Cynthia. They would stay at the park, despite its financial unfeasibility, its dwindling visitor numbers, its incitement of animal rights groups, the jokes people made about it, and its remoteness from any reputable retail shopping centres.

It would be inaccurate to say that Cynthia confided in Louisa, but Louisa was often present at closing time in the White Hart when Cynthia slurred her predicament.

One December night, Cynthia's lament coincided with a rare visit from Louisa's old falconry buddy, Nelly Carter, who listened to Mrs Bryant with some amusement.

'How am I supposed to find work, living here? Anyone can see how my profile has dropped,' Cynthia said. 'And I'm losing my independence.'

Louisa's coat was already around her shoulders, the empty sleeves hanging limp in her lap. Nelly made a wisecrack to which Cynthia seemed oblivious. She was yet to even acknowledge Nelly, despite his whistles and asides.

'I wasn't built for this solitude,' she said. 'I'm a social person. I need more. I mean, it's alright for you.' Cynthia waved her cigarette vaguely in Louisa's direction.

Louisa could probably have left without interrupting the flow, but she felt compelled to introduce her friend. 'Cynthia, this is Nelson Carter,' Louisa said.

'Hello,' Cynthia said, with a sidelong glance. 'And what is your first name?'

Nelly laughed, and Louisa left them to it, walking past Philip Cassidy, who was drinking quietly at the bar.

Louisa could understand Cynthia's unhappiness. She was a woman, too.

When Cynthia fell pregnant, she withdrew from life in Detton. David continued to try everything. He even abandoned the park for a week during the busiest season, and took Cynthia to the Canaries, but she came back pale. David caught the sun easily, and the disparity between their skin tones fired the imagination of Detton's residents. 'She had morning sickness,' David mouthed. Nobody pointed out that the sun shone all day in Lanzarote.

When he arrived, Christopher provided no liberation. At the nursery school, a trivial argument over an object not shared had ended with a little girl holding a bleeding ear, and Christopher sitting on the roof of the PE shed counting the tiles. It brought home to David what he had denied and excused since before the boy could talk: Christopher saw the world askance. That day, Louisa noticed the serene, accepting look on David's face as they walked through the fields between their houses. 'Cynthia's taken it badly,' he said.

'What about you? Are *you* okay?' Louisa asked.

'It looks like we'll be doing battle with this thing for the rest of our lives. But he's my son. In a way, I can't help thinking there's some sort of order to this. That it was bound to happen, after what I did to that other boy.'

Louisa shook her head. 'David, that's rubbish. Sometimes I think you forget what happened, and to whom.'

Not long afterwards, Louisa took a hawking trip to the Yorkshire Moors. On her return, driving through Detton after midnight, she saw the white BMW concealed off-road near the pub, the front end tilted into the bushes and smears of filth like fingernail scrapes along the bodywork. Louisa had imagined such scenes before, and so assumed there had been a crash. She pulled over a few hundred yards down the road, and ambled back to the BMW. She stood behind the car for a while, studying the tyre tracks in the dirt.

Louisa took a step back when the passenger door opened. Nelly Carter tumbled from the car, his stance as aggressive as could be for a man off-balance with his jeans undone. He relaxed considerably when he recognised Louisa, and gave her an elated beam. 'Eh up, youth,' he said. 'What you doing here? I thought you were the pigs.'

'Bloody hell,' Louisa said. 'Have you not heard of a bed?'

'Well. Hers is a bit crowded, in't it?' He walked past her.

'Where are you going now?' she said.

''ome,' he said.

'How?'

'Bus. Me and her's had a falling out. You'll make sure she gets back, right?' He crossed the empty road calmly, zipping his jeans.

'Bye, Nel,' Louisa said.

'See you, duck.'

Louisa approached the BMW. The scene inside the car needed no help from the blue-tinted windows to convey the sullied, bottle-bottom mood. Cynthia lay back on the reclined passenger seat, skirt hitched, hands folded over her stomach. The leather gleamed in places.

Louisa opened the door and Cynthia looked at her and laughed. 'Oh. It's you,' she said.

'My van is up the road,' Louisa said.

'I can drive. There's nothing wrong with the car,' she said.

'I know there's nothing wrong with the car. Get in the van.'

Cynthia followed without much protest, in one of her increasingly frequent numb states. She got into the van and sniffed the air.

'Yeah, well,' Louisa said, nodding to two peregrines in the back. 'They probably don't think much of your stink right now, either,' Louisa said. Cynthia smelled of turps, milk formula, Malibu, saliva, Nelly's Asda own-brand aftershave, tobacco, semen, and Chanel.

'Don't tell David,' Cynthia said flatly.

'It's not the first time, is it?' Louisa said.

'First time with *that* prick.'

'Steady on. He's a friend.'

Cynthia spoke quietly, and without conviction. 'Of course. You introduced us. All the more reason not to tell David.'

'Don't threaten me,' Louisa said. Before, Cynthia would have screamed at a line like that. She would have actually cried. Now she just looked at her feet.

'I did introduce you,' Louisa said. 'So it *does* put me in something of a bind. I don't appreciate that.'

'We'll probably divorce anyway, but I can't afford to walk away with nothing. Tell me what I need to do to keep it quiet,' Cynthia said.

Louisa saw herself as if from the outside. She felt, as she often did, disconnected from reality and consequence. What did it matter what she said?

'I think you need to get away from all this,' Louisa said. 'I think that's what you need to do.'

Cynthia was gone by Christmas. In public they cited 'mutual distance', a strange phrase. Most people suspected that she could not handle life at the park. The divorce was amicable because

David bowed easily to her demands, gave her everything she wanted and took everything she didn't. Despite their low opinion of her maternal attributes, the villagers were stunned that Christopher remained on the hill. Such a thing was unheard of. Even Louisa thought that Cynthia would take the boy.

News came back, many years later, that Cynthia had done well on her second chance. She had kicked the drink. According to Bill Wicks she had even 'got herself therapised' and was an all-round calmer woman. David raised his glass to the news, said he didn't even mind paying for such a philanthropic act. 'Think of all the bartenders, waiters, shop assistants and service staff I've saved from her wrath,' he said.

Nothing to do with me, Louisa thought, happy to have another little secret.

When Cynthia left, Louisa felt the sort of manic joy sometimes associated with grief. Since living on Drum Hill, she had had several half-hearted affairs, mainly in an attempt to make David jealous. Now, she finally saw an opening.

On New Year's Eve, she was done up to dine at the country club. She knew David would be there. She wore a two-tone blue dress, darker and more sophisticated than the one she had worn to the Pony Club Ball all those years before.

Despite the schedule she had been devising for weeks, Louisa froze in the afternoon and ended up rushing her preparations. At the last moment, she remembered that she had not yet fed her young steppe eagle, Iroquois. She struggled outside on heels, and cast Iroquois into the wind. Iroquois did not come down on the meat she held, but on the exposed flesh of Louisa's forearm. She locked her claws into the soft underside, and hung upside down before flying over the house.

Louisa was bemused. Such attacks were rare, and it was rarer still that a talon broke the skin. Perhaps the shimmer of her bracelet had momentarily aroused the memory of light in a vermin eye. 'Surely I don't look that bad in a dress,' she said, when Iroquois eventually came to the fist. 'You're probably right,' she said, applying pressure to the puncture marks, and walking back to the weighing room. 'Mutton.'

She may have been in shock. The moonless evening did not help matters. She dressed her wounds absent-mindedly and drove to the country club through the dark lanes.

As soon as she stepped into the reception area, she knew the night was over. The concierge stooped as if to catch a dropping glass, and the other guests turned. In the poor light of the weighing room she had mistaken the blood, which had sprayed quite liberally from the original penetrations, for the darker shades of her two-tone dress. Now, standing beneath the bright lanterns of the club, it was quite clear that Iroquois had hit a vein. Blood speckled her cleavage. It had leaked through the bandage and dripped onto her lap while she was driving.

The guests were called to the tables. David, thankfully, had already taken his seat, out of sight. Louisa stood in the lobby for a moment, alone but for the receptionist, who busied herself with papers. 'That'll teach me to dress up,' Louisa said, spinning on her short heel.

*   *   *

A few months later, Louisa's father called. 'I've just spoken to David Bryant,' he said, uttering the words with a certain ceremony. She closed her eyes, and sat down. After all these years.

'What did he say?' she asked, looking at her glove splayed on the kitchen table. She imagined the words, not for the first time: *your hand. He wants your hand.*

'He said he shot that boy,' her father said. 'Not you.'

Louisa waited for the plates of her mind to shift. When she failed to respond, her father continued. 'He said he was never brave enough to confess. That you made a *massive sacrifice.* Now that your life is ruined, of course, he's come forward, which is big of him. He's told Lawrence, too. Nice little boost for a widower on his deathbed. Hello?'

Louisa cleared her throat, to indicate her continued presence.

'When he said it, I thought, *yes, I know.* Typical me, you're probably thinking. Typical know-it-all Daddy. But there you have it. If you took the blame to spite me, it worked, I suppose. And if you did it to test me, I failed. Either way it's been a bloody waste, hasn't it?'

'Yes,' said Louisa, to her father's surprise.

She went straight to David, confronted him in his office. 'You've made a liar of me,' she told him.

He sucked in his lips, as if he knew this was coming. 'I told them what you did for me,' he said. 'How amazing you were. I couldn't get straight with myself, Louisa. I couldn't have gone on with it any longer.'

'I could,' she said.

He opened his mouth to speak, but they heard Christopher

running through the hallway towards them. Louisa saw David smile, saw the new freedom in him, as he turned to welcome the boy.

It was as though they had one vial of strength between them, and they could not share it equally. It was the boy who completed David's recovery. Philip Cassidy stepped up his hours on the park, David committed himself to looking after Christopher, and they managed. He took single-parenthood on with humour and imag- ination. Louisa retreated, feeling the sharp stab of her redundancy.

TWENTY-THREE

Two weeks after she had called Adam, Maggie was driving towards Detton when she spotted Louisa's van in the car park of the Strutt Arms. The kidney colour was difficult to miss. Maggie pulled in beside it. She could hear the weir crashing below, and see the spume rolling in the late afternoon darkness.

The Strutt was a chain pub, and a good deal brighter than the White Hart. Through the big glass windows Maggie could see young families eating at the tables, and a group of boys gathered at the fruit machine. There were *people*, everywhere, in configurations she recognised from another life. And yet she was only four miles from the lonely house on the hill. She got out of the Land Rover and crossed the car park.

As she passed the Transit, Maggie saw Louisa leaning against the door. Louisa was smiling ruefully, her arms folded. When she saw Maggie approaching, Louisa's expression changed considerably. She became rigid, and her face began to flush.

'Hey!' Maggie said. 'I saw the van, so I pulled in.' She turned to Louisa's companion – she hadn't registered him at first, nor how strange it was for Louisa to have company. 'Oh, God,' Maggie said, and gave a startled laugh. 'Hi. Hello.'

'Alright,' said Adam.

Maggie turned to Louisa and tried to act naturally. 'So, how's things?'

'Fine,' Louisa said.

There was a silence.

'I've got to be off,' Adam said. He leaned towards Louisa and then stopped, put a hand on her arm.

'See you,' Maggie said.

He nodded and strode off to his car. Maggie waited until he had driven past, and then turned back to Louisa with a wide-eyed smile. She noticed that Louisa was wearing mascara.

'How's Diamond?' Maggie said.

'He's fine.'

'Hey listen, I hope I wasn't intruding on you and . . . '

Louisa let the silence continue for a moment. 'You know who he is,' Louisa said eventually, with some irritation.

'What, he told you we . . . ? I didn't think he was supposed to talk about other . . . '

'He didn't.'

'Well. It was a while ago, really,' Maggie said, choosing not to count the more recent brief visit. She smiled mischievously, but when she saw Louisa's reaction – a few stern deep breaths – she reined in the conspiratorial good cheer. 'Lou, I hope you don't feel weird about it. I certainly don't. These kind of services—'

'Do we *have* to talk about this?' Louisa said. 'I mean, are you finished with this *bloody* talk? I know exactly what you're thinking because everything's about sex for you, isn't it?'

'I wish,' said Maggie. 'Look, Louisa, it's okay. It's nothing to be ... you're a woman, you've got needs.'

'No I haven't,' Louisa said. 'It's not like that. You don't know anything about me and him. You don't know what you're talking about. I wish you'd mind your own bloody business.'

Louisa got into her van, and slammed the door. Maggie stepped back and waited. Louisa reversed and then drove away, leaving Maggie alone with the sibilance of the weir.

After a moment, Maggie went back to the Land Rover. Climbing in, she remembered Adam's face when he had come to the house last week. He had looked disapproving, almost repulsed. Maggie had been drunk but surely such a situation was nothing new to a man like him. So the question loomed: why was he unable to sleep with Maggie, when he was clearly capable of keeping his appointment with Louisa? Maggie studied her own face in the rear-view mirror. She had not been sleeping, and tender patches of dark skin swelled beneath each eye. The radio told of flash floods in the North-East; a man last seen alive trying to cross a submerged car park had washed up a day later by the cathedral five miles away. The weather was heading south.

She turned off towards Drum Hill, thinking of Louisa's smirk and slouch by the van. In the moment before she had seen Maggie, she had looked so at ease. It had taken a long time for Louisa to relax into such a posture, and Maggie knew she could take some of the credit. She tried to feel good about that.

*   *   *

That night, Louisa tried her best to pick a fight with Adam. They dined in a huge, virtually empty curry house on a back road out of town. The heavy pink curtains remained open, leaving the vast night sky visible.

'I'm sick of hiding out in holes like this,' she said, looking at the ceiling. 'We're like lepers.'

'You suggested the place. God knows I've got nothing left to hide. Why don't we go on back to Detton? Eh? The White Hart,' said Adam, leaning back in his chair.

'Don't be stupid,' she said.

'I'm serious,' Adam said, smiling. 'I mean, you're not ashamed of me, are you?'

'You know that's got nothing to do with it,' Louisa said.

'Besides. There's no *point* sneaking around, now.'

Louisa looked up from her food. 'Now *what*? What's changed?'

'Well. Your neighbour knows.'

'You think *she* was the only person I was keeping it from?' Louisa said.

'Yes,' Adam said.

'How dare you?' Louisa said, but she lacked conviction. She thought of Maggie's look of bewilderment outside the Strutt.

'She was always going to find out eventually, wasn't she?' Adam said.

'Only because she's always prying,' Louisa said.

Adam laughed. 'She pulled in to the pub because she saw your van, and she wanted to see you. It's probably because she *likes* you or something.'

'Why are you sticking up for her?'

'I'm not. There's no need to. She hasn't done anything wrong. What's she done wrong?'

'All these questions she asks,' Louisa said, trying to stoke the memories of earlier in the day. 'She doesn't know what's going on between you and me. She thinks she does but she doesn't.'

'And why doesn't she?'

'Oh, it's my fault is it?' Louisa drained her lager and threw down her pink napkin.

'Why does it have to be someone's fault?' Adam said. 'Why is it all about vendettas for you? It's not the mafia. You both live up there on that hill and it seems a bloody shame to do so alone. For both of you. Don't you want to be happy?'

She turned away and looked out of the window.

The next morning Louisa woke to the percolating sound of rain. She could not remember the last dry day; the sleeves of her coat were constantly damp inside. When the shower subsided, she dressed, tied beef to the lure and went out to fly Diamond. He was reluctant in the wet, and she kept the session short. She stood for a while with him on her fist. He shook his feathers and looked to the sky.

She remembered the day that Roy Ogden – of all people – had brought Diamond to her. Louisa had been in her early thirties. Maggie's age. It was the first time she had seen Ogden since that night in his underground garage. Eighteen years had passed. He had tried to send messages through Nelly and Baz, but she cut them off as soon as they mentioned his name. Until Ogden arrived at her house, Louisa had not considered the reality of the years gone by – it was just a smooth stretch of bitterness for her.

But there he was, an old man. He wore a long sports coat bought from the market and he carried a box.

'What do you want?' she said, stepping out of her cottage and closing the door behind her.

'Nothing. But before you boot me off your property, I've got a hawk for you.'

She looked down at the box, and then away, but she could not resist. She opened it, and – with some difficulty – took out a first season tiercel peregrine in terrible condition. Louisa examined him: swollen feet, fed-up, stunted feathers, the works. She shot a mean glance at Ogden, who looked down. 'Did you *find* this falcon?' she asked.

'No. He's mine. Pure perry.'

'You mean *you* let him get like this?'

Ogden winced. 'I've not the puff for him any more. I can barely walk dog.'

'You should have brought him in earlier,' she said.

'Aye. Happen I should,' he said. 'It's hard to accept though. He had me bound, did Diamond. Right bound.'

Ogden stood, head bowed, as if waiting.

'Okay. I've said I'll take him,' Louisa said.

'Right. Ta.'

Still he did not leave. 'What do you want, money? Here.' She took a few notes from her pocket.

'I don't want none of that,' Ogden said, meeting her eye. 'Well then,' he said. 'Cheerio.'

She watched him hobble away. He left the box.

Later that day she gave the bird a thorough health check, coped the beak, and filed the talons. So, she thought, Oggie had become the thing he most despised – a neglectful falconer. It was hardly surprising – hadn't he neglected *her* when she most needed him?

One thing was certain: Diamond's story was written on his feathers – nothing sentimental or pretentious about that claim. When a falcon is undernourished, the feathers cannot grow properly. A fault line appears, even if the bird is fed again. The fault is called a hunger trace. Louisa could calculate, from the growth of the feathers, how long Oggie had neglected Diamond for. She was furious with him.

A few weeks later, she saw the notice in the newspaper. *Shirland R. Ogden, 1928–1994. Known as Roy. Finally at peace after a long and painful illness.* The words stretched back over their last meeting. His physical appearance came rushing back to her. He had looked twenty years older than he should have. His skin had darkened, especially around the eyes, and she could see in her memory the rigging of his neck as it fed down into his coat, the papery palpitations of baggy skin. She recalled now that his moustache had gone, revealing the crooked line of his lip.

She put down the newspaper and went out to the weathering, took Diamond to the weighing room. In that cold white space she saw the hunger traces for what they really were – the flaring of Roy Ogden's illness, recorded on his bird, every half-grown feather a mark of his decline. Diamond had not eaten because Oggie had not eaten; Diamond had not flown because Oggie could not rise from his bed.

She sewed the moulted feathers of her other peregrines into Diamond's faults. She treated his bumblefoot with Preparation H. It was the last time she would share a bottle of anything until Maggie visited, a decade and a half later, with a litre of scrumpy.

Diamond had always been dominated by his body – its wild needs and marvels. The falcon with its leg snapped in half can breathe through the hollow bone. Its hormones descend before the mind can catch up. A peregrine will kill a bird in the morning and nudge it, confused, until the blood starts to flow. Louisa first noticed that with Diamond. It was as though there was another living thing within him, innocent of the body and its will. Louisa had heard people make such remarks about animals before, and always thought it to be bullshit.

If Diamond was helpless before his desires, they made him do the most incredible things. He gave Louisa the best flights of her career, the ancient whistle of his stoops arriving before his forked frozen self. He had rare wisdom: most peregrines will chase grouse into cover, allowing the quarry to escape while the falcon becomes entangled in the bush. When Diamond put a grouse into the bracken, he pulled up to his pitch, as though borne by water, thousands of feet in the air, and waited for the reflush, waited for Louisa, while the rain of his killing stink settled on the cover like a rumour.

Louisa could feel what he was doing even when she could not see him. That penitent second in the thin atmosphere before he fell backwards: suicidal, cannibalistic, self-enveloping and hungry, the transparent membrane slipping horizontally to sheath the giant eyes against the debris.

Moments later she would sit beside him with the kill, dig out the tiny heart and feed him the rich meat, which he loved.

Looking at him, now, the missing talon, the weak leg bones, the grey abrasions on the feet, she knew she would have to act fast to preserve his qualities for another generation. That's where

Caroline was supposed to come in. It would be another year or so before Caroline could breed, and Louisa had already designed the dual chamber with the viewing window so the two birds could get to know each other. Caroline would be bigger than Diamond by then. If left together without protection before a relationship had developed, she might try to kill him. Eventually, if everything went well, he would court her by plucking a small bird and leaving it at the window.

These plans for the expensive dual skylight breeding chamber, with its nesting sites and courting spaces, were sketched on the back of a utility bill Louisa could not pay. Any thoughts she might have had about pooling finances with Maggie were now forgotten.

She put Diamond back in his weathering, and walked out into the day, where the outside lamp still shone, turning the rain to sparks. Up on the horizon, she saw Maggie, dark against the smoky sky. It looked like a two-dimensional scene, like a crude toy from her childhood, as though Maggie were walking on the thin perimeter of a circle cut from card.

Most days she could see her at this range. She could hold the figure on the horizon between her finger and her thumb.

TWENTY-FOUR

Maggie was in the Land Rover outside Christopher's college when the call came. It was Philip. 'They've got the last ibex,' he said. 'On the building site where they'd seen him before.'

'What condition is he in?'

'They didn't say. He's alive, though. I spoke to the estate agent. Bit of pain in the arse to be honest. Should I go up there?'

'No, I'll go. Thanks, Phil.'

Maggie could hear the unmistakable rhythms of Christopher's boots on the concrete behind the Land Rover. She fastened her seat belt and started the engine.

'What are you in such a rush for?' Christopher said, climbing unsteadily into the passenger seat.

'Animal stuff,' Maggie said.

'Sweet Jesus,' Christopher said, rolling his eyes.

They headed for the estate, winding out of town into the green-belt. 'I don't suppose you fancy coming with me next week then, to look at the deer,' Maggie said.

'No can do. I've got other, erm, plans.'

'Yeah? What are you doing?'

'I'm going out with Louisa and Adamski.'

'Louisa and who?'

Christopher looked out of the window. 'Adam.'

They had reached a T-junction and it took Maggie a moment to make the connection, so thoroughly had she hidden Adam from the reality of her home life with Christopher. 'Why is *he* going out with you?'

Christopher held his hands out, to indicate the stupidity of the question. 'He's Louisa's boyfriend. God. It's blindingly, erm, clear.'

Maggie laughed dismissively. 'Oh Christopher, he's not her boyfriend. He's ... ' She had never said it out loud, and wasn't about to now. The words that came to mind were not Christopher-friendly. 'You shouldn't be hanging around with him, anyway. Neither should she, quite frankly,' Maggie said.

'He *is* her boyfriend. He told me so. He's round there every day. It's blindingly, erm. He practically lives there. I know true love when I, erm, see it.'

Maggie tracked back to the memory of Louisa and Adam out-side the Strutt. It was a strange place to meet someone like Adam. Maggie herself had never arranged a public appointment with him. *It's not like that*, Louisa had said.

Maggie put the Land Rover in gear and turned left. 'You said he's there every day?' Maggie said.

'Yes.'

'Do you mean every *night*?'

Christopher was becoming exasperated. 'Both. He stays over. They're probably going to get a joint account, for Jesus' sake.'

Maggie bit, and then slowly released her lip. Things began to make sense.

'This night out has been planned for ages,' Christopher said. 'I'm not calling it off now, at the last minute.'

'I'm not asking you to,' Maggie said, quietly. 'I'll go and see the deer on my own.'

'You can't tell me what to do. You have no, erm, jurisdiction,' Christopher said.

'I'm not telling you what to fucking do, Christopher.'

'There's no need for language.'

The first row of houses on the estate had already been completed, but the rest was a building site. A woman tottered out of the showroom. Maggie got out of the Land Rover, and – to her surprise – Christopher followed.

The estate agent was clearly perturbed. With her scarf ruffled at her collar, and her shuddering fins of hair, she looked like a pigeon cock on heat. 'You'll have to come with me,' she said, and took them towards one of the finished houses.

'Erm. Oh good,' said Christopher. 'I could do with looking at some properties.' He took a leaflet from the agent, and scanned it. 'Some, erm, dwellings, I mean.'

Maggie did not understand why they were going into the empty house. Her apprehension grew when she was hit by the odour of scent glands and dung as she entered the hallway.

'Erm, I like that new house smell,' Christopher said.

'I certainly don't know what is going to be done about *that*,' the agent said. Maggie noted her use of the passive voice.

The ibex lay by the French doors in the living room, breathing heavily, the metacarpus of his right foreleg snapped and protruding from the skin, and the infection clear to sight and smell.

'Who brought him in?' Maggie said.

'Nobody. We *found* it here this morning. No idea how it got in. It's certainly made an absolute mess of this living space.'

Maggie ignored the comment and crouched down by the ibex, who looked out of the window at the future back garden, the churned earth revealing caramel swirls of clay.

'Erm, erm, blimey!' Christopher said, still examining the property details. 'Two hundred grand for this flimsy thing. That's ridiculous. It's made out of papier mâché.' He banged on the wall, which shook.

'Please don't do that,' said the agent.

'Well. Erm, it's no wonder he's used the place as a toilet.'

The big grey boards of the floor were dotted with ibex shit, some of it trodden in by a workman's boot. Sweat and heat from the animal had caused a damp patch to form on the wall by the French doors. Maggots squirmed in the wound. When Maggie pressed lightly on the upper leg, the ibex flinched, the noise startling Christopher and the agent.

'Christopher, can you give me a hand?' Maggie said.

'No way, I'm not touching that dirty article. Erm, it stinks to high Christendom.'

Maggie took a breath. She turned to the agent, who was hugging herself. 'Do you think you could call a couple of fellas over to help us lift him into the car?'

'They're working. We can't spare men. This is your responsibility.'

'Okay,' said Maggie. She stood, and started to walk out of the room.

'Where do you think you're going?' said the agent.

Maggie turned and looked down at the woman. 'I'm going to get a captive bolt gun, or a heavy dose of barbiturates, so I can put this animal out of his misery. Then I'm going to leave him here, because I can't lift him. There shouldn't be much blood, but he'll almost certainly urinate when he's dead, so you might want to change your shoes before you show the next couple round.'

She was learning, it seemed, from Louisa, even in her absence.

'I'll see if any of the men are on a break,' the agent said, and stomped outside.

'Two hundred thousand,' Christopher said. 'Jumping Jesus. For this s-house.'

Maggie went out to get the drugs from the Land Rover, and came back inside just as the agent returned with a workman. Maggie knelt by the ibex, sedated him and checked the pulse in his neck. Everyone else watched in respectful silence, even the agent. 'I'll be back to clean up,' Maggie told her.

'Don't worry. They'll just paint over it,' the agent said gently.

Maggie and the workman carried the ibex out to the Land Rover and laid him on the back seat. When the animal was secure, Maggie took her place in the driver's seat next to Christopher, and cleaned her hands with wet wipes.

'Erm. I'm sorry I couldn't help,' Christopher said. 'I think my disc has slipped.'

'It doesn't matter,' Maggie said.

'Is he, erm, going to die, at all?'

'Yes. His leg is broken and badly infected. It's better that he's asleep. He must have been very scared.'

'Erm, I know. Did you see her lipstick?' said Christopher.

Maggie laughed, and then Christopher laughed, realising he had made a joke.

The sky darkened quickly as they travelled home; the clouds were oppressively low. Maggie explained her plans to bring the deer to Drum Hill. Christopher approved. He wouldn't promise that he'd touch them, but he might.

'How do you think the goat got into the house?' Christopher said, looking behind him at the prostrate animal.

'The ibex? Difficult to say. What I don't understand is why this one broke from the pack. I mean, how did he end up over *this* side of town?' Maggie said.

'Well, he spun round and went through the woods as soon as he saw my torch,' Christopher said.

'What?'

Christopher gasped and stiffened in his seat. 'Erm, erm, erm. I mean. The torch of . . . erm, whoever.'

Maggie blinked slowly and sighed, but she didn't say anything. Christopher glanced at her, and then looked away.

They drove on for a mile in silence. It began to rain. Maggie rubbed her face. She could not believe she hadn't thought of it before, but she had been so certain it was activists. She imagined Christopher out there in the enclosures with the bolt-cutters, in the middle of the night. The thought made her long for David. Christopher began to cry. 'I suppose I'm going to get an absolute rollocking, now?' he said through his tears.

'No,' she said. 'No. It's okay.'

When they arrived outside the house, she put her hand over his shaking fist on the passenger seat. 'Did you do all of the releases?' she said.

'Leave me alone,' Christopher said.

Maggie shook her head and just sat there for a while. 'I'm sorry, Christopher, about—'

'So you should be,' he said. He cleared his sinuses, and swallowed. 'You knew they were daemonic all along.'

'I mean, I'm sorry for what I said about that man.'

'Adam?' Christopher said.

'Adam. It was wrong of me. He's probably very nice. I'm sorry. It's good for you to go out.'

'Yeah, right. Erm, what if?'

The rain hit the roof of the Land Rover like crackling fat.

'And Christopher . . .'

'What?'

'When I first came here, to Derbyshire, that must have been very difficult for you,' Maggie said.

'Looking back, it was abysmal,' he said quietly. She thought of his kindness back then, and knew from his tone that he did not mean what he said.

'Well, you were nothing but nice to me. I married your father because—'

'Because of financial concerns.'

'No. That's not why. I married him because we were massively in love. But if you must think in those terms, then you were the Christmas bonus. I knew I'd be happy with your dad, but I never expected to find someone as brilliant as you waiting for me here. I moved away from all the people I knew when I came to Detton. You know what it's like to be lonely. I couldn't have managed without you. Whatever has happened since, I want to say thank you for that.'

'I'm not lonely,' Christopher said. 'I've got friends. More than you.'

'I know.'

Christopher looked at his feet for a moment. 'Say it then, if you want to say it,' he said.

'What? Oh.' Maggie smiled. 'Thank you.'

She kissed him on the cheek and hugged his head. 'Best bollocking you've ever had, eh?' she said, and he grinned.

Maggie glanced over at the cottage, its lights strong in the thick darkness of the late afternoon.

LATE SEASON

Pheasant, partridge.

TWENTY-FIVE

It seemed obvious to the people of Detton that their village would be dismantled in this way: slowly and irresistibly turned over and picked apart. No panic, no explosions, just the crushing weight of the world. For the first few days of the flood, the village looked still, its people and vehicles and animals sheltered. The only movement came from the straining, tea-coloured ligaments of flood water, and the things it carried.

Louisa had seen the signs before most. Trying to fly Diamond at Ladybower had been pointless in the deluge, and she had observed the abnormal level of the reservoir, and the officials taking decisions down in the basin. She was on the road now, heading back through the diversions.

The problem, as always, was that Detton stood in the delta between two bodies of water. The ancestral barriers held back some of the Derwent's overflow, but when the River Ecclesthorpe broke its banks for the first time in 112 years, things began to move more swiftly in the lower part of the village. Houses were prised open. In Dewke Street, a patch of cream and maroon wallpaper stripped from a hallway a mile to the north got caught on the windscreen of a Toyota. Terracotta patio tiles, and blue and white bathroom tiles, spun gently into the Bottleneck Brook, where the weeping willows showed high brown stains of their drunkenness. Eventually, bigger debris – a mattress, pallets from the industrial estate – blocked the bridge near the confluence of the Derwent and the Bottleneck, and squeezed the brook like a tube. In the fields, the soil moisture deficit reached zero and the rain had nowhere to go.

On the radio of Louisa's Transit, an RSPCA rescue worker spoke of being called to help some horses in a waterlogged field, but finding an elderly couple trying to get their granddaughter out of a car as the levels rose, causing the doors to jam. 'It creeps up on you, water,' he said. 'Everything seems fine. It's so quiet. Then, before you know it, bang. Trouble.' Louisa thought of her hawks, and began to make plans.

The plate glass window of Young's Ye Olde Sweetshoppe down by the school gave way under the pressure, and the children who lived nearby awoke on Thursday morning to find jars of bon-bons, bullseyes and Liquorice Allsorts floating past their windows. Some of the children were struck by a sense of wonder, but concealed their excitement when they saw their parents sitting on the dry half of the staircase, watching their homes go to ruin.

Jessop Avenue was the worst hit. The residents waited to be evacuated as discarded clothes, garden furniture, and the bones of shallow-graved pets lodged in the tops of hedges. From his bedroom window, Richie Foxton saw a swan sailing in and out of the windows of the estate agent's, the red light of the alarm flashing but mute.

And still there was a sense of calm, even when stories came of the accidents, injuries and deaths across the county. A workman in Hilford died behind the Glow-Worm factory when his dumper truck tumbled into the river. A young man was missing after a night out.

At the bottom of the hill Louisa saw Christopher clambering into his brookside den, and was glad to rise out of the valley. The van shunted unsteadily, and Louisa saw rivulets coming together like the handles of divining rods, winding past her, and flushing the detritus into the village. An expert on the radio programme explained the 'vulnerability variables' at work in flood-related accidents: clothing, intoxicants, being asleep. Many deaths happen in vehicles, he said. People die in shallow, quick-moving water. 'Males are almost twice as likely to be injured taking undue risks and attempting rescues.' There had been a time when such a sentence would have drawn a derisive snort from Louisa, but no more.

The hawks, however, still came first. Despite their favoured location at the summit of the hill, water pooled on the weathering lawn, and had reached within a foot of some of the chambers. The old wooden stables which had served as an aviary in Louisa's early years at Drum Hill stood on raised ground to the west of her cottage. It had never been an ideal place for falcons, and she had abandoned it years ago, but it was huge, dry and could be warmed for the Harrises by heat lamps run off the outside generator.

Louisa got to work as soon as she got home, but the hawks

were reluctant to move in the rain, and it was an exhausting task. She started with the longwings, loading each into a carrier box and taking two at a time round to the stables. With the hood on her coat pulled up, she did not see Maggie until she was a metre away.

'Hi,' Maggie said. 'I saw you moving the hawks, and thought you might need some help.'

Louisa squinted through the downpour. Maggie wasn't smiling. 'I'll be fine,' Louisa said. 'You should go back to the house, stay out of this weather.'

Maggie did not move. She held out a hand for one of the carrier boxes, and after a moment, Louisa relinquished it.

They worked together in silence, Louisa erecting fence panel partitions for some of the more temperamental falcons, while Maggie brought Iroquois round from the lawn. The eagle remained calm on her fist.

Louisa put Diamond in last, lifting his tail, with the little transmitter wire she used to track him, over the block perch. She looked at her watch; Adam was due to arrive in an hour. Before they left, Louisa turned on the red porcelain heat lamps, and the place assumed the feel of a Christmas grotto. She padlocked the door.

'Thank you,' Louisa said.

'That's okay. I wanted to talk to you, actually.'

'Yeah, me too. Let's get dry.'

Maggie nodded briefly. They walked over to the cottage and went inside. The warmth and quiet was welcome as they stripped off their outer layers. In the kitchen, Maggie sat at the table beneath the coloured light while Louisa made tea.

'I wanted to apologise, first off,' Maggie said. 'I was flippant, in talking about Adam. I thought … Well, maybe you know what I thought. I hadn't understood the nature of your relationship.'

'Christopher filled you in, I take it.'

Maggie nodded. 'I'm sorry,' she said.

'It's understandable.'

'I guess that's why I haven't seen you for a while,' Maggie said.

Louisa brought the tea to the table and sat down, forced herself to smile. 'Yeah. Been busy.'

'Sounds like it.'

'It was nothing to do with you, and I'm sorry if it came across like that. You were right in what you said outside the Strutt. I felt strange about it, you know.'

'And do you feel strange about it now?' Maggie said.

'No. You know the truth, and that makes me feel a bit better. The whole thing is a disaster, anyway. It's a stupid situation and it's going nowhere,' Louisa said.

'Why is it stupid? Is he in love with you?'

'I don't know,' Louisa said, although she did know.

'And do you love him?'

Louisa did not reply.

'But because of his job … ' Maggie said.

'Yes.'

'Would he ever quit?'

Louisa looked away. 'It was ridiculous from the start, to think that someone like me could get into this kind of thing.'

'It isn't ridiculous,' Maggie said. 'It's certainly nothing to be ashamed of. You're an attractive woman. You're a great person to spend time with.'

'Maybe I was, once. I don't know. I made certain sacrifices.'

Maggie looked up at Louisa. 'David told me what happened, you know,' she said. 'With the little boy. He told me what you did for him.'

David had spoken to people about it. She knew that already. Louisa, however, had never told anyone, and nobody had said 'the little boy' to her, until now. She was struck hard by the boldness of the words, but the sensation gave way in her mind to clear pictures of that day way back in the past, on the borders of Oakley, her life unravelling from the barrels of the shotgun in David's hands.

'He let the lie go on too long,' Maggie said.

Louisa dragged her attention back to the conversation. 'It wasn't that simple. I wanted to do it.'

'You were just kids.'

'Very briefly,' Louisa said. 'And then, all of a sudden, we weren't. I look back and think, well, it didn't make any difference, really, taking the blame.'

'I think it probably did.'

Louisa fell silent.

'I've missed you,' Maggie said. 'It's good to be back here. Maybe we can just get on with things, now.'

Louisa closed her eyes. Such as she was about to say did not come naturally to her. 'Me too. I just feel guilty sometimes. I feel like we never would have been friends if ... '

'If David hadn't died,' Maggie volunteered the difficult ending. 'Yes.'

Maggie shrugged. Apparently this was not an original thought. 'I know you loved David, but it would have been worse for you had I been the one to die.'

Louisa ignored her protestation reflex. 'Why?' she said.

'After the warm welcome you gave me, I doubt he would have spoken to you again.'

Louisa let her head drop. These feelings had been between them for some time. 'I'm sorry. I hardly got behind the relationship, did I?'

'I always felt you were behind me. I just wanted you in front of me, where I could see what you were doing.'

Louisa smiled, but Maggie did not. 'I'm going to Norfolk this afternoon, to see the deer.' Maggie checked herself, realising how long it had been since she had spoken to Louisa at length. 'I've been thinking of purchasing red deer. I'm going to stay there a while, have a look at the way they do things. I just wondered if you might hold the fort while I'm gone.'

'What can I do?' Louisa said.

'Nothing much. Take the dogs out. I've left Philip in charge, but he's been weird lately. Maybe you could pop in from time to time, but really, I was hoping you would keep an eye out for Christopher. I know you and him are going out tonight. He thinks very highly of you. More than he thinks of me, anyway. If you could make sure he's okay.'

'Sure. How long are you going for?'

'A few days.'

'Yeah. I'll look after him.'

'He doesn't have many proper friends, you know?'

Louisa nodded. 'I know.'

'And it's been hard work making him believe that the world is an alright place these last few months. Hard fucking fraudulent work, I can tell you. If you feel like you might want to blank him, or say something mean, then it's probably best to just leave him alone.'

Again Louisa flushed, but controlled herself. 'I'll be around if he needs me,' she said. Maggie reached across the table and took Louisa's hand, smiling finally. The damp heat from Maggie's hand warmed Louisa's. They continued to smile, but there was a little anger in Maggie, a little force in the grip; Louisa felt it.

TWENTY-SIX

That afternoon Christopher sat at the back of his den, a notepad on his knees. Library books warped on the damp floor.

The last section of his essay – The Death of Robin Hood – was a daunting prospect. The demise of the historical figure was subject to much revision and debate, just as his life was, and Christopher had begun to find the so-called 'historical evidence' as shaky as the many representations in films and books. He wondered how a man could have multiple graves. They must have pulled him to pieces.

There were just so many versions. In the eighties TV series he'd watched with Maggie, Michael Praed found himself outnumbered by the Sheriff's men on a foreboding hill. He'd already been given a fairly pessimistic forecast by the antlered prophet Herne, so he knew what was coming. He told Marian to save herself. 'Dying is easy,' he said – and was swiftly proved right.

Christopher found the episode difficult viewing. In his father's stories, Robin always escaped. But here, hundreds of arrows were fired, a blur of colour slid down the screen, and that was that. Christopher could not help but think of the things they did not show: Michael Praed's body, riddled with arrows. There was indignity and humiliation in such a death. Later, in Nottingham Market Square, where he would surely have been displayed by the Sheriff (a scene also omitted from the Yorkshire Television production), the flies would have made short work of his model's complexion.

Christopher had wanted to talk to someone about it, but the kids at college had never seen the programme. Some of them had seen a recent version on TV, and the new film with that buffoon Russell Crowe, but Christopher did not want to talk about those. It said on his documents that he did not like change or new things.

What he wanted to talk about was the element of betrayal. In the very next episode, Jason Connery arrived, saying, 'Hi, I'm the new, blond Robin.' In Christopher's view, it took a traitorously short time for the merry men (and, more to the point, the merry woman) to accept him. The evidence built against back-stabbing Marian. Christopher found it easy to imagine Maggie Green finding a blond replacement for his father. He had seen *certain other people* leave Derbyshire before and come back virtually betrothed. Maggie Green and Carol-Ann were like Marian, Christopher thought. They were fickle, changeable, naïve. They lacked rock-solid values.

He thought, briefly, of Carol-Ann in the foyer of the Travelodge, the thick make-up which made her face a different colour from her pale neck and made it seem that her whole head had been constructed from bronze powder, right to the core. 'Aren't you going to sit down?' she had said.

'Erm, no,' he had said. 'I think a man like me has to be alone. I don't think I'll ever be a part of normal, erm, society. Erm. Bye.'

It may have functioned as an excuse to get out of the foyer, but he truly believed what he had said about normal society. And he also believed that if your face *had* to be a different colour from your neck, they should at least be colours that did not clash.

He had to admit that Cullis, for all his faces, was right about Marian: she was a flimsy addition to the legend.

The account of Robin's death suggested by the fourteenth-century ballad that Christopher trusted was incomplete. It was said that the readers of that time were so devastated by Robin's demise that they tried to destroy the manuscript. The remaining pages interested Christopher greatly, because, like all good stories, they combined death with love. So Robin, who was unwell, went to see his cousin, the Prioress of Kirklees – a cousin with whom he had been in love since they played together as children. Christopher let the incestuous element pass. The reason Robin visited the Prioress, against the advice of his friends, was to have his blood let. Christopher reminded himself that they were dark and sometimes medically ignorant times. And if men were men, then women, well. The Prioress was certainly a hard lady.

The ballad said that the Prioress bound Robin to a chair, shifted the buckets, took the bleeding irons to his forearms and opened the veins. The account of her actions after that were sketchy because of the missing pages. Some academics claimed that she was a backstabber, in league with Robin's enemies, and that she left him there to bleed to death. What amazed Christopher, what left him astounded, was Robin's profound trust in love. Of all the daring and skilful feats attributed to the outlaw, relinquishing his fate in this way to the woman he adored was surely Hood's most heroic deed. The fact that the object of his affection left him to die did not, at that moment, interest Christopher.

Of course he was disappointed that some of the pages of 'The Death of Robin Hood' were missing. For one thing, it left the door open for some halfwit to write a bestseller where it turned out that Robin Hood was actually Jesus of Nazareth or Robert Kilroy-Silk. But there were benefits, too. If the pages were missing, and the historical evidence was lost, then Christopher would just have to imagine the rest for himself. And in the dank comfort of his brookside den, with his eyes closed, that is what he did, the stout Prioress appearing in a torchlit room, the black silk of her robe shimmering, riding the contours of her thick calves while Robin's blood dripped into the pail. Herne stood behind the Prioress, his antlers clear against the light coming through the window. He wore a long green coat. 'Nothing is forgotten,' he said. 'Yes, yes, I know,' said the Prioress.

In the fire, she scorched the small wooden figurines that she and Robin had carved many years before as children, and she ground the blackened heads of these charms into the stone floor, to make a powder. She rubbed her calloused, squared-off fingers in the dark dust. Then she came towards him, her breasts heavy, her blonde hair spilling from her wimple, her soiled hand outstretched so that he could see the whorls and knots of her calloused fingerprints, and she painted the black dust onto the soft skin beneath each of his bright blue eyes. It was a sensual moment for the faint, captive Robin, his arms pulsing – as it was for Christopher, who woke from the reverie with an erection. He tried to think what film or story or book that scene had come from. He could not place it. The voice and shape of Herne was not that of the TV character, although it seemed strangely familiar. But he knew the face of the Prioress well enough. Yes, he certainly recognised *that* face.

The rain tightened its hold. In the grim light, the brook looked grainy and opaque but also nutritious, like the Japanese soup Maggie sometimes drank. The water had spilled over into the field again, and Christopher thought of the one hundred year event of which his father had spoken. He shuffled further into his den. Once, way back in his early teens, he had woken here to find that it had snowed while he slept; on another occasion, he had woken to find his foot covered with ants. In general, though, it was a place for peace and contemplation. He heard Louisa's van go past. He was going to the pub with Louisa and Adam later that night. Louisa had promised.

Fearing that the weather might scupper his big night, he had called the White Hart. Brian Wicks had confirmed business as usual. The pub was on a rise, Wicks had said, in more ways than one (Christopher liked that) and some of the evacuated families from Jessop Avenue were staying in the rooms above the snug for a reduced rate. 'There's special prices on bottled ale,' Wicks had said.

'I'll be rocking around the alcoholic tree tonight, then,' Christopher had said. 'I might lose bowel control.'

When he saw Adam's car climbing the hill, he walked up to the cottage, a jangling noise accompanying his rhythmic strides.

Louisa answered the door quickly. 'Come in,' she said. And then, when she saw his boots, 'Better stay in the hall.'

'Erm, just because Maggie's put me under your care doesn't

mean you get to boss me around,' Christopher said with a smile. 'It does mean you get to buy me absolutely, erm, vast quantities of alcohol, though. Is Adamski ready for the night of his life?'

'He's upstairs having a shower. He just got back from work.'

'Man's got to earn his daily bread,' Christopher said.

Louisa closed her eyes and nodded.

'I was thinking I might like to have a go with the falcons again,' Christopher said, looking at the battered wet glove on the table in the hall.

'Let's just take it one step at a time,' Louisa said.

*   *   *

Four or five drinks later, Louisa looked at the pictures of the village on the pub wall. She enjoyed the way each photograph, going backwards in time, stripped away more of the human traces: roads lost their stripes and curbs; the barn conversions became barns again, and eventually even the pub itself disappeared, replaced by woodland. The cellar had flooded that afternoon, so Bill Wicks had brought the metal casks upstairs, and sold colder-than-usual bottles of beer with a sulphurous smell about them, for half-price. The rain on the windows was like another layer of glazing, and Louisa stared deep into the blue bullseye panel, its comforting circles like a benevolent ghost. Adam bought the next round.

Christopher performed a splashy jig to Dr Hook's 'When You're in Love with a Beautiful Woman', and then sat down. 'Did you, erm, hear it, Louisa? "When you're in love with a beautiful woman, erm, erm, it's erm, *hard*." Do you get it?'

'Yeah, I think I probably do,' Louisa said.

'Dad taught me that one.' Christopher became serious. 'I often think of the time when I elbowed you in the face,' he said.

Louisa laughed.

'Erm, it wasn't amusing. Now that we're friends, I feel bad about it.' He paused. 'You know, there was falconry in the time of Robin Hood.'

'Tell me about it,' Louisa said. 'I take my birds to the Robin Hood Game and Country Show every year. Have to dress like a man in drag.'

'Is it the show in Newark?' Christopher said.

'Yeah.'

'Can I come next year?'

'You can dress up with me, if you like,' Louisa said.

'Really? My excitement levels would go through the, erm, roof. You could be the Prioress of Kirklees,' Christopher said, slurring his words.

'I don't have the morals,' she said, for she had never heard the story.

Adam returned to the table, set down the drinks and kissed her. Louisa kept her eyes open, and saw some of the locals look over. Christopher watched, too. Louisa squeezed Adam's wrist in protest but he persisted and she gave in.

Christopher went back to the juke-box, put on 'The Locomotion', and began dancing again. His Wellington boots squeezed brown water from the thin strip of red carpet by the bar. His arms flailed, and he knocked over a few of the contaminated beers, which smashed on the floor. He stopped dancing.

'Steady on, y'daft twat,' said Bill Wicks.

'Eh up,' Adam said to the landlord. 'That's not a very nice way to speak to patrons, is it?'

'Leave it, Adam,' Louisa said.

'I don't approve of swearing,' Christopher said quietly.

'The lad's a liability,' said Wicks. 'Louisa, keep him in check, would you?'

Louisa sighed. Adam ambled over, hands in pockets, lips pursed. The area beyond the bar was raised, so Wicks appeared even taller.

'He's not a liability, and he's standing right there – aren't you, Chris – so you can talk directly to him, an' all.'

'It's *Christopher*, not "Chris",' Christopher said, almost in a whisper.

Adam seemed much more comfortable than Wicks in the silence that followed. 'Come on, Wicksy, he's only a half-pinter. Have a pop,' Louisa said.

Adam looked back at Louisa with a smile, and kept the smile on for Wicks. Wicks backed down. 'Look, pal,' he said.

'I'm not your pal.'

'It's been a tough day, and I lost me rag, that's all. I've been bailing out bloody cellar all afternoon.'

'Well that's not his fault,' Adam said, nodding at Christopher.

'Aye, but that's four bottles a beer he just smashed. That's twelve quid odd.'

'That beer smells like you dredged it out at bogs.'

'Alright, alright. I shun't a said oat,' said Wicks. He looked at the silty brown water running under the door. 'I need a cleaner,' he said.

'What you need is a fucking wet nurse,' Adam said, leaning over the bar. Louisa heard it, but Christopher did not. Wicks chose not to reply, and Adam came back to the table, leaving Christopher to sway gently to the music, a bottle in his mouth, his eyes full of concern, like a hulking lap-dancer trying to play damsel-in-distress.

After a few moments, he returned to the table. 'Erm. There's a bad atmosphere in this joint. Erm, erm, erm. Bad vibes. Can we go?'

'Suits me,' said Louisa. 'We can have one back at mine.'

'You alright?' Adam said, smiling up at Christopher.

Christopher cracked a deviant smile of his own. 'Erm. Sometimes I have one too many.'

'Oh aye,' said Adam.

'Have you ever lost bowel control due to drink, at all?' Christopher asked.

'No,' said Adam.

'Or, erm, bladder?'

'You be careful of my sofas, you,' said Louisa. Christopher found this inordinately funny.

They left with nods and smirks, opening the door to let in a backwash of filthy water. The poor drainage in the car park allowed great pools of standing water to fizz with new rain. Christopher and Louisa were bomb-proofed by outdoor gear, but Adam had only a slim jacket, so he stayed under the awning, behind a curtain of water. Louisa became mischievous and kicked puddles at Christopher, mainly soaking herself. Christopher turned around, delighted, and kicked back. 'Fiend,' he shouted. 'Erm. Succubus fiend.'

'Accept it,' she shouted back. 'When you're in love with a beautiful woman, it's hard.'

They kicked up ropes and tunnels of water, until Christopher stopped, wiping the grime from his face. 'Oh. Erm. Nearly forgot, Louisa. I've got something for you,' he said.

Adam looked up as soon as he heard the bell ring in Christopher's pocket. It took Louisa a little longer to realise.

'Yours, I presume,' Christopher said in his suave detective voice, handing the mouse head key-ring to Louisa. She did not look at Adam, who remained a couple of metres away, beneath the awning.

'Where did you find this?' she said to Christopher.

'Wait,' Adam said.

'Erm. It was in the downstairs bathroom at home. I knew it was yours straight away of course. Erm. I'm no fool. You must have left it there in the halcyon days of you being friends with Maggie.'

Louisa closed her fist around the mouse head, silenced the bell. Adam walked out from under the awning, and grimaced against the rain. 'I *was* there,' he said.

'Shut up,' she said. Christopher flinched.

'I was there,' Adam continued, 'But I never did oat.'

She opened her hand, looked again at the charm and closed her fist. 'You know what? Fuck you.'

'Erm. Erm, now now, children,' Christopher said, bemused. 'Don't bicker.'

'I didn't do anything. You and me had argued, and I was mad, but I didn't do oat. Look at me,' Adam said to her. 'You know I'm not lying.'

'Don't try that fake nonsense on me,' Louisa said. 'I'm not some lonely housewife you can play mind games with.'

'Don't do this,' Adam said. 'Don't use this as an excuse.'

'An *excuse*?' Louisa said.

Adam's shoulders sank. And then he received a text message. The vibrations of his phone sounded like a throat being cleared, his pocket was lit green. Automatically his hand reached down, but he stopped himself. Louisa laughed. 'Answer it,' she said. 'Go on. Off you pop.'

'What's, erm, going on?' said Christopher.

'Adam has got work commitments,' Louisa replied.

'You can't go,' Christopher said. 'I've had a wonderful evening, and this could be it. It could be one of those nights. A night to remember.'

'I'd rather forget it,' Louisa said. 'I'd sooner forget all of it. You know what you are?' she said to Adam, who was already nodding. 'You're a decent fuck, and nothing else.'

'Aye,' he said, and started to walk away. He pulled the jacket over his head as he left the car park, and began to run towards the hill. Christopher shouted to him. 'Adam, wait. It's only just begun. We could be the fun-boy three. Erm. Youth.' But Adam did not look back.

Louisa and Christopher walked up the hill against the rain, because there was nothing else to do. Christopher spoke of the Game and Country Show, and of the death of Robin Hood, its various representations. He spoke of the Prioress, and her attractiveness. He slurred his words badly. 'Erm, erm. I can't believe she didn't come back to stop the bleeding. I think she would have done. She couldn't have, erm, forgotten because she had love on the brain. I mean, what about when they carved the figures together? Erm. Sometimes I take some Zuclopenthixol, and then I have one too many. It's a lethal cocktail, but it feels good at the time.' He laughed and then stopped. 'There must have been blood everywhere.'

Louisa could barely hear him. She walked a few paces in front. She pulled up her hood but let the rain run down her face unchecked and into her eyes which stung already. She was stuck between never wanting to see him again, and praying that the wheels of his Golf had sunk into the ground. They had not. She saw the flash of his car pass by near the top of the hill. He slowed down, but when she did not turn, he kept going.

By the time they got to the house, Christopher was shivering. He had forgotten to fasten his coat, and a bib of wetness soaked his jumper. 'I've got some letting to do myself, now. Some purging. Erm. Erm. I'm going to the toilet to commit perjury.'

He ran upstairs. Louisa took her time to work through his words, and worried for a moment. 'Christopher, what do you mean?' she said. But she could already hear him vomiting in the toilet. She went up to her bedroom, where she saw Adam's overnight bag, forgotten in the corner. She replaced her jeans with an identical dry pair. 'You okay?' she said.

'Erm. Yes. Like father like, erm, son, eh?'

Louisa descended to the kitchen, and looked at the noticeboard where she had pinned the postcard Maggie had sent about the van repairs, now coated with dust and bird particles. *Mrs Musters as Hebe.* Louisa noticed for the first time that the eagle was perched not on a rock, but on a dark, smoky cloud. Mrs Musters stared out with a strained smile. Louisa took out the pin and turned the card over. Maggie always flattened the 'M' of her name so that it looked like the distant bird that a child paints in a picture of a sunny day.

Louisa washed the nutrients from some beef in preparation for the hawks' morning meal and listened to the pressing insistence of the rain. The wild birds would be struggling, but her own were safe, if slightly unfit, in their communal shelter. She thought of Adam, of the proposal he had made in this house.

By the time Christopher came downstairs, Louisa was crying, her hands squeezing bubbly pink liquid out of the strips of beef shin in the sink. Christopher charged around the living room, rejuvenated after his purging. Louisa could not hold off the tears and it wasn't long before Christopher noticed. 'Oh,' he said. He crept, with comic quietness, to the computer, turned it on, and came over to Louisa at the sink with the same soft footsteps. Louisa could see his reflection in the kitchen window. He had stopped a yard from her back, and was peering round her, into the sink. 'Erm. Put. The meat. Down,' he said.

Louisa laughed. 'Oh shut up,' she said, sniffing. 'I'm alright.'

'Erm. Erm. Step away from the meat,' Christopher said.

Louisa let the strips of beef slide into the sink with a sop. She ran her hands under the tap, and dried them on her jeans, leaving slight traces of blood on the worn-white denim. She turned around.

'It always seems like there's, erm, someone missing from the party, doesn't it?' Christopher said.

Louisa nodded.

'There's never the, erm, full complement.' He studied Louisa's face.

'What's wrong?' she said. 'Never seen me cry?'

'It's not that. I've seen you cry loads of times. Erm, I've just never seen you cry whilst wearing make-up.'

Louisa wiped the darkness from her eyes. He had seen her cry loads of times; she considered that, and knew it was probably true. She looked at him. The vessels in the whites of his eyes had broken from straining to vomit. One of his eyes was blue, the other grey like David's. He had probably lost a contact lens down the toilet, Louisa thought.

'I've got something, erm, amazing to show you. It's absolutely first class. Blow your socks completely off.'

He knelt down at the computer, and shoved the chair towards Louisa, who sat down, shattered. Christopher went to the video search engine. Louisa did not know if she had the patience for a Jason Donovan song now. She rubbed her eyes, thought of all the women she knew whom Adam could have been with, that very moment.

Christopher typed *FPS Water Balloon*. A list of thumbnails appeared. He clicked one, and maximised the video so it filled the screen. A red balloon. A red balloon with what looked like a Stanley knife heading towards it, extremely slowly. 'Christopher, what is this?'

'Quiet,' he said, in a deep voice.

At the moment the tip of the knife hit the surface of the balloon, the red skin shed, smoothly peeling away in two directions from the point of contact, leaving a suspended balloon-shaped mass of bright white water, the surface rippling into the most incredible tiny peaks of silver light. Louisa could still see the line along which the balloon skin had broken, and the knife continued to travel slowly through the perfectly formed capsule of water.

Gradually, the shape became hairy, and gave way to gravity, but Louisa remained transfixed. The images resonated with the slow rhythms of her drunkenness.

'What—?'

'Slow motion, high speed camera. A thousand frames per second,' Christopher said.

Louisa frowned.

'It's what your birds see,' Christopher said.

Louisa took a sharp intake of breath, remembering the falconry display on the lawn, and Christopher's question about how fast the wasp was travelling. Meanwhile, on the screen, a bullet ran through a lemon, the skin of which opened slowly in a zig-zag pattern. 'It's amazing,' she said.

'It's certainly, erm, eye-opening,' he said.

'It's eye-*changing*,' she said, and they smiled.

'Erm. That's right. Before these cameras, nobody had ever seen what these things looked like.'

More images flashed up: missiles breaking their own circles of haze, televisions exploding decorously, the elements flying apart in perfect order. There were more water balloons, some breaking over people's faces like membranous sheaths. A face was slapped, the hand stroking softly but distorting the features, almost folding the nose over. The lips became cod-like as the waves of the blow passed through the skin like a crease being ironed.

It was beautiful, Louisa thought, and so considerate of Christopher. It was like something Maggie would do. Louisa decided not to mention this to Christopher, but the idea of Maggie's influence gave her hope. She glanced at the timer, which promised another nine minutes of high definition eruptions and disasters. The thing about seeing the world slowed down, she thought, was that you could watch something terrible unfolding, without the ability to do anything about it. Perhaps you would not even notice that it was happening.

Louisa yawned and ruffled Christopher's hair. He put his head against her shoulder, and she cradled it, closed her eyes. She could feel the pulse in his temple, the vessels constricted by dehydration. She could hear the rain, like words tapped out on a typewriter. She dropped down a level, into a half-sleep, and on this plain she saw Adam, his thick fingers on her thigh, his head turned away. He had a way of breathing through his mouth that left him parched. She blinked. Christopher's right hand had slid along the inside seam of her jeans, and up between her legs. His head was against her breast. She blinked again, and then realised what was happening. She stood sharply from the chair, grabbing his wrist as she did so and pushing him back. He fell against the computer. His look of fear did nothing to assuage her, just pumped the blood lust further. 'Never, ever do that,' she said.

'I'm sorry,' he said. She recognised the plea in his voice, the inability to go back and withdraw an action.

'It's completely off the bloody scale. I mean, did you *really* think ... ?'

Still on the floor, he let his chin drop onto his chest, like a little boy. She thought he might cry, but he flung out his arm and punched the table. The noise of it shocked Louisa, made her jump. 'Get out,' she said. 'Just get out.'

He got to his feet, and scrambled into the hall. The latch defeated him for a moment, but he soon worked it out, and was gone, leaving the door open, the rain sidling into the house, dis-colouring the rug. Louisa stood in her living room, with the outside spilling in, and a blank noise in her head.

She slammed the door.

TWENTY-SEVEN

A few hours before, Maggie had seen two red circles in the dark of that late February afternoon. The lights engorged as her eyelids drooped, sending a long shudder of warmth through her. They were just brakelights. But in her mind they were also the lamps of that pub by the Thames. And they were the only things keeping Maggie's anger at bay as she tried to drive east.

She had followed the red lights all the way out of Derbyshire, watching as those crimson eyes had multiplied into the distance with the incline of the road. She had been micro-sleeping for the last thirty minutes, releasing the brake every once in a while to roll forward a few pointless metres. The travel reports had warned against the M1 but the A-roads proved just as bad. Up ahead, there was an accident, a road closure, something. She did not know where she was, but she hadn't travelled far. Newark? Grantham? Sleaford? The journey felt longer because she had set off in daylight.

Maggie knew that a hundred miles to the east there was a red-bordered triangular road-sign with the black silhouette of a stag on a white background. She knew she would not see that sign tonight. Drivers up ahead had started to attempt three-point turns, and the ominous fact was that they could manage the manoeuvre safely, for there was no oncoming traffic.

She thought of the deer in their thick winter coats, exhausted by the rut, back in their single-sex groups. The two stags she wanted were in their fifth head. The man from Norfolk had sent pictures – front, flank and rear. All she wanted was to see them in the flesh. One little thing. She felt Drum Hill, and the tendrils of its bad fortune, reining her in. She needed a drink.

After another half hour, Maggie turned off the main road and found a restaurant connected to a small hotel. A huge pylon stood in the field just beyond the car park. She could hear the electricity fizz, could feel the pressure on her skull. The size of the pylon dwarfed the hotel and the cars, and made her suddenly aware of the view of the place from above.

She walked into the restaurant, took a booth, and ordered two whiskys. 'Will you be eating, madam?' the waitress said.

'No thanks,' Maggie said, handing back the greasy, laminated menu. She remembered once when she was a teenager, she and her friends had gone into a restaurant like this on the outskirts of London and sat in there for three hours, abusing the offer of free top-ups on coffee. The waiter had been forced to go to the shop to buy more. They were wired and choking on laughter, and they all had headaches.

'I'm afraid you can't have alcohol unless you're eating,' the waitress said.

Maggie took the menu back. 'Probably for the best,' she said. 'Soak it up.'

She ordered curly fries and decided to stay in the hotel for the night. She thought about calling home to tell someone, but she knew they would all be out. There was nobody, really, to tell.

At dawn she lay on one of the single beds, kept awake by the flat-line of the pylon and the hiss of the rain. Who stayed in these hotels? People on work conferences, tired lorry drivers, murder-ers, falconers. Maggie gave up on sleep. She turned on the TV in the top corner of the room, and watched the future: a shadow of low pressure was moving down from Iceland, over the east of England, to bruise its heart.

*   *   *

Miles away, Louisa opened her eyes. She had slept with the lamp on, and woke because it went out. Her digital clock was dark and numberless, a collection of possible eights. Powercut. The rain on the roof sounded like an engine left running. It was tireless, unremitting, mirthful. She smelled smoke, and remembered that this could signify the onset of a stroke. Later in the day, she would recall that thought, and wish it had been true, wish that the blood had simply drained from her brain. She rose from the bed, got dressed, and went downstairs.

The smell passed in and out of her senses as she moved through the house. In the living room she stood still and tuned in to the world. Outside, the lawn and surrounding fields had flooded. She had been right, she thought, to put Iroquois indoors, for her bow perch was almost completely underwater. The water

itself provided the strongest source of light, a dull glaze like a
dirty glass table.

The wind outside changed direction and she caught the smell
of smoke again. There was a base tone to it, which her mind iden-
tified before she was truly ready. She steadied herself on the back
of the chair and then hurried to put on her boots. The pulse
thumped in her head, and with every beat her vision greyed,
closed in from the sides.

When she got outside, she saw the dark arm of smoke rising
above the stables and whipping back around it. The centre of the
roof had already caved in. Louisa ran forward until four brief,
crackling explosions stopped her. She screamed and raised her
hands to shield her face. Fire had caused the right half of the shed
to collapse – her Harris hawks, a lanner, and Caroline. She could
smell the sweetness of feathers, the wood smoke, and the flesh.
She thought she might be sick, but she did not have time. The
other side of the shed remained intact, but smoke rolled in a fossil
black tail from the vent pipe. Louisa kept running.

Two slats of wood dropped away and she saw Iroquois, bating
in bursts, the leash pulling her down. And then she saw Diamond
through the smoke. A blue flame crackled in front of the hawks.
She did not know if the screams she heard were real or imagined,
or even if they were her own. She ran towards the door. The heat
did not get through to her – she was shivering – but the smoke
was overwhelming. She could not get any closer, so she sprinted
back towards the house, realising as she did so that the sprinkler
hose would not reach, and buckets of water would be futile. She
went inside, took her shotgun from under the sofa and ran back
out, loading cartridges and pouring extras into her pockets.

She tried once more to approach the shed, but could only get within ten metres. The flames fingered Iroquois's perch, took hold of the leash, spun up through the fibres and across the bird. Iroquois's figure appeared black within the orange light, and she opened her wings, dipped her head into the brunt. The sight put Louisa on her knees. She stood again, shouldered the shotgun and fired into Iroquois's breast. She fired two more rounds blindly into the blackened, crumbled half of the shed before reloading and turning the gun on Diamond. She aimed, but he bated. Smoke obscured the view. The fire advanced towards his block perch, but Louisa could barely see the bird. There was another blue fizz of wire igniting, and a dark shape arrowed through the roof and into the sky. It was Diamond, his severed leash still smoking like a blown-out wick. He tanked towards the woods. Louisa's first instinct was to raise the gun, but she caught herself, called and whistled. She ran across the waterlogged field, stumbling and splashing. It was useless. She stopped and watched Diamond clear the coppice, his wings becoming a distant tremble, before he was gone, beyond the range of Louisa's inadequate vision.

Louisa walked back through the wisps of ash to the centre of the field. She hit the ground, her knees slipping through the standing water and unstable earth, so that she fell forward onto her arms. She stayed like that while the shed folded in on itself like a rotting fruit.

TWENTY-EIGHT

Adam found her an hour later, dragged her home and called the fire service. At the time, Louisa did not wonder how he'd found the nerve to drive up the hill. She took whisky and Valium and fell into a disturbed sleep for a few hours.

When she came downstairs, Adam was still there, sitting in the living room. 'Is there anything I can do?' he said.

She stood in the middle of the room. 'Like what?' she said. 'Give me a back rub?'

He blinked slowly.

'Where is he?' she said.

'Who, the fireman? They've gone. It's extinguished.'

'I mean the boy.'

'I told you. I saw him down in the village. He's fine.'

'Did you speak to him?'

'No.'

'Look alright, did he?'

'Louisa, what are you talking about? You're not making any sense.'

'It's not the time for it.'

He stood and moved towards her, but she backed away. 'I could call the radio station, see if they'll put word out about the missing bird,' he said.

'I don't want their help. I don't want anyone to know. I don't want anyone touching him.'

'I see.'

'I don't think you do,' Louisa said.

Adam's face showed a flicker of frustration, but he held it in check. Louisa retrieved her soiled coat from the kitchen floor and put it on.

'What are you doing?' Adam said.

'I'm going out,' she said.

'You're not fit to drive, duck. Let me give you a lift.'

'Go home.' She was already out of the door when she said it.

Louisa waded through the mud and water to Maggie's house. The back door was open, so she went in. She knew Christopher wasn't there. She shouted from the hallway, then went upstairs and looked around. The place was empty. She did not know when Maggie was coming back, and she did not feel like she could wait. She dialled Maggie's mobile from the house phone, but it was switched off.

She went through to Christopher's room, took a suitcase from the wardrobe and began pulling his clothes from the hangers, and throwing them in. Back in the living room, she made the call, pulled in an old favour. There could be no refusal, all things considered.

Half an hour later, she sat in her van, ready to seek him out. The mud hung heavy on her clothes, patches of it drying like cracked skin. Christopher's suitcase lay on the middle seat. The smell of smoke now mixed with a chemical stink, something the firemen had used.

What had it been like for the hawks to see the flames coming slowly in ultraviolet, the world gradually blotted out with brightness and no way to get free? She closed her eyes and thought of the videos Christopher had shown her. She thought of him dropping a cigarette, too stupid or scared to put it out. She thought of him dousing the beams with petrol. How quickly would the fire have killed them? She found herself hoping they'd been suffocated, but she knew Iroquois had not been killed by the smoke. Iroquois had burned, the lines of her big body quivering in the heat as she thrashed. Louisa opened her eyes, closed both of her fists and smashed them into the dashboard over and over. As the plastic cut her hands, as the tissue compressed and burst the vessels inside, Louisa was possessed by a rage she had not felt since she was a child. She let it grip.

She found him in the Hart, an hour after most of the lunchtime crew had gone. He looked as she expected him to look – pale. Before him on the bar stood a coffee, a glass of water, and a pint of lager. 'Erm. Oh, hi. Hangover cure,' he said, quietly. 'Caffeine, lion's blood and hair of the dog.'

'Get in the van,' she said.

'I heard sirens this morning. Erm. What happened? I thought you'd, erm, called the Feds on me.' He smiled.

She took him by the collar of his coat and pulled him off the stool. He stumbled slightly. 'Okay, okay,' he said. For a boy of his size he came away easy.

She did not speak in the van, and did not look at him. His evident fear awoke no compassion in her; the sleeping tablets made her separate. Christopher looked at the luggage. 'Erm. I've got a suitcase like that. Are you going on holiday?'

'No.'

'Is it just a natural barrier against me and my wandering hands? I can understand that. Erm. Where's Adam? Have you made up? Erm, I hope I haven't created a triangle. Where are we going?'

She did not answer. They hissed along the tree-lined roads, past the burnished woodlands sagging with the weight of water. The railway crossing was flooded, but the van ploughed through without difficulty.

As they left Detton, Matlock, and Cromford behind, the lawns got neater and the cars more modern. After an hour of driving, Louisa pulled into a cul-de-sac, much flatter and roomier than the one which Adam had forced her back down all those months ago. The houses were the colour of crabs, their fleshy brightness hardly dimmed by the saturation. Louisa noted the water draining off the steeply cambered road, and the predominance of pea-shingle. She thought of the stables. How had the fire moved across the floor? The pictures came back into her mind – the heat, and the darkening shapes within.

'What's this soulless place?' said Christopher.

Louisa remained silent.

'I've been to dwellings like these before, with Maggie. I helped her with one of those goats. Erm. I didn't help her, really. I had a disc problem.'

'Number fifty-three,' Louisa said. 'Your mother lives there. She's expecting you.'

Christopher seized up suddenly, the seat creaking beneath him. 'Oh right,' he said. He ducked his head and peered at the purple door. 'But what about—?'

'You said you wanted to see her.'

'Erm. Yes.'

'Well then. Off you go.'

He opened the door slowly and stepped down out of the van.

'Your case,' she said.

'Oh right,' he said. 'Erm. How long am I staying?'

Louisa sighed. Christopher pulled the case down off the seat, bumping it against the paintwork and then the black pavement, as treacly and soft as the top of a Bakewell pudding. A business card floated to the ground, and Christopher picked it up and put it in his pocket automatically. 'These cases are virtually, erm, in, erm, destructible,' he said under his breath, and then louder he said, 'Louisa?'

'I can't take responsibility for you,' she said. 'Do you know what you did to me? I have absolutely nothing left.'

Christopher backed away from the van.

'Just tell me one thing,' she said. 'Did you mean it? Did you do it on purpose?'

He screwed up his face with the effort of thought. 'Erm. Sometimes I have one too many,' he said.

Louisa leaned over and shut the van door. She saw Cynthia standing on the front step of her house. She was still thin, her hair like a short curved blade. She did not look at Louisa. Both women watched Christopher as he marched towards the house, dragging his suitcase behind him.

*   *   *

Maggie had slept through her check-out time. She woke in a light just a few grades brighter than the night before. The car park outside her window was submerged, and the fire-escape rattled with the overflow of the drains.

Her boots squeaked on the marble-effect rubber floor as she approached the front desk. She could hear the muffled drone of a conference from one of the function rooms. The receptionist wore a badge that read 'Nick'.

'Any chance of me getting out of here today?' Maggie said.

Nick consulted his computer. 'It'll be tough to make it any further east,' he said. 'There's a big stretch of the A47 closed with the flooding. A17 is trailing way back, too.'

'Right. But it doesn't seem too bad, here,' Maggie said.

'It's heading this way,' Nick said, earnestly. 'You can get back okay. The roads are clear going inland.' He made one final check on his computer. 'Yep,' he said. 'Yeah, if you're going in the direction of Nottingham, you'll be fine.'

'I wouldn't say that,' Maggie said with a smile. 'Thanks.'

She began to walk out towards the restaurant. 'Madam?'

Maggie spun towards him.

'Don't you have any bags?'

Maggie smiled. 'I left them in the car,' she said, sure that she was not the only person in this hotel to sleep in their clothes.

She called the man in Norfolk and cancelled the visit. He was somewhat relieved, having been up before daybreak tending to storm damage on the farm. 'Some other time,' she told him, wondering when.

Maggie drank two cups of coffee and got back on the road. She called in on a vet in Derby and ran some errands in the city, setting out for the park in the late afternoon twilight. The weather worsened as she travelled home. It was like watching the world melt. Soon the land was glassy. Verdigris moss patched the stone walls; the power station towers rose in the distance. How had this place become home? She had known no such landscape as a child, and yet from the moment she arrived in Derbyshire, she had felt its resonance, as though the gorges and undulations were replicated precisely within her on some smaller scale. She had read that brain matter could physically change shape, could be carved out or soldered by experience. She believed that. She thought of Christopher watching his Robin Hood tapes in the living room. What shaped his mind? His father had died clutching the ground as though it were the sheer face of a cliff, like the joke about the drunk.

It was dark by the time she reached Detton, and parts of the village were now impassable. She took a high route, welcoming the pressure in her ears as she climbed Drum Hill. The flanks of the road had collapsed, and were running back down the slope in a thick rope of mud; Maggie thought of the thinning treads on Louisa's old van, and resolved to warn her.

When she got to the driveway she saw the water running from all sides of the diving platform. She heard the noises of the animals. But she did not see the ruin of the aviary, which was steeped in darkness beyond her vision.

Maggie took her bag out of the Land Rover and made her way to the house. Her curls stayed in the shape of the headrest. The house was cold, but there was no real flooding. A few leaks here and there, nothing urgent. She called Christopher's name into the dark, and received no reply. Nothing unusual about that, even when he was home. After keeping herself awake for the drive, the tiredness now hit Maggie hard. She climbed the stairs to bed without turning on a single light, and was asleep by seven, none the wiser.

Twenty-nine

Christopher had felt conscious of his filthy boots on the carpet. It was a light colour, and so springy that the platform of mud on his soles stayed firmly on the surface. It was like some kind of coral, and he was by no means employing false flattery when he said, 'This carpet is truly beautiful.'

'We think so,' said Cynthia.

His heart rate was, he acknowledged, through the roof. He did not really recognise her the way he thought he would. Her eyes were blue, her jumper was baby blue, and she had a bluish light in her skin, too, the way milk sometimes does. He decided not to examine her body.

'With the carpet in mind, do you think you could take your boots off?' Cynthia said.

'Oh right,' he said. He slipped off the boots without bending down. He used his toes to flip them out of the door and onto the path. 'Erm. Adios,' he said. 'Adios amigos.'

In his damp socks, and with the door closed to seal in the quiet,

Christopher absorbed the details of the place: spotlights on the ceiling, a clock which was just two hands stuck to the wall, and a professional-looking photograph of Cynthia, a man, and a little girl, all of them wearing black, posing in front of a white background. He laughed. Cynthia followed his gaze, and pointed to each model in turn.

'This is Mike, my husband. This is me, obviously, and this is Georgia, although she's grown since then. She's thirteen, now. She hates that picture.'

'Erm, erm. The teenage years are a time of turbulence and rapid change.'

'Yes,' said Cynthia.

'I found them quite, erm, turbulent myself. I shouldn't worry.'

'No. We're not worried. She's fine.'

'And then you've got to factor in, erm, sexual awakening.'

Cynthia looked away.

'Who actually *is* Georgia?' Christopher said.

'She's my daughter. You'll probably meet her a little later if you—'

'Oh *right*. My half-sister. I didn't know I had a sister. Or even half of one.' He stared at the picture and began to laugh again. 'You all look like you're out of a magazine,' he said.

Cynthia searched his face. 'Welcome,' she said, as if beginning a sentence. 'Welcome.'

As the afternoon turned dark outside, Christopher sat on a soft sofa with his arm along the back, warmed by the hot fin of the radiator. He had sat there, in such a position, for several hours. He balanced a cup of tea on the armrest and watched a film on the TV.

It was a western, about a stranger who helps a poor homestead family. It was a good film, but everything the characters did made Christopher feel like crying. When the funny little boy of the family asked his father if he could beat the stranger in a fight, Christopher found he had to hold his breath. He put it down to his hangover. And emotional turbulence.

Cynthia made phone calls in a room upstairs. She had work to do, she said. Her voice reached him in quick, faint tremors, like a quivering bowstring. 'Twang,' Christopher said out loud.

He turned off the television when it started to get too much, because he didn't want his mother to think he was a baby. The bare insides of his forearms had started to itch, and he scratched them vigorously. He remembered the business card falling out of Louisa's van, and he pulled it from his pocket now. *Adam Gregory. Public Accompaniments and Home Visits.* Christopher frowned, but before he could work out what it meant, he heard the front door open. The noise of the outside world – the rain and yawning air and motors – was shocking, and brought attention to the silence of the house.

A girl breathed heavily, out of sight in the hallway. She came into view via the mirror on the living room wall, her shoes in one hand as she walked to the coat closet. She was short, her hair wet and scraped back, dark-rimmed spectacles rain-blotched at the end of her nose. She took off her coat and hung it on a hook inside the closet. Christopher stood and walked to the living room door-way, his feet so quiet on the carpet that she didn't hear him approach. He could smell the damp wool of her jumper, a trace of smoke. She squeezed out four tablets of chewing gum, crunched them in one side of her mouth, then reached down under her jumper, pulled a packet of cigarettes from her shirt pocket and went to put them inside her coat.

'Howdy,' said Christopher.

She spun quickly and closed the door, trying at the last moment to hide her shock. 'Hi,' she said. Her eyes widened. 'Oh hi,' she said. 'Mum said you might ... I'm Georgie.'

'I'm Christopher Bryant.'

'Right.'

'Erm. Howdy.'

She smiled and held her breath. 'Have you seen my mum?'

'Erm. Yes. She looks quite nice but I haven't got to know her yet.'

Georgia laughed. 'No. I mean, do you know where she is, right now?'

'She said she was, erm, erm, working.'

'Thanks,' Georgia said. She turned and climbed the stairs.

The early part of dinner would have been quiet, but the powerful central heating gave Christopher nasal congestion, which meant he had to breathe through his mouth while chewing his food. It sounded like an eighties electric guitar effect. Cynthia kept her head down, while Georgia began to relax a little, looking from Christopher to her mother.

'Erm, erm. I like beans,' Christopher said.

'Good source of protein,' said Georgia.

Christopher laughed, thinking of his father's argument for carnivores. 'Erm. Protein is the building blocks of life,' Christopher said. 'And that's the clean version.'

Cynthia poured water into Christopher's glass. He beamed

and thanked her. 'Erm. I thought you'd be a right witch,' he said
to her.

Georgia gasped.

'Is that what—? Who told you that?' said Cynthia.

'No one. Erm. It was just a hunch.'

Cynthia shook her head slowly.

'There have been a lot of women in my life,' Christopher said.
He did not mention Louisa Smedley, but he spoke at length about
Maggie. Maggie Bryant, he called her. 'Erm. We were partners in
crime, in some ways.'

Nobody interrupted. Cynthia sighed and cleared her throat.

'She was really, erm, really fast,' Christopher said.

'What do you mean?' said Cynthia, quietly. Georgia looked at
her mother with an expression of surprise.

'I mean, erm, I could usually beat her over short distances. The
fifty metre dash. But anything longer than that, she would always,
erm, pip me to the post. We had some really classic battles. Erm.
It was Clash of the Titans, at times. Maggie's specialty was the
erm, uphill race. She had tireless stamina.'

'What do you mean, *had*?' Cynthia said.

Christopher looked up, finished his mouthful of chicken, beans,
potato, water. 'She doesn't run any more. Don't suppose she has
the, erm, time.'

The empty shell of a baked bean dropped through the water in
his glass, losing its colour as it fell.

Cynthia took the plates through to the kitchen and loaded the
dishwasher. Christopher could hear her muttering. He stared out
of the window at the dark wet street, the brakelights of the halting
cars spreading through the droplets like red thistletops. 'Where's

the man of the house?' Christopher asked, scratching at his arms, one after the other.

'Dad's at a conference,' said Georgia. 'Not back till tomorrow.' She had begun to look fragile again. She picked at her dark nail polish. On her little fingernail, there was barely room for a brush-stroke. They sat in silence for a while.

'It's my long-term goal to be, erm, man of a house one day,' Christopher said.

Cynthia marched back into the room and slammed a packet of cigarettes on the table in front of Georgia. 'Right. Georgia. These. On the floor of the closet,' Cynthia said, the pitch of her voice uneven, breaking.

Christopher reached across and took the packet, slid it under the table. 'Erm, erm, in the pocket of Christopher,' he said.

Cynthia and Georgia continued to stare at each other. Georgia's glasses, even with the lenses thinned, magnified her eyes. She was completely still.

Cynthia squinted at her daughter and then turned to Christopher. 'Christopher, if you want to smoke, please do so at the bottom of the garden. It is slabbed, so you won't get muddy. Your boots were getting wet, so I put them on some newspaper in the utility room.'

'Oh right. I don't really fancy a cigarette right now. They're great and everything, but I'm not in the mood.'

Cynthia left the room again, and Christopher turned to Georgia and laughed. Georgia did not laugh. She wore the same stunned expression as she had when her mother banged the packet of cig-arettes on the table. The same expression she had when Christopher introduced himself. Christopher stopped laughing and nodded seriously. He leaned over to Georgia and whispered, 'Erm. There's nothing cool about emphysema.'

'Thank you,' Georgia said, and left Christopher alone at the empty table. A few moments later, Cynthia came in, her eyes rimmed red. The colour clashed with her silvery blue eye make-up. 'Let me show you where you'll be sleeping,' she said.

'But it's only early,' Christopher said.

She looked towards the stairs and waited until he stood.

THIRTY

For the first few seconds of the day, between opening her eyes and getting out of bed, Maggie felt better. She was happy to be anywhere but the Pylon Inn. She rose, and walked to the window. Looking out, she saw the shell of the aviary. She did not panic immediately, but became conscious of variousfragments of conversations and memories, all of them unreliable.

Maggie dressed quickly and ran out into the steady rain. She crossed the muddy field, stooping to roll up her jeans as she walked.

The aviary looked like a splintered crown. Between the blackened props Maggie could see the deformed metals and plastics of the bow perches and tools. Feathers stuck to the tar.

Any hopes Maggie might have had about the safety of the hawks were extinguished when Louisa answered the door, haggard and red-eyed, her neck covered in patches of raw skin like scraped brick. Maggie put her arms around her. She barely noted

314

Louisa's rigid resistance. 'What happened?' Maggie said, smelling the staleness of Louisa's clothes.

'It's not completely clear,' Louisa said in one tone.

'How many?'

'All of them.'

'No.'

'Diamond got out, but I lost him.'

'I'm so sorry,' Maggie said, beginning to cry.

'So am I.'

Maggie tried to turn her friend so they could go into the cottage, but Louisa did not budge. 'Louisa what are you going to do?' she said.

'I don't know. Nothing.'

'You have to start again.'

Louisa bowed her head and let out a brief, crooked laugh.

'I can help you,' Maggie whispered. 'I want to.'

'Nobody can help me. I've let my guard down recently and this is the result.' She gestured to the ground with her left hand.

'What are you talking about?' Maggie asked.

'I'm not fit to be around people.'

'Louisa, come on,' Maggie said. She looked around her. She could hear the animals. 'Where's Christopher? At college?'

Louisa shrugged. The gesture would not have troubled Maggie, but then their eyes met. Maggie took a deep breath, her mind reaching for something that she could not quite articulate. 'Is he alright?'

'I don't know. I didn't know you'd be back so soon, actually. So he's at his mother's.'

Maggie did not understand. 'His mother's? You don't mean

Cynthia, surely? Why is he there?' There was a sharpness in Maggie's voice, and Louisa returned it.

'Because I took him there.'

'And why did you do that?'

'Why do you think?' Again she gestured at the ground, more vehement this time.

Maggie stepped away and looked at the aviary. 'He did that?'

Louisa shrugged again. 'A lot happened last night.'

'But Louisa, he wouldn't have done that. What happened?'

'Like I said. A lot.'

'He wouldn't have done that. Not on purpose.'

'What has purpose got to do with it? I'm not responsible for him. I couldn't be, after that. They're all dead. I was lenient. Anyway.'

'Anyway, what? He's not a well boy, Louisa. You don't know what this kind of situation could do to him. His mother didn't *want* him. She didn't even want to *see* him. It's been fifteen years.'

'Look. He's too frightened to hurt anybody, and he's got too much self-interest to hurt himself.'

'Fuck you. Fuck you for even thinking that.'

Maggie began to run back towards the big house, slipping and sticking in the mud. Louisa, a second of outrage still left in her, took a step out onto her path and shouted, 'He's old enough to know better.' Maggie did not offer the obvious reply.

* * *

As she stood before Cynthia Driscoll at the door of the house, Maggie recalled David describing her as 'a bit icy'. It appeared that he had been surrounded by such women; women with complicated roots of bitterness stretching back before Maggie was even born.

'I thought he'd probably just gone back to you,' Cynthia said.

'He hasn't,' Maggie said, and the woman almost shrugged. Maggie heaved the suitcase out of the door.

With a jolt, Maggie realised that Christopher was this woman's son, not hers, that the exchange was all backwards. 'So you don't have any idea where he is?' Maggie said.

'Look, he's a grown boy. I'm sure he'll be fine. You can tell Louisa that I took him in, though, so ... ' She raised her hands, as if to suggest that she had done her duty, that the problem was no longer hers.

Maggie had no time to argue. She tried to stem her growing sense of panic. 'Yes, thank you,' she said. As Cynthia closed the door, Maggie scanned the fields around the estate. Her vision of this landscape was blighted by lack of familiarity, and the rising waters, which had begun to rob the plain of landmarks. Cynthia's house was on high land, but lower down the villages were brown, the roofs of cars humped like pills in a blister pack. She hoped to God that Christopher wasn't drunk.

She started from Cynthia's road and drove towards home, snaking through the parallel streets at a slow pace. If Cynthia had woken at 6 a.m. to find him gone, he could have spent the night outside. Normally, Maggie would have willed him to keep to the country, away from the towns where a boy like him could find trouble, but the flood plain was a death-trap.

Back home she spoke to Philip and the other staff, none of whom had seen Christopher. Philip filled in the details of the fire. 'Awful business,' he said, and Maggie could see that he meant it sincerely.

She went to Christopher's room again, looking for clues. The wardrobe had been hastily emptied of clothes, leaving behind videotapes, childhood books, pornography. Shirts hung raggedly by collars where Louisa had tried to tear them free; some garments had dropped to the floor. The room smelled of Christopher's unwashed hair and the residual traces of David's aftershave. Clags of dirt were caught in the fibres of the thin carpet.

Christopher's bed was lumpy and unmade, the impression of his chin still on the pillow. Maggie leaned over the bed now and buried her face in the covers. Her grief was in the floors and ceilings of this house – the memories and signs of people who were too rarely in the same room as she was. On those summer nights when David had out-drunk her and she lay in bed, she would feel the resonant hum of his voice caught in the floorboards beneath her. If she felt too hot beneath the sheets, she would lie on the floor with her cheek against the vibrations.

And on those days when she came in from her first two hours' work out in the fields she would hear David getting dressed upstairs – the three pumps of the hairspray. She knew that his eyes would be narrowed and he would have one hand shielding them, as though he were looking out to sea.

One morning, after he had gone, she had woken to find the cover on the attic had slid across slightly, leaving a thin slat of darkness. It had made her feel helpless for reasons she could barely describe.

She knew she could not lose anyone else.

*   *   *

Adam tried to drive out of Detton, through the tunnel of pines. It was mid-afternoon, and the weather kept him at a funereal ten miles per hour. He felt a familiar sense of oppressive agency, some giant hand on the roof of his car. The windscreen was just a blue wash-out. He was struck by a sense of physical futility, and so stopped at the Strutt Arms on the outskirts of the village, got himself a pint and a window seat, and looked out on the crushing folds of the weir. The water was almost up at the bridge.

The pub was empty but for a couple of bar staff playing the fruity. Adam was reading the explanation of water-powered mills when his phone rang – a withheld number. Another recommend, probably. There was always work to throw yourself into, its sweet disgrace.

'Aye?'

'Erm. Howdy. Is that Adam Gregory?'

'Christopher?'

'Erm. No. It's a sexy lady and I just wondered if I could have a erm, erm, home visit.'

'Where are you, pal?'

'I didn't know you were an American Gigolo. I did think it was a bit strange that my new arch-nemesis Smedley had a boyfriend. Given her appearance and personality. Now it all makes sense. Erm. Does it mean I'm off the hook, at all?'

'Youth. Did you really do the aviary?'

'Eh? I put my hand on her, erm, leg, but it was just an affectionate gesture between, erm, friends,' Christopher said.

'What are you talking about? Where are you?'

'Two-faced Smedley dumped me at my mother's.'

'Your mother's? You mean Maggie?'

'No. How could Maggie be my mother? Erm. We're practically classmates.'

'Oh,' Adam said. He thought hard. Louisa had told him about Christopher's mother. Not good.

'But I've buggered off, anyway. I've decided I don't really like the bourgeois life. I could probably live quite comfortably off the land.'

'If you could find it.'

'Yes, it's not very, erm, clement out. Erm. I hate that saying: "it's raining stair rods". If it was raining stair rods, we'd all be killed. It's the magic of the greenwood for me, from now on. It's the only place I really fit in.'

Adam thought of Louisa, of the birds. Where would Christopher stay if he could not come home? 'Listen, do you fancy a pint, youth? I'm in Strutt.'

'Erm. No thanks. I've things to do. Besides, I don't drink, now. It's impure.'

'Is that because of what happened the other night?'

'Erm. Why does everyone keep banging on about the other night? I touched a woman's leg. It's not like I murdered anyone. It's not like I'm a bloody, erm, *prostitute*.'

'You don't know what happened to the aviary.' It just occurred to him. It was not a question.

'Erm. What?'

'You didn't go in there? Yesterday morning? The bird house?'

'I don't even know where it, erm, is. I went to college yesterday morning. Erm. I left at the crack of dawn.'

Adam swore under his breath.

'There's no need for that,' said Christopher.

'The aviary burned down, lad.'

'Oh right.' Christopher said. He was silent for a moment. 'Louisa must have gone ballistic. Oh. Right.'

Adam put his elbow on the table, which was sticky with cleaning fluid. He put his head in his hand.

'I don't think I need my Zuclopenthixol any more,' Christopher said. 'I feel just fine. A little bit dreamy, maybe.'

'Listen pal, just tell me where you are.'

'Phone box,' Christopher said, giving a grizzly laugh.

'Yeah, but ... Look. Y'ought to come home. You can't hang around out there. It's dangerous.'

'Erm. I'm not coming home. What's *home* anyway? I can make my home in the forest.'

'You'll catch your death.'

'That's a good one. Erm. I like that one.'

'You can kip at mine.'

'No thanks. I hate it when people say "ring off" as well. You don't *ring* off. Erm. What is it that rings when you hang up?'

'Eh?'

The line went dead.

'Fucking Ada,' Adam said to himself. The two bartenders looked round briefly, but a tinkling crescendo from the fruit machine regained their attention. Adam finished his pint quickly but then realised he had nowhere to go. He thought of what Christopher had said, and called the fire service.

'I wonder if you know anything about the fire up at Drum Hill,' he said.

'With the birds?'

'Aye.'

'Nasty one. You from papers?'

'No. I was there. I called it in. Do you know how it started yet?'

''Lectrical fire, that one. Likely as not. Can't say for definite how it cracked off.'

'Oh. It wasn't from a fag or oat like that, then?'

'No way. Wood were sodden. Wire and water, that. Been a few on 'em, this last few days.'

'Right.'

'One a them things, I'm afraid.'

Adam hung up. He checked his phone for details, but there were no clues as to where Christopher had called from. He thought of speaking to Maggie, but what good would that do, if she was away? It struck him, also, that she would not answer the phone if his name came up on her caller ID. Most people, he realised, probably did not assign a real name to his number in their phone memories. He had forgotten, temporarily, what he was to people. It hadn't really mattered before.

He caught sight of himself in the window. The thought of being in love – he had shot it out of the sky, before now. But he pictured Louisa in that field, mud all over her clothes, the smell of cinders and rain. The feelings were like nothing he had ever imagined, and he knew he could not change them.

THIRTY-ONE

Christopher had been unable to sleep, for one thing. The room that Cynthia put him in had clearly been Georgia's when she was a little girl. Rather than redecorate, they had simply started her teenage room somewhere else, and left the childhood one behind. A globular sky-blue lantern with rainbows on it surrounded the lightbulb. The remnants of half-peeled stickers glittered on the walls, and Christopher noted the assortment of wooden boxes with keyholes. By the bed, one of these small boxes was open, and four dried-out seahorses – two big, two small – lay on tissue paper inside. The bed itself was a narrow single, and Christopher's feet hung off the end. This did not trouble him so much, but he was accustomed to the huge room at Drum Hill, and here it felt like the walls were caving in on him.

On his way to bed that night he had heard Georgia in her room, crying on the phone. Perhaps she had called her father, Mike. Perhaps she had called a friend. Perhaps she had just been talking out loud, as *he* sometimes did, though Christopher doubted that.

He looked at the wooden boxes around the room, and tried to imagine Georgia hiding things in them, as a little girl. It was difficult. What was more bewildering was the thought that, as Georgia had played in this room, Christopher himself, at the very same time, had played only twenty or so miles away. When she was four, he would have been nine, still at primary school with his special tutor. When he was fourteen, wishing for wet dreams, and dangling his feet in the brook, she would have been eight. A whole life going on parallel to his own. It was difficult to imagine.

He didn't know her, but then again she didn't know him. For a few sad moments he experienced the situation from her point of view: the teenage years were a time of great upheaval, and the last thing you needed was some massive psycho turning up claiming to be your half-brother.

He thought of the woods back home. They were lush and junglish in the rain. With all the things Robin Hood stole, he could have redistributed the wealth and still had enough left over to settle in a decent castle. But he didn't. Sometimes it felt good just to knock the walls down and get to somewhere that's been there forever.

Christopher rose from the bed. He had not removed his clothes, just rolled his sleeves up to let his itchy forearms get some air. He tried to lift his suitcase, but it was too much of a burden, so he walked downstairs without it. In his coat pocket, he still had Louisa's US Air Force T-shirt, which he had stolen after vomiting in her bathroom, back when they were friends.

He walked through the heavy smoothness of the house, retrieved his boots from the utility room, carried them to the front door, and quietly put them on. On the driveway he turned and raised his hand in a stiff goodbye salute. As he walked away, he felt a twitch of light fall on the pavement, just for a second.

The night had not been so bad. He had a student bus pass, and once he got to Nottingham he had just sailed up and down the A52 on the Red Arrow, watching the rowdy young drunks swap cities every half-hour. The Red Arrow smelled of sticky sweet perfume and sticky sweet alcohol, mint sauce and red onion, and hair gel – the kind with bubbles in it. Christopher recoiled from the distorted appearance of a boy with a stretched condom pulled over his head, the seriousness of his face as he waved to the cars on the road long after his friends had stopped laughing. At one point, a lad wearing dog tags and a gladiatorial belt approached Christopher, and asked that most dangerous of questions between Nottingham and Derby:

'Eh up. Mate. Who do you support?'

'Erm. I don't support anyone at the moment,' Christopher said. 'But no one supports me, either. One day I hope to be the man of a house, and support a whole raft of children.'

The lad squinted in the glare of the reading light, considered the answer for a moment, and then went back to his seat. 'Nah. Not worth it,' he said to his friends.

The buses began to empty at around 3 a.m., and Christopher saw the slow blinks of the driver in the rear-view mirror. He had a wrinkly bald head and low eyes which made his face look upside down. Christopher cleared his throat conspicuously every ten seconds, to keep the driver awake, until, eventually, he fell asleep himself.

His rest was disturbed by a voice, and when he woke there was an old-style bus conductor standing over him. This would have been fine – he had a valid ticket – but for the fact that the conductor had antlers. 'Who the, erm, eff are you?' said Christopher.

'*Tickets to Cromm Cruac,*' the conductor said. Christopher handed him his Peak Saver ticket, in which the conductor made a little tear before returning it, and disappearing.

At 8 a.m., Christopher left the Red Arrow and spotted a bus in Nottingham station with the word 'Sherwood' on the display. He had been feeling a little anxious, and wondered if it might be a hallucination, but he got on the bus anyway. He told the bus driver that he was going on a pilgrimage. 'Just ring the bell when you want to get off,' she said.

Sherwood, when he got there, was just a normal urban area, with an average high street on a persistent incline. It had a betting shop, an Indian take-away, a few pubs, and a Co-op. It was cold and wet. The local youngsters must have been thankful for their woolly hats and hoods.

Christopher bought a tin of tuna and a bread roll from the Spar. 'Erm. I'm not very impressed with Sherwood, I must say,' he told the man behind the till.

'It's an up and coming area, mate.'

'Not many open spaces.'

'There's a pitch and putt up there, past the pub.'

'Oh right. Erm. Do you know where the forest is, at all?'

'Forest? You mean the football?'

'No. Sherwood Forest.'

'Oh. Where the Holiday Park is, you mean? Few miles from here. Follow the signs for Center Parcs.'

'Oh right.'

Christopher turned away.

'*Nothing is forgotten,*' the man said.

'What?' said Christopher.

'I didn't say anything,' the man said, shaking his head at Christopher.

Christopher had not bothered following the signs to Center Parcs. He had eaten his lunch on the first tee of the pitch and putt, caught the bus back to Derby, and then a train out to Detton. He had called Adam from the station.

As he approached Drum Hill now, he kept to the high side of the brook and off the main paths, tracking instead through the trees at the base of the hill. It was a good decision, for the brook had burst, and the wooden footbridge which crossed the water from the field was almost completely submerged. Only the handrails were visible, like the humped backbone of an animal. The fast-moving water was the colour and opacity of old women's tights.

Christopher edged along the gap between the brook and the steep rise of the hill until he reached the silver birch, which he used to swing himself towards the entrance to the den. Inside the den was a blanket, a sleeping bag, a torch, and a couple of copies of *Asian Bride* Magazine, which he had ordered thinking they were something else. Christopher removed his drenched coat, trousers, socks and pants, and dried himself off with the blanket. Then he wrapped it around his waist like a towel, and shuffled to the back of the den with the sleeping bag, where he watched the rain fall in the brook. It made him want to urinate. Shivering, he thought about taking a nap but his father had once told him that if you were stranded in the cold, you should not go to sleep, because your body temperature drops.

It's cold out, his father used to say. *Especially if you leave it out.* (It had taken Christopher a while to get that one.)

He had a whole host of sayings about the weather.

It's so cold, that when I took Monty (their old dog) *out for a wee, I had to chop him off a tree trunk.* (Christopher found that outrageously funny.)

Listening at a locked door, Christopher had once overheard his father say, 'We'll make a silk purse out of a sow's ear.' He had asked what it meant a few hours later, but his father had been shocked, and gave a muddled explanation about how brilliant Christopher was, and how nobody should ever tell him different.

Every path has a puddle. This was apt, right now. Christopher looked at his boot prints leading up to the den. Soon the treads would be washed away, the troughs filled.

Christopher decided to go when he saw the water coming in. Leaving his socks and pants at the back of the den with the blanket, he replaced his jeans and boots. His jumper was damp. He struggled into his coat, put his hand in the pocket, and was momentarily amazed to pull out a dry T-shirt. But then he remembered that it belonged to the Turncoat Louisa Smedley. After dipping it carefully in the brook, he balled the T-shirt up and hurled it across the water. It landed in the pooling water in the field. He looked down at his forearms, which had pink and white crosshatches from where he had scratched at the irritation.

He took an elevated route through the pines. Clumps of grass and earth came away in his hands like scalps as he climbed. The light reflected in the puddles and the sheen of bark played tricks on him. He closed his eyes, and when he opened them, he thought he saw movement in one of the boggy areas a hundred yards away. It was as though the mud was taking a human form, and standing up. Christopher looked at his boots, willing the vision away.

The funny thing about the woods, Christopher thought, as he arrived at the top of the hill amongst the swollen, naked trees, was that they were in you, as much as you were in them. Like that old saying about taking the boy out of the country, but not being able to whatever. And what was in you, was *your* woods, and once they took hold, it was pointless trying to find anywhere else.

That didn't mean the woods were always *nice*. Right now, the bare branches reminded him of the little vein things you see in biology diagrams of the lungs. Micro-villi. They were frightening when you thought of them like that: something turned inside out. A large drop of water ran off the end of a branch and went down his collar. Even from deep in the woods he could see the charred shape of the aviary out there in the fields.

Up ahead, between the trees, he saw the back of a man covered in mud. It was hanging off him like rags. Christopher was too far away to see with any great accuracy, but he could certainly make out that the man had a quite glorious branch-like set of antlers. It definitely wasn't the bus conductor. Christopher was not afraid; he wanted to know who the man was, and he tried to follow him, but the man was fast, and passed quickly out of sight.

Christopher trudged on, thinking back to the episode of *Robin of Sherwood* he had watched with Maggie, featuring Cromm Cruac, that village of the dead. Little John had dreamed over and over and over of his wife's murder. The outlaws had changed in his mind since then. They weren't very merry at all. They were disturbed and sorry and sad, full of regret and loss. Christopher had read of the crusades recently, too. Times, he thought, had not been pleasant.

He imagined the woods, crowded with the dead and gone: the last man to be hanged in Derby, who had sexual relations with a calf; the girl from his school who overdosed by her mother's grave; the ewe he had found trapped in the brook; all of Louisa's birds. That bloke who invented the Spinning Jenny.

Christopher heard the angry, shuddering blades of a helicopter moving overhead. It was one of those yellow rescue choppers, probably carrying some old dear who'd fallen off her roof. Christopher pulled out his Peak Saver ticket, and looked at the little tear.

If he imagined the dead inhabitants of the woods, and each of those individuals had imaginations of their own, then the place would be absolutely teeming with the loved and lost. Teeming. He said it out loud, and the word seemed to summon the antlered man, who appeared, closer this time. Christopher could see the frayed fabric where the antlers had burst through the man's hat.

The antlered man started to run away again. 'Wait,' Christopher said, marching on. He hoped that the man (and all of the other dead folk) had not heard him singing 'Hey Mona' earlier that week. It was very much a work in progress.

The diving platform looked like the champagne centrepiece of an ambassador's reception, the steps so worn that the water flowed down them, one to the other. It was quite stunning.

Christopher climbed the steps slowly, their rusted grids like grin-ning mouths.

When he got to the top, Christopher saw the antlered man one last time, standing at the edge of the platform. He had his back to Christopher, and appeared to be looking out over Detton. 'Erm, who do you think you are?' Christopher said.

The man did not answer. Christopher was tired. He tried to speak again, but the words sounded fragile. 'Why won't you turn around? I just, erm—'

The man held up his hand to silence Christopher. 'If I held you any closer,' he said, and Christopher began to cry, because he knew what was coming. The man shook his head, and started again. 'If I held you any closer, I would be on the other side of you.'

Christopher got down on his hands and knees and began to shiver. When he looked up, the man was gone. Nothing was left of him but the spiralled, velvety casings of the antlers, bloody inside. Christopher crawled to the end of the platform, and looked over the edge, but there was no sign of the man.

Should've known I'd get no answers from him, Christopher thought. Another one of his father's sayings came to mind: *Dead men tell no tales.*

Christopher wished they would. There were far too many miss-ing pages. But maybe it didn't matter. Maybe, if the true story of a man wasn't known, if there was no historical evidence, then Christopher had just as much right as anyone else to make it up himself.

When he looked down, his forearms seemed to be bleeding quite openly, the rainwater brightening the colour, washing it away as more came to replace it. It made him feel weak, but not unpleasant. Christopher tried to keep his eyes open. He continued to peer over the edge of the platform, watching the world gain weight.

THIRTY-TWO

The door to Louisa's cottage was open, so Adam stepped inside. He could smell spilt whisky, wet mud, and the overpowering stench of several kilos of raw meat and defrosting mice and chicks.

He found her upstairs in bed. Her lower leg hung out from the covers, thick all the way to the ankle. For a moment he felt sickened, as he sometimes did on visiting a client.

Louisa was not asleep. She turned her head towards him. 'What are you doing?' she said.

He stayed quiet because, in truth, he did not know.

'When did it become okay for you to just walk into my house?' she said.

'I've quit,' he said. 'I've quit my job.'

'At the golf course?'

'No,' he said.

She did not speak.

'And I need your help for a bit,' he said.

'What could you possibly need me for?'

'The lad. Christopher. He's gone awol.'

'No he hasn't. He's at his mother's.'

'He ran off from his mother's,' Adam said.

'How do you know?'

'He rang me.'

He could see Louisa take a moment to process that information. The world was not as predictable as she would have it. 'That's nice,' she said.

He stared at her. She sat up in the bed, keeping the covers at her chin. 'He'll be back,' she said. 'How long's he been gone? A day? It's nothing. I've already had *her* ranting and raving. I don't know what the fuss is about.'

'He sounded weird on the phone. He takes them tablets, doesn't he? And it's waist high water in the village. I'm just going to drive around.'

'Oh, I see. Yeah, of course. Why don't you and her go and look for him together?'

'What you on about?' he said, feeling his temper begin to rise. He found her self-destruction childish. 'I told you what happened. I didn't do anything with her.'

'Do you know what she said to me, today, at the door?' Louisa said.

'Do you know what you *did*? You dumped that kid.'

'He fucking burned down my—'

'He didn't. He didn't do it. Nobody did. It were an electrical fire,' he said.

'Rubbish. There was nothing wrong with my electrics.'

'I spoke to the fire service. Wire and water, they said.'

She looked away. He held out his hand. 'Look. I know you're torn up,' he said.

'You know nothing,' she hissed. 'All I ever asked was to be left alone. I gave my life to those hawks.'

He saw his gym bag in the corner of the room, and retrieved it. He slung it over his shoulder, but then came back to sit on the bed. Louisa glared at him, but he did not move. 'You said that one of them got out,' he said.

'Diamond. He's long gone. I fed him up. He doesn't need me any more.'

'I thought you kept them beeper jobs on them. On their tails.'

'I take them off every—'

But she stopped, as if receiving a jolt. Adam watched her stroke the back of her own hand, acting out some strange ritual. 'God,' she said. 'I didn't. I didn't take it off.'

She rose from the bed, forgetting her nakedness for a moment before quickly pulling on pants and jeans and a green combat jumper. Adam stood too, nodding. 'You're going to come with me?' he said.

'No,' she said, picking up her keys and a torch.

He followed her down the stairs. She pulled a clunky old telemetry transmission receiver from the closet, turned it on and started scrolling through the frequencies. The machine pipped. To Adam it looked as though Louisa had been resuscitated. 'Less than sixty miles,' she muttered. She pulled rope and leashes and her boots from the closet and put the transmission receiver into a bright orange rucksack, with the aerial coming out of the top.

'What are you doing?' he said.

'Going to find my hawk,' she said.

'You're fucking joking.'

'I'm not,' she said, quick and active now, tying back her hair. 'You and her go off and play happy families. The boy will be home in a bit anyway so make sure he doesn't catch you at it.'

'Fuck you.'

'Fuck *you*. All of you.'

Adam moved in front of the door. Louisa put her hand beyond him onto the frame but he knocked it away forcefully. She held her wrist and looked up.

'It'd be easier for you if I left, wouldn't it?' he said.

'Right now, yes.'

'You know what I mean. It would be easier for you if I walked away, so you could say, "*Adam Gregory is weak. He abandoned me. If I ever saw him again, I'd kill him.*" Same things you said about all those other folk you dumped. Because you fucking *did* fucking dump them. Christopher, me, her over the way.'

'Listen,' Louisa said.

'No. You listen. I'm not giving in. I'm not having you slating me to some cunt in that pub when you know . . . when you *know* you made a mistake.'

'*I* made a mistake?' she said.

'Yes, you. It's easier to just fuck people off than to deal with it. Well. I'm not going.' He threw his bag so that it skidded across the kitchen tiles. 'I will look for that boy, and I will come back here. Because what happened between you and me on that first night was right. Fucking right. I haven't felt like that since I was fifteen years old, and I haven't felt like *this* ever. And I know you've got it, too. Tell me you haven't.'

She looked at his bag, crumpled in the corner like a squeeze-box. 'Let me out,' she said.

'I'm going to look for the lad. But whatever you do, you're not fucking rid of me,' he said, nodding at the bag. He turned and walked out, shutting the door behind him.

The rain felt cool and pleasant coming down on the raised veins of his hands, and up through the soles of his trainers. Walking out to his car, he saw Maggie outside her house, loading the Land Rover and speaking into her mobile. He had not intended to go with her, but now it seemed logical. His car wouldn't get through the water in the village, anyway. He crossed the field. She saw him and gave a preoccupied wave of acknowledgement. Then she realised who he was and finished her phone call.

'Hi,' he said.

'Hello. Can I help you?' she said.

'I was about ask you the same thing.'

'My son is missing.'

'Aye,' Adam said. 'I know.'

Maggie narrowed her eyes, and then looked over at Louisa's cottage. 'I'm going out to look for him.'

'I'd like to help,' Adam said. The RAF helicopter made them both look up, imagining the worst.

THIRTY-THREE

Before beginning her search, Louisa sat in the darkened living room for a long time, listening to the measured pips from the transmission receiver, the red light flashing through the mesh of the orange rucksack. Her boy. Her diamond from the dust-heap.

She had waited for the sound of the Golf's engine, and when that was not forthcoming she had looked out of the window. Clearly, they had taken Maggie's Land Rover. Her anger faded to regret. She had practically pushed him into crossing the field to Maggie's house.

Adam's bag was one of those leather-look ones from the nineties, the top colour flaking away to reveal the yellowed sack-cloth beneath. It was typical of him that he still had the bag he had taken to his school PE lessons, as though normal life had stopped in his teens. She picked it up, along with her own orange ruck-sack, and took them outside. The rain pinged off Adam's car. It filled the drains on her roof, making the plastic creak beneath the weight. The familiar sound of rain against the mesh of the empty weatherings rang out – the regular dwellings of her birds were still perfectly untouched.

They would be looking for Christopher down in the village: the White Hart and the off-licence; the back of the Co-op where the cardboard boxes would be rain-beaten to the consistency of porridge; Foxton's butchers where he sometimes bought a cob filled with pork and apple sauce. They would be driving further out towards the college, and the houses of his teachers and counsellors and two-faced doctors, and to the homes of people he sometimes listed as his friends when he needed an alibi for some dubious mission.

Louisa reached down into her orange rucksack and turned off the transmission receiver. She walked towards her neighbour's land, leaving both bags behind on her front step.

They did not know his mind the way she did. She shared no blood with him, no official bond, and for much of his life they had ignored each other, but they shared a territory. She also shared Christopher's desire to walk away – to put a flat palm up to the intricate humiliations of life with other people. This time, however, she would not let herself do that.

Louisa spent an hour in the woods, which were dark and livid in the wet. All she found were the abandoned accessories of Christopher's childhood: a blue tarpaulin, an old tyre, a knotted rope snapped seven feet from the ground; beer cans in various stages of degradation, and a Power Ranger figurine, half-buried, with its legs in the air. Water had filled the mouth of the fibreglass tyrannosaurus, and now poured out between the teeth, as though the dinosaur was salivating.

The collapsing of sodden branches had given her a couple of false leads, but when she emerged from the trees, she did so without much hope. She sheltered for a moment beneath the diving platform, dodging the thick droplets coming down from the edge. Maybe they were right, she thought. Maybe he was in the village.

Walking back towards the cottage to get the van, she looked over at the ruins of the aviary, the black wood shining in some places like film. For a while, in the woods, she had forgotten the hollow pain in her chest, but she knew that it would never leave her for good.

She started the van and pushed off down the hill. At the end of the descent, the road swung left and ran parallel to the brook. It wasn't until she was half a mile down this road that she remembered the den. It had been built, after all, with her own cast-off materials. She remembered the moment with David in her kitchen, the steam from her mug, the boy coming into the room. She stopped the van.

For the first time since her arrival at Drum Hill, the field was completely underwater. The flood plain was almost still, the weaving flows and currents from various sources of water barely visible on the surface. It was a broken yolk. Louisa looked across at the den beyond the brook, and bit her thumbnail. She thought of David and the boy splashing and playing in that brook when it was nothing more than a trickle, when you could see the tiny fish in there and read the labels on the discarded packaging that floated by. Now the water was lapping at the entrance to the den. And the longer she sat watching from the van, the more certain she became that Christopher was inside. If he wasn't in the den, he was in trouble.

Then she saw the piece of clothing. It floated on the surface in the middle of the temporary lake, shiny and bloated. It was dark blue, and quite a distance from the den. Had she not seen it, she might have turned the van around and driven back across the little bridge – even though it would have taken time, time which she imagined to be running out. But as it was, the sight of the fabric was enough to make her get out of the van and run down into the field. 'Christopher,' she shouted. She could not have guessed the height of the flood, and she fell forward into the water immediately, smacked by the cold of it, her head going under and then coming up, the shock kicking in. She gasped, pumped her arms, and was reminded of the tingling feeling when she had fallen from her bike as a child, that numb purgatory before the pain took hold. When she regained her footing, she saw that the water was up to her chest. She called out for Christopher again as she waded towards the dark blue shape and heard her own voice, smeary and formless, echoing back from the pines. After a few more yards of slow progress, she could see that the piece of clothing contained no body, so she scanned the water, looking for any signs of movement. She was surprised by the effort it took to drag herself along, the outer layers of her body already heavy and devoid of sensation, like a granite casing.

She took hold of the garment, squeezing an air pocket from the cotton. She held it above her head, against the background of the pencil grey sky and the tall, sagging pines, and unpeeled the folds to see that it was her own T-shirt. Her stomach flipped as she tried to think of a rational explanation. She took three steps forward, still holding the T-shirt above her head, and then she was dragged under by the current.

In that flash of panic, the pressure of the culvert's suction contained such violence and intent that Louisa thought it was an animal. She got her head above water for a second, spat, gasped and was wrenched back under. A charge of pain rose up her leg as her right ankle lodged, and then cracked, against the grate of the inlet pipe. She fought to keep her left foot firmly on the ground, and it took several seconds – most of them submerged in the midnight of the floodwater – to regain her balance. She rose and spat the gritty mix until it was just saliva. The wild pressure from the drain tried to pull her flat, but she dug her left foot deep into the soft soil, tried to keep her chin in the air and the back of her head in the water. Her foot was trapped; the pain was constant and she knew the ankle was broken. Louisa was furious with herself. She took hold of her right thigh and tried to pull herself free, but nearly blacked out with the pain, and the effort destabilised her, caused her to swallow more of the foul water. She was now shivering wildly, and her body felt granulated, disintegrating.

As the moments passed, she grew calmer, and accepted the simple gravity of the situation. It seemed so strange to be standing upright, head just above the water, half a mile from her house containing her guitar, grill pan, ice-tray and Scotch. And yet she could not move. Such a predicament, she knew, would not last forever. She tried to think, but soon it became almost too cold to do even that.

Time moved on with the immeasurable blankness of the flooded field before her, and yet her temperature was dropping rapidly.

The nerves in her face sparked with cold and she was vaguely aware of her functions being stripped away. In the space of these stretched and silent moments, her knowledge of the outcomes, the stages and treatments of hypothermia came to her in a tangled mass. She had heard of animals that literally dug their own graves in a final act of terminal burrowing, and recalled reading that delirious sufferers often removed their own clothes. She remembered fragments of a list of symptoms from a first aid course. *Inertia, poor judgment and hallucinations.* With this in mind, she considered the sad possibility that she had been hypothermic for forty-seven years.

There were flashes of delirious wellbeing, but the pain was exhausting now, taking over. Soon she was fighting back the temptation to wish numbness upon herself. The loss of sensation, as it took hold, was so seductive, such a comfort. She nudged the trapped right foot just to provoke the distant hit of hurt.

Louisa began to notice gaps in her thoughts, little absences. She believed she saw Adam's sports bag float past along with Diamond on a duck's back, his wings outstretched. Her eyes kept closing; when they did, the culvert pulled her under and she had to haul herself back up, coughing up water as she broke out of the plummeting stoop. The last time she brought her head above the surface, she looked out across the dull void of the flooded field and stared up at the pines, which had never appeared so tall. This was a new angle. The entrance to the den was now submerged, and she thought of Christopher one last time, tried to will his name into a scream, although she could not move her lips. I have failed, she thought.

Closing one eye and then the other, she noticed that half of her vision was blue, everything a clean cobalt monochrome. As she withdrew into the stone of her body and relinquished herself to the pull of the water, she recalled a doctor on a TV news programme, commenting on a little boy trapped in the snow, his pulse slowed to a single beat per minute. *Doctors have a saying: you're not dead until you're warm and dead.* She had always believed that; lived her life by it.

She lost consciousness, and the water poured into her. Her breathing slowed, and her metabolism closed down with the cold. Some minutes later, her heart stopped.

Maggie was inside the hollowed chimney of the paper mill, staring up at the rain flashing in the circle of sky. It was the kind of place Christopher might have come to – abandoned, private, off-limits. But he wasn't there. Maggie quietly apologised to David, her words muffled by echoes, the sentences swallowing themselves. She walked back out to where Adam sat in the driver's seat of the Land Rover, his head bowed.

She had been unable to raise a substantial search party. Richie Foxton took his van out. The staff from the park, most of whom she dismissed as soon as they had fed the animals, promised to be vigilant on their journeys home. Philip Cassidy had gone out separately to search the pubs in Detton and the surrounding area. Reg Birkett, from the Parish Council, had refused to mobilise a team, claiming that most deaths and injuries in floods are sustained during ill-advised rescue attempts. The police told her much the same, said the best thing she could do was stay home and wait. If someone had spoken to Christopher today, as Adam had, then he couldn't really be classified as missing. They said she was overreacting.

In the Land Rover, she wound down the windows to clear the steam. Adam's familiar scent mixed with the fresh mud and wet stone smells from outside. 'Is Louisa going to look for Christopher?' she asked.

He kept his eyes on the road. 'Yes,' he said.

The field, when they reached it, appeared otherworldly, as if scattered with fragments of their premonitions: the fire and rescue team and the ambulance, its lights melting in the rain-twisted visor of their windscreen, the punctured vessel of the brook. The sight of the den, which Maggie had forgotten, now made her nauseous. 'Please, no,' she said, over and over. The rescue team were in life jackets and dry suits, some of them up to their necks in water, three of them surely carrying Christopher's body on a stretcher. She and Adam both jumped out of the van. Maggie plunged into the water and waded towards the stretcher. The men from the rescue team shouted at her to stay back. Philip Cassidy, who had arrived by the brook after searching the pubs and called the emergency services, went after Maggie, restrained her.

Adam stood for a moment on the road, his hands on his head, his lips pursed, for he had seen Louisa's empty van, the door open. He watched Maggie's reaction as Philip spoke to her. She frowned, and shook her head slowly. The paramedic called out to the men approaching the ambulance with the stretcher. 'We're going to have to intubate her. Nice and quick.'

Adam went down into the water too, but he could not move fast enough to get to the stretcher. The men in their dry suits passed him by, metres away. They looked like performers, their hands and arms moving in smooth powerful strokes as they loaded the stretcher onto the ambulance. Adam saw her. Just a glimpse of the body he had seen rising from the bed that afternoon.

Maggie was now calling after the last remaining members of the rescue team. 'My boy. Christopher,' she was saying. 'Do you know where he is?'

He was less than a mile away, but much higher. Christopher looked down from the diving platform on his woods, which were just a brown pincushion now, the silver slants of rain coming in through the opening lights of the houses and streets in the distance. An hour ago, Louisa had stood beneath him, run her hands through her hair, and pulled up the hood on her waterproof jacket. He thought of nachos and hot-dogs and whisky and cheesecake, and began to cry. In the distance, he could hear shouts and sirens. He started to move, to call back, because he thought the shouts were meant for him.

THIRTY-FOUR

From the corridor of the hospital, Maggie looked out on a poorly lit courtyard with a carp pond, a couple of benches, and a plastic heron standing at the edge of the water to deter real herons from landing there. Patients and visitors were prohibited from entering the courtyard because of the possibility of contracting salmonella from the fish. Maggie thought of what Christopher would have said on being confronted by such a rule. *That's ludicrous. I'm not going to have, erm, coitus with the bloody fish.* But he was not there to say it because he did not come to the hospital.

That afternoon on her way back to the house to make more phone calls, she had found him walking through the garden, in tears, his sleeves rolled up, his forearms out, a faint pink crosshatch of scratches on the skin. She held him, took most of his weight. He trembled against her. She took him into the house, gave him brandy and ran a bath for him. When he came out, she told him she was going to the hospital, and asked him to come along.

'After what she did to me?' he said. 'You must be insane.'

'But she was trying to—' Maggie stopped herself, realising what she was about to say, realising that Christopher would not be able to take it.

'Okay,' she said. 'Philip is downstairs if you need anything.' She held him again, couldn't help it.

It was after midnight when they finally stabilised Louisa. 'She's sedated,' the doctor said. 'The thing about hypothermia is that it's a preservative state. The cold protects the brain. We have to hope she got cold quickly, and that it did a good enough job. Her temperature is up now, so it's just a question of waiting.'

'How long will she be like this?' Maggie said.

The doctor turned down his mouth and shrugged.

'Will she get better?' Maggie said.

'Difficult to say. She was in cardiac arrest when they found her. She was almost completely unresponsive.'

That's just her way, Maggie had thought with a sad smile.

The vitiligo fish mooched around by the underwater lights, featureless. She thought of Louisa in that suspended realm, her body shut down, her mind alive. Maggie tried to imagine it as a pleasant place – somewhere solitary and clear. Somewhere Louisa would enjoy. The stillness of one long moment.

Adam came down the corridor in the dry clothes she had brought: Christopher's jeans turned up and gathered at the waist, a green polo shirt. His short hair was soft, his eyes red.

'Ta,' he said, pointing down at the clothes.

'You look ten years younger,' Maggie said.

'Any more news?'

'No.'

'Can I go and see her?' he said.

'Nurse said *family only*,' Maggie said, rolling her eyes.

In the early hours of the morning Maggie drove Adam back through the city, which was bright with the daubed reflection of its streetlight canopy. Out in the villages – where the power was down – the view was more sinister, the water lurking in syrupy, malignant pools. They looked away from the field when the headlights caught the reflective strips of swiftly erected hazard gates and signs. She pulled up by his car. 'Sake,' he said.

'You gonna be okay?' she said.

'I will if she will.'

Maggie nodded.

'We left it badly,' Adam said.

He got out of the car, unable to say more just then. His feet, in Christopher's too-big boots, sank into the pudding ground. Maggie left him with his hands in his pockets, looking at the two bags on the porch which loomed in the full beam, as if promising a holiday.

Over the next few days, there were complications in the ICU. An infection, pneumonia. Louisa was conscious but weak, unable to talk. Watching her strong-jawed, wide face, Maggie longed to see the brightness of her eyes.

In the intervals between these episodes, Adam and Maggie met in the pub across from the infirmary, or by the window looking out onto the carp pond. Adam told Maggie all he could remember of the last six months. Such was his way, he did not invent compliments from Louisa to Maggie, keeping instead to the real speech. Sometimes Maggie, delighted to recognise the behaviour of her friend in what Adam said, would laugh freely and then remember that they were sitting at the sorry end of the story. She would then stare into her drink, or at the sharp beak of the fake heron. The way Adam told it, Louisa was a different character to the woman who had tried to crush her hand when David first introduced them. That was something, at least.

They talked, too, of that day in the rain, of Philip finding her, how strange it must have been: her open van, the field so still and quiet, her head and shoulders lolling in the water, as though she was standing, peering into the flood. Maggie could not help but imagine the scene, although it upset her greatly.

Eventually, Adam told Maggie the truth about their argument that day in the house. He told her about Diamond and the transmitter, how Louisa had refused to join him in searching for Christopher. 'So when I said to you, in the car, that she was out looking for him, I thought I was lying. But it came true, I suppose,' he said. 'She did go and look for him, didn't she?'

After two days, Christopher came into the pub across from the hospital. 'This dump looks like a cabinet,' he said, taking in the dark wood panelling. 'And smells like my navel.'

'Have you come to see Louisa?' Maggie said.

'Erm. Yes. I thought I'd be the bigger man.'

He sat down. Maggie smoothed an errant flick of hair at the crown of his head, which sprang back to its original curl. He nodded briefly at Adam. 'I'm sorry, Adamski, if I caused any undue relationship tension between you and Louisa. It's difficult for me to read signals sometimes – it says so in my evaluation document. I certainly didn't mean to create a triangle of any kind.'

'It's no bother, youth,' Adam said.

'It'd be nice to create a square for once,' Christopher said.

Maggie put her hand on his back.

The floodwaters drained from Detton at the rate of two inches an hour, and underneath the water the village was a wreck. Filthy, shit-strewn, and covered with every kind of waste.

The RAF were drafted in to search houses, and the police prevented residents from gaining access to properties that were unsafe. People wanted to return to their houses, even if those houses were cold and wet and dangerous. They could not help it.

An amateur photographer had taken shots of Tim Nettles, the former postman, being winched through his skylight to the safety of an RAF *Sea King,* his aged body limp and dull, clashing with the bright yellow of the helicopter. The power of the image and the happy outcome ensured that this became the lead story in the local news. Louisa's accident was relegated to the middle paragraphs, a woman who became trapped trying to cross a field.

Looking out on the high street at the dropping water level, Brian Wicks asked, 'Who pulled plug?'

*   *   *

The rhythmic beeps of sound grew faster. The light from the transmission receiver flashed from Christopher's lap as they drove up past the reservoir. 'Erm. Why are we doing this, again?' he said.

'Because it's nice,' said Maggie, concentrating on the surrounding fields. 'It's a nice thing to do.'

'Oh right,' said Christopher.

'The signal is awfully, erm, stable,' said Christopher. 'We just keep getting closer and closer. Do you think that means the bird is, you know, deceased?'

Maggie looked up at the hilly fields on both sides of the road, and the sheep, bright in the gloom. 'He might be. We have to be ready for that possibility.'

'Do you think it will be like in *E.T.: The Extra Terrestrial*, where E.T. dies and the boy gets better?'

'I don't know,' said Maggie, pulling over.

'If so, we really have to *hope* the bird is dead, or mangled in some way.'

They got out of the Land Rover, climbed over a small stone wall, and walked uphill. The rain was soft, now. Christopher took the hand-held device and the big receiver with its unwieldy aerial, and Maggie carried a lure, some rope and a few strips of beef. Louisa had once told of a time when she had trapped a saker by getting his foot in the loop of the line and walking around him in slow circles while he ate.

The field had a fenced-off coppice, shelter no doubt for sheep or cattle that had been taken under more substantial cover this week. It was the only place that Diamond could be. Maggie put on Louisa's tattered glove and began to swing the lure. She headed for the trees, whistling, letting out the line a little more. Any moment now, surely.

Nothing.

'Diamond. Come on, sweetie.'

Maybe he was injured, or scared. The signal was close beyond its tuning now – a smooth tone – so Maggie told Christopher to switch it off. Christopher was ten metres behind her, creeping like a cartoon burglar. In the shadows of the trees Maggie saw Diamond's colour, the flash of the transmitter. She straightened and moved in quickly. But it was his dock feather alone, slate blue and slick, caught on the fence, the transmitter still attached with its little wire, the bird long gone. She unhooked the feather carefully, and turned to Christopher. 'Not gonna find him now,' she said.

'Oh, right,' Christopher said, standing up out of his frozen pose. Maggie walked back to meet him, and gave him the feather, which he studied. 'Oh well. For the best, I suppose,' he said.

'Really? Why?' said Maggie.

'Well. He was keeping Louisa cooped up in that house all day.'

Maggie closed her eyes and smiled. Christopher tapped his watch. 'Erm. Hint, hint.'

'What?' said Maggie.

'A little thing called *visiting hours*,' Christopher said.

Back in the Land Rover, Christopher talked about his plans for the future. Maggie didn't really feel like discussing such matters, but he was insistent. 'I've been to the local studies library, and they've said I can volunteer. They need someone to help with school visits.'

Maggie raised her eyebrows. 'They want you to do that?'

'Erm, yes. I like children, although I'm probably not in a stable enough financial position to have my own progeny. The manager liked my idea about having a story competition where children write their own versions of the, erm, Robin Hood myth.'

'Sounds great,' Maggie said.

'So, erm, you see, I'm going to be absolutely fine. And I'm going to patch things up with Louisa Smedley, when she can talk properly again.'

'That's nice.'

'After all, she put her life in mortal danger on my behalf.'

'Well. Yes.'

'Erm, so did you.'

'Well.'

Christopher turned on the transmission receiver again. It started to beep. He put the tip of his index finger against the little light so that the skin glowed red. 'Look, Maggie, look. It's like E.T. Erm, erm, erm. Phone home! Phone home!'

She looked down at the light. Given the dirtiness and length of Christopher's fingers, the impersonation of E.T. was effective. 'Oh. Yes,' said Maggie.

Christopher stopped smiling and held Maggie's arm. 'No, Maggie. Look. Seriously.'

'What?' said Maggie, slowing the Land Rover and looking into the now unadulterated grey of his serious eyes.

'*Phone home*,' he said.

*   *   *

It happened on £3.50 Fish Supper Night. Christopher thought that was a great way to celebrate, so they went across to the pub, but the aroma proved too strong for Maggie. She had been the first to speak to Louisa when she woke fully; they had all agreed that she should be. She had found Louisa surprisingly lucid. Louisa had nodded when Maggie told her the plans, as if she had been thinking the same thing. Alright, she had said. Maggie kissed her forehead.

Adam said that Maggie should go home and rest. She thought about asking him if he would be okay, but he looked suddenly able to deal with anything. He could not keep the smile off his face. 'If you get to speak to her again, give her my best,' Maggie said.

As she left the pub, a roar went up from inside, muted by the door swinging closed. She looked back through the window to see footballers celebrating on the plasma screen.

Back home, Maggie rang the man from Beamish & Fisher, apologised for the lateness of the call, and went through the preliminary formalities. It would take a while, and there was plenty to do.

She went to her bedroom and began to take her clothes, many of which she had not worn for years, from the wardrobe. Silky dresses hung untouched, in the protective sheaths in which they had arrived from London. She placed them all in neat little towers on the floor around her bed. The piles of clothes gave her comfort in the dark, and she slept solidly until late the next morning.

*   *   *

She heard Christopher talking to the postman downstairs on his way out to college. The door closed, and the house settled. She could hear animals outside. Through everything, their rhythms had remained undisturbed.

Maggie descended the stairs of the big old house in shorts and boots. The merest light funnelled down. Her long figure loped, the sinews of her high bare shoulders like the tangle of wires behind the TV. The heels of her boots kicked up dust from the faded red stair-runner. On the floor, there was a parcel addressed to Ms Maggie – no surname – and she sat down to open it. Inside, she found a buckskin glove. It was plain, but beautiful, the hide thin – a longwing glove.

Maggie took a document from the box – a handwritten invoice for the attention of Louisa Smedley. The glovemaker had written a brief note under the price, but it was too dark to read in the hall. Maggie shuffled round on her knees, bringing an echoey shush from the smooth stone floor. She held the paper above her head, so the light would reach it. The glovemaker's note read *Sorry it took so long*, but that was not what Maggie noticed. The paper had become transparent in the light. On the reverse was an outline of her own hand made in make-up pencil. Maggie let her shoulders drop, and flipped the paper over, remembering as she did so that moment, which seemed an age ago, when Louisa had drawn around her fingers in the bathroom. A different time.

She slipped the glove on, put her hands together, linked the fingers, and squeezed.

ACKNOWLEDGEMENTS

Every day I worked on this book with Emily Hahn, and I'd like to thank her for the care, imagination, and most of all love she gave me throughout the process. You're amazing, Emily, and this one's for you.

I also want to thank Julie Redfern, for her massive support and astute reading. Thanks to Pop and Blake, and to Ignês Sodré and Gabriel Palma. Thanks to Daniel Jeffreys, who looked at so many drafts, and to Emma Sweeney and Sarah Flax for their insights. It was great to talk to Andrew Brentnall about falconry, and to James Shand about medical stuff. Belated thanks to Keir, Alex, Al, and Ian, for the room.

Francesca Main made a huge contribution to this book; I learned a lot from working with her, and had a great time along the way. Thank you to the brilliant Veronique Baxter, and to Laura West of DHA. Thanks to all the great folk at Simon & Schuster. I'm extremely grateful for the support of the Desmond Elliott Prize, too.

Eddie Hallam ran a wildlife park at Riber Castle, Derbyshire, for many years. Despite similarities in location, this book is not about that park, nor is it about Eddie. He did, however, give generously of his time to talk about his work in conservation.